Dedication

This book is dedicated to my brother-in-law, Robert Putt, the sweetest and gentlest of men.

Patricia Hutson

PURPLE MICHAELMAS

AUSTIN MACAULEY
PUBLISHERS LTD.

A CIP catalogue record for this title is available from the British Library.

ISBN 9781786127525 (Paperback)
ISBN 9781786127532 (Hardback)
ISBN 9781786127549 (E-Book)

www.austinmacauley.com

First Published (2016)
Austin Macauley Publishers Ltd.
25 Canada Square
Canary Wharf
London
E14 5LQ

Acknowledgments

I would like to thank my husband, John, our daughters, Carolyn and Michelle, and our son-in-law, Peter, for putting up with numerous fast foods and very bad tempers when I first started writing, I know they suffered greatly and patiently.

I also wish to thank Elizabeth Robertson who edited my work giving it the professional touch I couldn't.

And most important of all, I really want to thank Austin Macauley for giving a complete unknown the chance to prove herself. I have always loved writing and that this publishing house has decided to give me the opportunity I will always be thankful for. I hope they like the second one too.

Chapter 1

Was it the warmth of the early summer sun touching my face giving it a light dusting of gold? Or was it a cat jumping up on my dressing table? Sitting up I glanced around the room taking in the avocado coloured wardrobes, and light cream carpet, no all was in order I whispered to myself. Looking down at my sleeping husband then tip toeing into the children's bedroom I could see they too were fast asleep. So what was it that had given me such a bad night's sleep and awoken me so abruptly? My heart was beating fast, mouth dry, hands sweating, all things combined told me that today was not going to be a good start to our weekend.

Having been a practising Medium for many years now I had come to recognise the signs that something unpleasant was either about to happen or had already taken place. Making my way into the kitchen and looking out into the garden I shook my head, it was a beautiful day, the kind of Saturday everybody dreams about and yet here I was my legs and hands shaking making it difficult to stand. Feeling in the need of a coffee I put the kettle on, filled the cafetière and sat down to try and pull my thoughts together, something that was proving rather difficult.

Looking out into the sun filled garden my eyes wandered round the variety of roses, small trees and bushes that I loved and tended carefully each year. Looking at the plants did nothing to stop the feeling of restlessness that just would not leave me so with cup in hand I wandered out into the garden making my way towards the Standard Rose that stood very proudly in the centre of the garden, when in bloom the flowers were the most perfect red, so deep as to appear almost black. This plant had been given to me as a gift from friends after my mother had died, so it was that whenever I felt lost or afraid I would stand near the rose and speak to her, to most people this would have been difficult or impossible to understand but not for me. Why am I so afraid Mum? Is it my sisters? I know Bill and the girls are fine, so who or what could it be? About to move away I felt a movement at my feet and looking down I saw a large tabby cat making his way through the shoots that were coming up at the base of the of the rose, plants that would not bloom till early September, the Michaelmas Daisy.

Once again my heart started to race but not this time in fear or terror of the unknown, it was the memories that this very simple bloom rekindled in me. Pleasurable ones reminding me what guilty secrets I had kept for many years now ones that a happily married woman should not have.

Making my way back into the kitchen in need of another cup of coffee, I smiled as I remembered sitting in Circle one night many years ago, when I was a Developing Medium and hearing Jim saying to me: "When the Purple Michaelmas blooms, your life Vicki will change." This had puzzled me as I asked: "How do you mean?" His reply was simple and to the point: "I feel it will take a turn for the unexpected and new experiences will fill your life." Feeling that I had to lighten the mood I had giggled softly slightly annoying Harry our Circle leader who tut tutted, turning to Jim in the dark of the room I whispered: "You don't think my life is full enough?" With this we both went on talking to others in the room also developing their Gift.

Remembering Harry and Jim brought me back to the series of coincidences that had appeared to fill my life for as long as I could remember from childhood to becoming an adult almost everything I did, places I visited or people I met it was always afterwards that I realised: "yes, it was always going to be so."

My introduction into the world of becoming a Medium began in just such a manner, the evening that Frances and Mark had chosen for their anniversary party and BBQ was at the end of one of those perfect spring days when the sun was high, a gentle breeze stopped the day from being too hot as it was a pleasant evening Bill the girls and myself walked to our friend's house. As we approached our destination we could hear music, the sound of children laughing mixing with the voices of the adults. Seeing Mark and Frances' sons in their impatience to join their friends our girls skipped ahead.

Making our way down the side of the garden no need to stand on ceremony here, we were soon in the midst of friends and family. Congratulating our friends on their twelfth anniversary the men soon got together to discuss the new groupings for the upcoming football fixtures and we the women wandered off to carry on with our own conversations.

Frances, looked a very worried lady: "Do you think everyone has everything they need?" She asked breathlessly. I smiled at my little friend saying: "You have provided the place, food and booze, if they can't have fun not your problem." She was about to answer when her attention was called away by one of the children falling over. I had to giggle as I saw her trying to rush, Frances was really the sweetest person she was not very tall and reminded me of one of the good fairies in Sleeping Beauty. With her dark hair piled up on her head in a bun, cherubic round face and sparkling blue eyes dressed in a frock of blue that matched her eyes perfectly and on her feet low heeled shoes. Fashion had never worried her, comfort and looking good were her maxims in life. As she hurried away she looked back at me with a mischievous smile and said: "Please talk to the elderly couple at the fish pond." Puzzled I looked towards a couple who appeared to be examining the Koi very intently. I was puzzled as I had never met them before and wondered what part of Frances' or Mark's family they were.

Making my way toward the couple I could see that the lady (I would later learn her name was Norah) was a lady in her late sixties, her rotund figure covered in a rather shapeless lilac dress, on her feet were a pair brown brogues. Her hair was completely grey with what appeared to be a natural curl this covered her very serene features and perfect complexion. I was amazed this lady looked as if she had not a care in the world, I would later learn why.

Looking at her husband Harry Blake as he introduced himself was a little taller than his wife but equally as rotund. Not a hair on his head the reason for the cheese cutter cap perched on the top, "stopping me from getting sunburnt." He mumbled as he took his cap off to introduce himself and his wife. His grey eyes were very light giving one the impression you were looking into a pool of ice cold water. He wore a blue suit one that had obviously seen better days and obviously only came out on what he considered important days and this was one of them. Mark had known them for many years having once been apprenticed to him as a boy when learning the plumbing job that he was very good at.

The introductions carried out I was a bit perplexed as to why I had to meet them so specially, at first there was a rather strained silence between us and hoping someone would come and drag me away I stood awkwardly waiting for something to happen or be said. I was not prepared for Harry's opening remark. "So, you are the Psychic?" He asked in the tone of voice of a person who had for many years been an asthmatic. "Sorry?" I asked, "What are you talking about?" Shaking my head convinced that the sun really had affected the old boy, I was about to walk away when he said: "Can you honestly explain some of the strange experiences you have had in your life." He stopped for a moment waiting for me to say something, rather quietly I whispered: "What strange experiences?" He stared into my eyes, his appeared to bore right into my soul making me feel that I would not want to hold a secret in my heart because he would find it. He then whispered, "What about the holiday trip you went on last year and before you reached your destination you burst into tears that you could not explain?" I stared at him absolutely dumbfounded apart from my husband Bill I had told no one not even Frances and Angie, it was an event that had worried and frightened me so much I had kept it bottled in me. "How did you know?" I asked quietly, for once rather afraid, he smiled and said: "In our work dear there are no secrets." Taking my hand in his rough work worn ones, he looked at me like a fond father about to tell his child that a nightmare she had been suffering from for many years was actually nothing to worry about.

"I know it is frightening and at times upsetting, when you had this experience you were not to know that you had picked up the death of a family at a railway crossing." I was so shocked at what he was saying I was now shaking and had to find a chair to sit on. The man before me was so accurate I could find nothing to say. Yes, I had been travelling with my family on a week of our annual holiday and as we neared a village in Sussex not far from our hotel. I suddenly burst into tears, something that upset Bill and the girls greatly and terrified me. Neither of us knew the reason for this only the next day watching the news on television did we hear that a car crossing the railway had stalled killing a family of five when the train struck. Bill and I had told no one – absolutely no one.

"You see my dear," Norah carried on the conversation, "when you have The Gift as we have." Moving her arms I could see she was involving me in this group "and you have not developed" she continued, "you are very open to anything or anyone in Spirit coming through, you need to develop and be protected. I feel you have a very special Gift." Having recovered my composure I smiled and thought, "Yea, how many people do you use that line on?" She looked at me and like her husband who I was convinced was into mind reading she said, "This is not an opening to all our conversations, we are very fussy who enters our circle and whom we develop." By now my head was spinning words like Circle, Develop what were these two old darlings talking about. Then Harry continued: "Please come and join us we meet every Thursday at seven fifteen and Circle starts promptly at seven thirty. We look forward to seeing you." Handing me a business card, he smiled tipped his cap and holding his wife's hand they walked away leaving me feeling as if everything that I had experienced strange and unexplained was about to be answered. That was the day I learnt in my world coincidence did not exist, everything I would face, every person I had met and would meet in the future, places I had visited and was yet to visit were all designed. For after all the Gift I had was to help other people there was no safety net for me.

Deep in thought I wandered back to Bill taking him by the hand I said: "I have something to say to you." Looking down at me from his great height he smiled his hazel eyes lighting up, I really did feel a very lucky woman as my husband was literally tall dark and handsome. Over six feet tall, his dark brown hair and suntanned face with his very understanding manner, I could not help thinking: "I could never do anything to hurt this man." Oh! How little did I know my future? As we walked home from the party that night and after putting two very sleepy children to bed sitting down with cups of coffee I told him everything that had transpired between the Blakes and myself. Expecting him to be angry with them or myself, I was amazed when he smiled and said: "If you want to try it love, by all means go ahead. You have to admit since I've known you a lot of strange things have happened." Giving me a hug and a good night kiss he turned round, smiled and said: "Who knows you might even get the pools." Grinning I replied with a, "That is never going to happen."

Having arranged with my mother to babysit until Bill got home from work, I made my way to Moulsham a small village near our bigger town. Promptly at seven fifteen I very nervously rang the front door bell, not knowing what to expect. I was amazed to find along with Harry and Norah seven other people including myself in the Circle we made ten.

I never knew what to expect and was amazed as to how the evening progressed, I learnt a great deal from watching those who had sat in Circle for many years and I was definitely the fledgling as all new and developing Mediums are described.

There was Heather a soft spoken Norfolk girl married to an Essex man, Jim and Julie husband and wife and the man who along with Harry would have the greatest impact on my development, Jean a lady who was a Nurse, Malcolm and his new wife Rose they had married in middle age and Donald a builder and someone who did not look as if he believed in anything even vaguely spiritual let alone join a Circle. All these people came to have a very strong and good influence on me and my work and were for many years firm family friends as they came to know Bill, Hannah and Lottie too. However, it was the words Jim used that stayed with me the longest and were the most haunting. "Vicki," He spoke into the dark of the Circle, turning my head to follow the sound of his voice I asked: "What's up Jim? You sound worried. "I am my dear. Do you know what the flowers known as Purple Michaelmas look like?" I giggled at this it was a well-known fact my gardening was very bad and knowledge of blooms non-existent. I replied with, "No, you going to tell me."

"After we finish but I must continue for now, when the flowers bloom your life will change. There will be indescribable joy and heartbreaking pain." Leaving me with this statement he went on to talk to someone else, leaving me feeling not only worried but puzzled. How could my life change, I didn't want it to change, why should it change? I liked everything as it was. Happily married, great husband and kids never wanted to play away from home what was Jim talking about. After we had finished a sacred rule was broken, we never discussed what had been said in the room upstairs, but I had to know more. So I asked for a special dispensation to be set. It was explained that the purple flowers I had always considered to be weeds, were not they were so entitled because they bloomed in September at the time of the feast of Michaelmas. I nodded smiled pretending I knew and understood what they were talking about and tried not to think of it too much on my drive home. During the coming weeks I never thought of it at all. How little did I realise that in the coming years I would doubt my Gift as a Medium, not knowing my own future.

Feeling a movement round my feet I looked down seeing a large tabby cat wandering in an around the green shoots at the base of the rose tree, these I knew with certainty were the flowers that would bloom during the end of August and September Purple Michaelmas. Why had I doubted Jim? Why had I felt I knew more about my life than someone who had been a Medium for so many years? My own over confidence in my ability to run my life would be my undoing.

Picking the cat up and holding him close smelling the summer sun on his fur, I held Spikey close to me. Spikey by name, Hunter by instinct and killer by nature. "Come on," I whispered into his ear: "No good thinking of the past and what could have been changed, I'll have another cup of coffee and you a big bowl of cat food."

Together we walked into the kitchen me to sit down with coffee in hand and Spikey now joined by Tarzan a big black and white cat with none of the killer instincts of Spikey eating their breakfast.

For some reason I could not shake the feeling of terror that had awoken me and neither could I stop thinking of the past. In my mind I kept going back fifteen years and the day I heard Mark, and Tom saying to Bill: "You know she is going to kill you." We had been standing at the rail of the bar at the Football Club, as usual the men down one end and we women at the other, this arrangement suited us as we did not always want the men privy to our conversations and frankly we were not too interested in who was going up or down in the premier League. However, this particular piece of conversation really did catch my interest especially when I heard my husband reply with: "Well Vicki, won't mind he is handsome, charming and quite a few other things and he speaks English."

Now I really was interested, so walking over to the three men who had now been joined by quite a few others all obviously waiting to see my reaction I asked in a very quiet tone of voice, the one I used when working with an awkward Client or a local Councillor whom I was quizzing. "Just what am I not going to like my dear darling husband?" At this both Tom and Mark touched my shoulders blew on their fingers pretending that they had been burnt by my anger. "Ah! Yes," Bill stumbled a little: "I've been meaning to tell you that Peter can't stay with us next week, he's moved." he mumbled his voice fading away.

"And this means he can't stay with us?" I spoke very quietly and deliberately. "We have numerous people in the club who don't live in Little Barham." I continued. I could feel a "you don't understand" coming on and I was not wrong. "You don't understand," my husband's voice began to tail away and it was Tom who took up the rest of the explanation: "In Germany if you move out of your town you have to join new clubs, they are very home town orientated." He explained, "More like very small town minded." I mumbled, "go on surprise me who are we having then?" I turned to walk back to the ladies following it up with: "Not that great big fat bloke who broke Sam's dining chair two years ago," Then giggled until I was floored by Bill's almost apologetic. "It's Dieter Schmidt, the good looking one." At that I stopped, turned on my heels and marching back squeaked, "Who?" The weak smiles on the men's faces told me this was no joke, it was real, the man to whom I had never spoken a word, not even been introduced to but felt a hearty dislike for was to be my house guest for a whole weekend and for future weekends to come.

"Why don't you like him?" Frances who had now joined us with Angie walking beside her, "he is charming, handsome, great fun. I honestly don't see what is to dislike." I had no easy answer to this as I had no reason to give. What could I honestly say? "He frightens me." That sounded as weak in my thoughts as I knew it would in words. So I just took refuge in a shrug and a mumbled, "Well I just don't like him." I walked quietly away taking refuge in the one place a woman can be alone while still in a crowded place – The Ladies Toilet.

I stood there for a few minutes, looking down on my shaking hands, my legs feeling like jelly gave way making me sit down so sharply I jarred my back for a few seconds. "Are you OK?" I heard Angie call through the cubicle door. Sighing I replied with, "Yes, I'm fine can't a girl be left to do her business in peace."

"All right what do you want to drink?" she asked I could never remember what my reply was I just needed my friend away for a few minutes so that I could get my thoughts back together.

Staying sitting I cast my mind back two years previously, when Peter had stayed with us, it was the usual Friday night when the men had arrived, it was the first time that I was to play hostess to one of these guests as Bill had been to Germany for the first time the year previous and it was our turn to reciprocate. Peter had been a tall grey haired man very much on the lines of how we imagined an early nineteenth century Prussian gentleman to be. Gentle, courteous and charming. Dieter Schmidt was very different. We had bumped into each other accidentally in the car park, Dieter had gone out for a cigarette and I had been to get something out of our car, we walked towards each other in the dim light of the early evening and instead of passing comfortably by I had stepped on a stone that caught my high heels tipping me forward into Dieter's arms. For a moment we stood almost in a lover's embrace till I had the strength to pull away. I had run into the Club House, my knees knocking, breath coming fast and eyes misty as if I had been kissed – passionately. That was how I had felt but: "You are a silly cow," I grumbled to myself trying to get rid of the uncomfortable feeling that the previous encounter had left me with. I had never told anyone of this and really had no intention of ever doing so, yet here now I had been told that this man who I felt could be my Nemesis was to be with me for a whole weekend. I could still remember as if it had been today his comment as his bare arm had touched mine his husky, deeply accented voice whispering to himself: "That is very dangerous – very dangerous."

How cruel a fate was laughing at me? Especially as I realised that the original date given for the visitors had been changed they would be arriving during the second week of September, the time of the Purple Michaelmas flowers coming into bloom. Suddenly Jim's words came back not to haunt me but to slap me in the face: "When the Purple Michaelmas blooms your life will change."

Having cleared my thoughts, pulled myself together I made my way out into the Club once more trying to ignore the puzzled looks Angie and Frances were giving me.

"Everything OK?" Frances asked.

"Yep fine, would like a drink I feel parched."

A gin and bitter lemon was soon waiting for me, glancing down at my hands and realising they had stopped shaking I felt I could very safely pick up my glass nonchalantly take a drink from it and smile while looking very normal. "God! Vicki you should have taken up acting." I smiled to myself.

"Want to share the joke?" Angie asked lighting up yet another cigarette.

"Nope no joke just reality." At this I wandered away knowing my friends as well as I did I knew I would have to be on my guard.

By now the Saturday morning was turning into one of those beautiful rare sunny warm days. I knew it would not be long before my family were up and my time for daydreaming at an end, what worried me was that I could not shake the feeling left from the night previous. It was making me aware that something was about to happen, something that was both frightening and would affect my life for ever but what I had no idea?

Drinking yet another cup of coffee, fed both cats I sat down on my window seat once more, allowing my thoughts to drift back to that September evening. The warmth of the day was disappearing and a chill had come over the marshes that surrounded the rear of the Club house, accompanied by Angie and Frances we made our entrance into the noisy smoke filled interior, casting my eyes around the crowded room it was Frances who said: "You looking for Bill?" I nodded how could I answer her in any other way: "Over there in the corner, with the most gorgeous hunk you have ever seen." I wanted to slap her, he was my property for this one weekend, surprised at my feeling towards my friend I quickly pulled myself together. I nodded then started to make my way towards my husband and the time bomb that was to be my guest for the next seventy-two hours. "Oh! Dear God what is going to happen to me?" I muttered as I made my way across the dance floor, nodding and smiling at friends visitors and those whom I did not know in fact anyone, while doing this I managed to control my hands, the shaking of my legs, knees there was not a part of me that had not been affected. By now I was close to where the men were standing Bill and Dieter in close conversation as he spoke excellent English. Tom and Mark standing a little awkwardly with Fritz and Hans as their knowledge of English was very limited so the conversation was interspersed with a great deal of hand movements and "do you understand?" To which the visitors would smile and nod, I was never sure if they had, but it made for a very entertaining tableaux.

Within a second of Bill noticing me Dieter had also seen me approaching, his green eyes boring into mine and for a second I thought he looked a little flustered, had that been the case he covered it over quickly. Much to Bill's amazement I walked up to him and planted a kiss on his lips, standing back he smiled and said, "Am I to be lucky tonight?" I replied with a quick, "You could be." All this was said and done while I was looking into a pair of passionate eyes, that were trying very hard not to show more emotion than necessary for a stranger.

"This is your wife, Bill?" Dieter asked.

"Yes, the love of my life." He replied slipping an arm around my waist and pulling me close. I stared into Dieter's eyes and I could see the same look of puzzlement in them that I knew were in mine. How could two people who had never met for more than a second many months ago, never exchanged more than two words have so much emotion running between them, we both knew there was no need for speech no explanation necessary. By now Bill was introducing Dieter, Fritz and Uwe to us all and I was having my hand vigorously pumped by both Fritz who was a tubby little man with a shock of red hair and very bad taste in clothes. With his red a hair a plaid shirt in pink and green trousers were really not the best way to dress. Uwe, was a little more dapper dark hair, grey eyes and dressed in a much more conventional manner, grey trousers, white shirt and cardigan across his shoulders, as the years would go on and I grew to know him better I would realise that he always dressed like this, the cardigan was always across his shoulders no matter the weather. Then it was my turn to be introduced to Dieter, how I was dreading this, as I felt his long slim fingers wind themselves around my hand I looked into his eyes and could see the same expression that I was sure was mirrored in mine, utter bewilderment. We were both strangers to each other, married happily to other people yet suddenly feeling a desperate need for each other. As he held my hand for a second longer than was polite, he smiled and in it was a promise that some way somehow we would come to mean a great deal more to each other – soon.

"I don't need this, I am a happily married woman I love my husband and family."

"Yes, mother I know you love us but why do you feel you need to tell yourself." Looking up I saw my youngest daughter standing in front me her brown hair tousled, eyes the same brown as mine her pyjamas in her favourite colour pink. Charlotte or Lottie as she was known among family and friends was quite the most gregarious of our two daughters even though she was now twenty-two Lottie could not make her mind up about anything regarding her future and was a great source of frustration to both of us Bill would shake his head smile and say, "Lottie you have to grow up and take life seriously."

"Plenty of time for that Dad," she would reply, toss her long brown hair and walk away from us.

Helping herself to a cup of coffee she sat down on the floor at my feet, holding Tarzan in her arms as she stroked his black fur she said: "You slept badly last night," looking at her I asked, "What do you mean?"

"When we came up to bed Hannah and I could hear you as we walked into the bedroom you were tossing and turning, I think you muttered a name but not too sure. So what were you dreaming about? Not naughty thoughts you are keeping from Dad?"

I smiled holding her hand "No, love just a bad dream but can't remember what it was." By now Lottie was bored with the conversation and was making her way to the bathroom, leaving me in the same state of bewilderment as I had been in when I woke up.

By now Bill and Hannah had also woken up and were joining me in the kitchen, Bill was a tall man and well-built for his age the dark hair he had once had now a little sparse, his waist not as slim as before but he carried himself with a quiet confidence that made people admire him, his tone of voice was quiet with just the hint of the East End of London dialect that gave away his ancestry. Hannah was our eldest daughter and as different from her sister as chalk and cheese. Her brown hair was shorter and framed her heart shaped face, she spoke quietly very much like her father and her concentration lasted a great deal longer than that of her younger sister. Like Lottie after kissing my cheek, Hannah said, "What was wrong with you last night?" By now I was tired of the night previous and the the constant questions, so pushing it aside I went for the obvious: "Who wants bacon and eggs for breakfast?" A show of hands gave me the answer I needed.

A little later on the day Bill gardening, our daughters deciding on the important subject of what they would wear that evening for a party, there were three years between Hannah and Lottie but in height and looks people often though they were twins until they realised that Hannah was the serious one and Lottie quite different. I was standing at the fence talking to our dear friends and neighbours George and Joyce, we had known each other for as long as we had lived in our home. George had during the war been ground crew for the RAF and would often regale us with stories that were funny and interesting. He was small in height and very slim, a dapper dresser his thin hair now covered with a flat cap as the sun did affect him and of course the usual cigarette rolled between his fingers and placed between thin lips. Joyce, would look at her husband disapprovingly having given up smoking many years ago she felt rather superior to him and would often show it either by word or gesture. Joyce was the same height as George small and round our daughters described her as looking like a character from a children's book Mrs Pepperpot, her grey hair always smart no make-up and a beaming smile for our daughters, wearing a grey and black summer dress she and her husband were preparing to go out for the day but there was always time for a gossip.

As we stood talking Bill joined us we heard the phone ring, in that instant I knew my nightmare was going to come true. Bill put down his shears and made his way into the kitchen to answer it, I wanted to shout to him: "Don't answer it please. We don't need to know who is at the other end." As the blood drained from my body and tears started to fill my eyes, I knew without any Psychic Gift being present that my life was never ever going to be the same again. I really did not want to know who was at the other end of the phone. Please Dear God don't let it be I stopped myself afraid to put things and thoughts into perspective.

Bill walked out of the house thoughtfully and quietly, holding my hands he said: "We need to go to Germany, Dieter has been injured in a road accident on his way home from work."

I whispered one word, "Fatally?"

"Not at present but Monique is not sure if he will make it, that was Uwe on the phone." Monique was Dieter's wife and Uwe his friend and brother-in-law.

Joyce who had met Dieter was shocked she turned to us and said, "You must go to Germany don't worry about the girls we will look after them."

We both nodded silently made our way indoors, told the girls who both burst into tears, as Dieter and his family had long been very much a part of their lives, this news had shaken us all to the core, me especially but again as with everything in my life over the past fifteen years had to be kept secret.

Quietly we went up to pack as I carried out this job I was asking the fates to whom we owe our lives to not take him from me, not rob his wife and family of his endearing personality, husky voice his ability to love and I would make any promise they needed so that the Kismet that put him into my life would save him not just for me – Oh! Please don't let him die, I will give him up.

"Sorry love, what did you say about dying?" Bill asked

"Oh nothing, wasn't sure I had said something." I turned quickly away afraid that he would see the utter hopelessness in my eyes.

Chapter 2

We went about the business of packing in silence broken only by the inevitable: "Do you know where my toothbrush is?" answered by "In the bathroom."
Where are my good shoes?" Trying to keep my patience I replied with, "in the shoe rack as normal," this brought the reply: "No need to be sarcastic." I was trying desperately to keep my patience and was quite pleased with the way in which I was doing so, until Bill with his head stuck in a suitcase muttered: "I suppose to be really prepared I should take my black tie, any idea where it is?" At this I nearly flew at him but instead of being violent I sat with a jerk on the side of the bed wanting to hold my head in my hands, fighting to keep away the tears how was my husband to know that in the fifteen years we had been friends with Dieter my life had changed so much, I had gone from being a young rather naive housewife and mother to a woman in every sense of the word. Though I knew Bill loved me and I did love him too, the feelings that were between Dieter and myself far outreached any emotion I had ever experienced with my husband so the thought of never seeing Dieter ever again was the most traumatic event in my life. My future without the man I loved most in life

stretched ahead lonely, bleak and dark so how could I answer Bill when he asked about his black tie without bursting into uncontrollable tears that I would be unable to explain away so it was with my head stuck in the suitcase a pair of trousers muffling my voice I replied with: "Well lets be positive, take the purple tie instead." This seemed to satisfy him, everything packed and ready we waited for the cab.

Phone calls having been made seats booked on the flight to Cologne we waited restlessly for the taxi. By now George and Joyce had joined us as we sat with cups of coffee making conversation none of us could remember or meant anything. Until, Joyce said: "I do hope your young friend survives, he is such a charming young man and so good looking too." With a wicked glint in her eyes Joyce looked at me and said, "Had I been younger I would have given you quite a run for your money." She chuckled at this George carried on with, "My wife was quite a girl when we were younger, I always had to keep an eye on her when the men were around." Looking at the aged couple sitting in front of us I found it hard to believe they were ever anything other than a sweet, loving elderly people. Joyce in her shift dress to cover her large frame and George small, thin and bald, smiling for the first time since that phone call I chuckled then Bill made a statement that awoke every ounce of guilt in me: "Oh! I have never worried about Vicki, she is the perfect wife and mother. Business like when needed, caring with the kids and as a wife I could never doubt her loyalty to me, nope not my wife." I was so shocked by this comment of his that my hand jerked as I was putting the cup to my mouth spilling the coffee on the table, calling myself a couple of silly names I quickly mopped everything while trying to stop the shaking of my hands.

"Mum, Dad the cab's here." I heard Lottie call out. We hurriedly said goodbye to the girls knowing they would be safe in the care of our friends and neighbours and left for the airport.

Feeling that the cab driver was going to ask, "Where are you going on holiday?" Bill soon made it clear to him we were not in the mood for empty talk and our journey was a serious one. Bill sat looking out of the window at the passing scenery trying not to show how tense he felt. Curling myself up in the corner of the cab, while hanging tightly on to Bill's hand, I desperately needed that feeling of someone close to me – it was not the person I wanted or needed and I felt awful placing my husband in second place but what could I do?

Every bump in the road affected me, each time the car got stuck in a traffic jam I wanted to scream out loud, "Get out of our way!" I could not do this and knowing that the holiday traffic, the sunshine and the day being Saturday every road our car went down appeared to be jammed, glancing back at us the driver smiled and said: "Trying to get you to the airport as soon as I can, horrible when you have bad news to deal with." At this point I did come back rather rudely, "It's not bad news yet." This brought a scowl from Bill that said, "Calm down, he didn't mean anything." I smiled an apology. Cuddling into Bill's arms and in a desperate attempt to forget traffic jams and my need to scream I began to remember when Angie, Frances and I were having one of our usual monthly lunches in an old Pub some ten miles out of Little Barham when our topic of conversation turned as usual to how we were to treat our visitors from abroad. I was still remembering that fleeting moment when Dieter and I had bumped into each other so many months ago, the memory had haunted me ever since this being my reason for not wanting him to stay in our home. My thoughts were disrupted as I heard Frances say: "You will feed him well, won't you?"

"Feed who well? What are you talking about?" I tried not to sound churlish "You," Frances replied "Out of the three of us you are the cook," she carried on "I have to admit having seen him I think I could offer him more than food."

"I am not that kind of woman," I almost shouted back at my friends seeing the look of amazement on their faces I realised that this time I had perhaps protested too much. So, giving a weak smile I ordered the soup as the young waitress approached us.

For the first time in all the years that we three had been friends there was an awkward silence between us, knowing it was my fault I knew I had to say something and fast nothing German related. Giving a sigh as I slipped my shoes off under the oak dining table, I glanced around the Pub it had once been an old house during the twelfth century but had now been turned into a fascinating inn even having its own resident Ghost that I had found and had worked with. She had told me her name was Sara while the people in the village of Carndean had always thought she was called Catherine. I had been told by her she was no Witch and had been murdered by a very unpleasant Uncle and her baby too had been killed by him. As my friends hadn't known me at the time these discoveries were made when I spoke about it they found it fascinating. I had long known when talking about my work people would be either completely interested or pretend to be totally disinterested while still asking questions.

Looking at Angie I smiled as I often wished I could live in her world, Angie was small, slim and dark-haired. She was adored by her husband Tom and in Angie's world nothing ever happened to disrupt it, whatever she wanted Tom provided sometimes I envied her as I had never seen her lose her temper or be put out by anything. Sighing once more I could not help thinking, "I do wish I was you Angie." But, I was not and though I was not too sure, my world was about to become a great deal more complicated.

"Here we are," the cab driver's voice brought me back to reality with a jolt. After thanking and paying him we made our way toward the booking in hall, for a moment I glanced back almost as if by that look I would be able to hold onto reality and saw the driver still standing where we had left him, a sympathetic smile on his face and a thumbs up as though he too knew my secret. "Oh! Don't be so stupid not everyone knows how you feel about Dieter, it's amazing how a guilty conscience can make you think and feel." I mumbled.

"Think what love?" Bill asked, I looked up at him for a moment not knowing what he was talking about "Oh! That, sorry I was thinking about something Angie said last week." He glanced down at me puzzled then taking me by the hand hurried me towards the departure lounge as the announcement was given.

Making our way towards the plane and finding our seats as we had been a late booking we had to take what was left. Having placed our bags in the overhead compartments Bill sat down by my side, "Want a drink?" He asked I shook my head I really was not in any mood for talking or drinking so resting my head on my husband's shoulder as the plane shook in its first throes of the take-off procedure I closed my eyes and drifted back to the past once more.

It was the Friday night and I had been tense all day knowing that by eight o'clock all my nightmares would become reality. How could someone who was happily married, content with her life end up in this state and all because she had accidentally bumped into a stranger and that one was now going to stay with her.

Bill came home from work showered and met up with Tom and Mark and headed off to the Club where they would pick up a coach that would take them to a Pub a few miles away where they would meet and greet and dine with their guests before bringing them back to meet us in the Club.

As we would be out for the evening and return late I had arranged for my mother to look after the girls. So washing and putting our daughters into their night attire took them to my mother's home. Knocking on the door I tried to look as relaxed as possible, worried my mother would be able to read my thoughts as she knew me very well. The door opened and framed in it was a small, silver haired elderly lady. Wearing a purple dress with black and grey flowers printed on it, she opened her arms to her granddaughters with the words: "Your tea is on the table and the TV on." No backward look from the girls, they were happy to be with Nan as spoiling was the only name of the game here. Giving her a wave I made my way home to prepare for the evening ahead or was it the weekend I was never sure.

Lying in my bath, trying very hard to relax by pretending that this was the start to just another uneventful weekend, I could feel the warm scented water caressing my naked body, touching every intimate part lovingly. Closing my eyes I tried to keep out the vision of black hair and emerald green eyes a memory that was so strong that it set up a trembling in my lower limbs. Feeling that I had gone too far in my imaginations I stepped out of the bath, shook myself like a puppy and began to towel myself dry.

I had known in advance the dress I would wear it was old but new, hung in my wardrobe for some months and this was its first outing. Subconsciously I had saved it for just tonight. It was a bright red, ruched down the front the neckline was very low and where the hem was it lifted up almost as though hem and neckline were trying to meet but separated by the rest of my body. Make up in place and stiletto heels on I was ready for battle. Tonight I was not wife and mother, but the eternal female. A wanton animal needing to be free but at the same time demanding a cage one made for her by the mate of her choosing except tonight I did not know which mate I wanted or needed?

Taking one last look in the mirror I smiled saying to myself: "Come on girl, go for it, things won't be so bad. When you see him again you will realise there was never anything there in the first place." One last look at hair, make up and dress I was prepared to do battle. With my experience I should have known that Fate loves to laugh at the over confident, there is always a nasty sting in a tail.

All my armour in place I was prepared to do battle, making my entrance into the lounge I saw Angie waiting for me, one look at her face and I knew I would have the required effect on everyone especially Dieter! "What the hell have you got on?" I heard my friend gasp, "Oh! Nothing just something I bought last year," hurrying her out of the house not really prepared to be lectured by the expression in her eyes I knew something was brewing.

Grabbing her arm I hurried her down to where our cars were parked pushing her into hers I climbed into mine waving her on I called out: "See you at the club."

My mind was running riot with a great deal of what ifs? I was so busy thinking I actually jumped a red light, pulling up at the car park at the club house I stood waiting for my friends to join me this they did with Angie looking furious: "What the Hell are you playing at? Didn't you see the red light and the cars crossing? You are so lucky not to be in hospital now." I smiled at her in an effort to make light of everything I replied with: "Gosh that would have been a waste of a great outfit." Grabbing both girls by their elbows I hurried them into the Club itself. The buildings had been rescued from a construction company and with the help of club members they had been turned into a Club with changing rooms, showers for the teams after their games and the larger of the buildings was the one that had the bar with a long counter that at one end served small snacks, opposite it was the lounge area where those not wishing to dance could sit, relax discuss football or any other sport and perhaps watch some television it was decorated in a mushroom colour with a deeper beige carpet. The main area was the place where the dancing took place with a stage in the corner for the Disco, singers or whoever was in charge of entertainment that evening, this too was done in mushroom but the flooring was parquet, no carpet here. Tonight the lighting was subdued with music playing as a background as there was to be no dancing tonight. Once the men arrived back from their evening meal there would be introductions, cases being carried out and a great deal of laughter. Frances, Angie and myself made our way to the bar as we were the drivers we would have our one and only drink Angie her usual dry white wine, Frances also a wine but hers would be a red and I? The mood I was in I could have drunk a pint of Vodka but stuck to one with a Tonic with shaking hands and to the amazement of my friends I swallowed it in one. "Honestly," Frances said, "you are acting so odd, you afraid of something?" Turning my back on both of them as I really did not want them to see the expression in my eyes, I replied with, "No, just really fancied one – got a problem with this?" Realising that I was in no mood to say anything further they walked quietly onto the dance floor so that we could talk to some of the other ladies who were like us waiting for their husbands and visitors.

There was Lucy married to the Club Chairman Danny, a large, unpleasant woman who had never really learned how to dress she always wore her clothes too tight accentuating her size and tonight her violent red hair vied with the puce of her dress. We were joined by Natalie and Christine new to the club and very nervous about foreign guests, "Nothing to worry about," Frances said with a wicked smile, "If they don't understand just shout." I nudged her in the ribs smiled at the ladies and explained that these men probably spoke better English than many people we knew. Just then the cry went out: "The coach is here."

That was my queue to go to the ladies, here standing in a cubicle with heart beating fast I was able to pull myself together. Shaking my shoulders, adjusting my dress and taking a deep breath I was ready for something not really knowing what it was.

Making my entrance into the club house I could see that it had certainly become a great deal more crowded, among the melee I tried to find Bill but there was too much coming and going with the arrival of the men the room large as it was had also become full of cigarette smoke and the dull lighting made it doubly difficult to find anyone.

Suddenly I felt a hand on my arm and heard my husband: "Where have you been?" I turned to look at him with my heels on I was able to look him in the eyes: "Loo".

He smiled, relaxed he had found me, "Come on I want to introduce you to Dieter," looking at me he carried on with: "You look nice and I know you will like him."

I wanted to reply: "That's what I'm afraid of, I might like him too much." Obviously that reply was never made, instead stumbling a little as he pulled me unceremoniously across the floor to where a group were standing, they were Tom and Frances, Angie and Mark two German gentlemen I recognised as I had met them before. Fritz a red haired, rotund little man whose English was a little doubtful with many an American phrase inserted into a sentence making it difficult to know if he had understood what was being said. Then there was

Uwe the brother-in-law of Dieter and his best friend though unable to speak English he could understand so it was easier for Angie to communicate with him. Finally taking a deep breath I turned to the dark-haired man standing in the corner a cigarette dangling from his fingers, placing my hand in his ostensibly to shake it I was shocked by the intense power of emotion that coursed through my body and looking into Dieter's eyes it was obvious he too was feeling the same. Forcing a smile and finding my voice from somewhere: "Good evening Dieter we have met before."

He smiled, nodded and replied with: "Yes, but it was very brief." I had forgotten just how husky his voice was trying to bring myself back to normality I thought, "Um too many cigarettes." That did nothing to help my composure.

In the years that I had been a working Medium when helping people to bring their lives back to some kind of normality, I had so often heard them say, "I wasn't looking for an affair." I loved my wife or husband, "I don't know how it happened." And of course the usual, "It just happened." I had never had any understanding of these people and their mistakes and here I was about to do the same. Pulling myself together I thought: "I am not going to make a mess of my life." Extracting my hand from his I said: "Welcome to Little Barham, we will try to make your stay an enjoyable one." He never replied just smiled enough to let me know that our feelings for each other were reciprocated.

Feeling I needed to get some strength into my arms and legs making some excuse to the men I wandered off to join the ladies who were by now trying to decide how they were to entertain our visitors. Angie said, "Lunch on Sunday is going to be difficult." With Frances quickly replying: "Yes, we all know what a fantastic cook I am." For the first time that evening I laughed wholeheartedly, yes it was a well-known fact that when Mark needed a meal he would either get a take away or we would feed him and their two boys. I remembered one such special event when Angie was going to cook something special. She burnt the chicken, destroyed the boiled potatoes and the lemon meringue ended up a melted mess on the oven shelf. No, I had to step in here or her visitor was never going to survive. Looking at my friends I suggested: "Why don't we all get together at Angie's house? I will cook the beef, Angie can do the vegetables and you Fran can buy a good desert and bring the drinks." By the look on Fran's face it was obvious she was very relieved though Angie did say, "Why my house?"

"Because your dining room is that much larger," I replied smiling.

By now the evening was wearing on and we soon heard the bell for last orders, as I approached the men I heard Dieter ask: "Why the bell?" Bill then explained to him the last orders rule unless special permission has been granted, something the club had for the Saturday night. It was obvious from the look of puzzlement on the faces of our visitors that in Germany this rule did not exist. It was Fritz who said: "As long as someone is in the bar it stays open." I had no answer to this so smiled.

Now we had reached the end of the first evening I was really growing worried as for tonight there would only be Bill, Dieter and myself in our home never having been in the position I now found myself in, for the first time in my life I did not know what to do. As Bill collected Dieter who was by now more than slightly drunk and behaving very silly and found his suitcase and leather jacket we made our way to the car. As I opened the doors for them I heard Dieter mumble: "A woman is driving not in my house." I looked at him in the mirror seeing the glint in his eyes and knew he was laughing at me replying with: "Good thing it's my house then and if you don't behave it's a long walk there."

"Oh!" he replied "The lady bites,"

"Very hard" Bill laughed.

The journey home was quiet I guessed that Dieter had dozed off in the back having had a long tiring day and too much to drink everything was taking its toll of him. For a second I allowed myself to gaze at him asleep and wondered how he would look in bed until I heard, "What the hell are you doing?" You nearly missed our turning." I mumbled an apology and quickly swung down our street.

Bill woke Dieter up led him into the house and into the room that he would be sleeping in, it was normally used as the place where I did my Psychic Readings but for the weekend it had been turned into a bedroom. Seeing the slightly sleepy look in his eyes I suggested that Bill show him the bathroom, enquire if he wanted a coffee before bed and tell him what time we would be doing breakfast as the men had to catch the coach early for their trip to a London football game. As I left the men without thinking I asked: "Do you need anything else?" He replied with, "My Frau always kisses me when I go to bed." As Bill had his back to Dieter he never saw the smile and puckered lips in my direction. I threw back over my shoulder: "Good thing I am not your Frau then, good night."

I heard a muttered: "That is not a good woman." In my heart I thought it's because I am a good woman that there would be no good night kiss I was terrified as to where it would lead.

By now my memories were beginning to flood in and was making me restless in my seat, when I heard Bill say; "The landing lights are on, we will be on the ground in a few minutes." I came back to the ugly reality of why we were flying into Cologne today not for Carnival or a visit but to see how the man who had become so important to me was surviving, "Do you think he is still alive?" I whispered.

Bill looking down on me as we disembarked from the plane said: "I am sure he is, I won't believe how bad he is till we see him." This did something to allay my fears Bill had always been the common sense in my life and I saw no reason to disbelieve him now.

Leaving the airport we made our way to the Taxi rank and finding one of the big yellow Mercedes cars we gave the address in Kirschweiler and sat back in silence for the relatively short trip to our destination. By now my fear was having a very bad effect on my legs as I was finding it difficult to walk, sit or in fact do anything normal every turn of the car's wheels seemed to be saying, "Dieter, Dieter."

Eventually we found ourselves outside the Hubertus Brau Haus it was an old inn that had survived the war years and was now the centre of life in the village. Making our way to the front door we found it being opened for us by Walter and his wife Louise both looking as if they had been up all night and that she had spent many hours crying. As we entered they grasped us in bear hugs Walter muttering: "It is such a pity," and Louise just sobbing on my shoulder for a moment I let my guard down and allowed some tears to fall but I had to keep a tight rein on my feelings after all I was a friend from abroad not the woman whom he loved so much. For the first time since we had received the phone call only hours ago though it felt like a lifetime since that dreadful phone call. I allowed myself to glance down at the amethyst and gold circlet on the third finger of my right hand lifting it to my lips I gave it a surreptitious kiss the memory of the day Dieter placed this on my finger in the Cathedral in Cologne was just one of my precious memories to be brought out and visited. Slowly we made our way into the Hubertus to be greeted by a variety of friends, male and female.

Having been guests in this village for many years we had come to know many of them as they knew us and we were used to entering the Hubertus to music and laughter but the sombreness of everything around me was positively frightening. I wanted to shout and scream, "He is not dead yet." But once again I could say nothing. Friends came over quietly to greet us, there were the cousins Paul and Frank, along with Karl Heinz, there were so many people all with the same idea in mind the health of a dear friend.

I suddenly felt myself trapped in three pairs of arms one belonging to Maria, and the other two were Christoph and Markus. We had seen these children grow up, now in their early twenties I was amazed how they had developed. Extricating myself from their arms, and trying to smile my heart breaking when Maria said in a soft voice: "Uncle Dieter is very ill." Holding her to myself again I whispered back: "I know darling but we will pray for him." She looked so much like a miniature version of her mother except for the hair colour. Dressed in black trousers, white and gold blouse, smart pumps on her feet, and her blonde hair cut into the latest style. Next to her stood Christoph and Markus both as tall as their father, Christoph with his light brown hair, teeth now straightened without the braces and the most charming smile. Markus the heartbreaking image of his father and already a hit with the girls in the village I had been told in the past. From his dark hair and green eyes with the appeal that was his father's. Both boys dressed in jeans and tee shirts had obviously been crying. Holding all three, what could I say? I was as afraid as they were. Life without Dieter there was no thought that could go beyond that.

Having greeted us, both boys felt they should go home to their mother, who had been with the Doctor.

Maria went over to join her father, leaving Bill and myself with the others.

Needing to be on my own saying to Bill, "I'm going up for a bit." He smiled, I knew my way up the curving stairs to the room that was always ours, opening the door and leaving the bags on the floor I threw myself on the bed and for the first time in hours was able to allow my tears to fall, in that moment I knew the true feeling of heartbreak, now I understood what many of my clients had been through when they came to see me. A shattering of everything that you held dear, darkness that saw no light and pain that was so searing there was no coming back from. I could not lose the love of my life.

As my tear drenched eyes began to close in the God given mind numbing rest we call sleep, slowly I allowed my memories to drift back one last time to that first evening I took Dieter to my home.

The journey was silent Bill tired, while Dieter and I were aware of the tensions that were filling our bodies and very souls we were crying out for each other but unable to do anything about it.

Entering the house Bill looked at us yawning: "Sorry folks can't stay awake any longer must sleep." I said I would need one last coffee, not something new for me as I often had a cup before bed. I tried not to look in Dieter's direction as I heard the little gasp he made knowing that my coffee was his cue to know I would wait for him.

As I left the bathroom from the room opposite my work room now Dieter's bed room a soft, "Vicki, I am waiting." I looked up to see him standing at the entrance wearing a pair of pyjamas the like I had never seen before, they were in burnt orange, a tee shirt type top that clung to his muscular chest, the pants more like long shorts that clung lovingly to his thighs making me want to caress them. Looking at his shorts I could see the swelling that told me exactly how much he needed me. He stood silently arms open murmuring: "I know this is wrong but what can we do?" Silently I walked into the waiting embrace our lips met at first in an exploratory way then catching fire from each other. I felt his hands undoing my zip allowing the dress to fall to the floor. I was incapable of thought, not once did I think this was my house and that of my husband too.

The only feeling running through me now was the passion taking hold of us both, new to us we had never experienced anything like this before. Having removed my dress, he went on to remove my underwear making it obvious he had no patience with anything dividing our skins from each other as I had by now removed his pyjamas too. There was no thought for anything or anyone only the man holding me. I experienced kisses that I had never shared before with Bill, Dieter could examine every nerve with his lips where they did not go his hands did, once this was satisfied he allowed his tongue to assist. For the first time in my life I was not just being made love to I was being worshipped, adored, a goddess on the altar of love. I returned every caress, suddenly I was a pupil again and there was so much to learn. The man in whose arms I stood was my tutor, my interpretor and I so much in love only too willing to learn and study his philosophy.

Dieter whispered as we were close to crossing a bridge that we could never come back from: "No, Liebchen not yet and not like this." For a moment I was stunned I had been about to give him everything I had – myself and here he was refusing. Quickly pulling my clothes on feeling ashamed I had allowed myself to be made a fool of, realising how I was feeling he placed his arms around me once again whispering: "Yes, mein schatz that is what I also want but not like this we do it in love not satisfaction." Planting a kiss on my lips with a little smile he walked into the room and shut the door.

As I finally felt sleep take hold of me I cried out to God: "If you are there I promise you anything, please let him live. Not just for me but for his family too. I am prepared to never see him again just knowing he was on the same planet would be enough don't take him dear God please don't."

The promises we make when someone we love is in mortal danger.

Chapter 3

"Wake up Vicki" I could hear the soft voice of my friend Louise calling me out of the sleep I did not want to stir from. "We wait for you in the breakfast room." It never ceased to amaze me that though I did not spend too much time in Germany the moment I heard the language to me it was as understandable as listening to English. "Come downstairs Bill is already eating, we have your favourite bacon." Rousing tiredly and rubbing my hand across my eyes I gave a weak smile. "Child you did not undress last night," she smiled "you did look very tired, come." I climbed stiffly out of bed allowing Louise to give me a hand. Though she was married to Walter a very proud German Louise was in fact a Croatian from Zagreb they had met after his divorce from his first wife and he had been on holiday in that country with some friends. She was a well-built lady with dark hair, slight streaks of grey, laughing brown eyes and could, much to her husband's annoyance pour a beer faster and better than he could though he had been born to the trade. Though she was a foreigner to the village Louise had soon won the hearts of all those she came across and was well known as Tante Louise.

I made my way slowly and slightly unsteadily into the bathroom to prepare myself for whatever the day would throw at me. Washed and dressed I followed Louise down the stairs to the breakfast room from the sound of voices I knew that Bill and Walter had been joined by Dieter's brother-in-law Uwe. On seeing us enter the room he jumped up enveloping both of us in a bear hug that threatened to break our ribs, I could feel the emotion in him by the shaking of his body. "We can go and see him today," he whispered "but first it will be Monique and the boys."

At this I wanted to scream, "No not her but me." Of course that was not going to happen she is his wife I am not.

Silently I nodded letting him know that we understood. "How is Monique?" I asked.

"You know my sister she cries a lot and walks round the house quietly like a little mouse, so we wait." I nodded knowing Monique as I did her brother had described Dieter's wife perfectly.

In appearance Monique and Dieter were a perfect foil for each other she was small always impeccably dressed with a perfect taste in clothes her blonde hair never out of place and her make-up perfect, in personality she was quiet and unassuming. He tall, handsome and virile with his raven black hair, green eyes and muscular body he was the total opposite to his wife yes they were the consummate picture of the ideal couple. So, it was that I understood Uwe when he said she walked round the house like a little mouse.

Our first meal of the day was a difficult one with many gaps in the conversation, after what appeared to be a very long and painful time it was decided that we should go to see Monique and then accompany her and their two sons to the hospital. It had already been decided that she would be going into the unit that was caring for her husband then once given permission accompanied by the rest of us we too would enter the ward. All the arrangements would of course depend entirely on the surgical team that were in charge.

As we walked along the street that would lead us to the house I could feel a terrible dread, questions were running through my brain such as: "Perhaps Monique has heard that he is worse and she hasn't phoned. Maybe she will say it is better if Bill and I don't visit." That and many more questions were running riot in my feverish mind. The neighbourhood appeared very quiet almost as if everything and everyone was waiting, normally on a Sunday morning there were numerous cars travelling on a variety of missions from football games to handball and tennis courts but today none of that appeared to be happening. As Dieter and his family were very much a part of the fabric of village life I felt that they were all waiting for news good or bad.

Eventually after a few minutes' walk Uwe led us up the path leading to the front door of the house, I could hear the voices of their two sons normally deep but today they were muted and a little frightened. As Birgit, Uwe's wife opened the door to us I could see that she too had spent the night crying, the red of her eyes and her swollen face expressed my feelings entirely but as family she was more able to express herself than I a mere visitor and a foreigner as well, could not.

Birgit was about my height and very slim, she had red hair with a natural curl that she did try to keep straight but never completely succeeded in doing. She was dressed perfectly, no matter where she was or what she was doing, Birgit never had a hair out of place or an outfit that did not fit the occasion., Today she was dressed in a grey track suit, with black sandals on her feet and the inevitable shoulder bag slung over her.

On seeing Bill and myself accompanying her husband Birgit threw her arms around us both sobbing, having extricated himself from her clinging arms Bill called out to the two boys Christoph the elder and Markus the younger, on hearing my husband's voice both boys came out of their bedrooms and greeted him, no longer the children we once knew, but young adults. Today these young men were far more reserved, looking at them I felt they had grown up a great deal since I had last seen them, this recent event with their father suddenly forcing them to face life and all its problems.

Having said hello to Bill they turned to me looking down into my eyes, I felt they were begging me to tell them everything would be all right for them and their lives would return to normal these were promises I could not make no matter how desperately I needed it to be so for my sake as well as theirs. Christoph now in his early twenties with his brown curly hair, hazel eyes in a heart shaped face with a well-defined mouth, took his year's seniority over his brother very seriously. Looking at Markus the younger one by three years having a bigger build than his brother his hair as dark as their father's, and his eyes were the same green as Dieter's, his face and cheekbones well defined and a smile that normally had mischief written across it today that little touch was sadly missing. Both boys were very sporting Christoph like his father enjoyed playing football, Markus loved skiing and ski jumping to the concern of his mother.

Taking us by the hand they led us into the living room where their mother sat with the television on but obviously not seeing anything. Having grown used to seeing Monique so perfectly dressed every time, I was shocked at the young woman I saw standing before me today. Her normal blonde hair was totally unkempt, for the first time since I had known Monique I saw her without any make-up her slim body looking dishevelled in a blue track suit that had seen better days and pink socks on her feet. On seeing the pair of us like her sister-in-law she too broke down in tears, clinging to Bill as if afraid to let go. I stood helplessly by needing someone to give me comfort and solace but knew that the only person who could do so was the one in this instant for whom it was impossible.

After the inevitable cups of coffee Monique went to prepare herself for her visit to the hospital, there was the usual discussion as to what time we should arrive. I sat quietly in the corner of the room pretending to be looking at a book while every nerve in my body screamed out that I didn't want to waste any more time I had to get to the hospital but as usual I said nothing just giving a weak smile when necessary.

Eventually we were all ready the boys looking every inch the young men their father was so proud of. They walked on either side of her, protection of their mother in every move they made. Monique, almost looking her normal self, a taxi that would take us all had been ordered it had been decided that would be best as Bill and I did not know the whereabouts of the hospital where Dieter was.

The journey to the hospital was carried out in almost perfect silence apart from the boys discussing what they would do for "Poppa" when he came home, how they would care for him and what they planned to say to him, no one had the heart to tell them as he was unconscious he would not take in anything. I would later learn how wrong I was in this presumption.

After the cab had traversed the many busy and one way streets of the large City of Cologne I was informed that we were not too far from the hospital, looking straight ahead I could see a number of large white buildings with parking areas for ambulances and doctor's vehicles as we pulled up the drive Uwe spoke to the driver making an appointment for the time we would be ready to leave. As I had only just arrived I really was in no mood for coming away again, in fact I was more than prepared to spend nights at the hospital something I knew would never be allowed not without some very awkward questions being asked.

Uwe knew the name of the ward Dieter was in so there was no time wasted, we made our way along brightly lit and impersonal corridors up and down stairs taking left turns then right turns till Uwe finally stated we had arrived. There facing us was a room with the number 8A, the blinds on the windows facing into the corridor were closed as was the glass panel on the door giving everything a feeling of total emptiness and loss this frightened me. Suddenly, we were faced with a young nurse who asked who we were when Uwe stated we had the patient's family with us her demeanour changed, she ushered us into a relatives waiting room. Here there had been a little touch of trying to make family members more comfortable. A large brown leather sofa in the middle of the room, with two armchairs, a table in the corner with the inevitable coffee making machine and some books in a stand and also a TV should anyone be interested.

We sat down in the various seats provided once again in silence, even the boys were now quiet, each one with their own thoughts and afraid of what we would find behind those blinds and closed doors. Eventually we heard the rustle of medical gowns as the door opened to allow a group of three people to enter, one was Professor Gruber a tall thin man with a slight stoop, pale face sporting a full beard and moustache his bright beady eyes gave me the impression of a sparrow, for a second I had the impression that the Professor recognised me but I dismissed that as a moment of fantasy. The second was his assistant Herr Doctor Seiler equally as tall as his superior but bigger made and blond his blue eyes had a very understanding look and a mouth that looked ready to smile. I would learn at a later date that Rugby was his favourite game and he would often come to England to play and watch the game. The third person was the little nurse we had first seen, her name was Nicola a small blonde who took delight in asking us to call her Nikki she stated that she was Dieter's special nurse and on call with him for as long as he needed her. At this point I nearly shouted out that it was I he needed not some slip of a girl but once again I had to hold my tongue. The introductions made we were informed that as he was still very ill it would be Monique, her brother and the boys who would be the first to go into the room. This they did quietly and nervously like us left in the waiting room afraid of what would face them behind closed doors.

The time the little family spent visiting Dieter seemed to go on endlessly, we glanced at the books in the room then put the TV on and off numerous times as nothing could catch our attention. Birgit and I tried to talk to each other about anything that entered our heads but the conversation would always tail off into nothing every time we heard someone walk past. Eventually, we heard the door open and Uwe came out accompanied by

Monique and the two boys, it was obvious that mother and sons had been crying Uwe was trying to keep calm for the sake of his sister and nephews. As they entered the room with us we were informed that we could go in now but not for long.

As we entered the room Bill first, then Birgit I trailed along last – afraid. I was never sure what I expected to find but was surprised to see that the square room was bright and almost cheerful, one wall was a window that overlooked a garden. The wall facing the bed had a mural of Cologne Cathedral on it and a third window overlooked the corridor but it was the one at the head of the bed that caught my attention that was where all the medical instruments to help keep Dieter alive were positioned. Finally, having looked round the room I allowed myself to look at the man I loved so very much. There were drips and tubes attached to almost every part of his body, from an attachment to his mouth into a machine that I was later told would for the moment breathe for him. Blood pressure monitors and much else besides. At last I looked at the man in the bed his usual suntan now missing, what little I could see of his face was pale and drawn, I noticed that his hair was swept back from his forehead, for a second I wanted to pull it forward as I knew he normally had it styled. My heart ached to see him looking so helpless, "Oh! Dear God!" I cried out in silent prayer no doubt many others in the same room with an identical entreaty, "Please let him live and be well, I will promise you anything." Birgit called out to him to let him know she was there, Bill touched his right shoulder I just spoke his name. I was never sure if it was my imagination or whether he really had heard me because I was so sure that there had been a slight movement of his mouth. After some minutes Nikki came to tell us we had to leave as the medical staff had to do some work with him. As we walked away I realised that I had left my bag in the room, asking them to wait for me I hurried back picked up my bag was about to leave but the temptation was too great for me at last being alone with him I walked over to the bed held his right hand in mine and gently placed a kiss on his lips again I felt a movement was it imagination? I didn't think so straightening up as I made my way to the door I saw Nurse Nikki looking at me she gave me an understanding smile, a slight shrug of her shoulders and went over to the tray that stood in the corner with the medical needs for Dieter.

Slowly I rejoined the group apologising and saying what a very silly person I was, in my heart though was a tiny piece of sunshine. I had seen Dieter, he was still alive and I was sure all would be well. Climbing into the cab I thought, "How am I able with my Gift of Clairvoyance to help others but totally unable to help myself?"

Chapter 4

Our return journey to their home was done in complete silence even the boys had nothing to say.

On our journey to the hospital we had all had so much optimism but faced with the reality of seeing Dieter in that hospital bed the feeling had left us.

Leaving the people carrier and walking up the short footpath that led to the front door of the small terraced house, past the little hedge and plants that Dieter tended so carefully every weekend as relaxation from his normal working life in the Bank. We stood at the foot of the two steps while Monique opened the front door, stepping into the small square hall to the left were the stairs leading up to the bedrooms and bathroom. Walking across the brown stone tiles, "Ordered from Portugal." I remember Monique telling me with pride and Dieter's reply of: "At great financial cost," did almost make me smile, we made our way into the living room, walls tastefully painted in cream, with a large brown velvet sofa that curved facing the dining table and chairs, along the other wall was the bookcase that held Dieter's favourite books and family photographs, one was of the two of us on a Sunday in the park when the boys were very small, how happy we looked. Though it was now four o'clock and coffee was being made there was no offer of the usual cakes, today was not one of those days.

Finding it difficult to sit still I walked over to the book shelf, as I touched the spines of his favourite books I could almost feel Dieter's long fingers covering and caressing the back of my hands. Behind me I could hear Uwe's stilted English and Bill's broken German as they tried to make conversation. Normally, this would not have been a problem as Dieter had always been there to help usually with mocking laughter as either man made a mistake.

Hearing "Vicki," I looked up into Uwe's eyes: "What do we do if he does not come home?" I knew what he meant by the question, something I had been trying not to think about since yesterday's phone call. Picking up a book to hide my eyes now swimming in tears I mumbled, "Uwe, please let's not talk like that it is upsetting the boys." He apologised and went into the kitchen to help his wife and sister bring in the coffee tray.

It was growing late when we finally said goodbye to Monique and the family, Birgit had said she would spend a few nights with her sister-in-law. So it was when we left the house Uwe accompanied us to the end of the road then he turned left to go home and we went on to the Hubertus.

It was not difficult to see the Hubertus as in the main street it was quite the largest building there, having been built at the start of the 1850 era by a very enterprising entrepreneur, having seen that the village would grow and would consequently need a place that would become the centre of everything and that it certainly had from Football Club meetings to Christmas Parties and Carnival celebrations and of course the hotel, all life really was there. It was typical in design of the mid nineteenth century the outside done in brickwork with a castellated roof and bay windows overlooking the street, the entire outside gave the appearance of a prim school teacher but the inside was totally different.

The bar was divided into two areas the first was where the tables were for dining, drinking and holding club meetings, walking past the tables and down a narrow walkway led to a large square area here they would hold dances, parties, weddings and of course the wonderful carnival celebrations times that held so much magic for Dieter and myself.

Looking around the Hubertus, everything was so familiar from the people to whom it was a local to those who used it as a night out for special occasions. Walter had decided for reasons only known to him, when he had first taken charge of the hotel and bar from his father, that he would alter what he considered the old-fashioned décor. So, he had it designed and built to look like an olde worlde Galley.

The bar area resembling the forecastle of the ship, the tables in front of it, the poop deck, then the narrow walkway resembling that of a gangway, where there was more seating for those who wanted to eat but be away from the smoke and noise of the bar itself.

The walkway ended in the square room at the end that had been designed for dancing, parties and weddings also very useful at Carnival. To the left of this area was the door that led into the secret area known as the Kegel Bahn, in England a bowling alley. It was only opened to those who were club members, and for all the years we had been visiting and almost adopted by the people of Kirschweiler, not once had we been allowed to enter its no doubt hallowed hall.

Dieter had often joked that perhaps they all played in the nude. Hence, the secrecy.

No sooner had we entered the smoky atmosphere then conversation stopped, all eyes cast in our direction and the long awaited questions were aimed in our direction. We did the best we could to answer in German and English, eventually feeling exhausted we sat down for an evening meal just the two of us in silence both of us lost in our thoughts. Bill thinking of his friend, and me? Well my thoughts were with my lover.

As Walter approached us I had to ask him how this accident had happened as no one had explained anything to us, he went on to inform us that it was a common problem with the autobahns. He explained to me that on the autobhans there were incidents caused by drivers known as Gheister Fahrers – Ghost Drivers who would take the wrong turning on the road and drive the wrong way up so colliding with oncoming traffic, this had happened to Dieter.

With the Bar emptying out and having paid our bill against Louise's wishes we made our way along the hallway that led to the stairs that were semi-circular. Bill walked ahead, with me following behind, as we walked I trailed my hand on the bannister feeling the strength of the wood knowing that Dieter's hand had on previous occasions done the same thing.

Entering the room we pulled the curtains and started to prepare for bed, looking around the room I took in the coffee coloured carpet, the heavy oaken wardrobe and dressing table to match and the bed too giving proof of Walter's Bavarian Ancestry. The bed too was one of heavy oak and with the bed covers the same colour as the carpet not beautiful but serviceable. I watched as Bill entered the bathroom newly decorated, I felt so sorry for my husband as he looked suddenly very old he had never been in such a situation before and did not know how to handle it.

Turning out the lights Bill reached for me, I turned into his arms prepared to give him what he needed but not with my heart. As his lips touched mine I had to fight the sobs that were waiting to surface. At this moment in time I couldn't do what I had done in the past when my husband made love to me, it was Dieter's face I thought of and saw.

With Bill sleeping soundly I turned my back to him, trying to sleep, but all I could see was the hospital room. So, once again I slipped into memories of happier times.

Chapter 5

For the first time I could remember sleep and I had not been the best of friends. It was with relief that I finally saw the first fingers of dawn strike my bedroom window, setting all my ghostly fears of the night before to flight. I had lain for hours at the edge of the bad not wanting my feverish tossing and turning to disturb my husband's sleep as he would ask questions I could not answer. Then of course there had been the usual thoughts of: "Idiot woman you know you have played into his hands, you are a bet he has won." Numerous other thoughts like this raced round in my mind none of them answerable.

So many questions and no encyclopaedia to give any quick answers to give me comfort. As I was finally out of bed, dressed and ready for whatever the day threw at me. Entering the kitchen I was about to start breakfast having discovered what they ate in Germany I wished to offer our guest the same but Bill had other ideas. "Bacon and eggs with some fried bread," he mumbled as I started the oven: "What?" I almost shouted back "Do you want us to return him home ill?"

"No just satisfied." This word almost threw me into panic "satisfied?" What did Bill know? What had he suspected? Until I realised he was talking about his eating I was thinking of something else.

There was so much for me to worry about but all of it came down to one word "Guilt." Because I knew that the minute Dieter placed his arms around me again or attempted another kiss there would be no refusal only a silent yes. I was for the first time being made to feel like a woman. Walking through the hallway into the living room I caught a glimpse of myself in the mirror, the same one I had glanced in the night previous. Thinking if only I had known the night before what was to happen, would I have changed anything? "It's all right being a Medium to help others," I whispered to myself, "but no bloody good if you can't help yourself."

Busying myself in the kitchen with pots and pans, Bill having gone to bring our children home. I could hear the shower in the bathroom being used, Dieter whistling and the quietly soft aroma of his aftershave drifting into the kitchen. I nearly screamed, "How can you be so normal? You have made my world different, what are you going to do about it?" To my relief I heard Bill and the girl's voices coming up the path and Dieter opening the door to them.

Walking quietly across the lounge with the sun coming in through the now open windows, the brightness seemed to mock me while making a path across the carpet. Here was the mirror we bought cheap, but one of the first things we had bought as husband and wife. The surrounding walls covered in mint green and white regency stripe wallpaper. Pictures, paintings, photographs and ceramics we had gathered together over the years and for the first time I felt a stranger to them or was I just feeling a traitor? Afraid to answer this I made myself busy laying the table and waiting for the family to join me including the disturbance that had now found me.

As the smell of grilling bacon, frying bread and eggs started to fill the air I heard a voice that shook me to the core: "Look what I have found, aren't they beautiful." There he stood looking every bit as handsome as before, and very rested. Wearing blue jeans, open neck tee shirt in bright red showing the dark hair that I knew grew profusely on his chest. He did not look as I felt I did, frazzled and worn out. I looked at him trying very hard to appear normal as he was not in the doorway alone he was in fact holding the hands of my two daughters. He looked so vibrant and natural standing between them, my heart gave quite a jolt.

"Yes, my friend," Bill replied picking Lottie up and placing her on the chair that she quickly wriggled out of as she wanted to sit near Uncle Dieter they had both soon given him this name and so it stayed. There was a little tussle between Hannah and Lottie until their father very wisely reminded them that two could sit either side of him. Smiling their satisfaction to Bill the matter was soon settled.

Once the food was laid on the table I took myself back into the kitchen feeling unable to eat, but so very proud of my family. Sorting out the washing up I was not prepared for the voice that addressed me from the door way: "Liebchen, you must eat or you will not have a good day." I turned to him and in a frantic whisper. I turned my unruly hair all over my eyes, almost blinding me

"A good bloody day, that was ruined the moment I saw you." The hurt look in his eyes took me by surprise: "Do you think this is what I want also?" Brushing the hair out of my eyes I turned back to the sink, "No I suppose neither of us wants this." Taking my hand kissing the open palm he whispered: "Please darling for your children." Sighing I gave in and followed. "What took you so long?" Bill asked.

"Nothing much just showing Dieter how to use a washing-up sink, his wife has a dish washer." This had long been an argument between us: "Yea, I know," Bill laughed with a mouth full of fried bread "Me. Cheap, and good." This little joke brought everything into perspective and I was almost normal for a while.

I allowed the conversation to carry on around me, each little brown-haired girl trying to outdo the other. Hannah as the older by three years felt her seniority gave her more chance to speak intelligently and grown up. Lottie the brown-haired slightly rabbit toothed youngest just felt her personality outweighed all of us and could shout louder.

"You're very quiet," Bill remarked.

"A rare lady," Dieter replied. I felt quite annoyed that both men had singled me out in this fashion. "Just thinking what to do today, when you men are out being little boys." I was of course referring to the football match in London that they were going to. Putting a cup to his mouth Bill replied with, "Aren't you going shopping with Angie and Frances?"

"Oh! Ouch!" Dieter came back grinning, I did hit him this time with a wooden spatula. "No not this time I am taking the girls to Foxton on sea." Now I really had made a promise I could not break as I had two pairs of arms round my neck and kisses too. "Lovely, lovely Mum." Was it guilt that had made me make my promise? No, I defended this I had discussed the matter with my friends days before the arrival of storm force Dieter. As

63

we would not be spending much time with our children it was decided that the Saturday was theirs.

As I was beginning to feel almost normal Dieter walked up, stood behind me and said, "Can I hug your mother too?" Looking at the laughing green eyes and the mischief in his face I would happily have stuck a knife in him. But instead mumbled, "No time, got to get the washing-up done." Making my escape I could hear the men laughing and Bill asking: "So, old son what have you done to my wife, never known her behave like this before she's almost nice." Shaking my head I walked into the kitchen with shaking hands and legs and continued with the clearing up of breakfast.

There was a knock on the door, opening it I saw Tom and Mark looking as if they were naughty school boys allowed out of school early. "Are they ready?" Mark asked his fine fair hair glinting in the sun. Both men were dressed in black and white football colours, I presumed that was the team they were going to visit. Calling out to Bill and Dieter I said, "Your chums have come to play, ready?" this was greeted with a groan from Bill "Typical, you women just don't appreciate a good game." I laughed as there really was no answer to this.

Holding the door so they could make their escape I was unprepared for the purposeful way in which Dieter's fingers brushed mine as he walked through the door it shook every fibre of my being. He just looked back and smiled.

The day I spent with the children in Foxton on Sea was wonderful. With these two magical beings I was able to forget the night before and the upset to everything in my life. I could push the name of one man behind me and just be normal.

As Foxton was the largest seaside town to London, it was never empty. From Bingo Halls to the inevitable penny machines that no one ever won on. Hearing the piped music coming from the adventure land that had been designed for the children it wasn't long before we three were all being carried away in the excitement. "Mum," I looked at Hannah as she sucked her way round a multi coloured lolly pop something in the normal course of events I would never have allowed her to eat again that word "guilt," came to me. Looking down at her as we walked past a family of northerners enjoying the southern summer sun, "Um, what?" Smiling at me she said: "That Uncle Dieter he is very handsome, even more than daddy." In an instant I was brought back to reality, children. Looking at her I said, "Well because he is foreign he just looks different." And before I could say anything else Lottie filled in with, "He dresses differently too." I was not prepared for any more talk on "Uncle Dieter" so quickly changed the subject.

The day was now getting quite late and I had to get the girls home, changed and back to my mother's house before the men returned. I also had to prepare for the evening myself that would take up a great deal of my time.

Once home the children bathed and very sleepy were taken to my mother who had their room ready and as I had given them quite some rubbish to eat I did prepare her that there might be consequences that night something she should be prepared for.

Making my way home and very tired as there was no sign of the men I decided that a long leisurely bath and a short doze would prepare me for the evening ahead. I had heard it was going to be a barn dance and a BBQ.

"Should be fun," I thought as my eyes slowly closed in relaxed sleep.

I was rudely awakened by Bill and Dieter falling in through the front door having lengthy and loud conversations about which had been the better team. I thanked God that before I fell asleep on the sofa I had put on a track suit and not stayed as was customary for me after a bath in my dressing gown.

I heard, "Guten Abend, Liebchen," mocked the gentle tones of the voice I had longed to hear all day.

Feigning indifference, pretending I had not heard and determined to appear unshaken, I lifted the cup of coffee to my lips that I had quickly made on hearing the men enter the house. Thankful that in the gathering gloom of the early evening he could not see my shaking hands.

"Oh! Sorry Dieter I didn't hear you come in was it a good game?" He replied with one word, "Liar."

Then burst out laughing and I knew it was at me.

Our visitor was followed closely by Bill who rubbing his hands together said: "Coffee, great got any more?" Disappearing hurriedly into the kitchen I called back: "Plenty." there was of course an obstacle to my entering the kitchen it was Dieter who had planted himself fairly and squarely in the open doorway. To get past him I had to slide sideways and make myself as small as possible seeing my discomfort made him laugh louder than ever before. As I did this I felt the tips of my breasts come in contact with the lean firmness of his chest. The tension this created in me was intense. Had his hand not grabbed me when it did I felt sure I would have fallen.

Hearing the song of the birds in flight as they headed home, I wished I could be like them free and able to go where I wanted not tied to the present and unwanted emotions.

With a start I sat back listening to the two men talking amazed at Dieter's knowledge of English, when Bill asked him about this he explained that he had been taught this as a second language, where most other pupils learnt French he had chosen English. Explaining further that at the time he had not known why throwing a sideways glance in my direction he grinned and said: "Now I know why." I pretended to ignore this while at the same time wondering why it was a word or a letter in the English language could not be pronounced by him and it would almost come out like a lisp making his speech very endearing.

Fighting the urge to walk over to our guest and plant a kiss on his sensual lips, I called out: "It is time we were getting ready, I've told the girls what time to be at the Club let's not ruin Frances' record for being late." Bill laughed at this as it was well known among our group if we wanted Frances and Mark to be anywhere on time we gave them a half hour difference in time and to date it had worked. Bill explained all this to Dieter as both men walked away to prepare for the evening.

I sat sipping another cup of coffee as a variety of smells issued out of the bathroom door, I knew the one that Dieter used, his was a muskier one whereas Bill's was slightly sweeter. "A sign of the difference in both men."

Coffee finished, I decided to go up to the bedroom and prepare myself. As I entered the bedroom I saw my husband standing in front of me wearing a pair of grey slacks which suited his long legs perfectly. He wore a light blue open neck shirt and round his waist a leather belt with the Union Jack in silver as a buckle. On his feet were a pair of light blue loafers, as Bill never danced I knew these shoes would be no deterrent to him moving on the dance floor. His dark hair and hazel eyes glinting in the light of the bedroom. Feeling very proud I walked up to him planted a kiss on his cheek and said: "All the women will envy me tonight." His smile said "Thank you."

With Bill going down I was now free to get dressed and put my make-up on, this time I was not dressing for me but for someone else.

Slipping out of my tracksuit I stood for a moment naked in front of my mirror, running my hands up and down the length of my body, unable to dismiss the thoughts that flitted furtively through my mind. I was like a barn owl on the hunt, searching while at the same time afraid of discovery.

"I wonder what Dieter would think if he saw me as I am now?" Hearing the question spoken frightened me galvanised me into action and it was not long before dress and make-up were on albeit with shaking hands.

Tonight I need not have worried what effect I would have on the men, with the clever use of make-up, the black tights and high heeled shoes were all the perfect complement to the dress. It was not new just never been worn before, the red dress clung lovingly to my body, covering it like a soft glove smooth and soft with not a wrinkle or a bulge. Dabbing perfume behind my ears and little between my breasts I now felt prepared for anything. All I needed was the look in the eyes of one man – not my husband's.

Afraid of slipping down the stairs in my shoes I took the descent very carefully as though making an entrance that was at first ignored as both men had their back to the stairs and were in deep conversation. It was Bill who caught sight of my legs descending asking, "What have you got on? Hope it is decent."

The stupidity of the married male never ceased to amaze me, they would admire on any female an outfit they would not approve of in their wives. Well this one was married to the wrong woman.

"Told you it wouldn't take long for me to dress."

By this time I had cleared the stairs and was in full view to the two men. Out of habit I looked first at Bill just to see his expression. It was as I expected admiring but reserved. Then with pulse racing and heart pounding I challenged breathlessly: "Herr Schmidt, do you approve of your hostess?" I will thank forever the fates that for that moment my husband's attention was drawn away from Dieter and myself for those precious moments. His eyes were large in a face gone suddenly pale, I could see a nerve twitching in his cheek as he took in the picture I made.

Brown eyes emphasised with the clever use of colour to make them appear larger than normal. Cheeks highlighted so accentuating the cheekbones and lips outlined with a darker pencil then glossed over to make them appear full, pouting and ready for passionate kisses. The dress clung to every curve of my body. High heels, black tights and silver shoes finished off the ensemble.

He replied with two words, "I like." My reply was soft, "Do you?" The words sounding so unimportant and facile. Yet the expression in our eyes were to be studied exclusively by two people Dieter and myself.

"Come on you two," Bill called shaking the car keys in front of us: "we are losing valuable drinking time." Making us both smile and come down to earth. As we walked towards the door he whispered, "We are not free, this is not good." I had no reply to make as he was so right.

Sitting in the back of the car and still trying to put the recent events into perspective, I found myself playing with my wedding ring a little smile playing around my lips. How proud I was the day Bill slipped that gold circlet on my left hand, why was I now contemplating destroying everything that stood for? Surely not just sex? This ring that had once been a symbol for everything I held dear, was now feeling like a tight band, restricting the blood flow in my hands and tightening its grip round my heart making breathing very difficult. By now we had reached the club and as I was stepping out of the car the sudden realisation of everything that I had gone through made me trip, bringing Dieter to my aid: "You all right Schatzie?" He whispered, I nodded dumbly quickly pulling away and walking as fast as I could towards the lights and music of the building ahead of us.

The warm autumn evening was filled with the scent of late blooming flowers. I could pick out the scent of jasmine from a neighbour's garden, roses that had been planted to make the approach to the club appear more attractive and looking up at the sky I could see that the stars were coming out in force. Everything appeared so normal, why then was I so different?

We were met at the entrance of the Club by Danny the Club Chairman and his wife Lucy. What a picture they made? Looking at the pair Bill and I had to stop from laughing out loud, Dieter just stood in awesome silence. Danny was of Italian descent and short and rather fat, with his dark unruly curly hair, swarthy complexion and brown eyes he normally looked like a bad copy of an American Mafia man. Tonight, however, he looked ridiculous, dressed in a complete cowboy suit from jeans, too tight for his rotund figure, covered by leather chaps, the plaid shirt and cowboy hat did nothing to make him look attractive or smart. Lucy, appeared even more absurd she too was short and fat with slate coloured hair just long enough to put in bunches tied up in mauve gingham ribbon. Her pale face covered in make-up too bright for her skin, her blue eyes seeming to disappear into her face with the make-up covering them. Her figure was covered in a purple and white gingham dress, with white socks that had a lace edge to them on her fat legs and black flat shoes with ankle straps. The picture they made was just the funniest thing I had seen in months and for the first time in many hours when on my own I was able to have a really honest laugh – of course at the expense of Mr and Mrs Binecchi.

As it was a warm evening there was no need for coats, the men kept their jackets on and we ladies just stayed as we were. Tonight the Club's main dancing area was set up to look like a barn. It was obvious that Danny, his wife and the committee had worked very hard at setting everything up. There were bales of straw set at intervals, the soft lighting was a pale pink mixed in with shades of green. The curtains tonight were made to look as if they too were made of stalks of plants and on the stage was the group that would be entertaining us for the evening by the name of Shiloh. They consisted of a guitar, banjo, mouth organ and what could best be described as a modern copy of an old fashioned piano the kind normally heard in western films, fronting them was the singer and he was quite the largest man I had ever seen. Gary, had to be over six feet tall and almost the same in circumference he also had a voice to match making it easy to understand why he was the caller for the group.

Looking out of the side door into the normal football field area I could see that a BBQ had been set up and the gentle smell of coals warming up, added to onions and burgers being prepared it promised to be a great evening. If only I felt more like myself.

Feeling a movement beside me I realised that I had been joined by my friends Angie and Frances.

Looking at them I forced a smile as both had taken the opportunity to dress for the occasion. Angie in a flared blue and white polka dot dress also with flat heels and Frances in the best that Laura Ashley could provide in pink. Linking my arms with them we made our way towards the bar to join the men. Bill, Dieter, Tom and Uwe had now been joined by all the others of the group and there was a great deal of talking and hand movements going on: "Honestly," Angie said laughing, "these men have been together all day, seen the same match but still got tons to talk about." As we walked down into the well of the dance floor to find a table for ourselves Frances said: "Let's face it, it keeps them happy. And they won't be dancing."

I smiled it was a well-known fact that we three girls loved to dance but our men were quite happy propping up the bar not something that really worried us. Tonight, was different I did want to dance, I needed to be touched but not by my husband but someone else's. "You should be ashamed of yourself." I mumbled "Ashamed of what, love?" Frances asked. "Oh, nothing just thinking rude things about our Chairman and his wife." My friends laughed, "Well that's nothing new, is it?"

Eventually, we found a table, it wasn't difficult as tonight was a special night the dance floor area was curtained off from the saloon part of the club, where the members could enjoy a drink, listen to the music but be away from the rest of the merrymaking. Sitting down we made ourselves comfortable, I made sure from where I sat that Dieter at the bar was in my eye line and looking up I could see he was thinking the same for a second our eyes met and the blood coursed through my veins. "You've gone red what's wrong, blood pressure?" Angie asked.

"No, just bending down to tighten my shoe strap." I received a disbelieving "Huh!" Looking at Angie I realised that I would have to be careful as she was a very astute lady and nothing much slipped past her. Having been friends for so many years we three were more sisters than friends and very close.

As we sat down prepared to be entertained Frances said: "So, what's it like?" Looking at her puzzled I asked "What's what?"

"Your feller"

"What Bill, he's OK." I had decided to play obtuse.

"No, my dear that rather dashing piece of German machinery." Pretending to search in my handbag afraid of them reading the expression on my face. I replied with, "He is a man same as all the others, why?" Looking at Frances and Angie who both had very strange looks on their faces as they replied in unison, "Oh, nothing just thought you both looked interested in each other." Staring at them feeling a cold and hot shiver run through me, surely I could not be so transparent. I continued with, "I am looking after as best I can, yes he is good-looking but so too is the man I am married to. Let's dance." By now the group had started up and I had no intention of suffering the third degree any further.

As the music started up and Gary took his place microphone in hand: "Right ladies and gentlemen, we are here to enjoy ourselves, don't want anyone sitting down, all up and dancing. The first dance is a reel." This of course had to be explained by the English to the German visitors who had never been to a barn dance before. This was the start of one of the most hectic and feverish evenings ever spent in the club. The dancing was not fantastic, there was not too much agility but the laughter more than made up for it. How I wished I could have enjoyed it more but my mind was always on the green eyed devil standing beside my husband.

"Got an important question to ask," Angie said into a moment of silence as we had sat down to take our breath, long drink of orange juice or coke as we were the designated drivers. Afraid to ask what the question was it was with relief that I heard Frances enquire instead: "What important question?" Looking at the two of us Angie continued with: "Well tomorrow lunch?"

"Yes, after the game that I know our men will lose," the girls looked at me, "looking at the drink they are putting away."

"Yes, I had noticed," Angie replied giggling.

Because we had already discussed this the day before, it was a simple matter to arrange a time to meet at Angie's, "How about combining everything in my house." This was something we agreed to with alacrity and it was decided that all we had bought would be taken over to Angie's house and we would cook the meal together, preparing it before the football match so all would be ready when we got home.

I was relieved with so many of us present at the table there would be no need for Dieter and myself to be alone at any time.

There had been an unspoken agreement between Dieter and myself that we would not be seen together that evening. Eventually Gary informed us that it was time for a break and that the food was being served: "Would you like to go and join the young ladies now cooking your burgers for you." Angie, Frances and I looked at each other holding back rude laughter: "Young ladies!" we giggled, "Young they might have been but young and ladies?" With this we left the club and walked out into the warm, dark evening to the barbecue where Lucy now joined by Rita a close friend of hers and quite the opposite in appearance, whereas Lucy was short and fat, Rita was tall and very thin with over bleached hair, pale face too much make-up and in green gingham, "What's with this gingham?" Angie asked.

"Don't know," Frances whispered, "but it is giving the men a giggle." Looking at the expression on the faces of our visitors was fun, they had obviously never seen anything like these two before.

We ladies had decided that our men would not leave the bar so we took trays placed the food on them and walked over to the table, Angie walked over to them and asked them to sit down and eat. "Good looking, waitresses you have here." Dieter stated.

"Oh! Yes and very efficient too." Frances laughed simpering as Dieter placed his arm around her waist, for once I could have hit my friend I felt so jealous. It should have been me, I thought.

Once the food had been cleared away, we held a raffle, this really did amaze our visitors as they had never seen anything like this before and Bill and Tom went on to explain that the money raised would go towards a charity. Dieter explained this to Uwe and Fritz who nodded though probably not comprehending too much.

The lights were once more dimmed for dancing, by now our men had decided not to go back to the bar but sit at the tables. I was in no mood for sitting around, I had to be on the move the only way to get a release from my pent up emotions. So it was we grabbed male after male to get them up and dancing, at one point I glanced in the direction of the table at which Bill and company sat to see Dieter lounging with his long legs sticking out, his eyes not leaving me and a cigarette dangling from his fingers. I felt such a rush of emotion that for the next few minutes I danced like a Dervish. Until, a sudden feeling of loneliness over took me, here I was surrounded by friends enjoying myself and yet I felt all alone. At this point on the pretext of visiting the Ladies I made my way out into the now quiet field. All the food cleared away, the barbecue out nothing but the smells of the night air to keep me company.

In the still autumn evening with just the occasional breeze to stir the leaves, I walked blindly, tears of self-pity misting my eyes. From the distance I could hear the music and laughter, instead of filling me with pleasure it only served to heighten the intense feeling of loneliness now engulfing me. I meandered around the grounds deep in thought, convincing myself that there was no great love between Dieter and myself I was no Helen to his Paris. We were no star-crossed lovers as in all the great myths and legends. No, we were just two suburban people who had for a moment felt a sexual attraction and Jim's words about Purple Michaelmas were not a Spiritual Message they were just words to which I wanted to fit a situation.

Shrugging my shoulders I decided it was time to rejoin the enjoyment, but as I turned a gasp escaped me as I saw the dark shape of a man standing behind me, angry at having my privacy invaded I called out, "Who is there, what do you want?" The softly answered,

"You," was all that I needed. Slowly I turned into the waiting arms neither thinking nor caring if someone else walking round the fields would see us. For now I had all I needed, the man I had grown to love so deeply in such a short space of time.

As he held me he whispered, "I saw you leave and was worried, are you O.K.?" I could feel his smoky breath on my face as he said into my hair, "People were worried about you, no one has seen you for a little time." He carried on, muttering into his jacket I replied with. "A bit late now."

"What do you mean?" He carried on, looking up at him I said "I haven't been OK since you walked into my life yesterday." Pulling out of his arms I carried on with: "Anyway why does everyone need to know where I am and what I am doing, even I like to be alone sometime." This reply made him laugh and his "Yes, Greta Garbo we will try to leave you alone." Laughing he pulled me back into his arms, "You must know you will always be needed by someone, Bill, your children, friends and tonight it is I who needs you." pulling me into a deeper darkness he whispered, "I have such a need of you my darling."

I felt his arms close around me, drawing my quivering body ever closer to him. Our breathing was laboured filling the air around us. Moments before his lips covered mine, I heard him whisper, "This is dangerous, very dangerous." I nodded agreement but I was like a wanderer in the desert, needing the relief offered by an oasis while knowing that there were hidden hazards. The air around us was filled with electricity, I needed those lips on mine. Instead, he appeared to hold off, allowing his hands to wander at will across my body. Lingering on my breasts, now taut my nipples rigid with pent up emotion. Had I been a cat the only sound I would have been capable of would be loud purring.

As his lips eventually met mine, plundering them like a pirate of a bygone era, the storm of desire that filled me was overwhelming. Though I was not an inexperienced woman I was still unprepared for the feelings within me. It was almost as if were a virgin waiting to be taken for the first time. Knowing there were a myriad ways in which to delight each other, while at the same time afraid of the consequences. As we kissed and caressed out there on the dark football pitch the strength of his desire was as obvious to me now as it had been the night before. Taking it in my hands, I caressed and played with that toy of nature given to man for the sheer enjoyment of woman. The erotic feelings racing round me were new and exciting, like nothing I had ever felt before.

As I was beginning to feel we would soon reach the point of satisfaction, I felt him pull abruptly away turning his back to me as he adjusted his dress. I stood feeling rebuffed, hurt and dirty. Not knowing what I had done to be treated in this fashion. Not till he spoke did I fully understand.

"What we do is wrong, we must never be alone together again." He said, his voice still shaking and rough from unsatisfied desires. He carried on, his English now sounding strained and faltering: "It is not the game of growing children we play, we have two separate lives, different countries and others who depend on us, we cannot let them down." Then his voice broke a little as if the tears filling me were in his heart too. "Darling Vicki, please understand we are not for each other, please help me to be good." As he said this as if impossible to help himself he bent his head to brush my lips with his and I felt the tears on his face mingle with mine. It was little compensation to know our pain was mutual, fate had invented a cruel game and we were the ones chosen to play it.

I let Dieter make his way back into the Club and bright lights, once I thought that a proper interval had passed I followed him back into the smoke filled atmosphere, now the music that I had enjoyed earlier appeared to me loud and brash how I needed to be out of it. I was grateful that no one had noticed our absence, or so I thought until feeling eyes on me I noticed both Angie and Frances staring, coming up to me Frances said: "I know you have eaten and drunk but your make-up looks really messed up, not been up to anything I hope?" Feeling that I could not at this moment give a proper reply I shrugged and ordered another orange juice.

To my relief the end of the evening was announced and Gary informed that he would play a record and a nice slow one to allow people to calm down. Knowing that our husbands would not be dancing this the three of us made to walk off the floor but Uwe and Fritz had other ideas and taking hold of Angie and Frances led them in a very gentlemanly manner onto the floor my friends looked surprised and delighted. I knew no one would dance with me so continued back to the bar, until a pair of firm hands slipped slowly round my waist and pulled me close to him. I just did the most natural thing in the world and folded into his arms.

The voice of Leo Sayer singing "When I Need Love," held us both in a trance, we swayed in the semi darkness of the dance floor oblivious to what people might think we were two people in love albeit a forbidden one.

As the last words of the song faded away and the bright lights came back on, I felt I wanted to scream, "Leave me in my secret world, please." But of course this was never going to happen reality was never far away. I saw Klaus pulling Dieter aside and whispering something in his ear that made him look very angry, I promised I would ask what his sly countryman had said. Stepping up to the bar I felt a finger poke me in the ribs, turning to look at my now two furious friends I asked, "What is wrong with your two?"

"Wrong with us?" Angie squeaked: "You didn't see yourself dancing out there, is there something we should know about?" I shook my head in silence and whispered: "Please girls give me a chance, I am going to need your help and support but not now please." Saying this we all parted going to our various vehicles and calling good night to everyone.

It was in silence we made our way home, Bill sitting beside me Dieter having kept his promise to stay away from me sitting quietly in the back.

Once we arrived home on the usual pretext of a headache, I prepared for bed I knew there would be no sleep just recriminations, guilt and a dreadful unfulfilled longing.

Chapter 6

I must have eventually fallen asleep riven with guilt memories kept coming back to me, including the night that Bill and I were introduced at an Ice Rink in London. The days we spent with each other until finally deciding we wanted to marry, the birth of our children two beautiful girls, my mother and family, his family the memories kept coming so did the tossing and turning until eventually exhaustion finally took over.

Finally it was time to wake up and resume normality, going down the stairs to start breakfast I heard the phone ring knowing it was my mother I answered with a bright, "Hi, mum everything OK? Girls sleep well?" My mother was the kind of person easy to fool so I had to be very cool, calm and collected. "Yes, dear" she replied, "Looks a lovely day you are very fortunate with your weekend." She then went on to ask, "Enjoying yourself love?" How could I honestly answer that, so a mumbled, "Yes, fine."

"Good she came back with." Then continued, "You taking us to Church or shall I get a cab?" By now Bill was up and dressed and standing beside me. Talking into the phone he said, "That's OK Mum I'll take you." Then turning to me he said, "I'll take the three of them, you get on with breakfast." With the situation settled very much against my will Bill got in the car and left. Now I was alone in the house with Dieter my lover and alone, something neither of us wanted. I also realised that I would need to wake him up.

On trembling legs and with racing heart I walked towards his room, Dieter's room for the weekend but from Monday it would return to being my work room.

As I gently knocked on the door hoping he would answer it fully dressed, I thought, "If he slept well

I will kill him."

The silence of the room told me that he was not awake, opening the door I looked in, the room was still in darkness as he was fast asleep and so the curtains were still drawn. Glancing at the painted lavender walls and the cream coloured woodwork. My filing cabinet and diaries on the work surface everything looked as it had the day previous, the only thing different was the spare bed borrowed from my mother and of course the person sleeping on it.

I could hear his soft breathing, silently I approached the sleeping man and stood watching his face, secretly glad that this was my time to watch him completely unobserved. My eyes having become accustomed to the dim light picked out his every feature. The high cheekbones and perfect mouth, black tousled appearing as if restless hands had run through it constantly. Though his green eyes were hidden by the long lashes now covering them, I felt as if I knew every expression they were capable of once he was awake. Allowing myself the luxury to continue studying him with no one to observe, my eyes followed on down past his face to the strong neck, the pulse beating there for a moment I wanted to bend down and kiss it but quickly drew back "No, Vicki he is not yours." My eyes wandered to the wide shoulders and muscular chest, dark hairs looking as if they were painted on. The nipples peeking through the dark foliage, I could feel the familiar desire welling up in me and the fear feathering its way up my spine afraid to give in I pulled back with a gasp.

A deep sigh escaped me for it was obvious that Dieter too had spent a restless night, as he had dislodged the duvet. Leaving only part of his bare body hidden from my wandering eyes. Following the line of hair down to his flat stomach, past his navel I tried desperately to tear my eyes from the large bulge just hidden from my eyes by the cover. My mind was in a quandary, should I cover him up again? I really should wake him for breakfast and the day ahead what should I do? What should I do? The final decision was taken out of my hands when I heard a voice ask, "Well how do I look?" Stepping back, a horrified gasp escaping me, I had been so busy studying the man before me I had been completely unaware that he was returning my scrutiny.

"So, how do I look good or no?" He whispered asking the same question again.

Once again he demanded an answer from me, I was incapable of answering. My eyes taking in the picture he made, now sitting up in bed those green eyes filled with the look of a sleepy but mischievous faun. Before I could move further from the bed so leaving a distance between us, he had manoeuvred himself up so that he was resting nonchalantly against the headboard. His brown skin looking darker than ever against the white of the pillows.

"I like the valleys of Essex," he whispered.

"Valleys, what valleys?" I was now feeling irritated not in the mood for any games.

"These," with this he placed a finger gently between my breasts. I had been so intent on the man in front of

83

me, it had quite slipped my mind that not only was I still in my nightdress minus dressing gown but in bending forward to awaken him it had fallen forward so exposing my breasts.

We both heard Bill's car returning from his trip having taken our family to Church. Dieter asked, "Bill?" I explained where my husband had been: "You did not go?" How could I honestly answer that question today. So I just turned away. Hearing Bill opening the front door I ran to the bathroom to prepare for the day. Hearing Bill say, "Well old son, today we show how England can win a football match." I smiled hearing both men laugh and at the same time wishing things could be different. That Dieter and I could just be friends nothing more but the fates were never going to allow that.

As Breakfast started the two men were teasing each other as to which country would win the game, when my opinion was asked for I shook my head not wishing to enter the conversation as I knew nothing about the game and really was not in a mood for talking.

"You are very quiet," Bill said.

"Yes, I didn't sleep too well last night." I knew my husband would want an explanation so I continued: "Trying to work out how we would be arranging dinner at Angie's today." This answer satisfied him and both men continued with breakfast. Looking at the time I realised that my mother and the children would now be ready to be picked up and before Bill could come up with any further ideas I got the car keys and made my escape.

I brought the children and my mother home the girls would stay with us for the rest of the day and I felt my mother should meet our guest.

The moment Elizabeth Hutchins my mother shook hands with Dieter I knew she was lost. My mother was a small woman with perfectly white hair, a slightly rotund figure and a complexion that belied her advanced years, she had laughing brown eyes and had not worn make-up for many years. Her dress of purple background with a black design on it suited her perfectly. She and the children sat down to have breakfast with us and it was not long before there was a great deal of laughter as my mother along with the children had all fallen under his spell. Eventually, Bill announced: "Well Dieter, come on get your boots out, it's England Versus Germany once more and as in the sixties we are going to thrash you." Laughing at this vast exaggeration Dieter replied: "We will see, no medals are won till the game is over." Almost as if on cue we heard the sound of a car announcing the arrival of Mark. Looking out of the window I could see Uwe in the back of the car with Tom. Waving good bye to them all wishing my husband, Mark and Tom the best of luck and we would see them later I went in to clear and tidy up breakfast, take my mother home hoping she would not be asking too many questions I could not answer.

The ringing of the phone brought me out of my thoughts, guessing it would be either Angie or Frances and at the same time hoping not to have too many awkward questions. She had phoned to discuss the lunch that we would all be preparing in her house. Having discussed all this at length we then decided what time to meet to go to the club everything arranged I decided I really had to smarten myself up. So hair washed, make-up on I was now ready for battle.

As we approached the clubhouse I could not help thinking how things had changed for me in a matter of hours from the Friday evening to the present moment. The only difference from the Friday evening was that now the sun was shining, birds singing and I was accompanied by my children, apart from Bill the most important things to me keeping me in line. Holding their little hands in mine I thought, "You cannot possibly do anything to hurt these little people, they trust and love you." A gasp of desperation escaped my lips: "You OK Mum?" Hannah asked.

"Yes, just a little out of breath too much rushing." This answer was accepted and we continued our approach to the collection of low wooden buildings to our left.

As we entered, the sound of music being played was coming over the PA system, we could hear voices yelling encouraging the various players, as is always the way with football those watching knew more of the game than those playing. "Where's Daddy?" Lottie asked looking out into the playing area it took me a couple of minutes to find my husband, as my eyes were taken by the man dressed in green and white and standing in goal. "Over there," I pointed as Bill dressed in the team colours of maroon and black went running across the pitch. Forcing my attention back to the children and the others in the club we waited for the end of the game. Angie did ask of one of the regulars, "How is it going?" he laughed and replied with the words, "Expected result." But never followed it up with any more of a reply. Till the end and I knew what he meant, yes a team had been thrashed but unfortunately it was ours. Laughing we waited for the men to shower and change and join us, as Tom walked past the studs on his shoes hitting the ground he called out: "Hey, Vicki coming to scrub our backs?" As I shook my head a familiar voice walking past whispered, "I am ready." Turning my back on Dieter I made my way back into the smoky and noise filled club.

After the game and the men had rejoined us, Dieter and I made every effort not to be in each other's company or alone. With the children present and so many friends who had come to spend a normal Sunday afternoon in the Club it was not difficult as there was always someone who wanted to talk either about the game or our visitors.

As I wandered out onto the now empty pitch I heard a voice ask: "Any of the lads staying with you?" Looking in the direction of the voice I saw Wally, that was the only name we had ever known him by, he was sitting on one of the benches left over from the barbecue of last night. I nodded looking at the frail old man I was now seated next to. His white hair, wrinkled skin and arthritic hands told a story we didn't know in its entirety. Holding his hands in mine I said "Does it hurt?"

"What my hands oh! All the time especially..." I stopped him here, "No, having the men here from Germany."

"Oh! That, no love these boys are what thirty, possibly a bit more than that the age my children would have been no-no animosity there at all." We then went on to talk of the game and friends, songs the sort of things people comfortable in each other's company discuss. We then went our separate ways him to his pigeons and me to the family.

As I walked back to the clubhouse I remembered being told that while Wally had been away fighting in France his wife and two daughters had been killed in an air raid we had no more information than that and no one had ever asked for more.

Angie was waiting for me as I entered, "Spending a lot of time on your own aren't we?" She asked, "What is wrong with you?"

"Nothing, just looking for some quiet time."

"Huh! Got to be a first with you." Taking me by the arm and leading me towards Frances we passed the bar where the men were standing as we passed behind them I felt Dieter turn to stare at me but refused to turn my head in his direction.

It was obvious that both Frances and Angie wanted to talk about the lunch and the afternoon that had been arranged in a Manor House near Little Barham. Deep in conversation it was with relief we heard the bell telling us that drinking time was up for today. "Ah well this time tomorrow all will be back to normal," Frances muttered standing up straightening her dress and walking towards Tom. I had been about to stand up too but this comment of hers suddenly put into perspective that tonight was the last time I would see Dieter, tomorrow he would be on his way home to wife and sons. Feeling as if a hammer had hit my heart I sat down unable to breathe. "You fall down love?" I heard someone ask as they walked past.

"Yeah, caught my heel in the carpet." This answer satisfied all around me, so picking up my handbag, collecting children, husband and Dieter we made our way to Angie's home.

Lunch that afternoon was a noisy affair with a great deal of laughter, the inevitable teasing of the English not being able to play football and the children running in and out of the house. Even I was able to enjoy the normality of the afternoon making sure that apart from offering a piece of roast beef, potatoes or a drink I had no other contact with Dieter.

"Is it true we are going to a really old house?" Lottie asked, I nodded.

"Will there be ghosts?" Aaron, Frances' son asked, turning to look at the blond-haired boy I nodded, "Bound to be."

"Can you deal with them?" He continued.

I smiled and said, "Probably." This of course led to me being asked why I could deal with the so called dead.

Before I could explain about my work Bill interrupted and told them all about my work as a Medium and Exorcist, this of course caught the interest of the visitors and for some time the discussion was all about my work. "So," Dieter interrupted the talk by saying, "this means that even when I am dead I will not be free of you." I stared at him why had he made this statement? What was in the back of his mind? I almost shouted back, "Don't talk like that."

"Calm down," Bill said, "he was only joking." Taking a deep breath I did the normal thing for me and disappeared into the toilet once more.

Hearing Angie and Frances starting an argument about the game, both of them having sons were always very involved in the football games and today according to Frances it was Joe's fault the game was lost. Before they could get too deeply into the game stepping in between them, putting my arms through them both I smiled and said, "Come on ladies, game over for a couple of years," at this my heart sank, "let's get on with washing-up and heading off out again." To my relief both friends agreed to call a truce and we prepared for the afternoon ahead.

Everything tidied up, we got into our respective cars and headed off to the Manor House known as Harlesden Manor. It was an Elizabethan building standing in its own parklands and we had been given permission to use it by a Club member who was a Bank Director in the City.

On reaching our destination I was impressed by the gatehouse and the liveried keeper who welcomed us. Lottie said, "Makes me feel ever so posh." The enquiring look Dieter threw me in the back obviously wanting the word explained, I just shook my head making it obvious there was no explanation. The gatekeeper checked our names were on the invitation list and he showed us where to park the cars. Making our way long the long, sweeping drive past oak trees, rhododendron bushes and magnolia that would burst into bloom in the spring. Having seen that the gardens we passed were beautiful we were little prepared for the Manor itself. A typical Tudor building with the bay windows and having once stood in a moat that was now turned into a garden.

Leaving our cars we headed for the imposing ivy-covered entrance. Here another man dressed in the red coat with gold epaulettes, grey trousers and matching top hat greeted us. Having welcomed us with a smile the large silver-haired man then handed us over to the attention of a younger and slighter man obviously his subordinate to take us to the area designated for us. We walked along a lengthy corridor with a plain carpet on the floor and the walls covered with tapestries, paintings and some modern photographs. The corridor appeared to go on for a long time, leading us ever deeper into the house. I began to imagine how this house would have once been the families who would have lived, loved and died here. Were their children like ours noisy healthy and boisterous or were they sickly and quiet. Did they lead good God-fearing lives? Or were they less than honest? All this and more ran through my head keeping my thoughts free of the man walking between my children now.

I looked at Hannah and Lottie, they appeared so comfortable holding Uncle Dieter's hands, looking up at him as though they had known him since they were born. He answered all their questions about his wife and sons very patiently only now and then glancing in my direction.

Reaching a long oaken staircase with solid no nonsense carvings on its side, we were lead along a thickly carpeted hallway towards a room where the rest of the men and women were gathered.

Here in a room where once the music of possibly Greensleeves and Handel was played, today it was a record player belting out the music of the sixties. Finding a vacant group of seats we made ourselves comfortable. Angie who appeared to have sunk into her part of the sofa muttered, "If I have to get out of this thing in a hurry I am stuck." Looking at her discomfort we all laughed very unsympathetically. A slim dark-haired young lady approached us enquiring what we would like to drink, making a note of our order she disappeared as she left us, Marie as we discovered her name to be, told us in a delightful Irish accent: "If the children wish to play they can go outside." There was no further need for our six they were up and out each one shouting louder than the other as to what they should do or what tree to play on. "Be careful," Bill called out, "don't want to visit any hospitals today." We were never sure if they heard or if they had any intention of listening they were out and free.

Now it was not just the children who had wandered off Bill accompanied by Dieter and the rest of the group had wandered off as well. I knew they would be heading in the direction of the room in which was the bar and the dartboard. Angie looked at me with a smile: "Men, they have to be competing all the time, never mind gives us a good excuse for a real chat, the first during the weekend." I knew what was coming and was not interested, so decided to start another subject. "Have you seen Connie and dear Lucy sizing each other up for yet another argument?" I looked in the direction that Angie was facing and I could see Lucy the Chairman's wife and Connie a lady equally as unpleasant as Lucy, she was as large and as obstructive as her enemy, both these women had disliked each other for years somewhere there was a rumour that Danny had married Lucy when it was always thought that Connie would win. Looking at both women I smiled and said to Angie: "Frankly, it doesn't matter which one he married both are as unpleasant as the other." This give my friend the idea that I was really not interested in a girlie chat or in someone else's life if only she had known my own problems were outweighing everything and everyone.

Feeling restless I began to wander round the large room in which we were sitting, glancing up at the high ceilings I was amazed at the work that had gone into it. Part of the ceilings were I was told, timber from a ship that had once sailed the seas during the time of Henry VIII, on the panelling were large oak leaves carved and plaster cherubs. I was amazed that the masons of centuries ago could do so much and all with love and care. As I walked slowly round the room I realised that where I stood would once have been three rooms now made into one.

Leaving the area where the women were seated, I made my way down towards the room where the dartboard was located, in time to see Dieter throw a dart that apparently was very good as all the men cheered. Glancing in my direction he smiled and said, "My lucky charm." Feeling I was in no mood to talk I made my way out of the building and into the parklands also away from where the children were happily playing.

As I made my way towards the outside I passed a beautiful black varnished grand piano, gently caressing it I wondered about a quieter time and wondered about the people who might have played it. Standing looking at the instrument I allowed my fingers to caress the closed keyboard, imagining that I was playing something by Liszt, or Brahms, suddenly my peaceful thoughts were shattered as a pair of long, brown fingers gently covered mine as together we played the same mysterious tune, silent and spiritual both of us one and indivisible. Feeling afraid that someone might notice I turned in his direction, smiled weakly and said, "Hi Dieter, enjoying yourself?" I had tried to speak in a normal tone of voice but it came out in no more than a whisper.

When he failed to answer I looked up at him to see what was wrong. He was staring at me, no glint of laughter in his eyes, no smile on his face his expression was empty except for one expression the same that filled my heart, it was a feeling of pain, longing and desire. We both knew that tomorrow there would be hundreds of miles and water dividing us, today was all we had.

Bending to pick up a piece of sheet music that had fallen he whispered: "I need to touch you," flicking through the pages as if we were discussing the composer, I replied: "We can't," glancing round to make sure we were still unobserved. "Not here."

Glancing out of the window as if showing me a plant he whispered, "This I know, but I will go in the garden, there is a big tree that looks broken," he pointed through the window in the direction I should take: "meet me there, please." Then added, "Soon." This last was said in a voice of complete dejection.

I nodded as I too had seen the tree and was perplexed by its shape almost looked like a monkey puzzle tree. How could I refuse his pleading? It was after all what I wanted and needed too. I nodded smiling acknowledgement.

A few minutes later I walked down the stairs having told Bill that I was going to take a walk round the garden, he knew my interest in gardens and trees so was not surprised by this. Walking down the oak stairs and out of the side gate that led into the garden I made my way towards the strange tree to discover it was an old yew tree centuries old and knowing that these trees had very spiritual qualities I was not surprised that Dieter had chosen this, it was meant for us.

Standing before the tree I touched it, realising that at some time it had been struck by lightning; instead of breaking completely apart it had stayed in the twisted tortured shape that stood before me. Though gnarled and bent, it still carried a beauty and charm along with being a home for numerous birds and small animals. It was here that we were to meet but where was he? As Dieter had left the room before me, I had taken it for granted he would be awaiting my arrival, as eagerly as I. Had he changed his mind? Perhaps he was laughing at me, maybe some of his friends were standing close by so they could laugh at the silly English Frau. Having decided that I was to be a made a fool of I decided to run while I still had some dignity. As I turned to move I was brought to a standstill as a hard, male chest blocked my way.

"What is wrong, why are you going?" I heard him whisper. The relief I felt was so strong, that all my earlier thoughts were silly foolish imaginings the kind that guilty people conjure up.

No reply was needed, he was here and so was I. Looking up into his beloved face, was answer enough.

"Leiberlein, little love," he breathed, pressing me back against the tree. The feelings arising in me were so turbulent as to make me immune against the pain I might have felt from the hard, unforgiving surface of the oak's bark. We stood at first allowing our eyes and hands to wander at will over each other, until gradually our lips took over. He seemed to explore every inch of my face, eyes, hair and ears. Finally when I felt it impossible to take any more his lips met mine, taking and holding them with a power no other man had held over me. I was like a flower that had been dying from lack of light, no sun had shone on me before, no light so strong as that reflecting his passion.

"I love you," he whispered into my mouth, his clean breath filling me, seeming to give me a new life, bringing every part of me tinglingly alive. "I must have you," he continued.

"But you said we should not." I was never allowed to finish my statement as taking command of my mouth again he said: "I know but I cannot breathe without you. When can we make love?"

Knowing that the children would go to school from my mother's house and that Bill would be at work very early I told him that would be the best time for us both to become one.

As we stood our arms wrapped around each other, I could feel the slightly softer movement as his hard lips again found and held mine. So we stood breathing heavily, lips, hands wanting, needing each other. Our clothes acting as the only barrier. There could be only one end to satisfy our needs and we had tried to deny this but now could no longer do so.

Breathing a sigh of relief, he renewed his onslaught of love on my mouth and body. Realising we were in danger of reaching a point of no return a voice calling me name broke in on the haze enveloping us. Slowly surfacing from the sea of passion we turned to see Angie and Frances bearing down on us.

I had never seen my friends look so angry before: "What the bloody hell do you two think you are playing?" Angie shouted not caring who might be hearing. Even normally quiet spoken Frances had joined in with Angie: "Honestly do you want to ruin the weekends for the rest of us?" She said in a loud and trembling voice. Feeling like a child caught doing something very wrong I kept my head down, these women had been my friends for many years better than sisters and now I felt that I had not only let Bill down but these two before us.

"Do you have any idea what Bill would do if he found out?" Frances said her tone reproving. I stared at them both dumbly, as Dieter was about to say something Angie pointed in the opposite direction: "I suggest Mr Schmidt you take a long walk away from here, a cold drink and don't come back here at all." Looking at me he turned and rather like an animal that has been badly treated walked quietly away, leaving me with my friends.

Standing with Angie and Frances staring at me I should have felt really ashamed at having been found in this compromising position, but I didn't all I did feel was annoyed that someone else knew my secret.

"Angie, Frances you girls are my friends and I value this friendship, but please understand, you don't and can't live my life."

They both nodded in acceptance of this statement.

"I have to do what I want, in my way. Just be there when I need you both. Because believe me, I am going to need you both very, very soon." Having begged my friends' support, I stood waiting for their reply. Hoping they would realise this was not just a mad fling, a second's flight of passion.

I was for the first time in my life not in love but I had grown to love someone so completely and in so short a time that my life could never be the same again.

Angie answered for them both: "Stupid, you know we will always be there when you want us, just make sure you don't get caught."

Pretending innocence I asked: "Caught, how can I get caught?" forcing a smile: "and what would I be doing?"

Giving a sigh: "I'm not bloody stupid, now come on, it's time to leave, that's why we came to look for you." As I walked away in front of my friends, Angie dusted my back and turning to look at her she said, "Twigs, can't explain that!" The three of us burst into helpless laughter, giving those watching our return the impression of very good friends enjoying themselves, how little they knew.

Of course Bill had to have his say: "Where the hell have you been? He asked crossly, "Honestly every time we go anywhere this woman always goes missing, she's worse than the kids." He made this last remark to Dieter, who like me was finding it hard for our eyes not to meet.

So we drove away from the Elizabethan Manor and back home.

As we drove home Bill having forgotten his bad temper said to me: "I hear Lucy is cross there is no dancing tonight and no extension to the drinking time." This was no surprise, Lucy was always complaining about something. Tonight as the last night and the men having to leave early in the morning, many people like Bill having to work it would not be a night of music and dance quite the reverse in fact.

Arriving home I prepared Hannah and Lottie for bed, packed their school uniforms in their overnight bags and took them to my mother who would take them to school in the morning. Kissing them and my mother goodnight I made my way home feeling very much a hypocrite knowing what Dieter and I had in mind for the morning.

As I entered the house I heard Bill ask Dieter: "Did the children say goodbye before they left." He nodded silently then said: "You have beautiful children." Bill smiled and nodded and added "Look like their mum." Touching my hair as he walked past. "Come on let's get for our last night together." It was this last sentence that nearly knocked me off my feet, yes tonight was the last night.

As tonight was not a night for revelry there was no rule as to what to wear, so I just put on a pair of jeans, tee shirt and tied my long hair back in a ponytail leaving my face free of make-up.

Going down to join Bill and Dieter I found it hard to believe how in the manner of seventy-two hours my life had changed. Seeing the two men standing waiting for me, I wasn't sure what I felt, ashamed of what I was planning to do in breaking my marriage vows or looking at the man who had to come to mean so much to me.

"Come on guys, let's go." Dragging both men by the arm we walked out to the car.

As we arrived at the Club I tried not to notice that the coach the men had arrived in on the Friday had been brought out of the garage in which it had been parked and was now standing ready for the forthcoming journey. My breath caught in my throat in a sob of despair. Dieter hearing this tripped up and nearly fell on the hard stone of the drive way: "Watch out, Dieter!" Bill said, "Don't want to send you home damaged eh!" Neither Dieter nor myself could answer honestly so we said nothing.

Entering the clubhouse tonight was different, there were records playing but as background music, tonight was for talking taking phone numbers and addresses if needed. Then there was the presentation of the shield won by the German team in the game earlier that day. So much had happened in these hours that everything seemed to have happened in another time and to a different Vicki Johnson. Talking to Angie and Frances we then walked round with Fritz and Uwe. I even shook hand with the dreadful Klaus and there were others whose names I would one day remember but for now the only one of any importance was standing as far from me as possible. With the shield presentation Dieter was called upon to give us ladies a present from Germany, it was a variety of toilet items all with the scent of 4711 the perfume of Cologne as he presented each item to the ladies he gave them a kiss, when it came to my turn we both knew no matter how small the kiss there would be a problem. As I approached him my dear friend Frances who never did anything to attract attention to herself realised the awkwardness of the situation stepped forward with the words: "Dieter, if you don't mind I'll take this as Vicki only wears Chanel." Ignoring the stunned look on his face she took the box out of his hands kissed him on the cheek and walked back to me grinning. Bill and Mark stood dumbfounded she had never done anything like this before, Mark asked, "Are you mad?" What make you think Vicki didn't want one of those boxes?"

I smiled at him and said, "Actually your wife is right, that perfume is too sweet for me Frances can have it."

Turning my back I went over to the bar to talk to Josef and Paul two school teachers in a senior school known as a Gymnasium.

I could feel tears welling up in me so taking a deep breath I made my way outside, when we had left home the indigo skies were full of stars but looking up now they had disappeared behind heavy clouds. Taking a few deep breaths looking at the mist that was creeping over the grass, I looked up at the starless sky and called on my Spirit Guardian, Guides to help me. "You are always working with me to help others now for the first time I really need you please be beside me, don't leave me I am frightened." As a gentle breeze played with my hair I waited for answers that up to that moment had not come.

Entering the lit building once more I was in time to hear Philip who had been playing the records say: "Ladies and Gentlemen it is time now to say goodbye, I am sure you will have made a lot of good friends and will meet again, our record for the weekend is Every Time We Say Goodbye."

"Now come along the visitors should dance with the ladies who cared for them so well." This last instruction was given by Danny. I really wanted to shout: "Mind your own business." But of course could do no such thing.

Watching the English Ladies and the German visitors pairing up I could see that Connie and her guest Fredreich were laughing, I envied them as I heard

Frances say: "Pity that is not the kind of friendship you and Dieter will ever have." Looking at me with sympathy she put her hands out to Fritz and allowed him to lead her away. Angie and Uwe were already on the dance floor in fact I was the only one on my own. About to leave I heard: "We must do this, it does not look good." Looking up into his eyes it was obvious he had been trying to put the moment off, but it looked more conspicuous with me on my own. So, once more I allowed myself to fold into his arms, both of us shaking with emotion as the song took hold. Goodbye such a simple word but with such deep meaning.

Eventually the song and the evening came to an end, Bill saying goodbye as he would not be at the coach the next morning and we made our way home. When we arrived I made it obvious that I was not staying downstairs and I made my escape.

Waiting for Bill to come up I remembered talking to Angie and Frances, both of whom sympathised but yet felt that I was being unfair to Bill and ultimately Dieter's wife. Somehow I never really thought about her as I felt we would never meet, how wrong I was. "I suppose you think you and Dieter are in love?" Angie asked, I shook my head and replied, "No not in love but we love each other."

Puzzled she asked, "There is a difference." I nodded, "But that's why you married Bill surely." She carried on and I had no answer to give really no answer so we had left the subject of love at that point.

It was still quite dark when I got up with Bill and saw him off to work. Once I was alone in the house with Dieter I stood in my living room not sure what to do. I should really go up to the bedroom lock my door and not come down till it was time for him to leave and catch the coach. But that's not what I wanted or needed.

I stood outside his door from now on my workroom would in my heart always be known as "his room."

"Do I knock?" I asked myself before I could think of doing anything the decision was taken out of my hands, as I heard the door open. Looking up from bare feet, to brown muscular legs, along the length of an equally suntanned naked body. A gasp escaped me, this man was truly perfect. In silence he held out his hand. Taking it I was led into the room, the pungent smell of cigarettes lingered heavily in the air. So we stood facing each other, I in my dressing gown and nightdress and he – naked.

"So, my darling you came to me." He whispered

Nodding, silently, I stood like a child before Father Christmas, seeing her presents but afraid to reach out and touch.

He had no such fears. With hands that were steady my nightdress was removed, dropping round my feet that were fast losing their strength. I then felt myself being carried over to the bed, still ruffled from his sleep. As if I were a goddess, he laid me reverently on the coverings. No words were exchanged.

We were two people in love, knowing only one way to perfect our desire for each other. The world at this moment containing only two beings Dieter and myself. My eyes closed in an agony of anticipation. I could feel his hands wandering up and down the length of my now naked body. My taut nipples were possessed by his hot lips. Once he had taken his fill his mouth wandered to places Bill had never even looked at, let alone touched. These had the most vibrant effect on my nervous system. I began to respond in a way, until now completely unknown to me. My breathing became laboured, my already hot fevered body gyrating and groaning, needing him to take me. But, he seemed to hold off till the pain of suspense and agony became too strong. A cry of demand left my lips. "Take me, take me Oh! Dear God make me yours." In the light just filtering through the bedroom curtains I could make out his smile. It said, "That's what I wanted to hear." As I felt his hand parting my thighs, for a moment I restrained myself and him. Then with little persuasion I gave in to his desire and mine. As he took possession of me, a feeling of shock took hold. Bill had been the only man I had ever made love with, so was completely unprepared for the size and strength of Dieter. I had no need to worry, with gentle handling, passionate kisses and the words that only lovers know, I became Guinevere to his Launcelot. We rode the tide of love and need together. Neither giving nor taking more, both sharing the joys and pain that comes only with true love. As I felt my poor body could take no more, with a crescendo we reached our peak. Both of us crying with the intensity of emotion. Our senses had been truly fulfilled, the reason for my living now truly known to me. I had been born for Dieter, his woman, his life.

Later having showered and dressed we sat down to a very sad breakfast, neither of us were in the mood for food. So, having drunk a couple of cups of coffee we decided it was best to leave. He did offer to help me wash up, touching his arm I said: "No, please don't. I can't take much more, just let's go." He understood.

Having checked that all his possessions were packed including presents for his wife and sons, placing the case in the boot of the car I called out: "Ready?" his reply was swift and expected: "No." I smiled ruefully as I climbed into the driving seat.

As we arrived it was obvious that we were the last, Angie came running up to me: "What happened? I was going to phone you." Turning I smiled at her and replied "Heaven Happened."

She screamed silently: "Oh dear God you have gone and done it." I walked quietly away not ready for any recriminations not today.

Herbert the coach driver was calling all the men together informing them it was time to leave. I watched in silence as they made their way laughing onto the vehicle, calling out words, of thanks and short messages for those who were not present.

Dieter was one of the last to get on the coach, he made his way to back seat so that he could look out of the window in that moment green eyes locked with brown both had tears in them. They waved I waved but for now I was numb.

I made it obvious to my friends that I did not want to be with them just need to get home, this I did in record time. It was the blindness caused by my tears that made my drive home difficult. Walking through the front door at last I was alone and would be allowed the luxury of self-expression. I cried, for the first time fully conversant with heart break. At this moment the rest of my life seemed very bleak. "How can I continue," was the thought torturing me as I wandered aimlessly from room to room. Everything seemed to be so empty except for his aftershave.

I walked into his room, so empty and yet so full with his personality. Touching cigarette ends that his lips had touched, placing one between my own lips, then looking into the dressing table mirror hoping to see his reflection there.

However, it was the indention of two heads on the one pillow that was my final undoing. Throwing myself on the bed in a fit of despair, the tears and sobs came, with nothing and no one to prevent them. Even the ringing of the phone, just impinging on my consciousness, could not stem the dam that had burst. Finally, worn out, my emotions drained I fell asleep where he had lain.

Chapter 7

Once again my memories of a wonderful yet painful time had helped me to deal with the shock of seeing Dieter lying in that hospital bed. Sitting up in bed I felt an anger against an unknown person take hold of my body, how dare they destroy life? How can they not take care on the roads? This and many more ideas ran through my mind like rivers crossing and criss-crossing keeping me awake. Looking at the clock beside our bed I could see it was still very early in the morning but sleep and I really were not the best of friends. I needed a cup of coffee and not having eaten properly I was both in need of a hot drink and something to eat.

Putting on the light and a dressing gown given to me by Tante Louise, looking at it I did smile as it was a very old fashioned green candlewick one I had not seen since before my mother passed away. Making my way down the stairs I walked quietly past the entrance to the flat where Louise and Walter lived on to the landing that led to the ground floor, bar and kitchen. I could hear the soft padding of feet walking up and down the hall, smiling I knew who that was. Calling out to them in a whisper so that there would be no barking, I crept quietly into the bar and headed towards the kitchen. Having been here so often before Bill and I now used the Hubertus as though we were home.

Making my way through the rubber swing doors that divided the kitchen from the bar, I saw my old friend's two very large, long black haired Alsatian dogs. Both looked fierce and could be, but not with friends. Dreamie the female stood beside me as I put the percolator and Vidor her male partner sat by the main entrance to the Inn. These guard dogs were always on duty when Louise and Walter were either out or in bed and Bill and I had come to know them since puppies so they had no problem with me.

Coffee and Frikadelle in hand I sat down on one of the long seats in what looked like a poop deck of an old sailing ship.

With the bar completely empty I had a chance to study it at will taking me back to the first time I actually come to Germany and Kirschweiler.

Listening to the chill, autumn rain beating against the window, driven with a harshness that comes as we are being prepared for the true cruelty of winter. I wasn't dismayed by the pitiless attitude of nature; she only echoed my feelings. In the weeks since Dieter's departure, my life had been spent in a world that contained no sun. We had not heard from him at all, except for a short phone call to Bill thanking him for the weekend. I was amazed on listening to him talk to my husband how impersonal and detached he sounded. How could he? After that morning of love-making we had experienced to not even enquire about me when speaking to Bill was unbelievable.

Turning to look at my husband, curled up and relaxed in sleep. The twelve years of our marriage had been contented ones. Never for an instant had any man interested me till Bill's friend had entered my life, leaving me with the feeling of having experienced one of life's tornados. Once again, staring through the dark windows seeing nothing but my own reflection, my mind drifted back to Dieter. Thoughts like: "If he really loved me, I'd get a phone call." or "is he laughing at me, am I the topic of conversation at his drinking hole?" Having given him not just my body, but my innermost thoughts too, I felt his treatment of me to be Cavalier at times making me feel quite dirty, because I had given him so much than I had ever given my husband.

One afternoon, some days after our visitors had returned to their homes, the children at school I had decided to give myself a long weekend. Having problems of my own to deal with had been preventing me from working honestly with clients coming to me for readings, this was obvious from the mistakes I had been making. Putting on the radio, I sat down tea in hand to listen, suddenly, the Disc Jockey announced that a "special listener" name unknown would like a request and I heard the strains of "Help Me Make it Through The Night." This was too much for me, I burst into tears as the song filled the air around me.

Lost in a world of self-pity I had not heard the back door open, nor my friends calling to me. Not till I felt Angie's arms close round me, and Frances' sympathetic tones did I realise I was no longer alone. By then it was too late for my tears to stop, they would have put the Niagara Falls to shame.

A smile did cross my face, as I heard Angie exclaim: "That bloody Kraut, I'd cut his balls off," turning to look at her, I couldn't help making a little joke: "That would be a terrible waste," then started crying again.

"You have got to talk about this, the mood you've been in lately has got a lot of people worried and what's worse talking." Frances continued.

This advice was unnecessary, I knew my temper had been very short. Irritated by everything and everyone, no time to spare for family or friends. Nodding my head, I walked away from the two women sitting beside me. Knowing my shortcomings was one thing, I had no idea of talking about my problems with any one when I needed help I turned as I always had to my Spirit family and friends.

This time however, it was different and I did need some earthly guidance. So we sat with me telling my friends everything from the time we had met two years previously to our most recent time. I had honestly thought by talking to my two best friends I would feel better, but that did not happen in fact bringing everything out and looking at it in the cold light of day actually made me feel a great deal worse.

I called out to my friends as they left: "Is this all my life will be now, a memory of one amazing moment." Giving me a quick hug both of them left.

The Saturday dawned cold and damp, climbing stiffly out of bed as I had once again slept badly I went down to make the family breakfast. Once it was ready I called them together, looking at Hannah and Lottie once again made me feel very guilty after what I had done – but as I entered the kitchen I could see my friend and neighbour making signs to me through the kitchen window. So, I replied mouthing words and with a lot of arm waving. I could hear Bill and my recently become a teenager eldest daughter laughing at me. "Honestly mum," my brown-haired beauty said to me: "How can you and Aunty Jo have a full blown conversation through glass." Smiling with tray and toast in hand I replied: "Simple. We understand what we say." Ever since we had lived next door to Jo and her husband Philip because our kitchen windows faced each other, she and I had learnt a way of having full conversations.

Sitting down at the breakfast table, she asked, "What did Jo say?"

"Oh she was just remarking on the weather and they were having trouble with their car." Looking at my family's faces I could see how amazed they were. "How could you learn all that in silence?" Hannah asked "We just understand what we say."

Walking to get another cup of tea, Bill said to the girls: "Beats me how your mum and Auntie Jo can understand each other so well like this." Lottie answered with, "because our mum's clever." Facing my daughter, in her rose-pink pyjamas, my heart ached a little. How ashamed they would be of "their clever mum," if they knew the truth.

Smiling at the girls, Bill continued in tones that were conspiratorial, "We have a secret don't we girls?" they nodded. Then he continued, obviously out to annoy and irritate before giving me the facts. "Do you think your mum deserves a break?" Again silent agreement from the girls. By now I was really coming close to being violent. "OK I have had enough, what is it? When is it going to happen and what's more do I want it?" Nodding and smiling Lottie said, "Oh, yes Mum definitely you will want it."

Turning to look at me Bill said: "We have a special birthday present for you."

My head shot up, "Present, what present?" By now thoroughly enjoying my annoyance all three burst out laughing as Bill said, "AH HAH, your mum finally comes alive at the word present." By now I had reached screaming point: "What is it?" Lottie said to Bill, "Tell Mum the present is for all of us but at her special time." Yes, my birthday was a couple of weeks before Christmas, but what on earth could Bill have got me that was for all of us and so special. I was soon to find out.

I was not prepared for his announcement: "We are going to Germany for a long weekend." I was stunned, never had I expected anything like this. "Germany, did you say we were going to Germany?" I stumbled trying not to show how happy I was. "Yes," Bill replied looking very happy with himself and his arrangement.

He continued with, "I have been speaking to Dieter while at work and we decided that you deserved a treat as you have been working so hard and look so tired." Again I was made to feel guilty, yes I had been busy, I always was in the wintertime, but my reasons for being tired was guilt and love of two different emotions for two very different men.

"When was all this arranged?" I asked trying not to show how excited I felt at the chance of seeing Dieter again so soon and unexpectedly. "Where will we stay?"

Walking into the kitchen dirty cups and plate in hand, whistling answered: "With him, get the two boys to bunk in with him and Monique and you the girls and I will sleep in the boys' room. No arguments all signed sealed and delivered."

This was an arrangement made by my husband that I was never going to disagree with. The rest of the weekend drifted by in a haze of happiness and deciding what to take with us, as I knew Northern Germany was very cold.

It wasn't long before I was on the phone to both Angie and Frances: "Hi, I've been given my birthday present." I told Angie.

"A bit early, still got two weeks to go."

"I know that," I replied but we will be using it this coming weekend."

"Oh" she replied,

"Yes, we're going for a long weekend."

"That's nice, where?"

I replied with one word: "Germany." The silence at the end of the phone was shattering. She then replied with one word: "Help."

Phoning Frances the reaction I received was completely different: "Ah, yes." She replied to my news, waiting for her to say more I was surprised at her words: "Do you good to go,"

I asked "why"

"Well," she continued, "you probably need to see him again. This time in his own family setting, see how he belongs and you don't." She then continued "Let's face it you were never going to get over that Hun, and waiting for two years to see him again would turn him from man to god. Yes, good idea go, but do try to behave." Trust Frances to come up with the common sense solution. I was so happy over the coming days that even my Readings improved.

The weekend of our journey was damp and cold, with sleet, rain and little specks of snow. Bill muttering: "Why can't you have a summer birthday?"

I grinned back, "Not my fault, should ask my mother."

As we were driving along the motorway to Dover, we had decided to travel by Hovercraft, this excited the girls and myself as we had never seen one let alone travelled on one. Arriving at Dover, passports cleared the four of us drove onto the craft, parked the car and it wasn't long before we took off. The rubber skirts billowed with air, there was a loud noise as we hit the water with speed then we were off. I didn't mind the smell of diesel, or the odd bottle crashing around me as we hit a wave in the channel all I knew was Dieter was at the end of this journey.

Driving down the Autobahn, if we had thought the English weather was bad, the continental one was far worse. Here there were no slight flakes of snow they were heave and large. "Good job I got new windscreen wipers," Bill mumbled, I nodded. We stopped along the way in Belgium for a break because of the darkness around the children could see nothing, though we did give little history tips as we drove along. Eventually, Hannah called out from the back "Dad, how do you spell Cologne?" I was about to spell it our way when Bill reminded me, "It begins with a K – Koln. Why?"

"Because I have just seen that funny spelling," she replied. We waited till the next intersection and saw the name of the City so we knew when to turn off.

Leaving the Autobahn we then had to find the village, this was done with a great deal of difficulty as every road we went up appeared to look like the one before. Though Bill had been here before, it had always been with a coach so he was as lost as we were. Eventually I saw something coming out of the murky darkness it was a name, "Bill, what is the name of the place you go to?" I asked excitedly.

"The Hubertus," he replied. Pointing in the direction we had just come from, I said, "We have to go back, we've just gone past it." Swinging the car round, we headed back in the direction of the bright lights we had just come past.

We finally saw the Hubertus in front of us, with a large parking area for customers only. Leaving the car there we stumbled stiffly out of the car, holding two very tired and hungry little girls. I suggested that Bill go into the hotel first, because I suddenly had a dreadful attack of nerves. My feet felt like jelly and hands were sweating. Looking down at me Bill said, "Come on, they won't bite." Looking at the girls I said, "Yes, but the girls…" I never got to finish this sentence because as Bill said, "This is Germany, children are more than welcome in the bar. Not a problem."

I saw our two daughters picked up in two strong pairs of arms and carried into the Hubertus, they were Paul and Frank, cousins.

Entering the outer porch my eyes took a few minutes to accustom themselves to the brightness of the Bar. Looking at the cousins each one holding a bemused child by the hands, the two men were related but did not in any way look alike.

Frank, the younger by ten years, was quite the better looking. His grey eyes in a thin long face, high cheekbones giving him a Slavic look. His thick dark hair in unruly curls, forcing him to keep it cut very short. Although well over six feet, it was his strength that most people, especially the women, remarked on. He was almost Herculean.

Paul, on the other hand, was completely different. Short and fat with mousey brown hair thinning in the middle. His eyes were of the same grey as those of his cousin's but there the similarity ended. The older man had the appearance of a fighter who had lost rather too many rounds, due to his days in the ring when doing his version of the German National Service "Bundeswehr," Uwe had once said that, "Paul loved to fight, but was not very good at it." Looking at him, I did believe this.

Both men had come to meet us dressed in jeans. And jumpers to keep out the cold.

The men and the children entered the smoke-filled bar before me, I walked behind dragging my feet while thinking: "Why am I here? What made me come?" What happened at home can have no meaning here, we are two separate people."

"Will you hurry up," Bill called out to me holding the door open: "Its freezing." Nodding in agreement I did as I was asked.

I had never been to Germany before, so this was a real education for me. I stood blinking, allowing my eyes to grow used not only to the light, but also the acrid smoke that filled the room. For a few seconds after we had entered there was silence, giving me even more reason to wish we had not come on this visit.

The happenings of the next few minutes, were to remove all my doubts and fears. Not only did the babble of voices resumed, but everyone seemed to know Bill and had heard of myself and the children. They approached us as one.

Words of welcome, greetings and good wishes came directly from the heart. I felt that here was genuine friendship. Suddenly realising I had not seen our daughters for a few minutes, I looked around the room to see them seated on stools in front of the large oaken bar, they had bowls of steaming hot soup served to them, accompanied by glasses of Fanta and bowls of ice cream and fruit waiting till the soup was finished. Bill and I smiled as he said: "Well the girls are settled." Yes, they were but would I be any minute now?

Having seen that the children and Bill were settled and happy, with a glass of Kolsch beer in my hand I was free to take in my surroundings. The Hubertus was family owned, as were most of the restaurants, bars and hotels in Germany. The name of the owners were Louise and Walter Gruber. Though born in Cologne, Walter's family stretched back to the Bavarian Alps, he was a tall soldierly gentleman, with quite a touch of the Prussian about his demeanour, tall and slim with laughing blue eyes his straight grey hair hung rather lankly about his ears forcing him to constantly sweep it behind his ears, Walter's most distinctive feature was his nose giving him the appearance of an eagle. Tonight he was dressed in white shirt, green flannel trousers and mustard coloured waistcoat. Louise, his wife was from Croatia a large lady, with silver-grey hair, a round happy face with naturally red cheekbones, she too had blue eyes. Tonight she was dressed in a blouse and skirt that came almost to her ankles, with comfortable shoes on her feet, I was later told that Tante Louise as she was known was the person that anyone and everyone with problems would go to. Her life's experiences in the war had made her a very understanding person and that was how she and Walter had met, though neither of them talked about it. I learnt once when asking about their earlier lives: "What is passed is history," she would then smile and walk away. I very soon discovered that Walter, cooking and the bar was her life. She did have three sons who would one day run the Hubertus, but not yet.

Looking around the area in which we stood, I could see that it was very strangely designed to look like the Forecastle of an old sailing ship. To the left of me was a raised area which contained dining tables and could be the poop deck. A few feet of space in front of the elevated area was given to those who wanted to stand and drink, as there were a couple of raised tables set just for a person to rest their elbows. The space now taken over by those standing to drink would during Carnival become a very crowded and crushed dancing space.

Standing on tip-toe and looking down a narrow walking area in which dining tables were also set I could see a second dance floor with yet another door leading out of it. Asking Bill, "What's in there?" He smiled, "That is the Kegelbahn." Puzzled I looked up at him: "The what?"

"Kegelbahn, a kind of nine pins."

"Oh, could we go." I was never allowed to finish the sentence because Franks said: "Only the club members go in there." This was the first time I realised that the German was very jealous of two things, their Heimat or place where they were born and any club they belonged to. Looking past the Kegelbahn I could see another larger square room, that would be used for weddings, parties and of course a dancing area for Carnival, this led out into the garden that we were told was opened in the summer.

Having finished my first German beer rather too quickly and warned by Bill that though the glasses were small the contents were quite lethal, "So drink slowly, you are not used to this." By now having become accustomed to my surroundings, I now needed to know where Dieter was and how long before he came to fetch us as I could see the children were now very tired.

Trying not to make it obvious I was looking for one person, I was deep in conversation with a rather large, jolly lady by the name of Agatha whose speech was so fast and in the Cologne dialect that understanding was difficult even though I did speak German. I felt I nodded rather too much and shook my too little. Suddenly, my senses came alive as the door opened and cold air was allowed into the stuffy bar room.

My hands began to sweat, my heartbeat gathered speed, all familiar symptoms. I knew without turning round that Dieter had entered the room there was no need for: "Hi, Dieter," then turning to touch my shoulder: "Look who's here, Vicki." For a moment I was rooted to the spot but somehow managed to turn from Agatha to Dieter with my hand out stretched to take his.

Taking in the picture he made, there he stood as handsome and striking as ever. His black hair was wet and slightly windblown from his walk through the damp evening, making it look as if tiny beads of diamanté had been studded between each tendril of hair. His skin when I had last seen him had been suntanned, that was now gone, yet there was a glow about him that no other man possessed. Slung across his shoulders, seemingly oblivious of the cold, was a green corduroy bomber jacket, over a jumper that would have rivalled the tail of a peacock.

With great strength of will I tore my gaze from his, terrified he would read my mind. I wanted him to come to me, at the same time afraid how I would react were he to kiss me in greeting.

I need not have worried, as he took my hand in his, he smiled and said: "So, Vicki you have arrived, that is good." Oh! God, that voice. There was a great deal I wanted to say instead: "Yes, we got lost, silly."

He nodded. "Yes, our little village is not easy to find," he then turned to Bill who was now holding Hannah and Charlotte by the hands. "How did you feel about driving on our roads?"

Bill replied that, "It wasn't that difficult," the men then started a lengthy discussion on the rights and wrongs of driving on different sides and road systems. I was amazed and angry, I had gone for weeks with not a word from him, travelled over three hundred miles and this was how I was greeted. So, turning my back on my husband and Dieter went into deep conversation with Agatha and the four children she had, all daughters and how difficult it was to look after them. What I really wanted to say to Agatha, was sod your bloody kids, stuff your husband, I'm going back to England. Instead I stood listening totally bored and very angry.

Finally, when all the men had finished deciding the best way to drive, Dieter looked at me and said: "Come, I will take you to meet my wife and we will see Uwe and his wife tomorrow when we take you to Koln."

I nodded dumbly, now really hurt. His greeting of my family had been more affectionate than any given to me. This gave credence to all my doubts, I had just been a quick lay for him in England.

"Well buster, you played with the wrong goal-keeper," I thought as we made our way to the car with Dieter sitting in front to show us where to go: "This one is off limits to you now, I only get made a fool of once." Making up my mind was easy; carrying out my resolution was another matter, but I was strong-willed and had every intention of succeeding.

The earlier drizzle had settled into a fine, winter rain. This rain we were told by Dieter would, through the night probably become snow, this made the girls very excited. "Will there be a lot of it?" Lottie asked Looking at Dieter's face reflected in the rear view window and lit up when passing street lights, I saw him smile: "No, not that much, enough to make the stalls in the Christmas market look good." His husky voice and laugh, still had the power to affect me, as he spoke to my daughters. He then went on to give Bill directions that would lead to his home, listening to the two men talking, I realised that apart from our initial meeting Dieter had not addressed one word directly to me. I realised then that the time he and I had spent together really had been something for us both to forget, there would be no romantic reliving of the past. There had been no love there only a sexual need and ultimate gratification both of which I had given him.

So, deciding to discard my shattered dreams, and begin to rebuild my destroyed self-esteem by looking on Dieter as nothing more than my husband's friend. Easy to say but it would prove very difficult to do.

A close study of the streets we were driving along gave my tear filled eyes something to concentrate on, the lamps compared to the ones at home appeared small and old fashioned. Unlike most of the houses we had seen before entering Kirschweiler, I had noticed that some attempt had been made to keeping the houses individual and I did mention this to Dieter.

"Yes, my father's friend rebuilt most of Kirschweiler, after the houses and streets had been destroyed." He answered my question in as impersonal manner as if he were talking to a stranger.

Ooh! Fancy destroying people's homes." Lottie said, tonight was not the night for talking about war.

"Yes, darling I agree and remind me to explain when you're older." I thought that was a good escape but children have a way of not letting go as she continued with: "Uncle Dieter, Mummy has a lot of explaining to do when Hannah and I are older," turning her head to look at me she carried on with: "Every time we ask a

120

question she always says I will explain when you are older." to this he gave a soft chuckle, my heart just leapt.

Turning my attention once more to the houses around me, I could see some beautifully designed bungalows decorated on the outside with stone coloured fascias; small terraced houses, and one or two blocks of flats. Trees grew in abundance along the pavements giving the effect of an avenue, their branches now bare seeming to reach up to the cold dark sky.

Eventually we reached our destination, it was one of the most attractive houses in the area, one of four built in what appeared to be a red ochre brick. Climbing out of the car, I was unaware of the rain beating in my face. The children were already standing under the porch as Dieter bounced proudly onto the step. Taking each girl by the hand he tapped on the door with his foot. The young woman who opened the door as if she had been waiting just for this sign. No sooner had he knocked then the door was thrown open. I had so wanted to find Monique plain, unattractive and unpleasant but the young lady who stood framed by the hall light was none of these things.

Monique was petite, her hair a natural blonde, her skin pale and creamy complimenting her complexion perfectly. As we were introduced she turned her eyes in my direction and I could see that her blue eyes were so deep in colour they were almost violet. Looking at me with a genuine smile of welcome.

While Dieter and Bill were bringing in the suitcases and they were taking them up amid a great deal of laughter, hurriedly hushed as both Christoph and Markus their sons were asleep. Monique showed the children and myself into the living room, leaving the front door we walked across a small hallway with brown and cream terracotta tiles on the floor, this led into a square uncluttered living room that carried on the same colour scheme as in the hall way that of cream and a light brown. There was a large settee that would easily seat about five people, the corner of one side curved into a very clever sofa, a bookcase stood in the corner and a three cornered cabinet tucked into a corner wall with family photos, a collection of china and a variety of scented candles. This young housewife was nothing like me, again the floor was stone tiles with a couple of rugs thrown down.

As I spoke German it was not difficult for Monique and myself to communicate. Going into the kitchen she called back to me: "I am sure the children will be tired, if they would like a hot drink then they can go to bed." Glancing up the stairs and listening to the men laughing she carried on with: "I am sure they will have the beds ready, soon." I smiled feeling awkward never having been in this position before, talking to a woman whose husband I had been to bed with.

Shrugging and sighing I nodded and waited for the men, while our daughters drank hot steaming chocolate. "Beds ready," Bill and Dieter had now joined us slightly out of breath. I looked at Bill and enquired as to why it had taken so long. Looking at Dieter he laughed and said, well the bunk beds and the one we will be sleeping in were difficult to get round, not a very big room." I nodded, then took the girls up. It was not difficult to find the room we were sleeping in, at the top of the stairs and on the right, rather like the rooms down stairs it was not very big but square. In the centre of the room was a double bed, that I later learned had been borrowed from a friend, to the left were a set of bunk beds that I knew belonged to their sons. The girls were soon undressed and ready for bed, once they had settled the argument as to who would take the top bunk.

Children settled, I now had nothing and no one to concentrate on but myself. Sitting down at the dining table in the other corner of the room, with Dieter opposite me and Bill seated beside me, while waiting for Monique to bring in the rather wonderful smelling Gulasch Suppe, a meal quite normal in Germany and very filling. Once seated for the first time I looked directly into Dieter's, for the first time since arriving we made eye contact; mine asking, "What do you want me to do?"

His reply was simple: "Please like her, we have to talk."

While I was a guest in another woman's home, I was not about to start anything that would upset her or my husband.

Making herself comfortable Monique said having placed fresh bread on the table to accompany the soup: "I though you would be late, so I made this for you." Nodding my head, as my mouth was full of the delicious bread and soup was the only reply I could give.

Eventually, meal finished I offered to help take the used crockery into the kitchen, we entered this room via an archway, this was an attractive room with white walls lined with pots and pans in copper, shelves containing china tea pots as Monique explained to me they were all collector's items handed down from her family. There was also a large picture window that I guessed would look over the back garden, now shuttered against the cold and dark. For a moment I stood looking for dishwasher, washing machine but could not see either until Monique smiled and informed me that those items along with an indoor washing line were in the cellar area, the basement being widely used in Germany. Once the food was cleared away and the circular dining table placed tidily away in the corner, I saw Monique place a candle decoration in the centre, there were five candles set among holly and ivy leaves. I knew what this meant it was the Advent Candles, each one a different colour and lit each Sunday till Christmas Eve. There were two candles to be lit.

Once we were seated on the sofa, my mind drifted, being brought back to reality only by the sound of a husky voice asking: "Vicki, you will have a coffee or wine, Bill and I are having a beer." I agreed to a coffee while my hostess had a glass of white German wine. Smiling, she said: "I was cooking for a long time," I smiled in return we all need a pick me up at some time, but the one I needed and wanted was not going to happen.

Our conversation over the next hour or so covered a wide aspect of things, from how I came to speak German, explaining that though I was born in India, I had gone to a boarding school run by German nuns and I had picked the language up there. On hearing that I had gone to a convent School, I heard Dieter chuckle and say: "So, is it true what they say about convent girls?" I decided to ignore this, but not Bill: "You should know what my wife is capable of." There was a silence, looking at Dieter I knew what he was thinking, "I know." Making me feel quite hot and uncomfortable.

Standing up stretching giving a huge yawn, Bill asked to be excused as having driven so many hundreds of miles he was really tired. Monique, a few minutes later also informed that she was going to bed. Leaving Dieter and myself alone for the first time in a very long time.

It was a well-known fact that I never went to bed early, so my refusing to go up with Bill now was really no surprise.

Turning halfway up the stairs my husband said: "Don't let her talk you to death."

Smiling at me with a wicked glint in his eye, Dieter replied: "Don't worry I will look after your wife."

Sighing, I turned to follow my host back into the lounge.

Now we were alone, there was a hush between us. Not the friendly silence that had existed when we had company, but one filled with tension. I sat on the edge of the sofa, rigid, almost frozen. We couldn't make love, not here, causing thrills of delicious fear to run up and down my spine. As if in a dream I saw him stand up, walk round the coffee table and hold out a hand to me, the first physical contact we had made. As if incapable of standing on my own, I allowed his arms to take my full weight. So we stood, arms around each other, each one breathing life into the other. For seconds we stayed like this, then I felt his lips begin to explore my neck, as if resurrecting a nearly forgotten memory. The pleasure and excitement this man was giving me was beyond belief. No dream or fantasy could ever come close to this reality. With a groan, his lips finally took complete mastery over mine. First with little kisses, then longer, lingering ones. I could have died from the joy he was giving me, I could only try to return a little of what he shared with me. My hands began to explore his body. Lifting the jumper out of his waist band I allowed my fingers to run up and down his back, feeling the hot skin beneath growing ever warmer with my touch. Needing more satisfaction I explored further, finding his zip I was about to draw it down when he took his lips from mine.

"No, darling, not yet, not now."

At first I was disappointed, pulling away about to ask why, when with a secret smile he whispered: "After tomorrow, we will be one." I didn't understand what he said, but was prepared to accept he had a secret we had yet to share, as he pushed me away saying: "Now go to bed, before it is too late."

As I tumbled into bed tired but not satisfied, Bill asked: "I hope you didn't bore that poor man." Smiling a little secret smile, "No dear, I don't think I did that at all, good night."

"Vicki, Bill, breakfast." Dieter's voice came through the half open bedroom door. It took a few moments before I could remember where I was. Over the past few weeks I had often fantasised waking up to the sound of Dieter's voice. Now that I had, it took sometime to work out the reality from the dream. Afraid that my husband might have seen the glow on my face the night previous, I had not put the bedroom light on. Now, I had a few minutes peace in which to inspect the room.

From the wallpaper covered with, Star Wars, Yoda and the actors from the film, it was obvious that this room belonged to two little boys. The green carpet was covered with football stars, and skiers flying down mountains. It was obvious that both boys were like their father very much into sporting activities. As I hadn't met the boys yet I did not know which one was into what sport. On the bedside table was a lamp also with football stars. To our left were the bunk beds pushed up against the wall so that the double bed we had slept in could be made to fit in the room.

Looking at the beds we could see our daughters fast asleep, quiet and peaceful not something that would last once their eyes were opened. Bill, standing behind me now also washed and dressed both of us in warm jumpers and tracksuits putting an arm round my waist he said: "Looking at them like this you would never believe what a pair of devils they can be." I smiled, when Bill nuzzled my neck my heart breaking as he said: "I love you." Gently I rubbed his head against my shoulder unable to return the endearment, honestly especially knowing what I had in mind and yet loving my family so much. "Why oh why did I ever meet Dieter?" I asked myself as I supervised two little girls getting washed and dressed: "I used to be so happy once." These were questions I could not answer so in an effort to return to normal, got Bill to take one daughter down and I took the other.

As we made our way downstairs Bill asked just before we entered the kitchen: "What did you think of Monique?" My reply of, "She is very sweet," was answer enough. A sudden rumbling noise that made the four of us jump and the other family to laugh, proved to be the shutters going up automatically. As Dieter explained to us, "It is set for the summertime and winter." With the shutters up we could see the weather more clearly and the promise of the chill of the night before had proven to be accurate there was now a light smattering of snow on the ground. Giving the streets an almost unearthly glow.

As we entered the kitchen and then the living room in which the dining table had been set normally only for four, with my family we were now eight so seating was at a premium, it was decided much to the delight of the children they could take their breakfast, some cushions, sit on the floor and eat in front of the television. But first a very important job had to be done, Markus and Christoph being introduced to us. "Do you think they will like us?" Hannah the serious one asked, "I am sure they will." Bill replied.

So it was that two pretty little girls were introduced to two very smart little boys, the first one was Christoph, as the elder he felt his introduction should come first. He was the same age as Hannah ten, but a great deal taller than her, with brown hair, hazel eyes, a cheeky smile showing teeth that would one day need braces. Dressed in jeans and thick jumper in red and white and a skiing motif, he was obviously the winter person.

Markus, was seven years old a little shorter than his brother with dark hair almost the same shade as that of his father, he had his father's eyes – green, and a rather serious expression on his face. When meeting him for the first time I felt that he was deciding whether to like us or not. He made me feel quite nervous, in case he could or would read my mind. Unusual for me, allowing for the work that I did. Eventually both boys decided that we foreigners were acceptable, taking their rolls, cold meat or cheese from the table they sat in front of the TV. Bill and I were a little worried as neither girl understood the language, but the first programme was a cartoon and regardless of language everyone understands them.

Sitting down to a typical German breakfast of fresh brewed coffee for the adults, hot chocolate for the children, rolls, a variety of cheeses and cold meats, it wasn't long before we were all tucking in.

"Hungry?" Dieter asked.

"Um," I answered, not wanting to look at him, because I knew his question to be double-edged. I had found sleep difficult to come by after we had started to make love the night before, as my body had yearned for the satisfaction only he could have given me but, for reasons known only to him, had refused.

"So, how did you sleep?" Was he determined to trip me up? Luckily Bill thought the question was aimed at him, for it was he who answered.

"Fine, that bed of yours is really comfortable."

"The bed belongs to my parents," Dieter replied: "I have borrowed it for you."

Changing the subject from beds and sleep, I asked: "What are we doing today?"

We are taking you to see the Kriss Kringle Market in Koln, this brought a shout of sheer joy from the boys and a look of puzzlement from us. "Kriss Kringle?" I asked.

"You call it a Christmas Market." Dieter carried on with: "It is a special market and people come from all over the world to see it," at the time I did think it was an exaggeration until later on in the day I realised that in these places you could hear practically every language in the Western World.

Continuing with an itinerary for the day, Dieter carried on with: "Then we will visit Die Dome, the Cathedral in the City centre and I will show you where the Three Wise Men are buried." Now, I was sure he was teasing me, looking at him I asked: "Seriously, the Three Wise Men?" both Monique and Dieter smiled and said, "Yes, the Three Wise Men, I will show you."

"After we have given Bill an education into the architecture and commerce of our City, then," this was said tapping Bill on the back, "we will take you my friend to some good beer-drinking places." With motherly concerns I asked: "the children?"

"No, problem, we can take them with us, this isn't England, we like to make the family atmosphere."

As Dieter was talking in the plural, I took it for granted that Monique was coming with us, but she soon told me this was not so. As she had visitors and had quite a great deal to do, she would stay home but would be with us tonight when we went to the Hubertus. Monique went on to explain that she wanted to speak Andrea a friend of hers who would be looking after the children overnight when we went out. She had bed linen the children's nightwear to take, I went up to get the girl's nightdresses and washing things for the following morning. As I was sitting down to another coffee, there was a knock on the door. Monique opened it for her brother, sister-in-law Birgit and their daughter Maria.

As Monique opened the door I heard the deep tones of her brother Uwe, plus the softer tones of someone I took to be Birgit, his wife. There was also the lighter tones of a child obviously their daughter Maria. Coming down the stairs it was not long before I found myself engulfed in a hug so tight that breathing became a problem. I heard Dieter who was now standing behind me whisper, "Lucky man, he can do in public what I can't." This did fluster me a little. Looking at Uwe and the way he was dressed never ceased to amaze me, as I could not think of any English man of our acquaintance who would dress like this. From Uwe's well-groomed dark hair, beard and moustache to the pristine condition of his clothes. Over his shoulders was a yellow and brown ski jacket to complement black ski pants in a kind of Lycra. Tucked into the pants was a black skinny rib jumper. Black made Uwe appear taller than the average height he shared with his sister.

Bill, having greeted Birgit in the way of old friends, it was now my turn to be introduced. As we shook hands for the first time, I could see why Bill and Joe had been so impressed when they had met her for the first time. Though not overly attractive, she was a bundle of dynamite. A person who oozed a sense of fun. Her red hair was warm and rich like her voice. As she welcomed me to Germany and Kirschweiler, I felt there was a genuine note to her voice, in contrast to the reserve that was at first present in Monique's when she and I were introduced. Like her husband her mode of dress was perfect, not a hair out of place, or a colour that didn't match. She too wore black ski trousers, but with a white jumper, her ski jacket matching that of her husband, not unusual I was soon to discover, as by a strange German custom the women loved their men to dress in the same colours as themselves. Something we didn't dare suggest to our far more conservative Englishmen.

Their daughter Maria was very much a child of her mother's. She too had red hair, was very slight and slim and for the age of ten small in height. She, like her parents was also dressed in a ski suit but of yellow, a colour that matched her hair perfectly. Her face was elfin in shape, with sparkling blue eyes and a mouth that seemed to be made for laughter. Her fingers were very long, we later learnt that Maria was in fact being trained to play the piano. On her feet were a pair of leather boots, it was obvious that for Maria no expense was too much.

We headed out to the two cars, Hannah and Lottie with us in Dieter's, while Uwe, his family accompanied by Christoph and Markus took the other. Giving a final wave to Monique out of the rear window we headed off to Cologne and the Christmas Market.

I sat in the back to enjoy the journey. Seeing the streets daylight was a great deal different to the night before. Then I had been tense, tired and afraid, unable to take in everything around me. However, with the events that had taken place between Dieter and myself, I was now relaxed, allowing me to appreciate the light dusting of snow and frost, the white icy fingers seemed to coat the streets, nothing had escaped the sugar-coating effect trees and roofs were all dusted the same.

We drove past the Hubertus, where we had waited for Dieter the night before. Past churches, schools and small shops and the odd supermarket. As a child I had heard so much from the Nuns who had come from the Cologne area that I was really excited to see this city that had such history to it. We drove past the football Stadium where Dieter had once played, but had to leave due to a knee injury, that was why he was now in banking. Now and then I would look up and see Dieter looking at me in the rear view mirror, just that little glimpse of his eyes looking at me was enough to turn my legs to jelly.

We drove for a few minutes in silence. I must have drifted off into a doze for Dieter's voice woke me with a start. Opening my eyes I could see that we had now entered the city proper. The houses and flats were like those in all inner cities, given more to utilitarian than attractive. Driving past an enormous cemetery with a Roman name we followed the trams lines. "Look Schatzie!" Dieter called excitedly. His use of the German for "Darling" quite took me aback, afraid my husband or daughters might remark on it. If Bill had heard the endearment he never remarked on it. Following Dieter's pointing finger. There was no mistaking what had him so excited. Even though we were still some distance from the city centre, the twin spires of Cologne Cathedral could be seen reaching into the cold grey skies.

"It is when we see that on the skyline, all Koln boys and girls know they are home." There was no false pride in his voice, only a genuine feeling for his home town.

Mindless of the fact that neither Birgit nor Uwe spoke English our children appeared to have adopted them. Accompanied by Maria, Hannah, Lottie, Christoph and Markus followed Uwe and Birgit where ever they went, all the children chattering like magpies. What amazed us the adults the most was the fact that though the boys and Maria spoke no English and our daughters spoke no German all the children understood each other perfectly.

Leaving the modern shops behind us, we were led by Dieter and Uwe along some narrow side streets in the Old Town, rebuilt since the end of the war. It was Uwe's call of turn left, an instruction we carried out to be faced with the most amazing scene. Facing us was a square that instantly transported me into another century, that of the world of the Brothers Grimm and their fairy stories.

All around us were stalls covered with green roofs, the light smattering of snow the night previous added to the magic.

Some with chimneys sticking out, these were the one selling hot, fascinating foods. Then there were the stalls that had wooden toys and Christmas decorations, Gluhwein a hot red punch something I tried but had little liking for. All around us there was hustle and bustle, I could hear every kind of language the people selling and working in this market were dressed in the national costumes of Germany, Leder Hosen and Dirndl's, the children, Bill and I were fascinated, the look of delight on the faces of our friends showed they were as happy as we were with the morning's trip.

Suddenly we heard a scream of delight from the children, walking in their direction we saw them standing by a very tall man, dressed in something similar to Father Christmas but with many differences. He was busy handing out sweets, chocolates and gingerbread men to all the children who ran up to him.

"Who is he?" Bill asked, Dieter answered: "That is Kriss Kringle." So he was the German Father Christmas.

So we spent the morning watching the children enjoying themselves, eating a variety of foods some I would never try again and Bill enjoyed a few glass of cold beer on a freezing morning.

"You like our market?" Dieter whispered in my ear.

"It's beautiful. No fantastic." I breathed, trying to hold on the atmosphere. From somewhere a band was playing, nothing that could ever hit the top ten, but very much in keeping with the centuries we had been transported into.

"Cold?" Uwe asked.

I nodded feeling a chill creeping in.

"Come we will have some Gulasch Suppe," This was something we all agreed to.

Leaving the magic of the market behind, we were led along the side roads to an old bar, belonging, we were told to friends of theirs, Karl Heinz and Bertha. In an alley that tourists would normally walk past, was a little oaken door with a small glass set in the centre. Uwe, knocked and it was opened very swiftly by quite the largest lady I had seen in some time. Showing us into the bar, which looked like someone's front room.

The floor was a dark wood, no carpets here. There were wooden tables and chairs lined up against the walls, all of the same dark wood. The bar ran along the right facing tables and chairs, and a door that obviously led into the kitchen facing the door we had just come in. There were no Christmas decorations here, this was a working bar for working people and the odd friends who would pop in.

A man jumped out of the dark to welcome Dieter, Uwe and the rest of us, when introduced to Bill he pumped his hand up and down like a pump. The Birgit and I were held in a bear like grip, the children were greeted with hugs and handshakes.

"Who is he?" Hannah asked quite out of breath from his greeting of her.

Dieter answered, "His name is Karl Heinz, and we have been friends for many years: He went on to explain, "Bertha his wife used to cook for Walter and Louise, and Karl Heinz used to work in a factory." He then went on to say that both had retired from their normal work, had always wanted a bar of their own and purchased this one.

Karl Heinz was of medium height, with very thin grey hair, hands that were like iron. His pale blue eyes behind thick horn-rimmed glasses blinked a lot and he was dressed in a grey-green cardigan, grey shirt and green trousers with sandals on his feet.

Bertha, a large lady found dressing in a plain shift, with her long tied up in a bun a lot easier. She had dark hair now liberally peppered with grey, and like her husband, pale blue eyes behind glasses that were constantly steamed from her cooking, her feet were encased in a pair of warm slippers.

As with the Hubertus the previous night it wasn't long before all of us were sitting down to large bowls of this incredibly satisfying and tasty soup with the inevitable beer for us the adults and something warm for the children chocolate or sarsaparilla.

While sitting and eating, Dieter noticed that our daughters were whispering together, obviously having a question to ask but reluctant: "So, little ones what do you want to know?" With all our attention on them, they both looked embarrassed until Hannah finally asked: "Lottie

135

and I want to know how the city got its name?" She blurted out in one breath.

Dieter translated this question to the others, who all looked like they wanted to give an answer especially the boys and Maria. Putting up a hand, Dieter went on to explain: "The answer is simple our city was named after a Lady who lived in the Roman times, her name was Colonia Claudia Ara Agrippine (C.C.A.A.) he then went on to give us a potted history of Cologne, one that we found fascinating. It was obvious from the way in which he spoke, that Dieter and his family had a great love for the city that was their birthplace.

As we sat talking, I allowed my imagination to drift back to how the area might have looked during the Roman era. How fascinating were their lives and how did they live them as life was very short and hard?

"Hey, sleepyhead where have you been? Bill asked

"Back to Rome of course." This made them all laugh.

"My wife is a terrible romantic." Bill smiled at me fondly.

"Perhaps, Vicki dreams like I do, it is possible to live in your mind." Dieter answered. Now we had been joined by Karl Heinz and Bertha, having served lunches to other clients they were free to talk to our hosts.

Bill, the girls and I sat and discussed the morning among ourselves, as with the other five talking among themselves we had no chance of understanding a word they said, as they were using the Cologne Dialect.

Out on the streets again, the day was now growing late, the sun that had been with us most of the day was now growing chill. The damp mist covering the river was drifting inland, giving everything a dreamlike quality. Fighting against the cold wind we found ourselves heading toward the Station: "Where are we going?" Bill asked, Dieter's reply of: "To the most beautiful church in the world." I thought was a compliment too many as I had seen many a beautiful church and would no doubt see many more.

Until, we entered the square and there facing us, The Cologne Cathedral or Koelner-Dom being its German name. "Don't you want to see this beautiful building? I am sure you will want to go inside." He continued. I could not understand his excitement, but it was rather catching.

It was Bill who answered: "Vicki will love to go inside, she loves churches." and laughing entered the cathedral with all the others, leaving Dieter and myself to follow.

Standing outside for a few minutes, I was amazed at the beauty of this Gothic building. Dieter then went on to explain to me, that it had been started in the mid thirteenth century and he gave me numerous facts about this amazing place they were now in. The others were now walking around the sides looking at the beautifully decorated windows, tombs and other holy statues. Dieter insisted on making me walk up the aisle towards the altar where I could see three gold boxes, Dieter would tell me that these really were the final resting place of the Three Wise Men, having been stolen from Milan in the twelfth century this and many more facts he gave me as we continued to walk up the aisle totally oblivious to all around us.

As we continued along the aisle Dieter whispered: "We look like a bride and groom." I smiled, as he was now holding my hand very tightly in his.

By now the look on his face appeared to be causing him some strain, feeling that he had perhaps given me too much history, I suggested: "Come on, let's get back to the others."

His reply of: "No, let Uwe explain to them, what they don't understand they can read. Please sit beside me." By now I was totally puzzled, until Dieter put his hand in his coat pocket and brought out an old jewellery box,

"When did you go to church?" He asked me his voice faint.

"Why?" I asked, not understanding what he was saying or why.

"Please Darling, answer it is very important." His tone now breathless, "I must know."

"The week before we came here."

"Did you receive communion?"

"No."

Can you tell me why not?" His tone was now demanding. Wanting an answer I found it hard to give.

"Because I was brought up a good Catholic girl, and I had been dreaming of you and me in bed together." I said this hurriedly, afraid of being embarrassed. To my surprise he did not laugh, just lifted my fingers on the right hand to his lips and kissed them.

Worried we might be seen, I looked around the ancient building, but Bill and the others were deep in conversation at the back of the church with what appeared to be one of the church's canons.

"Come with me." He walked me quietly along a small side aisle that led directly to the altar. Here he asked me to kneel, then out of his breast pocket he took out a tiny jeweller's box. From its design it was obviously very old. As he opened the lid prisms of light bounced off the stones on the ring held captive in its depth. Almost as if on cue a choir rehearsing began to

138

sing the Hallelujah Chorus, a song of happiness and thanks.

"I have this for you," Dieter then took the ring from its box, placing it at the tip of my third finger on the right hand, this was I knew the ring finger on the Continent. I was silent too amazed to say anything. Still kneeling Dieter asked: "Do you love me?"

At first I nodded, but he urged: "Say it please."

"I love you Dieter, I cannot imagine my life without you."

"That is good, I Dieter Bernhardt Schmidt, promise that I will love you for always, whether we are together or not." Placing the ring on my finger he continued: "Alive or dead, you Victoria and I Dieter are now one." So saying he slipped the sapphire and diamond circlet on my finger, emotion had taken such a hold of me I was unable to speak or stand. We knelt in silent Prayer for a few minutes, not sure if we asked for forgiveness or a blessing. From the first moment of our meeting we had always known we belonged together as man and wife.

Still in silence we left the altar and made our way towards the group waiting for us. Seeing my husband my children and his standing waiting for us to join them, I asked, "How can we do this?" Placing a finger on his lips, he whispered: "You and I belong together, we are and always have been one."

"I have thought of this for a long time. My grandfather Bernhardt gave me the ring many years ago, it once belonged to my grandmother. He said to me, "Give it to the woman who will mean most to you." Kissing my hand once more he whispered, "You."

This token of love was beautiful.

As we neared the door he said: "I cannot take away the promise made to my wife, before we met. But we have now exchanged spiritual vows before the Three Magi who lie here. They looked for a dream and found it. You are for me that dream."

"I have nothing for you," I whispered.

"Makes no matter" he replied: "You have promised to love in life and death, that is enough."

As we walked out to join the others, my heart filled to bursting, soared with the birds overhead.

Catching up with family and friends, I should have felt guilty at the promises made in the church, but when Dieter and I were together everything seemed just right. Thinking how I would explain the ring, was simple. A lot of little jewellery shops around us I would have seen it in the window and bought it should the question ever arise.

Bill asked as we climbed into the car: "What were you and Dieter talking about so intently?" I replied with: "Oh, he was just airing his historical knowledge with me. Fascinating place Cologne.

With this I closed my eyes and feigned sleep, my daughters cuddled up to me.

It was dark when we returned to the house, I was worried how I would face Monique but once we arrived at their home all this was taken from me as Andrea was also there.

Andrea, a friend of the family was a lady in her mid fifties, with the most beautiful smiling features I had ever seen. Her dark brown hair was naturally curly, with a complexion that owed nothing to make-up. She had smiling blue eyes and was once a school teacher, of medium height and a buxom figure, she would be taking the children for the night as her husband loved children and they had unfortunately never had any, her English was also perfect, having met this lady I had no worries about our girls eager to be on their way.

With fresh day clothes and night attire together, we received a wave from all four and Andrea and they were off.

Monique, made us coffee and offered us a variety of cream cakes. Feeling it would look odd if I refused, I forced a very sickly cream cake down then, making my excuses went up to prepare for the evening ahead. It wasn't long before Bill had joined me and Dieter and his wife were also getting ready.

We prepared for the evening out in silence, except when interrupted by the odd tuneless whistling from Dieter, or Bill giving a quick burst of Jim Reeves. The atmosphere was one of companionship. The shutters had once again been closed, the only light coming from the bedside lamp, throwing its gentle pink glow over everything. As Bill and I fought for space in front of the one mirror, we laughed and talked about the events of the day. The kind of small talk that comes from long association, and the familiarity that only true friendship between husband and wife can bring.

"So, how do I look?" Standing before my husband, waiting for his response.

"Not bad, but a little risqué for this lot, don't you think."

Laughing I replied: "If Olivier Newton-John can wear it so too can I."

He nodded, raising his eyes to heaven: "What did I do marrying an extrovert, surely there was some dull little woman waiting for me – somewhere?"

"How boring your life would have been? You would have hated it."

All I received in reply was, "Umm."

I had decided to wear a pair of black Lycra pants, with contrasting top of pure red, showing my full breasts to their best advantage. My high heels giving the impression that my legs were much longer. My make-up in place, I once again donned my other self. Not now the housewife but the woman searching for and having found true love.

Patting my bottom Bill whispered, "Do you want to go out, or shall we?" staring at the bed, "retire."

Ducking his searching hands, while laughing: "You retire, I'm going out."

"Not without me, certainly not in that outfit. I'll even have to watch my friend Dieter."

Shaking my head: "No way, not with a wife like Monique, I don't stand a chance."

Turning to stare intently at me for a moment: "Would you want to?" He asked, "By the way," holding my right hand in his and studying the ring, a puzzled look on his face: "where did you get that, you didn't have it this morning?" Smiling I explained about the little second-hand shop near the cathedral, breathing a sigh of relief when he accepted my explanation.

Leaving our rooms the four of us met on the small landing, each one of us eyeing the other. Monique looked lovely in a midnight blue dress that deepened the blue of her eyes, cut very simply with a V neck, fitting bodice, knee length skirt and white high heels. Her hair styled to look windswept, and her make-up simple but effective. For a moment I felt envious, her beauty was simple but in some way far more effective than mine.

Glancing at Dieter I hid a smile, only a German could dress as he had, in red trousers, green silk shirt, fawn slip-on shoes and a brown cotton-padded bomber jacket thrown over his shoulders. On anyone else this outfit would have appeared comical, on this man it was dynamite.

Bill, was dressed in a far more conservative style but it suited him, Grey slacks, light blue tee shirt, and royal blue blazer and on his feet blue loafers the same colour as his tee shirt.

Looking at the four of us Monique said: "We are a very good-looking group," a sentence that I translated for Bill who smiled nodded and said: "Of course."

As the four of us walked in the direction of the Hubertus, I marvelled at the events that had taken place in the last twenty-four hours since our arrival in the village. My life in England seemed so far away. I tried not to think of our leaving on the Monday. Refusing to think about it any further, I joined in with the laughter the other three were sharing. Linking arms we marched in step, Dieter calling out the rhythm in German.

It wasn't long before we were entering the Hubertus, leaving the cold behind and entering the hot, smoky atmosphere of the bar. On first entering and taking our coats off the place appeared to be crowded to overflowing, everyone dressed for an enjoyable night out. No, sooner had we been seen then Bill and I were being greeted by the men I knew and recognised from their last visit to Little Barham, I was then being introduced to their wives. It wasn't long before names and faces all drifted into a blur.

"What are they doing here?" I asked Monique: Smiling she replied: "No, they are all here for you and Bill. We have never had a visit from husband and wife here before so it is a special event." This made me feel rather embarrassed as I suddenly remembered Angie's words when she and Frances had found Dieter and myself by the tree: "Do you realise that you two idiots could destroy the weekend and friendships." I quickly pushed this errant thought aside, tonight I was going to enjoy myself and worry tomorrow.

Walter and Louise with great aplomb showed us down the long narrow aisle towards the large area reserved for dances etc. There tables and chairs had been set in a horseshoe style. The four of us accompanied by Uwe and Birgit, were sitting at what would appear to be the head of the table. Birgit dressed in a green catsuit, and Uwe dressed far less colourfully than his brother-in-law was wearing a white shirt, black trousers and grey shoes, The rest of the company found the seats they wanted and with a lot of noise and laughter the company was assembled. Food had already been ordered by Birgit and Monique, so we didn't have to study any menus. Beer or wine was served at the table, |I was puzzled by the little marks that were being placed on the beer mats in front of the men. "That is to tell the waiter what drink you have had and they add it up at the end of the evening." I thought this a wonderful idea, that way Bill could pay for us with no problem at all when the evening was finished.

The meals that were served to us by two very smart young men, specially employed for the evening. They were brothers who would one day work for their parents in another guest house, so were being trained by Walter and Louise. Their names were Ferdinand and Christian Bauer, both very slight and small with blond hair, dressed in black trousers, and pale blue shirts. Their family we were told had originally come from East Germany.

So, the evening started, alcohol flowed freely and so did the talk. Between Dieter and myself we managed to translate regularly for Bill so that at no time did he ever feel left out. Once, as Dieter walked behind my chair he

144

bent forward and whispered, "Enjoying your wedding meal?" I was so shocked by this comment, I choked on my drink causing a great deal of laughter.

And so the evening went on, until once the meal was finished Bill and I were informed there was to be a special treat, a band. But before the music could start, Frank who ran the football group stood up and made a little speech welcoming Bill and myself to the Village, this brought a little lump to my throat as I thought we were being welcomed to Kirschweiler and all I wanted to do was be with Dieter. We had been promised a musical treat once the speech was finished and we got it in the shape and sounds of an Oomph Pah group. Once they struck up no one was sitting down for long. We were up dancing and laughing for a little while I forgot impending heartbreak. Eventually the evening came to a close and we were again enveloped in hugs, kisses and promises that we would meet again. As we walked out into the cold night air, Bill placing his arms round my waist said: "That was a great night, we will have to try it again." I nodded quietly waiting to get back to the house, I so desperately needed to be with Dieter.

Once back at home with the coffee pot on, we all retired to the bedrooms to put on more relaxed clothing, Monique put on a pair of pyjamas and I slipped into a halter neck night dress and dressing gown, and the men jeans and tee shirts.

Bill, said, "I felt quite like King Arthur tonight, with the Court all around me." Laughing Dieter replied with: "Then Vicki must be your queen, can I be Launcelot?"

Laughing Bill agreed: "Provided you don't try to steal my wife." he answered. "She might be a pain, but I love her." as Bill had left to help Monqiue bring in the coffee cups, he never heard Dieter's, "I don't have to try, she has always been mine." Saying he raised his glass of Asbach Cognac to his lips in a silent toast to us both.

Once the coffee was finished both Bill and Monique said goodnight, Bill remarking to Dieter "Don't let her keep you up, my wife hates going to bed early." Smiling Dieter replied, "No, we will be with you soon."

Suddenly, the room seemed very empty as we were left on our own. I sat waiting on the sofa for some kind of move from Dieter, but nothing seemed to be happening. Afraid of making a fool of myself I stood up muttering: "Think I will join Bill," this simple statement galvanised Dieter into action. "No, not yet we have not finished."

"Finished what?" I was about to ask Dieter before his arms and lips were around me and on mine. His hot breath full on my face as our lips met in a kiss full of pent-up longing and passion.

I had no reason to worry, for still kneeling before me, I felt him move between my legs, slowly pulling my nightdress up till my lower half was exposed to his sight. For a moment he was silent as he stared at me, I experienced no shyness at his study of me: "Oh! Vicki, every part of you is perfect, even this." I felt his hands as they moved ever further along my body, rivers of fire flowing where he touched. My breath was coming in short, sharp gasps. The pain from my desire for this man was so strong, I felt that if it was not assuaged soon, I would surely faint.

I had realised that I only came to life when in the aura of this man, whether we made love, or just sat together. He had become the very centre of my existence, so I could deny him nothing.

Standing up he drew me with him, till we stood facing each other. His hands, and fingers trembled with

146

anticipation, as he slipped undone the pearl buttons on my dressing gown. I felt him slip it off and saw it fall to the floor. Glancing down at him, there was little doubt of the effect I was having on him, for the evidence was there, his penis stood strong and deliberate, making its intention clear. Pulling aside the halter neck of my nightdress he placed his lips round each nipple in turn, like a baby he suckled them as if needing the nourishment only I could provide through the love we held for each other. As though not being able to get enough, he eased the nightdress off my shoulders, till it too fell to the floor. Leaving me naked before him.

Opening each button on his shirt I followed with my lips, till I cried with the pain of my needs. His shirt open, I moved his jeans, holding imprisoned the love that could give us both the freedom and release we needed. Wishing to return the actions he had carried out on me earlier, I knelt before him pulling the zip undone, allowing his trousers to fall and join my clothes on the floor. The sight of his manhood exposed to its fullest before my eyes, was quite breathtaking. Still kneeling, I took that embodiment of love in my hands preparing to give the satisfaction he desired. A look of understanding crossed his face: "No, Leibchen," he whispered, drawing me gently back to my feet, "Not tonight, there are other ways of bringing joy to each other."

So began our adventures of rediscovery, like all explores we were at first careful with each other, then as knowledge and familiarity made us grown ever bolder our demands of each other grew stronger.

There was no more reasoning, only desperate need. With fingers, lips and tongues our journey of experiments soon became one of understanding. There was no need for words, only the giving and receiving of pleasure. We talked. Oh, how we talked! Such nonsense. The gibberish of true lovers, dreams and desires all woven together. As if speech also could give an outlet to our sensuality. It was only after the moment of climax, when we had climbed the mountains of Olympus, dined with Aphrodite, and feasted at the table of desire with Athena, were we content, once more, to part.

With trembling fingers, we restored the garments removed so hastily only minutes before, that seemed like hours. We had learnt so much about each other in those heavenly journeys of discovery.

"Now we have consummated our vows," Dieter's smile was one of total satisfaction, as he referred to the events that had taken place in the cathedral that afternoon. Sitting back, like a contented cat who had finished the complete bowl of cream, he lit a cigarette, holding open his arms for me. I snuggled into the cavity made for me.

"Now you are truly mine." His tone grew deeper with the knowledge of possession, "You have all I can give."

Feeling the flame of desire begin to grow once more, we decided that it was time to part, before we were caught in an act that stemmed from love but could be turned into one of anger and hurt by those who felt justifiably wronged. He walked me in silence to the top of the stairs, here we kissed once more, long and lingeringly, before whispering good night.

As I climbed into bed beside my husband he opened an eye looking at me. "What took you so long?"

"We were discussing the Greek classics."

He was so tired, "Oh" was all he grunted, falling back into the deep sleep I had interrupted. As exhaustion claimed me I slept with the memory of the scent of a hot musky body claiming mine. Taking me completely, body, mind and spirit. There was nothing left for me to give anyone else ever again.

Chapter 8

My sleep that night was filled with dreams. Impossible fantasies, an earthly paradise in which I walked with a green-eyed god. Our island was filled with a golden sun, azure blue skies and grass the colour of my lover's eyes. We were a population of two, no one else existed for us. And yet, all the time we walked, talked and loved I felt as if a nameless horror stalked us, always waiting, knowing its time would come.

"Mummy, mummy, did you have a good time? We saw Star Trek in German, it did look funny when Mr Spock was talking. Do you think he really knows the language, or did someone else do it for him?" this was not the time to go into the technicalities of voice overs and translation. Instead, I sat up in bed while two excited little girls, giving good impressions of human tornados bounced all over what had once been a haven of peace, the bed. As I was still drifting between the halcyon shores of my dream island and the earth I must now inhabit, I would have appreciated a little peace from my offspring.

Taking a deep breath, I asked, "Who brought you back, was it… Dieter? Again that tiny pause, that excited leap of my heart at just speaking his name.

"No, it was Andrea," Lottie carried on where her sister had left off, "she and Uncle Ernst are ever so nice, they made us cakes and hot chocolate, but we missed you." Instant guilt, at the moments spent with my lover I had not thought of my family at all. How the innocence of children could turn the screw on a mental rack of agony and pain.

"I'm very glad you did," I replied, smiling. "I'd have been very upset if you hadn't, now shoo I have to get up."

As I was about to slip out of bed, the strap of my nightdress moved, causing Hannah to shout: "Mummy, you must have hurt yourself last night." A puzzled frown crossing her face. "Did you fall out of bed?"

Not aware what she meant, I answered without thinking: "No darling, why do you ask?"

About to accompany her sister and leave the room, she glanced back and pointed: "Haven't you seen that funny scratch?" she said, as she and Lottie headed out of the door. Both shaking their heads.

Following the line her finger had pointed to earlier, I realised it was the top of my left breast that had caught their attention. At first I could not see what it was that had seemed so interesting, until an involuntary movement of my head allowed the light from the bedside lamp to bounce off my flesh. Bringing the night back to mock me was a red mark, one that had been left by Dieter's teeth. With careful, deliberate steps I made my way towards the dressing table. Having completely discarded my nightdress as I walked, I stood inspecting the mark, now turning brown at the edges on my skin. I stared at my body, feeling proud that it was still pleasing to the eye. "You may be over twenty-five with two kids, but you're not bad my girl," I mumbled. Running my fingers the length of my body, I had no wish to hide the scar, as I felt it to be a badge of honour, one that recalled the events of the previous night. With difficulty I fought the desire that was rising in me, like a tidal wave threatening to engulf all my senses. With gentle fingers I caressed the spot, still tender from the grazing of his teeth. So I stood, in silence, my mind and body completely divorced from each other.

A husky voice, seeming to come out of my dreams, broke into the mist surrounding me: "It is better if I do that."

Turning, I faced the man, making no pretence to cover myself. Why? I was already his, to do with as he pleased. The smile on his face and light in those eyes was enough for me.

Without the use of words I invited him in. Checking the landing, ensuring he was not seen: "Our friends Andrea and Ernst are here," he whispered. "You must come down."

I nodded once more incapable of speech. On reaching me, he had lifted both breasts in his hands, cradling, then kissing each brown nipple in turn, with gentle yet demanding lips, as if he had the need to draw my life's force to him. As we stood close I could feel the regeneration of his desire. "This is not good, we will soon both have a problem."

This was an outcome I could for see as all the desires of the previous night rose within me, like the sap that fills a tree in spring.

Pulling away, unsteadily I raised my voice in an effort to sound normal: "Have you got a plaster?" By now we were standing a few feet apart, our breathing hard with the strength of our unfulfilled desires.

"Why?"

I pointed to my left breast and the red mark.

"Me?"

I nodded. His laughing reply was typical of the man.

"It is clear I do not need a dentist, then." His laugh seemed to linger as he left the room. "Don't cover it, that's a present from Germany."

Smiling, I turned back towards the wardrobe, preparing to dress for the day ahead. I could hear his tuneless whistle, as he headed into the kitchen.

Having dressed in jeans and tartan shirt, I followed the sound of voices, and the smell of freshly percolated coffee. I could recognise all the voices except one, this obviously belong to Ernst, Andrea's husband.

With a catch of pain in my heart, which I knew was caused by guilt, I stared into the little room. The scene was one of such domestic bliss that for a moment, even though three of those in the room were my family, the thought that I was the interloper "the other woman," a term I had always hated but that was in fact what I had become crossed my mind.

Surrounded by the aromatic smells of fresh coffee, hot bread rolls and her sweet, gentle perfume, stood Monique. Dressed in a pink cotton knit jumper tucked into blue ski pants, I watched as she placed plates before the four children, making sure they had enough. Dieter and Bill were seated side by side at the dining table, busily discussing the events of the previous evening and the forthcoming visit from the English to Germany in the following September, something I really was not prepared to contemplate just yet, it meant leaving my lover and not sure when we would meet again.

Sitting on the other side of the table was Andrea and a man, her husband Ernst, a tall thin man, with a bald head, beady eyes behind very thick glasses. His pale complexion made his face look as if it were cast from papier maché. He had a very endearing smile and loved children. Both Andrea and Ernst were dressed in thick black roll-neck jumpers and jeans.

Seeing me standing at the door Ernst stood up came over to me and in a very courtly gesture shook hands and said what delightful children we had.

"Nice to see you have decided to join us," Bill exclaimed. The turning to the gathered company, he continued with: "The trouble with my wife, is she hates going to bed, but can't wake up either."

The group smiled at this husbandly statement, Dieter translating it for Monique who burst out laughing.

No sooner had I entered the room than breakfast was laid out in front of me. The usual quantity of cheeses, cold meats and beautiful, fresh warm rolls. Filling my mouth with the tasty, crusty pieces of bread. I turned to Monique: "I wish we could get breakfasts like this in England," she smiled and said: "but if you had this at home, it would not be holiday for you here." The logic did not escape me.

Soon the conversation was general across the table, children and adults the noise was quite deafening, everyone had something to say. It was almost like the night previous a truly fun time.

With breakfast finished Andrea and her husband had to take their leave. Everything tidied up, we sat quietly for a while, the four children played a board game. Until, Monique said: "Let's go for a walk in the Forest." I looked puzzled: "The Forest," Bill went on to explain that a short walk from where we were there was quite an ancient wood, with some beautiful trees and plants. Feeling that I did need a walk I agreed that we should explore.

Dressing warmly we headed in the direction of the trees that I could see, this took us up a little hill and past a cemetery. "That is where we will go on day." Dieter said pointing up the hill and to the left. Suddenly I felt the horror that had stalked my dreams of the night before. "Please Dieter, don't talk like that." I begged.

"But you believe in life after death," he stated.

"Yes, I do," I replied. "If I didn't I could not do my work."

"Then you have no fear of death," he carried on.

"No, I have no fear but neither do I want it to come too soon. The physical parting hurts very much and though the Spirit helps. It is the lack of touch, not hearing a much loved voice." Before I could continue Bill brought everything back to basics: "No sex mate." Walking ahead of us he turned to look at us: "Blimey a place with no sex," shuddering he carried on with "I am not going."

At this we all laughed, though I could not lose the feeling of fatality that seemed to haunt us.

As we walked through the trees, past the odd Brau Haus where people would go for a warm drink or a family meal especially on a Sunday, we were also told by Monique that often in the summer these inns would have parties and dances to celebrate the spring and summer.

"Sounds good to me," Bill laughed, "we love a party, don't we?" He said placing an arm around my waist. "Umm," was my reply as I was busy looking at a winter flower in full bloom a beautiful mauve it seemed so full of life and hope in the dark, empty woods.

Watching me admiring the plant Monique said: "When I had our sons, Dieter gave me lots of flowers."

Laughing at this I replied: "Bill, I am afraid is not a flower person. When I had Hannah I received a small box of chocolates and when Lottie was born I got a knitting pattern and some wool." At this everyone laughed: "Well I gave you something." grumbled Bill.

We walked on a little more in silence the children off on some mysterious adventure known only to them. By now the boys were trying to teach the girls German and our daughters were trying to do the same with the boys, I did smile because often Markus would pronounce a letter or word like that of his father, with what appeared to be a lisp, a very endearing sound.

As we walked and talked, it seemed to be the most normal thing in the world, just being here in this little village I had never visited before. We seemed to fit in, Bill and I had met so many people the evening previous we knew that a lasting friendship had been formed with Uwe and Birgit and their daughter Maria. With Frank and his far from attractive wife but with a heart of gold, Agatha and her four children. There were so many people and so many memories, the thought of leaving them the following day and especially that of not seeing Dieter was positively heart wrenching.

I was so lost in my thoughts that I did not see the frozen patch on the footpath, I lost my footing, slipped over and went head first into a bank of prickly bushes, proving to all the assembled company that I had been a very apt pupil at picking up some of my husband's more lewd language.

By now it had started to snow, this time a great deal heavier than the day before, and it was growing darker. Dieter, looking at his watch suggested we return back to the house as Uwe, Birgit and Maria were coming over for a final meal with us before they all got ready for work and school the previous day.

"Yes, and we have to leave early make sure no traffic jams on the way back to Calais." Suddenly the whole weekend began to collapse in on me. Fighting back tears that were threatening, I caught Dieter looking at me and it was obvious he was feeling the same.

Turning and calling out to the children we started to retrace our steps, this time no conversation all of us busy with our own thoughts.

Walking up the short path, we were soon engulfed in the warmth of the house, coffee pot on and cakes placed on the table. As I helped Monique set the table up with the afternoon fare, I asked where she got these beautiful cakes from, she told me that all the villages had their own bakery that would be open from early in the day for the rolls and bread till just after three for the cakes, they were always family businesses.

Once these were finished we got the children washed and dressed, so that once the evening meal was done they could all go to bed and prepare for the following day. A knock on the door told us that Uwe and his family had also arrived.

Now that the three families were together, we decided that the last evening should have a party atmosphere, we three women got on with putting the food together and the three men their self-imposed tasks of bringing up the beer and wine from the cellar.

When Bill was offered some beer his reply of: "Can't drink too much got a long drive ahead." Taking a long drink from his glass: "Just think this time tomorrow, we'll be at home sitting in our own front room." He said, turning to look at me an innocent and normal enough remark to make to his wife, but he had no idea of its effect on Dieter and myself.

He was not to know the sudden shock it had given me, controlled only in a hastily stifled gasp. I had desperately wanted time to stand still, but that only happened in fairy tales. This was no work of fiction, it was real life. Looking across the room I could see Bill's words had the same effect on Dieter, for he had gone quite white around the lips.

As the evening drew on soon Maria and the other four were giving huge yawns, so Uwe and the family decided it was time to leave as he said: "We have to return to normal tomorrow."

"Normal, what was normal?" There was no part of my life that could ever be like that again, looking at the ring on my right hand I could see the incandescent light being picked up by the table lamp in the corner of the room and glancing up I saw that Dieter had also noticed my move with the ring making him smile rather sadly I thought.

The buffet and empty glasses and cups tidied up, leaving just four coffee cups for us, the children in bed. We sat in companionable silence, by now the shutters had come down so keeping the cold night out and us safe and warm inside.

With a heavy heart, I listened to the conversation that went on around me as soft music played on the radio. My pensiveness was noted by Monique, who mentioned this to her husband and translated by him for Bill, whose arms were round me as we sat on the sofa together. Touching my hair gently he smiled and said: "Vicki, hates goodbyes." That was all the answer that was necessary. With everyone looking at me there was nothing I could say too much, so I nodded and filled my mouth with the black bread I hated so much.

Having felt the strain placed on Dieter could not possibly get any worse, I was proved wrong once again. For the disembodied voice of the radio announcer, informed us that he about to play a John Lennon song. Into the quiet of the lamp-lit room the words of "Woman" slowly filtered through. The words we so evocative of our feelings for each other Dieter and I, for once uncaring that our looks could be intercepted and interpreted, just looked deeply into each other's eyes, tears filling green and brown ones alike.

So the evening drew to a close. Dieter had to be in work early, the boys off to school and we driving through the snow to Calais.

One last cup of coffee and we would be spending our last night in Kirschweiler, as we sat drinking this Bill asked how Dieter and Monique had met, something I had at times wondered about. For a moment there was silence, then with a grin he replied: "I was a young man in the army, and Monique worked in a shop. I had to buy some shirts for a night out, my little one here was serving." Looking fondly at his wife's bent head, He caused the knife of jealousy to enter ever deeper into my heart. "She was the most beautiful thing I had ever seen, so I couldn't resist, the rest you know." feeling he had answered the question adequately, Dieter then turned the tables on Bill, asking the same question. The answer when it came was predictable. It was the truth, with much exaggeration and embellishments all giving added length to an already ridiculous story. But it did help to lighten the atmosphere.

Feeling it was now my turn to get my own back on the man who had turned my life upside down, looking at

Monique from my still reclining position, I said: "I suppose Dieter was quite handsome when he was young." Before his wife could reply a cushion flew across the room, missing me and hitting the floor as Dieter squeaked: "What do you mean when I was young?"

Following up on the thrown cushion, he stepped across the floor placing his hands around my neck, pretending to strangle me. He once more proved his power over me. With his head lowered over me, looking as if we played an innocent game, feeling his breath on my cheek, I heard him whisper: "I am not old, after Saturday you still need proof." It was at this moment as if his very spirit entered me. Saturday night would stay forever in my memory.

Turning to Monique, I laughed and said: "OK, I give in your husband is still an Adonis." It had now been mutually decided that an early night was called for.

Monique had already gone to bed and Bill followed sometime later. Dieter and I sat silently for some minutes after the sound of Bill's feet had faded into the bedroom and our door had clicked shut. I stared at a speck on the rug, as if hypnotised.

"Will you be OK?" A whisper reached me across the room.

"I'll have to be, won't I?" My eyes were drawn from the floor to his.

"That is not the way, please Schatzie, don't be angry."

"Angry!" I tried not to raise my voice. "I'm not angry, only frightened, terrified, not knowing how I am going to cope when I can't see you every day." Then almost as if I were begging: "Will you write?"

"No." the answer came without hesitation, forcing me into a reply I regretted the moment it was out.

"Oh! I see you've had your fun, now I've gone you can forget me." No sooner had I finished talking then he was across the room, his hands shaking as they clasped my face between them.

It was the glisten of tears on his cheeks that gave me my answer, making words unnecessary.

"I have not been having fun with you. I did not want this to happen, but it has. Now we must live with it." Then turning me, so that my back was to him. "Can you see me?" Silently I shook my head, puzzled. Can you feel me?" This time I nodded, still silent, "Does it feel good, to know I am here?" Now he had turned me to face him once again, arms closing round me like a vice. "My darling, don't you understand we don't have to write, it is enough for us to know we are alive. The same sun and stars that cover you are mine also. We have our dreams, I will come to you in them." Now his voice was growing more ragged with emotion. "God forgive me Vicki, I love you more than my life, but there are so many other lives to consider." I stared at him, the smile of a lost, lonely child on his face. "Now go to sleep, tomorrow we can worry about when it is here."

My feet seemed to drag, as I walked up the stairs to out room. Opening the door I could hear the deep, even breathing of my husband. Smiling into the darkness a quizzical look on my face: "Bill, my darling man, you are so uncomplicated," I whispered, kissing him on the cheek. A move that did not disturb his night's rest at all.

"Come on Mummy, Daddy said you have to get up now."

Opening eyes still heavy from my night's restless sleep, I forced a smile: "OK darling, tell Daddy I'll be down in a minute. Just go to make sure everything is packed."

Listening to young feet flying down the stairs to the kitchen. I heard my daughter pass the message on. With a heavy heart I climbed out of bed, having washed and dressed, I walked round the room, packing last minute items, checking in the girl's area that everything had been put away in the suitcase before I closed it with a decisive click.

Then wandering round the room, making a double-check that nothing had been left behind, I finally decided that I had no further excuse for staying upstairs. Walking down, I heard Bill say: "Nice of you to join us." About to make some kind of waspish retort, my eyes came in contact with Dieter's the look in his was enough to silence me. Pain they said was not mine alone, he too was going through the agonies of the damned.

Sitting at the table, the room looked so reminiscent of the morning before. With the fresh smell of coffee, and new baked rolls. I could almost have fooled myself this was Sunday all over again, but for a couple of subtle differences. There was no light coming in through the kitchen window, as it was so early the shutters had not opened and the winter darkness persisted. I was also surprised to see Dieter dressed as I had never seen him before, but looking just as handsome.

He was wearing a black business suit, a silver tie and smart black shoes. The boys also in uniform, grey long trousers, yellow shirts under grey jumpers. The girls chattered on, giving Dieter many messages for Maria. These he promised to pass on. Bill and Monique talked, via Dieter, discussing the weekend. So much was going on, I was relieved no one noticed my silence.

Thoughts ran wild in my mind, studying every facet of my lover's features, each nuance of his voice. I had to have something to take back with me, I was so afraid when we were no longer together I might forget some part of him, this was something I did not want to even think of.

I saw Dieter check his watch, an involuntary movement, as if he had to be somewhere else, but at the same time not wanting to bring our parting to its climax too soon.

"What time do you have to be at the Bank?" Bill having noticed the movement our host had made.

"You don't have to hurry, it makes no matter if I am a little late," Dieter replied hurriedly.

"Well we must be on our way, don't want to miss the Hovercraft." Then, turning to me Bill carried on: "And having Madame here as navigator is no help. This time she'll probably take us into Holland." Standing up he called to the girls who had gone to have a last word in broken English and German with the boys. "Come on you two, say goodbye." I had never known two words could hold so much horror for me.

My heart sank, I could feel my feet sweating, as if I walked a tightrope, "Oh! Dear God" a voice moaned in my very soul."

"I can't leave, he is everything I ever wanted, I need him." As usual these thoughts had to stay shut up in me, only to be released when my tears could also be allowed to run free.

The children joined us and with Dieter's help the cases were brought down, and packed into the car, along with a couple of presents Monique had bought for the girls. "Not to be opened till Christmas." She had informed them.

"You would have thought we had come for a month," Bill muttered.

"I wish you had," Dieter replied, smiling.

"Maybe next time," Bill answered. Making my heart leap, there would be further visits.

We stood by the car, surrounded by the cold air filling the dark still morning. Overnight no further snow had come down, but what had fallen the day before was now frozen over, making movement on the icy pavements treacherous. The children launched themselves at Dieter and Monique saying goodbye. Then Bill followed suit. Thanking the couple for their hospitality, I stood alone for a few seconds, still vainly wishing a miracle would happen and we would be able to stay, but that would only succeed in putting off the inevitable, anyway I had appointments made for the week coming where I would have to help and advise people perhaps in a similar state to myself. I would need my Spirit Guides now like I had never needed them before.

The others having said goodbye and in the car, it was now my turn. I could see that Monique was quite upset at our parting. Placing our arms round each other we stood for a while in companionable silence. Then I pulled away. Now it was my turn to say farewell to Dieter. This was going to be very difficult. It had to be done so that I appeared to be no more upset at leaving him than I would be with any of my husband's friends, an almost impossible situation to be in. I walked up to him, holding out my hand prepared to shake his, till Monique said, laughing: "I don't mind if you kiss my husband." turning to glance at the younger woman, I wondered what she would have said were she able to read my mind.

Quietly, Dieter placed both arms around me, my own closed round him. We stood like this for seconds, both of us with so much to say, and yet neither the time nor the place to say it. Our warm breaths mingling in the frosty air, coming out of us like ghostly apparitions. Once again I felt as if the promised Land that had been glimpsed was now being cruelly snatched away.

"I love you," he whispered, then: "Remember we have our dreams, nothing will ever part us."

I nodded wordlessly.

Then turning to Bill: "Drive carefully, we want you to phone us on your return to England."

Bill made a promise that he would do this. Then we were in the car, and driving off, the children waving out of the back till the car had turned the corner. I did not look back, because even though I knew the dawn was beginning to break, and a watery, winter sun was coming through the clouds, I could see only the dark, long winter ahead. No knowing when the summer would shine for me again, if ever.

Settling back in my seat, I prepared for the journey home, family and friends. Knowing I had left the best part of myself in a little village I had never heard of until a few years ago.

Chapter 9

The dark winter days following our trip, left an empty echo in my heart. Even the festivities of Christmas and New Year's Eve could not lighten my spirits. Events I normally entered into with great enjoyment, now appeared bare and devoid true life. But, afraid my family may grow suspicious, I had to become an actress in every sense of the word. Leaving me drained at night, so making sleep possible.

Everywhere I looked, Dieter seemed to be, from visits to the club to standing in my kitchen surrounded by well-wishers and friends popping in for the Christmas drinks that had long been a tradition with us. My thoughts seemed to focus only on one thing, "What was he doing now? Was Dieter being kissed by women wishing him Happy New year? Did he enjoy it?" Oh! God, I had to have peace, but I knew that was impossible. What I wanted was a letter, a phone call, anything, but these needs would never mature. I knew once he made his mind up there was no turning back. We were to have no contact whatsoever.

That weekend seemed like a dream, the only tangible reminder was the ring on my right hand, flashing in the light thrown from a wall lamp in my lounge. Hoping no one would notice, I lifted my finger to my lips, sealing with a kiss once more the love that had placed it there.

On the evening of New Year's Day a new war film was to be shown on television. Knowing this would be of little interest to me I wandered off to the kitchen, whiling away my time making coffee, tidying up and generally fussing around, that was until Bill called me:

"Vicki, come here quick."

Running into the lounge, afraid one of the children who had been playing on the floor near him might have hurt themselves, I stopped, out of breath, seeing that all was well with the girls, who seemed unconcerned with the tone of their father's voice. I was cross, because not only had he interrupted what I was doing, but also my thought. Filled once more with the German.

"What do you want? I'm busy."

"If you were less impatient, and looked on the screen, you might see something of interest to you."

Turning, I followed his gaze to the small screen in the corner, all I could see at first was a room obviously set in the Head Office of the Gestapo, turning to Bill, shrugging: "What? You know how I hate war films."

"Oh! For God's sake woman, look will you, anyone there remind you of someone we know."

Still puzzled, I turned my glance back to the screen, dumbfounded. For there in full colour stood Dieter, dressed in the uniform so familiar to everyone. As the actor began to talk, even his pronunciation of English, was so reminiscent of my lover. I could feel my heart beating faster. The green-eyed actor, with the dark hair and mischievous smile, brought all my secret desires and longings once more to the forefront of my mind.

However, after long months of practise my self-control had become such, that nothing could break through my composure apart from Dieter actually walking into my life again. Pretending an indifference I was far from feeling replied: "Should I recognise anyone there?"

"Woman, Can't you see. The Gestapo Officer, don't you think he looks like someone we know?"

Once more I shrugged.

"Honestly you can be so dense, can't you see he's the image of my mate Dieter."

"Yes, I suppose there is a likeness, but to be honest it's so long since I saw him I can't really remember what he looks like." Pleased with my attitude and lies, I wandered back to continue the washing-up, my feelings so numb I could feel no pain from the heat of the water, I had just placed my hands in, because of the agony filling my heart.

That night as we lay in bed, I could feel Bill's hands searching for me, holding me close. I knew he wanted to make love, but I was in no mood. Preparing to make some excuse, I began to pull away, till the picture of a man stood before me, green eyes filled with passion, the hot musky scent oozing from his body, as it was covered in the sweat created by our love making. Suddenly, I found myself responding to my husband's demands with such passion that as he turned over on his side, preparing to fall into a satisfied sleep, he whispered: "After all these years it's still good between us." As the soft tenor of his breathing told me he was asleep I turned my face into the pillows; soft, slow silent, heart rending sobs of self-pity, sorrow and guilt filling me.

One day as I wandered aimlessly around the kitchen I bumped into my mother who had come in through the kitchen door. I had been so intent on once more examining the beautiful sapphire and diamond ring, while thinking of the man who had placed it on my finger that I had been completely unaware that she had entered the kitchen.

"Darling, are you all right?" she asked. "Since your return from Germany your mind appears to have been very distracted."

"Don't be silly, Mum. I was just admiring my ring."

"Yes, it is pretty dear," she replied picking up my finger to examine the article in question closer. "Where did you say you got it, somewhere in Germany?"

Trying to hide my impatience, as really did not feel like resurrecting the lies I had invented to cover the sudden appearance of this piece of jewellery, I went once more through the story as to how it had come into my possession. All the time nagged by the guilt that here I was once again lying to someone else whom I loved and who loved me. Was that to be the story of my life, nothing but lies?

Having reached the end of my story, I turned to put on the kettle, at ease my story had come to an end. Hopefully, there would be no further questions as to my purchase. There was silence between us for a moment or two as my mother seated herself, taking a biscuit from the plate I offered. Biting it, an air of concentration on her face: "You know, I don't think it's a dress ring you bought." I heard her say.

"Really mother, it's not from the Crown jewels, why must we keep discussing the bloody thing." Now I really was getting annoyed.

"Well honestly, I just thought you would want to know what it is you really have."

"How would you know? Have you ever been to Germany?" I knew now I was sounding like a petulant and slightly frightened child.

"No dear, but remember there were many business people your father and I knew who were German." Her voice took on the dreaming sound, I knew and recognised. One that meant that the old days were once more being remembered.

I sat playing with my teaspoon, letting my tea grow cold as she renewed old memories. Many that were new to me, some that I recognised. All of them having a meaning for my mother, this way keeping my father alive for her. I sat locked in the time warp with her, until she said suddenly: "Now I know why I recognise the ring, old Frau Feidler, the woman whose family owned the shoe factory."

I nodded, still not knowing what my mother was alluding to.

"Don't you remember her wedding ring?"

Once more I shook my head, puzzled.

"It was a Sapphire and diamond ring identical to yours."

At last understanding was dawning, yes my mother would know the ring I wore was a wedding ring, even down to the inscription were I to let her see it. The elderly lady she had mentioned earlier, would often tell us of the story behind the family heirlooms that were hers and how these rings were both engagement and wedding rings as well.

Recognising the bloodhound look on her face, I decided it was safer for both of us if I could change the subject. However, luck was on my side. Before she could try digging any further in how I had come by the ring, I heard the front door bell. "Saved by the bell," I muttered, hurrying to answer the summons, relieved to see my two friends looking very cold and in need of a cup of tea. I could have kissed them so pleased was I at their timely intervention.

"What are you two doing?" I asked leading them into the warm kitchen.

"Got fed up with looking at some of the silly soaps, so we decided to come and see you for a gossip." Angie grinned at me, having already acknowledged my mother by placing a kiss on her cheek. "How are you Mrs Stracey? I hope this weather is not too bad for you." She carried on looking out at the afternoon sky, heavy with a promise of snow to come.

"Thank you for asking, dear. I'm fine." My mother smiled as she stood up, tea finished, making it obvious she was about to leave.

"No need to go because we have arrived." Frances muttered hurriedly.

Smiling my mother's answer was typical: "No, dear you are not chasing me away, got some sewing to do." As she got to the door she threw one more spanner at me: "Do you girls know where my daughter got that antique and very expensive ring from?" With a little wave she was gone.

"Phew," Frances said: "Your mother is no fool." I nodded my head in agreement. It was obvious my mother was very suspicious and rather like a pit bull would not let go. I was now forewarned, and would make sure the question of the ring did not arise again.

Cups of tea on the table accompanied by more biscuits, Angie placing a hand on my shoulder asked: "How are you?"

"Me, I've never been better." Then carried on talking as if a dam had been broken, so allowing the water to run free. I carried on: "Great weather we're are having, might snow they say, won't the children…"

At this point I realised both my friends were staring at me as if I had taken leave of my senses, their expressions silencing me as nothing else could have done. They were dumbfounded.

"Shut up." Angie demanded. "You don't have to put on an act with us. Now tell the truth how do you really feel?

"Like shit." I said, no other words necessary.

At this my friends laughed. Taking the cups of tea that had been prepared we sat down in the living room.

A more ill-assorted trio of women could never be found.

Looking at Angie I smiled. She had proved on many occasions what a good friend she could be. From helping out with babysitting to an almost complete understanding of my situation. Looking at Frances, I smiled she lived in what we called Frances' world, her husband Mark absolutely adored her and spoilt her unmercifully. She saw no wrong in anybody and had the worst dress sense possible. Without Laura Ashley Frances would be lost. But today these girls were my best friends and the best support anyone could ask for.

Frances looked at me and for once I could see that she was really moved by the situation I now found myself in, placing an arm round my shoulder she said: "You do know we are trying to understand, please let us help."

I shook my head to this as they and I both knew whatever help they offered would never be enough to fill the gap that was in my life Dieter not in it.

Afraid that the atmosphere surrounding us would be too much for my self-control; normally quite strong but now and then chinks would appear in the iron curtain I had tried to build around me.

"Come on girls, who died?" I asked my voice sounding over loud even to my ears.

"No one, just wondering what you planned on doing with the rest of your life," Angie asked, lifting her eyes from the tea cup that seemed to have held her concentration for so long.

"Living it, darling," I answered. Then continuing: "In exactly the same way, that I have managed for the last thirty-five years."

"Prove it." Frances demanded.

"What's to prove," I asked, my back now turned to my friends, afraid they might see the quiver of my lips. "There was life before Dieter Schmidt. Therefore, there can be again."

I felt an arm go round my waist as Angie muttered: "God I hate that bloody man." This was said with such heartfelt fervour, I felt she was thinking of herself as well as me.

"How about hearing some music?" Frances asked as we sat down again, magazines open before us, a little respite before picking the children up from school. This was not the first winter afternoon we had spent this way. Drinking tea, and chatting. Putting the world to rights often leading to friendly disagreements. Yet, here we were faced with a very real problem and completely unable to deal with it.

As the silence seemed to draw on interminably, the voice of the radio announcer could be heard informing us that a "Golden Oldie" was to be played. The Platters started with "Ooh Yes, I'm the great pretender." At this tears finally welled up in eyes that had been fighting for so long to stay dry. Placing my head in my hands, and to my friend's great consternation, wept because my heart was breaking.

I could see once more the look on Dieter's face, as he had smiled at me stating from now on we had to be "Great Pretenders." So these words were almost like an echo of his own.

Having allowed me to cry for some minutes, Angie stated matter of factly: "Look, you're in no state to pick up the kids from school, or feed them. I'll take them back to my place. And when I feel you are ready return them to you." then turning to Frances she said, "Coming?" the other woman nodded silently. In an action completely alien to both women, they bent over me, placing a kiss of friendship on my cheeks. Then I felt the cold air blowing in through the open kitchen door as they departed, leaving me completely alone.

I stared at the shelf by the telephone, a pen I had not noticed before, now taking on great importance. An idea had struck me: "I could write a little letter, let him know how wretched I felt.

Frantically I searched for some paper, and putting some of my perfume on it, I began.

"My Darling Dieter

I need to write to you. I am so lonely without you. Please tell me you really love me. Did you mean all those things that were said when you placed the ring on my finger? Oh! My darling..."

At this sanity returned, no I would not, could not, post this letter. What would we do if Monique found it. No there were some things better left unwritten. Taking the piece of paper in shaking hands, I walked over to the cooker, turning on the gas I watched as the blue flames licked around the piece of paper, now and then a word becoming legible before it disappeared into the heat surrounding it.

One Friday as the golden crocuses began to poke their heads through the earth, now much softer, the ice and snow having melted, preparing the ground for the new life that was to come. I sat silently gazing out at the afternoon that slowly darkening before me. The children lying in their favourite positions, stretched out on the floor watching television. My mind so numb, that it was not until Hannah shook me out of my stupor. "Telephone," she stated, somewhat superfluously I thought, as she was shaking the instrument at me.

"Who is it? Your Dad?" I asked, expecting a call from him.

"No," she whispered: "I think it's a foreigner."

Suddenly every nerve came alive, trying not to rush I stood up. While at the same time deciding if it were Dieter, this call would be best taken in the kitchen.

"When I pick up the other set, put this one down." I asked Hannah, not wanting her to hear what might be said between us.

On legs that appeared to have grown leaden, I walked towards the kitchen. Making myself comfortable, I picked up the handset: "O.K. Darling, I'm here now." I said to her, knowing the caller, if it were indeed Dieter, would know the message was also for him.

"What took you so long?" the husky tones I had wanted to hear for so long came over the wire to me.

"Hullo." I was amazed and annoyed that for months now I had wanted to speak with this man, and now I had the opportunity all I could say was hullo."

"I miss you." He continued echoing my thoughts.

"How are you able to call me?" At last I had found words, and the breath to use them.

"Monique is not at home so I decided to call you." He sounded so pleased with himself.

"Dieter, do you still love me?" I asked trying not to sound too adolescent.

"I have told you, where we are concerned love is forever, even when we are not here anymore." His disembodied voice came back over the wire. For a second or so silence reigned between us. It was obvious that the same emotions filling me, were affecting him too,

"I was going to write to you." I found myself saying.

"Good, I am glad you did not." I could hear the smile in his voice. "There would have been a big problem if my wife found had found the letter." I heard the sigh I was unable to hold back: "It is better we appear only to be friends."

I nodded, knowing he was unable to see my action. We had so much to say to each other but were unable to empty our hearts. I, all the time afraid of discovery by my children, and he, well his wife would be back any moment now. So we tried to talk with stilted sentences, till hearing a commotion at his end I knew his wife had arrived home. Even before the hurriedly whispered: "I must go now my love." Followed by the dialling tone.

I sat for some minutes, shaking as if in the aftermath of a typhoon. Then standing up, straightening my back, I reached a decision. From now on I was going to put Dieter out behind me, we were to be only friends and if given the chance to visit Cologne and him again I would refuse the offer if and when presented. I also vowed that my friends were not to be told of this phone call, in this way

I could start the process of forgetting what a fool I was.

The Saturday evening I found myself in the drive to the large house in which Frances and her family lived, was one of the first truly spring evenings. Though the nights still closed in early, they held a warmth not contained in the chilly winter nights just gone. Even in the dusk, roses could be seen bursting out on the new, green stalks, with leaves still the tinge of pink common to these bushes when first coming to life after their winter sleep. I could feel the promise of new life all around me, yet I was unable to look enthusiastically on anything now. Not since that fateful evening when I had reached my decision.

"Hi," Frances smiled as she opened the door to us. "Go in, Angie and Joe are already here." Bill and I did as invited.

Leaving the large pink and grey hall with its assortment of paintings and family photographs, we made our way into the large square lounge. Two large bay windows took up the main front wall, the other three walls were painted in a pale lilac shade. This form of decoration had been chosen by Mark, as Frances was always changing her mind as to colours. We often laughed at the time when on one wall in the kitchen there were fifteen different sample colours, Frances just could not make up her mind to what colour schemes she wanted. The three piece was large and cumbersome but like everything in this house expensive. This too was in a light shade of coffee, contrasting nicely with the pale pink of the thick, luxuriant carpet. On the far wall could be seen an elegant rosewood cocktail cabinet, now open, the light inside illuminating the variety of drinks inside.

Sitting down, kicking my shoes off, I smiled accepting the Bacardi and coke placed in my hands by Joe. Glancing at the large fireplace that Mark had built in a corner of the room, an almost exact copy of a medieval

177

one recently seen on television in a castle newly renovated.

This evening was not an unusual event, at least once a month we three couples would try to dine together, or failing that, meet at one or the other's houses.

On getting the invitation from Mark, I had prepared myself for any talk there might be of the Germans and the impending journey our men had arranged for them in September, when they would be the visitors and the German people the hosts. It was not long before Joe brought up the subject.

"What date are we going to Kirschweiler? I need to tell my deputy that I will be away." As Mark was head of a bank in the City, we knew he had to make provisions for any leave he might take.

"The second week in September," Bill replied, glancing at the large wall calendar.

"What will you girls do while we are away?" Mark asked.

"Worry about you." Frances replied, caustically.

"Why?" Mark demanded

"You lot can't handle English beer, so how can you manage the stuff out there." Was her laughing reply.

"Well we do try to hold up the British end." All three said at the same time, laughing.

The three men were talking as were we the ladies, my ears however did pick up when I heard: "Have you told them yet."

"Tell us what?" I asked, prepared to say, 'No.' without knowing the question.

It was Bill who dropped the bombshell, one I had not been expecting: "We three fellows felt a little guilty, because we were to have the long weekend in Germany, and you had worked so hard at making their time here almost like home... we could not explain to our husbands why Angie and Frances had such a sudden joint attack of choking at these words.

"To continue," Bill carried on annoyed that his moment in the limelight had been spoilt by the two women. "We thought you might like a long weekend over there yourselves around Easter.

"No," I found myself almost shouting.

"What is the matter with your, I thought you enjoyed the visit over there." Bill replied, staring at me. Anger apparent on his face. "Women, you try to please them and…"

Touching him gently on the arm, hoping this apologetic gesture would soothe his obviously ruffled feathers.

"Darling, you forget that time of the year is very important in the Catholic countries. Visits with families, going to Church, not like the heathens here." My voice trailed off into silence.

The men looked at each other, understanding dawning between them, my explanation had obviously been accepted.

Never mind we'll take you some other time, "Bill replied giving me a forgiving hug.

I had not got the heart to tell him he would never be taking me back to Germany or that village ever again. Looking at the faces of Angie and Frances I knew there was no need to give them any apologies, they understood as true friends do.

"Actually, I agree with Vicki." Angie replied coming to my aid:" After all you will be there in September, why inflict any more agony on those poor people then they have to endure." she burst out laughing ducking as her husband threw a wine cork in her direction.

I sat back in silence, as the conversation flowed around me. No more talk about Germany now, it was filled with the more mundane things, covering politics to fashion male and female. My mind once more filled with thoughts I had endeavoured to keep at bay.

As it was said, "In Italy all roads lead to Rome." With me it was different. "All thoughts lead to Dieter, my Waterloo."

Chapter 11

The sound of bird song woke me from a less than restful sleep. Reluctantly, opening one eye to stare at the bright spring sunshine breaking through the curtains. About to get out of bed it was the sound of whispers quickly silenced that made me quickly shut both eyes pretending to still be asleep.

After minutes of silence I decided some acting was necessary. Turning on my back, stretching as if in the luxury of relaxation and contentment, I opened both eyes, this time gasping in real amazement, for I was staring at the yellow petals of a daffodil, that had found its way onto a tea tray, accompanied by very soggy looking cornflakes and burnt toast. Only the coffee appeared to have any real substance to it, having been prepared by Bill.

"Thank you darlings." I kissed both my daughters in turn, thanking them for their thoughtfulness in preparing this sumptuous Mothers' Day treat. They wandered off, scampering down the stairs pleased with their offering, while I prepared to discard food that was completely inedible. Bill burst out laughing as I hastily place the unwanted food in a plastic bag that he handed me. "One of these days you are going to have to tell these two you can't eat what they give you."

"What, and hurt their little feelings?" Shaking my head at this unthinkable idea. "No way, they will improve," adding as an afterthought "I hope."

Still laughing, Bill walked down to the kitchen, so that he could prepare a proper meal for us both.

As I dressed for the day, a rogue thought flashed through my mind: "I wonder if they have Mothers' Day in Germany, and do their two sons also make a treat for Monique helped no doubt very ably by their Father.

It was not the sound of Bill calling me that attracted my attention it was the excited tone in it. "Hi, Vicki, guess what?" Looking up at him I asked: "What?"

"Got a letter from the Tax man he is giving us some money, quite a lump sum." Bill continued.

Looking at the letter I was delighted with what we had received, then there was the inevitable question: "What do we spend it on?" By now the children were standing with us, as excited as we were and with their ideas of how the money should be spent. Opinions like a large Wendy house, and other very imaginative ideas, until Bill came up with: "Lets hire a camper and drive through France, Switzerland into Germany," my heart speeded up then dropped as I remembered my promise to myself so long ago, as Bill continued talking to the girls now: "We could spend some time in Kirschweiler, visit Dieter and his family, you can see how big the boys have grown." I was about to say that was a stupid idea, when looking at the three faces looking at me I did not have the heart to spoil anything, so dumbly I nodded agreement.

Walking away from them, I shrugged: "Who am I to argue? Anyway, I'm a big girl now, I can handle anything that comes my way." There was no need to wonder if anyone heard me grumble, Bill had gone to the garden and the girls making so much noise they couldn't have heard an explosion had there been one.

My feelings during the intervening weeks varied between feverish excitement and panic. Did he still love me? Had Dieter ever loved me? Were my feelings for him still the same? Had he just become a beautiful fantasy or... here I had to stop afraid that I might overstep the boundary between sanity and madness.

"Enjoy the holiday, take each day as it comes." Was my last waking thought the night before our European trek began.

The morning of our journey started with great promise. A strong July sun shone overhead making everything appear brighter. Trees looked greener, colours on the flowers fuller. I stood watching as Bill, accompanied by his brother Charlie and our children, filled the camper we had hired for the holiday, with clothes, food and drink.

"Well Madam, are you ready?" Charlie stood smiling at me, his hands pointing me in the direction of the open door. I could see the excited faces of our children as they stared out of the windows, misting it with their hot breath, waving to my mother who had been seconded into looking after house and animals. Placing a kiss on her unwilling cheek, I set my foot on the step leading into the cab, trying to hold back the tingle of excitement that feathered its way along my spine. I had always been a gypsy at heart, now I was to have the opportunity of partially fulfilling some of my dreams as a traveller. "Yes, but what waits for you at the other end?" A voice whispered in my mind. "We'll worry about that when we come to it." I silently argued back.

Though I had made all the travel arrangements, I had been adamant when speaking to Germany: "You talk to him." I had replied to Bill's "Can you phone Dieter, see if he can find somewhere for us to park?" Thankfully he had not argued the point.

We had mutually agreed to invite Bill's unmarried brother Charles along with us, not only because he was good company and a firm favourite with our children, but because he would be able to help with the driving. When Bill had asked if I was interested in being co-driver, I had flatly refused.

As he was to be the second driver it was only right that Charlie should sit beside Bill in the cab.

The girls had chosen the two long seats at the back for themselves, when put together at night this would make a double bed for them. The bed Charlie had chosen for himself, would come into being when we parked for the night, and it looked like a hammock slung behind the cab itself, instead of being made of soft material it was in fact a long seat similar to the ones the girls were using. The bed for Bill and myself was a double bed above the cab. With all our seating and sleeping arrangements taken care of and food and clothes stored away we were off on our journey.

I marvelled at how well this vehicle had been appointed. It was painted in muted shades of cream and coffee, with matching accessories of seat coverings and carpets. A small stainless sink was situated over a fridge crammed full with cans of food and drink, plus some perishable foods for breakfast. As we had never travelled this way before, I had prepared for all eventualities.

"Just as a matter of interest, what have you got in that suitcase?" I heard Bill ask his brother.

"Only a few outfits to impress any lovely ladies we might meet on the Continent, I'd hate to let the British male side down." Charlie replied laughingly at his brother's mocking description of the large holdall he had arrived at our house with.

Looking at our newly acquired navigator, I could not help thinking how dissimilar these two men were. Whereas Bill was tall and well proportioned for his height and smart, Charlie was quite the reverse. Approximately the same height as my husband, and three years younger, his hair was an untidy black and grey tangle over a face that was completely moon shaped. His eyes appearing bleary through the bifocals he wore which rested on cheeks of a ruddy complexion. The beard and moustache surrounding his small mouth was the same colour as his hair and as unkempt. In all the years I had known my brother-in-law, I knew that he and sartorial elegance never suited each other, so it was that his comment on numerous outfits to impress the ladies made us all laugh.

Having fought our way through the inevitable traffic jams that accompany holiday traffic, we arrived at Dover almost too late for our hovercraft, once on the sizeable craft and its skirts billowing out to hit the water with speed, I knew there was no turning back and only one destination Germany and Dieter.

As the sound of its engines could be heard I waited, unaware that I was holding my breath. Thinking once more of the first time I had entered this miracle of modern engineering, and the ensuing events.

"Dreaming, sister dear?" Charlie smiled at me.

"Oh, yes, just thinking. It's amazing how they get these things to float." I had become such a good liar. Turning my eyes once more to the Channel. Looking out of the port holes, I could see the spray from the water now being sprayed over all the cars with the force of its giant engines.

As it was early evening when we arrived on the French coast, it was decided that we should stop for an evening meal at some roadside restaurant, then settle the now tired children down for the night.

Finding a quiet road we travelled along for some time into the darkening evening, until Bill noticed what looked like a bungalow with flowered curtains in the windows, and green shutters on the outside. There were a couple of cars in the car park so we decided this would be an ideal place for a meal and a rest for Bill who would drive well into the night.

For a moment I felt as though it was an English country cottage I was to enter, not a French farm building.

However, having crossed the threshold the smell of highly perfumed continental cigarettes, cheap wine and strong coffee soon put these ideas to flight.

It wasn't difficult to find a table, apart from a couple of French labourers the little place was quite empty. We had some problem in giving our order, as we spoke no French and our host no English, it was a miracle that our requests came up as anything edible. It resembled an English stew, the adults had coffee and the children orange juice. While we were eating Bill gave the children a mini history lesson about the land that surrounded us and the events of the First World War, this they listened to with the equanimity of the young who had only ever known peace. He talked about Pill boxes and much else besides

Having satisfied our hunger we were soon on our way, girls in pyjamas, I too had prepared for the night and we were settled comfortably for the night excited at being in Switzerland when we awoke the next day. Bill having driven the first part it was now Charlie's turn to take the wheel, a task he took with alacrity.

As the sun settled ever lower, preparing the children for sleep was not difficult as their eyes were closing even as the bed was made up for them.

"I've never slept on a bed that moves before," Hannah called out to the two men.

"I have," Charlie replied, "regularly, on my return home from the Rowing Club."

For this useless piece of information Bill gave his brother a smart kick on the ankles, bringing an. "Ouch, that was not called for." But it did silence him.

With the men taking it in turns to rest, our journey through the night was carried out quite effectively. We travelled at speed, stealing silently across farmlands and through villages, like thieves.

Every time we entered a small town or village there would be the inevitable lights of a large church or cathedral rising out of the dark, the only signs of life appearing in the form of grinning gargoyles that inhabited the brightly lit towers of these large buildings. Like ghosts, they came out of the blackness, seeming to hover unsupported in the night mist, then disappear. Sometimes a lone owl would hoot as if offering to join us on our lonely journey.

The moon having taken over from the sun, gave everything around us an unearthly glow. Its silvery fingers giving mundane bricks a touch of majesty and mystery.

I must have fallen asleep, as it was the sudden shaking of my shoulders that woke me up.

"I thought you'd like to see this, Bill whispered, afraid of waking the other occupants.

For a moment or two I was bemused, having fallen asleep while the camper was in motion. It took some moments to realise that at some time during the night we had pulled up, in this way giving both men a few hours' rest.

Climbing gingerly from my bed over the cab, I tiptoed across to the window near the sink, where Bill was already stationed. The view that unfolded before us was breathtaking, I stood for long seconds in complete silence. We were on a plateau surrounded by green fields dotted here and there with wild meadow flowers. The last time I had seen the sun was as it set in France, it now appeared to have changed direction and was rising from a bed of mountains. With its golden glow touching the snow on neighbouring mountains, everything around us was painted a burnt orange giving the impression of flames rather like the Olympic Torch.

Each snow covered top appeared to hold a luminescence I had never witnessed before. Slowly my eyes wandered from the glory of the dawn to the lake below. This was in complete contrast to the mountains above, as its blue echoed the colour of the sky, each one appearing to vie for brilliance with the other. As the snow shone with fire, the azure blue of the lake held light bits of silver glimmering and shimmering in the sun's light. In the distance could be seen houses huddled round the lake.

As the sun was not quite high, the air around us still carried a chill that made me shiver. An action that Bill noticed, placing an arm round my waist and holding me close. This husbandly concern for my welfare gave me a momentary pang of guilt, as for a second I had wished it was Dieter's arms around me.

Preparing for the day ahead was chaotic to say the least. Though the camper had been designed as a six seater, it had never allowed for everyone wanting to wash at the same time, get dressed and a great deal else besides.

During breakfast it was mutually decided, as the town before us appeared to be uninteresting, we would journey on till reaching Berne, the capital of this tiny but rich Banking country.

Our itinerant holiday began once breakfast had been tidied up, Charlie had decided that he would take the wheel this morning, so allowing Bill the luxury of being passenger and sightseer. The mountains stood around us as if guarding the magnificence of the scenery, imperturbable sentinels, these monoliths of nature stood as if defying man and nature to spoil what was perfect.

Suddenly, the sky dimmed and darkened, giving us what appeared to be day turned into night. The skies that had so far been cerulean blue turned into night were now rent apart with the anger of the heavens, treating us to a further display of nature's might. All around us lightening crackled and thunder roared, as if proving that the Scandinavian God Thor did exist, wielding his hammer of terror. As the lightening flashed around us, rain pounding on the windscreen of the van, making vision impossible.

"Charlie," Bill called to his brother: "See that parking place, pull up till this passes over."

With obvious relief, my brother-in-law carried out the request, wiping imaginary sweat from his forehead: "Phew, I'm glad you came up with that idea, I didn't fancy driving through this little lot."

So we sat watching the storm play about us, tea and soft drinks taking on a great importance.

The hours in which the thunder and lightning played their little games seemed to hang heavy on our hands, making us restless and the children irritable.

As soon as it became obvious the weather was lightening, as the heavy downpour became a drizzle we were eager to be away from our hiding place in the lee of the mountains.

"Right folks, let's restart our journey."

Taking his place in the driving seat, Bill began making his way through the hot, steaming puddles that had accumulated on the greasy road surface. With the movement of the vehicle, the atmosphere brightened like magic. Driving through the shallow rain-lakes on the tarmac, with the sun now once more showing her face, it was hard to believe the wrath of nature that had surrounded us earlier.

Sitting back in my seat, I watched the ever changing faces of the valleys we travelled through. Never two the same, so boredom did not set in, even with the children. It was as we travelled through one of these alpine villages, filled with the sounds of cow bells coming from the pastures covering the side of the mountains, that a sign hanging harmlessly over a leather shop: "Dieter Schmidt Lederwaren," brought a feeling of fear as memories were once more unwrapped.

"That reminds me," Charlie remarked, pointing to the notice I had already noticed: "Does your friend know I have joined you on this holiday."

"Oh, yes, we warned him!" Bill continued laughing: "Told him we were bringing the biggest drinker in England with us." Then turning to me my husband asked, as if needing this statement verified, "Didn't we, dear."

"You did darling, remember, I didn't speak to him."

"Yes," he replied, already tiring of this conversation, as he had seen something on the mountainside that needed his full attention for a moment almost forgetting he was not only an engineer but a driver as well. It was Hannah who brought his attention to this fact, as he and Charlie became engrossed in a conversation about Hydro Electrics.

"Daddy should we be aiming into that mountain," She asked.

Having made the necessary correction we carried on with our journey without any further mishap. Though it took sometime longer for my heart to stop its fast beating due to the unexpected excitement that name had conjured up.

"Is it true?" Charlie asked turning to me from the front seat: "Is what true? I may be psychic, but mind reading has never been my thing," I replied. "About the Germans," he continued: "What?" I was now growing really irritated, I just wanted to be on my own in my mind. "That they are really big drinkers." Looking at him, I said: "No more than anyone else, they have one little fellow, I hope we don't meet Klaus. Nasty little man, drinks like a fish and very rude when drunk." Looking at Charlie's face this time I did read his mind: "And no, you will not be starting any competitions with him." It must have been the expression on my face that silenced him.

Not wanting to spoil the atmosphere, I walked along the swaying vehicle, kissing him on the cheek in unspoken apology.

"If this happens every time I annoy you, I must do it more often." he replied laughing, making a great show of touching the spot where my lips had touched.

As the word friend had been used, a mental picture of a young woman with blue eyes and blonde hair flashed before me. How could I possibly be her friend? I was certainly going to try. For now I was intent on enjoying the moment, we had many more hours of fun in this beautiful country. Lots of places to explore.

It was as the sun was setting at the end of a perfect day, even allowing for the cloudburst we had experienced earlier that, we realised we had reached the town of Berne, our objective.

Now all we had to do, in a strange place at the start of a dark night with not a star or moon in sight to assist us, was to find a camp site. Being inexperienced this was going to prove difficult as had no idea what signs to look for.

It was Lottie who said: "Mum, that could be what we want?" Pointing to what appeared to be a pine forest: "See, there's loads of cars and what looks like a camper like ours."

Following her pointing finger in the darkness surrounding us, I could just make out the shapes she had described.

"Bill, head in that direction, darling." I called out.

"Referring to me like that, how can I refuse." My husband laughed.

We headed for the trees in the distance, following the vast line of hedges. Like a blind man tapping his stick against the edges of a wall we soon found the entrance. A large wrought iron gate with the name of the campsite and opening times.

"What's the time?" Charlie asked.

"Just after ten," Bill called back.

"Don't think they will let us in."

"Vicki, can you check what is printed on the wall." Thankfully it was in German as well as French.

Reading the notice, my heart sank, I had to agree with Charlie we were too late they would not let us in.

"No, problem." Charlie replied: "I'll use my charm." and Bill placing his hand in his wallet pocket joined in with: "And I will use mine."

Both the brothers walked over to the camp manager's office, with Charlie using his hands a great deal, a lot of head shaking and some nodding it was obvious that Charlie was getting nowhere. Eventually, Bill took over realising that the manager was of French nationality, who spoke only a rough patois, so making it impossible for either man to understand him and he could not interpret what they were saying. After a few minutes and I could see the movements of all three men were growing ever more frustrated with a little anger involved, finally I saw Bill resort to something he knew would work. In his daily work Bill often had to deal with delivering to factories and large establishments, when those he was to deal with were less than willing to bend a rule. Bill had long realised that one little helper always worked – money.

Placing his hand in his back pocket, bringing out his wallet I could see some paper Swiss Francs exchanging ownership, and finally there was the nodding of a French head, the gates swung open and both Bill and Charlie were back in the van and we were driving through.

"Blimey, that was hard work." Charlie said to Bill, a big grin on his face: "Thank God you thought of that."

Smiling and obviously feeling very pleased with himself as he should Bill replied with: "In my work, trust me I know a fiver works every time."

We followed the little man who had been driving in front of us in a beat up old jeep, eventually after driving along lines of parked vehicles and tents the little man got out of the jeep and pointed to a corner telling us we should go in the corner. I watched the little man standing before us, dressed in a dirty, sweat-stained red cotton shirt with black trousers crumpled along the legs, his feet encased in open-toed sandals. His face was wrinkled and brown like an animated prune. It was impossible to make out the colour of his eyes, as they appeared to have shrunk into his face. All that was obvious was the bad teeth showing in a slimy grin. His grey hair like the rest of him was dirty and unkempt. I saw his left hand place the notes Bill had given him earlier in the top pocket of his tee shirt as his right hand was raised in a wave of farewell to us, watching Bill back the camper into the corner provided for us.

So after this very eventful day, all of us were exhausted and it wasn't long before we were all asleep.

I was awoken by a ray of bright sunlight breaking into the van through the canopy of trees under which we had parked. From the open window a warm breeze blew gently across my face. Excited and eager to explore our surroundings, I scrambled out of bed. Having dressed I began to prepared breakfast for the family. Asking Bill and Charlie to set up the camping furniture, purchased but as yet unused, it wasn't long before a good meal was set up, and enjoyed by us all in the fresh, open air.

This first meal of the day was not a quiet one, the children chattered like magpies. Bill and Charlie pored over maps, discussing the routes we should take on leaving the site. Having exhausted this topic of conversation they then turned their attention to what we would do while in this town. While all the family were busy, I had the golden opportunity of taking a few precious moments for myself, allowing my attention to wander, investigating our immediate surroundings.

Whether by accident or design, because Bill had handed over quite a substantial tip the night before, we appeared to have been parked in the most picturesque spot, beneath a roof of pine trees and almost hidden by a high hedge from our neighbours. On the other side of us was a bed of flowers, a mixture of alpine plants and tropical blooms. Birds of every hue seemed to fly around us joining in with the buzzing of busy bees who were obviously making the most of the few summer months they had. Watching these little insects flying around, each one with its own chosen task, gave me a feeling of restlessness, jumping up I walked towards the river's edge. Looking down I could see the little holes made by the creatures that inhabited its banks. Now and then the beady eyes of a vole or river mouse appeared, only to disappear as fast, once they were made aware of our existence.

"Beautiful, isn't it?" Bill's voice reached me.

I had been so lost in contemplation of my surroundings that I had not heard my husband's approach, as his footsteps were muffled by the pine needles and thick grass covering the ground near where we had parked, it was also obvious that we were in fact the only vehicle in this area.

"Yes," I agreed, still too lost in my thoughts to give any other answer.

Gazing down at the fast, flowing water I wondered at the freedom it was given. Able to flow from country to country, knowing no barriers making its own boundaries: how I envied this water its momentum and liberty.

For a moment there was silence between the two of us, we sat at the edge, looking down at the river. Bill's arm around my waist, my head on his shoulder. Husband and wife in perfect unison. Eventually sighing looking up at him I smiled and asked: "Just how much did you give that little man last night?" Shrugging as he stood and pulled me up with him, smiling Bill replied: "No idea, but it was obviously good, look at this lot." Nodding and taking the hand he held out to me we walked back to the children and Charlie.

"Guess what we found?" Charlie called out to us.

Turning to look at me, Bill whispered: "Bet it's a bar."

"What have you found dear brother?" Bill turned, his arm still around me making me move with him.

"A shower, some proper toilets," this was one problem we had all discovered with the van, so the discovery of these proper facilities was very welcome, indeed.

"Plus," his voice grew excited.

"Here it comes," I whispered back to my husband.

"A bar, and guess what…it's open."

"How exciting," Bill replied, trying not to sound too sarcastic. "But you can forget that."

"Why?" Now Charlie's voice was defensive.

"Because, old son, not only have we just had breakfast but I intend we should all go for a nice long walk." At the astounded look on his companion's face, Bill started laughing in a way that was quite infectious, so raising a smile on all our faces, including Charlie's.

Placing an arm round his brother Bill said gently: "You are part of a family now, we enjoy each other's company. We do not spend all day in a bar, come on look around you, mate." Tapping his brother's arm and showing him the beauty that surrounded us.

Looking up at the sky, realising that even at this early hour it was really very warm, Charlie raised his arms in mock horror: "I Charlie Johnson am going walking with nothing but a cup of coffee in me, shock horror. Please don't tell my friends in London." Then taking his place between the girls he began to walk, slowly.

Heading in the direction of the gate we had driven through the night before, to reach this we had to make our way along stone paths that divided the variety of camping paraphernalia. Having almost tripped over the ropes that securely held a small ridge tent, inhabited by two young men. I found myself staring at a tent that was the complete reverse, this was a glorious piece of blue canvas, fitted with windows, a front door, and the sort of furniture that would be found in a home. There were many such canvas palaces to be found. Looking around I could see caravans of many shapes and sizes, from tiny ones that carried Eastern Block identification to their far more glamorous and wealthier neighbours with wheeled homes that vied with their canvas compatriots. Added to this was the mixture of languages spoken not only from the European Continent. Over the warm morning air the sounds of American and Australian could be heard, then the sounds of a Japanese family, elsewhere we heard more English accents all this and more added to the excitement that was the campsite. Having successfully traversed the many obstacles in our way, we found the gate open. Nodding to a middle-aged lady of much smarter appearance than the man we had seen the night before, we headed in the direction of the two signs, one indicating the way to the town centre and another bearing the name "long Road," having walked along it for over half an hour we realised it was not just a name but a reality.

This really was a long road, eventually as all of us were beginning to flag, our energies wearing out in the heat that was building up, coming out of the forest we got an odour that was familiar but at the same time unfamiliar. "What is that smell?" Charlie asked, at first I could not think then realisation dawned on me: "It's chocolate." Of course Berne was the centre of one of the biggest factories in Switzerland. Normally chocolate was a sweet enjoyed by us all. However, on this occasion the all-pervading smell of chocolate being made was enough to make us feel decidedly unwell. As our stamina began to leave us and we felt that indeed we would have to wait sometime before having something to drink we spied the parliament building standing on a hill overlooking the magnificent River Aare, the same river Bill and I had looked at earlier that morning but how different its surroundings were now. Still encircled by trees and hedges but the most important parts of the town were now growing ever more evident, the business of finance and banking. Everywhere we looked there were large structures, some old, a few new ones covered in glass, each one trying to be more magnificent than its neighbour. All of them vying with each other to attract clients and money. We walked past these buildings heading in the direction of a street cafe, serving cold drinks and to Charlie a beer.

Having satisfied our thirst and rested our legs, we wandered round the shops, finding the statue of a woman bearing a shield in one hand and a sword in the other. We never did discover the significance of this beautiful sculpture. Lunch was taken in one of the many snack bars that were interspersed between banks. After lunch we made our way down the hill to the river itself, here we could see the young people who worked in the offices surrounding us relaxing by swimming in the fast running river.

Having had our fill of Berne we made our way back to the campsite this time not on foot but in two taxis.

The evening began with the men heading into the showers, followed by the children then myself. I did find it strange knowing that I only had a limited time in the shower but I managed it within the allotted period, on leaving I could see a queue building up and was grateful that we had decided to use this particular facility before the others on the camp site.

Once our evening meal had finished, we sat watching the light of day slowly fade into the lilac of twilight, then the darker shades of night began to take over. Slowly lamps began to be lit, making the normal and ordinary appear ghostly and ethereal. The only sounds now to be heard were those of soft singing from a barbecue taking place some wagons away. A mouth organ in the distance could be heard picking up the tune. Then a guitarist plucked his instrument from another corner, adding to the sense of loneliness. But it was the sound of the concertina, coming from across the river, that started the yearning I kept hidden so well.

I wanted to be sharing this scene with a man who had emerald green eyes, hair as black as the night I sat in, and a voice as soft and husky as a piece of velvet being drawn over a comb. Thinking of him like this, made a shiver tingle up and down the length of my spine.

I knew that once again, as I had done on so many occasions before, this night I would sleep with a phantom lover. One I tried to forget, but time and circumstances made it impossible. Every step, each turn of the camper's wheels took me ever closer to him. As my eyes closed in sleep his words came back to haunt me: "We are married in spirit, you and I are one. The bond between us is too strong." How then, could we possibly be friends, after the relationship we shared.

Chapter 12

After that first night at the campsite, I grew used to awakening each morning to the sounds of voices raised either in song, or friendly arguments. Added to this was the chinking of cutlery and the sounds of pots and pans preparing breakfast accompanied by a variety of different smells, as not one nationality believed in their first meal of the day being identical. These sounds of confusion soon became normal to me, making my life in Little Barham seem like any other world.

Having seen all we wanted of Berne, our nomadic journey across Switzerland continued to Interlaken. Not quite the mercantile centre, more a place of outstanding myth and legend, a fact made obvious by the statue of William Tell standing at the entrance to the Town. As with our own Robin Hood, he too had been looked upon as the saviour of his country, songs and stories being written about him. Legend outliving the fact. I was soon to discover that the town had been given its name because it stood at the centre of two lakes, Brienz and Thun.

The former of the two was quite the smallest, with water so cold and clear the trees surrounding it could be clearly seen reflected in its waters, as if forming a subterranean jungle for water nymphs to explore. With the clarity of the water it also gave our daughters great delight in standing at the water's edge and watching the myriad of fishes swimming in and out of their legs, their squeals of delight and their giggles bringing smiles to our faces.

Thun however, being the largest and busiest. Clustered round its edges were hotels and houses, each one owning their own private boat parks, as those living inland would own driveways and garages. All around this large inland sea there were places to visit and explore. From a prehistoric cave that had once been the home of a Hermit, whose name was emblazoned at the entrance to the pier where we alighted to visit the St Beatus Holen, to an old castle with a cellar the children found fascinating as the contents were all kinds of torture implements. I was more interested in the beautiful gardens that surrounded this old Gothic fort. All these and much more could be reached with ease, as tourists were transported round the lake by a large boat.

This ship would ferry its passengers from one pier to the next. Winding its way across the busy lake cutting with ease across the paths of small boats or waterskiers all who appeared to have suicidal tendencies, for though they saw the ship heading in their direction many seemed intent on meeting it head on. As we cruised beneath the hot sun, I felt sorry that because this lake was so very busy it was impossible for the waters to be as clear and clean as its sister on the other side of the bridge.

Again having felt we had seen all we wanted of Interlaken, we began a route that was to lead us eventually into Germany, at this a little shiver of apprehension ran up my spine, as I was too afraid to think of the eventual meeting that would take place between Dieter and myself. So many months had slipped past since we had last been in contact. For a moment, as I sat in the back of the camper making our way to one of the many passes that visitors found fascinating, I even wondered if I remembered what he looked like.

Perhaps with the passing of time those eyes that I considered to be so hypnotic or the laugh that was gentle and mocking didn't exist. Maybe he was only a figment of my imagination. At this I looked down once more at the ring on my finger, gently shaking my head, no he did exist I had only to wait and find out what our relationship truly was and how it would continue, if at all.

We wandered from town to town, always studying the maps. Visiting the Jungfrua, that grand mountain that overlooked Interlaken, the waterfalls of the Trummelbach. Each day as we awoke to a new site or scene, I was amazed by the beauty of this country. As the morning mists cleared allowing the sunshine through it seemed as if during the hours of night as we slept some mysterious persons have given the place a clean down, preparing it for its visitors and inhabitants.

The excited look in our children's eyes were a pleasure, making this whole journey worthwhile. They loved the perilous trip that took us over the three main passes, Furks, Grimsel and Susten. The sight of the Rhone Glacier proved to be so breathtaking our two chatterboxes were silent for a minutes afterwards.

One day as we made our way across the route that was to take us out of Switzerland and into Germany, I was once more lost in the beauty surrounding us, never ceasing to be amazed at the civil engineers who had made it possible for us to follow this passage into another country. Across bridges spanning wide gorges, under tunnels through mountains, along roads that seemed to cling precariously to the mountains with no hope of any assistance if anything should go wrong all these journeys were made with the capable hands of Bill at the wheel, Charlie having seen what lay ahead of us having refused to drive along these routes.

The sun shone brightly through leaves that covered the road we traversed acting like a green parasol from the heat of the sun when Charlie turned in his seat to ask: "This guy Dieter," his tone was enquiring. "Bill says he's a handsome looking fellow, is he?" What a question. Answering this would be difficult, but I had to try. Clearing my throat, taking a sip of the drink I held in my hand, I smiled and said: "To be honest he's not really my type, but he does seem popular with the women." I was so pleased with my reply that I fell into a state of complacency.

"I don't think my wife is telling the complete truth." Bill replied.

At this my heart rocked guilt uppermost in my mind. What did he know or worse suspect?

"Oh!" I replied determined to find out, "and just what do you mean by that last remark, husband dear?"

"Well, you talk about the other women. I noticed when he danced with anyone but you or your two friends, daggers were drawn and knives sharpened. Claws also appeared to be a little obvious."

"What are you talking about?" Turning to stare at my brother-in-law, "honestly the things your brother remembers. It's been so long since the Germans visited us that I can't remember much of what went on, to be honest I don't think I can even remember what the man looks like." I felt at the moment as if I had earned an

Oscar, so deciding to change the subject I turned to the children drawing their attention to a chair lift that appeared to carry its passengers into the clouds, this helped the moment to pass, much to my relief.

We visited the Reichenbachfall where Sherlock Holmes met his arch enemy Moriarty in mortal combat. From crystal caves to museums, all around us was proof that nature held the best artists, she also took the upper hand on everything, for compared to her, mankind really was very puny creature. Once we had taken our fill of the majesty that Switzerland had to offer it was decided that we should head into Germany as Bill had phoned Dieter telling him when to expect us. Once again at the thought of meeting this man fear was uppermost in my mind and heart.

Our journey out of this mountainous paradise was to be made during the night, again with the men taking it in turn to drive. I stayed awake as long as possible, eager for my first view of Germany from a direction I had never taken before. This was something that never happened as exhausted with the day's walking and sightseeing I fell fast asleep, only to be awakened in the morning by Bill gently touching my shoulder: "Can you prepare us something to eat, we've reached Germany. I'm giving the old van a bit of a rest before we carry on."

As my eyes gradually grew used to the daylight, I was horrified to find no sunshine here. The sound of rain beating on the roof, and clouds hanging heavy overhead almost as if they were echoing the heaviness that was in my heart. For I had left safety behind me, and was now heading directly into danger. The day was still in its infancy so the children were not disturbed. Once I had prepared the required meal, I decided to take a little look outside the confines of our van. While the men ate and discussed the new routes they should take, I walked about outside the restlessness that had filled me on that first morning in Berne when I had looked into the deepest, dark river that had flowed past.

The camper was parked in the middle of a bank of trees, all huddling close as if trying to keep the rain out. I gazed up at the greenery covering us, amazed at the height and size of these magnificent Titans of the forest. The Schwarzwald, or Black Forest as it was more commonly known really was an amazing place to be. For even though there was no sun to make the day bright, and the trees grew close together there was still a brightness, almost a glow that that came from the translucence of nature growing all around us. How different this scenery was from the country we had just left.

"Vicki, come here quick." Charlie's voice came to me in an excited whisper.

Puzzled at what he might want I hurried back, tripping over rocks that lay on the leaf covered earth.

"What?" I asked

"Look," Bill whispered, placing an arm round my shoulders bending my head to look out of the window on the opposite side to which I had been standing. For a moment I was silent, holding my breath, afraid to move. For there in front of us stood a herd of small red deer, dining on the plants that grew all around us. They appeared to be quite unafraid as they moved slowly from one area to another. We stood transfixed by the beauty and serenity this little group provided, even the children who had by now awoken were silent, until as if at a signal the head of the animal clearly the leader went up, scenting the air he made a sound then with speed he and the herd went leaping back into the dense forest behind them, so fast was their exit we almost believed the scene had been imagined.

The men having rested, children fed we restarted our journey, travelling through villages that were nothing like the ones we had left the day before. These were smaller, the pastures that cattle fed on were not so high, and the presence of cuckoo clocks very evident everywhere and in everything.

Having pulled up at a little shop so that I could stock up on supplies, for the first time I was able to understand the language with ease. Turning to Bill and Charlie who had been seconded into carrying the goods I smiled and said: "That's better I can understand them. Now I know I'm in Germany." At this thought my heart went into a spin. Within a few hours I was to be face to face with the man who was my dream or nightmare I was not really sure.

With mutual agreement it had been decided we should carry on through Freiburg and its villages till reaching Heidelburg. As it was a Sunday the people we passed were dressed in their best clothes. Men in Lederhosen with little knitted jackets woven in such a way that it was possible for them to stay dry. Women dressed in dirndls of every colour imaginable little hats, and big black umbrellas to help them stay dry. No coats were worn, for though it was raining there was a warmth that would have made the wearing of coats superfluous.

"Do the bars open here." Charlie called over to me.

"This is Sunday and we have just had breakfast. Wait till we reach Heidelberg the bars are always open." Then shaking my forefinger at him I reminded my erstwhile relative that he had chosen to be co-driver, so too much alcohol was really not advised, certainly not in Germany. Grumbling about the cruelty of family he took over from

Bill, only smiling again when Bill said: "When we reach Kirschweiler there will be a couple of days without the van you can have a proper drink then – understood." A swift nodding of the head was agreement enough.

Our journey was now taking us from quiet roads to the autobahns, here the pace was much faster.

As we sped along these roads, I was amazed that the weather appeared to be echoing my feelings. The constant drizzle created a mist that hung heavily over everything, making the wine valleys we were now travelling across appear dismal and depressive.

"Would you like some coffee?" I called to the men feeling in need of some kind of action. My offer was accepted with alacrity busying myself carrying out mundane tasks, I missed my first sight of the thirteenth century castle the Heidelberger Schloss. This city had a very colourful history, being one of the first places to actually have a university. It was a mixture of the Gothic and Renaissance.

Bill having drawn my attention to the Schloss on the hill, I was now very excited as having been taught by German nuns, not only did they talk to me about Cologne but in Mainz and Heidelberg too. In fact their opinion had been that anyone in the teaching world whether medical or educational would have had at some time in their lives a basis in something that had come out of a university in Heidelberg.

Parking the camper we spent some time wandering round the ancient town, from its fountain to the numerous bars and restaurants filled with tourists and students. It was vibrant with life and a most exciting place to visit. However, it was our next stop that I was really interested in visiting that of Mainz and seeing a lady whom I had not seen for many years. A nun from my old convent, now living in retirement.

Leaving the City of Heidelberg behind we began to make our way towards the Rhine. Again, we had chosen a route that would take us away from the autobahns and onto what is known as the Romantic Route.

The course of the Rhine ran between great business parks, vineyards, around fairy tale castles with a folklore that was as rich as our legends. Past great churches and cathedrals where all kinds of saints were given birth to. Its many tributaries giving life to smaller villages as the main body of the river had given birth to the larger towns.

Allowing my imagination to take wing, I thought of the stories I had read and heard. Those of the Brothers Grimm, their princesses and knights who always came to the rescue at the right time. Until a little voice mocked me: "Not all the stories had a happy ending." I tried not to remember the tragedies, the stories of star-crossed lovers never destined to be together. "But, I live in the twentieth century." Before I could go further into my dreams I was once again being called on to once more put us back on the right road again, as Charlie had been unable to decide which route we needed.

After some little time we found the site that we needed to bed down for the night, the heavy rain that we had first experienced in Switzerland had caught up with us, again.

As the lights in the van went out, and signs of sleep affecting all the occupants except myself. Climbing up into my bed I turned my face to the small window, slowly pulling a little of the curtain back so that I could see, but without disturbing my sleeping husband. The rain was now stopping, with clouds like cobwebs moving away allowing a sleepy moon to rise. As her silver fingers began to touch the hedgerows and car bonnets. Wet grass tips glistening as if diamonds had been placed on them. Yes, tomorrow would be a beautiful day.

Yet, even as my eyes closed in sleep, my thoughts were once more with another man.

"Did Dieter see the same Moon and think of me on the road coming ever closer to him? Did he dread our meeting as much as I did? Or was he quite impervious to my forthcoming visit?"

These answers would have to wait for a day or two, as I was looking to my meeting in Mainz, with the only other woman apart from my mother who had been instrumental in forming much that was good in my life. Sister Melanie, the nun who had taught me in India.

Chapter 13

It was in bright sunshine that we crossed the bridge spanning the two rivers that made Mainz into the thriving business centre it was. I knew little of its history apart from its having been a Celtic settlement and the first town to have its own archbishop, and of course it held the Mother House of the nuns who had taught, hence my dear friend and teacher had come here to retire.

The people who thronged the streets and shops all appeared to be very happy, in fact at one point an elderly couple walking past us heard Hannah calling Bill and realising we were English the couple spoke to us in English wishing us a good morning. We were pleasantly surprised.

There was a question I had been waiting for ever since I suggested stopping in this town, so it was no surprise when it came:

"Do we have to visit your nuns?" Charlie had stopped outside one of the many bars that could be found on every street. "I'd much rather go in here."

Trying not to show my annoyance: "Look, I have written to this good lady and told her to expect us. Not one not two but a group of five."

"Well, you could go in." Bill was now joining in the conversation, "we don't really all have to." With an almost pleading look on his face: "Do we?"

"Well, we are going in with Mum, and you can't go in the bars because we have to drive again soon." Hannah came up with the common sense that was needed.

By now I was growing very cross, instead of having a full scale row in public, taking my daughters by the hand I strode off so forcing the men to follow.

Lottie, looking round at her uncle called out: "Mum is really angry, we know, don't push her."

We wandered round for some time trying to find the convent, there were so many streets and squares all appearing to lead into another that we were now quite lost and in the heat of the day all growing frustrated and angry. I heard a mumbled "You and your convent." From Bill but chose to ignore it.

Suddenly I heard: "What's this? Looks a bit secluded." Charlie called over to us, as we wandered past the same boutique for the third time.

Walking hurriedly back to where he stood, we could see how the entrance to this courtyard could be so easily missed. The approach was almost covered by ivy that crept over the wall into which a wrought iron gate had been set, so dense was the growth it would have been impossible to find by anyone not specifically looking for it.

Pushing past the foliage, we found ourselves standing on a cobbled footpath. The high stone wall we had first seen encircled the yard, as if protecting it from the outside world. The sound of running water attracted our attention. Looking round to see where the sound came from, we were amazed to see a stone fountain shaped to look like a sunflower, the base being the stem and the bowl the flower fully opened. The peace of the garden and the fountain were an attraction for the birds who came in their multitudes to bathe and feed.

"This has to be the place," Charlie whispered. I smiled the peace of this garden had even affected my hedonistic brother-in-law. I nodded feeling words were unnecessary.

The sound of a cough behind us, drew our attention. We turned to see a man, dressed in black shoes, grey pinstriped trousers, white shirt and black jacket his ensemble would not have been amiss in The City.

"Can I help you?" He asked, his English faultless. "This is a convent, I do not think you belong here.

Looking at the smartly dressed grey-haired man as he asked again: "Can I help you? This is a convent and private ground. I do not think there is anything here for you."

About to tell him who I was, a sudden movement in the doorway facing us stopped me, as at the same time a voice spoke: "Victoria Jane Stracey, my child I would recognise you anywhere."

Suddenly the veils of time had been thrown back, I was once more a child and one of the two women I loved and trusted in all the world stood before me. Words were unnecessary, I ran as if wings were on my feet. Her arms closed round me, as I felt the sweet softness of her cheek touch mine, and the Latin Blessing quoted as it always had been in the past.

Eventually we managed to pull away, tears of happiness on both our cheeks.

"So tell me, what are you doing here and who are these?" Sister Melanie asked, breathless from my hug. With pride, I first introduced her to Bill, then our daughters in turn, it was wonderful to see her hold them in the way she did me. Looking at the girls and studying their faces, Sister Melanie smiled saying: "Oh! Yes in the older I see your face, but in the eyes of the younger daughter I recognise mischief, come." Saying this we were led up the steps, past a very astonished man whose name we would learn was Engelbert, and was the caretaker for the "House." Last Charlie who appeared to have for the first time have nothing to say, he stood quite tongue-tied.

I stared at the face of my friend, realising that the passing of time really had not dimmed my memory of her. The only difference being, when a child I had thought she was quite tall, it was in fact the reverse as I had grown she appeared to have shrunk, I now looked down on her. Dressed in the black, long sleeved habit that was common to this Order away from the Tropics, her veil was black too with a white cotton band that came low over her forehead, emphasising the white of the skin on her unwrinkled face, and the sparkling blue of her eyes, her lips red, though they had never known lipstick, innocent of all kind of make-up. Her habit was calf length, showing only a little of her legs in their black stockings, feet encased in thick, almost brogue-like black shoes. As with all nuns she appeared ageless, clasping my hand tightly I was led with the rest of the family into the confines of the convent, and the meal they felt greatly in need of.

We sat down to the meal prepared for us, served in the nuns' refectory. A large dining room, where small windows set high in the outer walls let in little light, and no view of the outside. The walls were in dark panelled oak, with long, hard tables and bench seats in similar wood. At the main end, near the servery, was a large gold crucifix with a large lighted candle on either side of it. Behind the cross could be seen a great deal of hustling and bustling, as the nuns who were on duty in the kitchen area prepared to set lunch for us, It was obvious we were guests of honour.

"Come, sit," we were ordered. "The meal will come soon."

"No come we must talk, there is much to know and tell." For the rest of the time, as we sat and demolished the very tasty chicken meal and fruit flan served as dessert the conversation flowed, never stopping. As one of us ran out of subjects to talk about, so another of us began to talk. Until my dear friend started to tell my children about some of my schoolgirl exploits. This I had to put a stop to so:

"Please sister, how can I ever control these two, if you tell them about me." I broke in on her reminiscences.

"But, my dear, you will understand them so much better," Sister replied giggling then giving way to open laughter: "After all you will have done it before, no?"

One look at my face and the shake of head, Sister Melanie smiled knowingly, yes my friend understood.

Under cover of the conversation going on between the men and Engelbert with the children listening intently to the history of the ancient building, Sister looked at me and with the knowing look she had always when I was in trouble asked: "What is wrong? There is a heaviness about you I did notice, do you need to or wish to talk?" I nodded silently, afraid I might burst into tears should I try to speak.

Pushing her chair back: "We will go into the garden child, there is still much to talk about, and in here too much noise."

Leaving them to their discussions, Sister Melanie and I walked down the long dark corridors that seemed to run like rabbit warrens round this large old house. I had no need to wonder how all this was so sparkling and clean, as I knew in the convents no person is ever felt to be useless. Nuns who had grown too old for teaching, or other rigorous duties, were given other little tasks in "The House," cleaning being one of them. This they would carry out with diligence and love. Something made obvious with not a speck of dirt anywhere in sight.

Coming out of the darkness of the building, we found ourselves in a walled garden. I held my breath at the sight. If I had thought the courtyard to be lovely this was by far the most beautiful. The garden had been shaped round a large sunken pond, in which gigantic Koi were very much at home, darting in and out of the water lillies and other submerged plants designed for aquatic life. Along the four walls were planted rhododendron bushes of pink, red and orange. All colours seemed to intermingle here. Apple and pear trees grew like a mini orchard. Hiding in the lee of a north wall stood two peach trees and near the south wall was a gazebo, covered in grape vine, now rich with fruits.

"We make our own wine," I was informed, when sister Melanie saw me looking at them. The rest of the garden was a riot of colour and blooms. Added to this was a large aviary in which budgies and parakeets lived side by side, the doors were open in the day so they had freedom to fly in and out as she laughed and said: "We have no escapees." Everywhere I looked was a feeling of peace, happiness and contentment.

Taking a deep breath, I turned to look down in the face of the one person, I had been wanting to meet again, but in the light of past events I was afraid to.

"So, what is the problem?" Her gentle voice came to me.

"What would you say, if I told you I had broken one of your commandments?"

"I would say you have not broken anything I have made, only what God has asked you to do."

"I have done something very bad."

"Who is it you have killed?"

"There are some ways of committing murder without actually taking life." I answered, shaking with fright. Turning I went to walk away, the courage I had started with, now in tatters around me.

"You love another man." Her voice was matter of fact.

I stopped in my tracks. "How did you know?"

"You told me when we first met," she answered, pity in her eyes for the misery I was going through, but no judgement.

I was horrified, how could she have known what my feelings were.

"I never…" Before I could carry on, she held up a hand to silence me.

"You didn't need words, I read it when you introduced me to you husband." she pointed to a long wooden seat made from plaited ash tree. Once seated the good sister went on to explain. Though she had no outside knowledge of the world, she had come across enough of its pain and suffering to know the symptoms though not the answers.

For some time she sat, hands clasped on her knees, feet together in complete control of herself, while I stammered my way through a bad explanation of my passion. My companion appeared to be completely reposed. I was quite the reverse, tearing a tissue to pieces in my hot sweaty hands, feet that did not stop twitching the whole time. Eventually when I had finished, my voice trailing off into the distance, I waited for some kind of answer, not knowing whether I wanted her to expunge my guilt, or decry it and condemn me.

"Do you love this man?" she asked, her tone gentle.

"Yes," was my simple answer.

"But you loved Bill when you married him?"

I had been asked this question once before, and the answer was still the same: "Yes."

"I am not your conscience, my child. You know what must be done." Hearing sounds of voices coming in our direction, she carried on, as my family came into view: "They are your responsibility, look after them," Pulling me to my feet, she carried on in a whisper, "and He," looking at the crucifix that hung over the chapel, "will look after you."

I knew our visit had come to an end, I was not sure when I would see her again, if ever. But I knew she had not judged me harshly. As I was taking my leave, as in the old days I knelt before her and she made the sign of the cross on my forehead, then, kissing me gently on my cheeks, Sister Melanie said goodbye.

Having left the convent behind in a flurry of goodbyes and requests to visit them again we walked towards the parking place where our camper had been left, with Charlie muttering: "These nuns aren't all that bad, are they? I even got some beer there." And looking at the bottle of white wine in my hand: "And you got some wine."

Laughing, Bill replied: "What did you think they were like?"

Knowing our stocks of food were once again running low, I forced the men into unwillingly carrying some bags of shopping purchased in a supermarket near where we were parked.

"You don't mind eating and drinking, but don't want to do anything to earn it." I mumbled, annoyed with their grumbling and the fact I felt they were spoiling what had been a wonderful day.

"I've paid for it, wasn't that enough," Bill's pained reply came to me as he settled back in the driving seat.

Bending to the job of placing the food in the cupboards, I decided to ignore this remark. I was not in any mood for further arguments.

We decided to spend the night in Sankt Goarshausen, an ancient city going back to the sixth century AD and site of the famous Loreley Rocks said to be the home of the fabled water nymphs whose voices were so beautiful they would lure sailors to their deaths.

"These don't exist anymore, do they?" Lottie asked, and I explained they were only stories and not to worry about them.

We drove quickly through Rudesheim, the centre of the Rhine Wein area, with its bars and night clubs it was not the place to take children, as they were hungry we did find a little restaurant on the bank of the river and were able to park almost outside it.

Having found seating outside the restaurant we sat down, giving an order to the smiling waiter who had appeared like a genie from a lamp, once he felt we had studied the menu. The young man stood before us, resplendent in his white frilled shirt, black bow tie and black trousers the smile on his face saying he was eager to please.

Our meal finished, we sat at our table talking softly, the children sitting quietly, their drooping eyes telling without words that they were tired.

I sat listening to Bill and Charlie discussing football and the possible winners of the World cup. With the men so involved in their own conversation, I was allowed the freedom of my own thoughts. Within an instant they had flown to the city of Cologne, only a few miles along the river. Raising my eyes, I could see the moon, now lifting herself from the bed of the Rhine, looking more than ever like a dream machine. Slowly the orange glow turned to silver sparkles, shining down on us, suddenly turning the setting into a magical evening.

Magic! That was the one ingredient missing in my life.

Looking up at the silver shape growing ever larger, growing from strength to strength I wondered, would Dieter also be staring at the night sky, could he be thinking of me as I was of him? Was he filled with the same tensions as I? After all, so much had happened since we had first sworn our love for each other. Under cover of the tablecloth, I played with the ring on my right hand. Glancing down at it, the moonlight picking out the glow of the jewels, each one seeming to have a sparkle all its own, so giving it a fire, almost making it live. I was wrong, magic did exist. I carried it with me wherever went, in possessing the love of a man I had not seen for many months, but as long as I had his ring, I knew I also held his love.

The continuous yawning of the young people in our company told us it was time to start the penultimate leg of our journey once we had found a camping spot for the night. Driving along the quiet road running alongside the river, so bypassing the town filled with its bars, tourists and noise we felt we had now become rather old hand at finding campsites. Our first night in Bern seemed so long ago.

We had agreed to park in a field that was on our camping map, following the map carefully we made our way up into a hill, here we could see the sign for St Goarshausen a place we would investigate the following day.

Having started the last night's drive we were to make, we found ourselves driving into total blackness. We had left the sounds of cheap music, bright lights and noise behind us. At first the stillness as we drove through the vineyards, no street lamps here, only the occasional light from a lone house or passing car. At this moment we appeared to be totally alone, quite a new and frightening experience.

"Look! What's that?" Charlie interrupted my wanderings.

In the light thrown from the camper we could just make out what appeared to be a set of old farm gates, over these hung the international flag indicating this was a camping site.

"Thank God. Don't think I could have driven much farther." Bill's reply was obviously heartfelt.

We drove over rutted, grass covered ground till finding what we thought would be a good parking spot. Within minutes everyone was asleep, except me my heart racing, not with fear or anxiety, but with one thought, Dieter. Dieter the name seemed to wind its way round my system as surely as blood in my veins.

"Ooh! Fresh milk," were the first words I heard the following morning.

Where did you get it from?" Charlie continued, obviously speaking to his brother.

"The girls and I have been awake for hours, so we decided to take a walk. Finding a farmhouse for the milk, some eggs and fresh baked brown bread." Bill replied obviously pleased with his excursion.

"Come on sleepyhead, move."

This order I knew was for me, scrambling to my feet, the small of bread and eggs having more of an effect on me than my husband's threatening tones.

As we sat down to breakfast, Bill asked me: "What do you know about German fairy tales?"

"Nothing much, only what I've read, why?"

Hannah then went on to explain that as they had strolled around the farm, the three of them had also found two castles on opposite sides of the river and wondered what they were and why? As we were not leaving the field for a couple of hours, I decided to satisfy my own instincts and also investigate.

On leaving the camper the sun had become really strong making us blink our eyes. The air around us was so pure it was almost like being back in Switzerland. However, walking towards the gate by which we had entered the night before, I soon realised that the field was on top of a cliff. Glancing round I could not see any castles.

"O.K. If you were not dreaming, where are these castles?" I asked. Without any hesitation the children grabbed me by the hands pulling and dragging me across the uneven surface of the field.

"It's just like a fairy castle," Hannah called, panting while running backwards.

Presuming this was childish imagination at its best, I ignored the remark, only to have the statement corroborated by her sister: "Honestly Mum, I though Rapunzel would let her hair down over the water." Knowing this to be impossible, as a mother I smiled knowingly, while not understanding a thing until, as we turned a bend, it was my turn to stand and stare, silently.

At first it appeared that my view of the river and opposite bank was blocked by a clump of rocks covered in grass and moss. Only on close inspection did it turn out that these gigantic piece of stone had in fact been fashioned into the image of a castle. Everywhere we looked were more remnants of a medieval castle. Because of its age and state of decline it was impossible to tell where the bastions had been, or the chapel, even the portcullis was impossible to find. Of one thing I was sure, here was no need of ramparts or drawbridge, as there would have been no necessity for a moat as the Rhine flowing at its back would have been by far the best form of defence.

As excited as the children, I ran about trying to decide where the towers would have been, or the palisades that would have helped keep a small village safe, tripping over the hillocks of grass, or falling into little rabbit holes that had appeared in the soft soil. Wild flowers of varying colours grew free and undamaged here, giving the place a far from derelict air. Though no human life had been here for centuries apart from the odd visitors such as us, there was a form of natural life to be found under every stone. A lizard was seen basking on a warm rock under the hot sun, and wild goats defied us to get too close to them. Laughing at our absurd inventions about this place and its mysterious past, I asked the children where was the other castle they had seen.

"Look, Mummy." Lottie spoke to me as if I were a very stupid adult: "Open your eyes and just look."

At first, all I could see was the field we had camped in, then the animals surrounding us. A bit further in the distance the farmhouse my family had visited earlier that morning. Shaking my head: "I'm sorry kids, can't see a thing." I said.

"Over the river," Bill said, grabbing my shoulders and turning me in the direction he wanted me to look.

As with the first castle, I was equally stunned, for there across on a bend of the wide and busy River Rhine, stood what had to be the twin to the place in which we now stood. It was just possible to make out that in many aspects it was identical to "our one" as the children nicknamed the ruins we were standing next to.

I could see that from one of the stones a gigantic pine appeared to have taken root, growing ever taller as if with a previous arrangement with the sky. Bushes and wild flowers also had made the stones into homes for themselves and small animals. The view was breathtaking. From this height all the boats chugged up and down the river looked no large than matchbox toys. From the large passenger boats turned the water into tourist attractions to the working boats carrying every kind of cargo across the continent, even the smaller private high powered boats paled into insignificance beside the majesty that faced us, carved out forever in stone.

Suddenly, realisation struck me. Ever a fan of the Brothers Grimm and their brand of storytelling, I remembered where we were, and on what we stood. "I know where we are." Pleased with my discovery, I could not wait to tell the family.

"These are the Loreley Rocks."

Nodding their heads my family realised they had heard the stories before, but I went on to fill them in with more detail. Talking about the fairy folk who were said to live in these rocks, and their beautiful singing would lure sailors to their deaths as the rocks clashed together as that was the meaning of Loreley – Clashing.

I was suddenly brought back to reality as Bill said: "Well we will be meeting a very dry grave, if we are not in Kirshcweiler this afternoon as promised." Bill's tones rocked us from the world of the mythical to the present and for me the harsh reality of the approaching nightmare I dreaded so much.

Chapter 14

"So, you find my country boring, you sleep while travelling through it."

I tried to ignore the voice until a light finger flicked across my face.

Within seconds that familiar feeling of tension had returned to my body. This was no dream. Opening my eyes, heavy with the sleep I had fallen into, caused by the late and restless night plus the early morning I had been forced into, I was totally unprepared for our arrival in the village of Kirschweiler and my first meeting for months with Dieter.

Slowly turning my face in the direction from which the voice had come, I could see the outline of a man his shadow dark, accentuated by the light entering the camper from the afternoon sun. The glow coming in from the window was so bright that it exaggerated his height, so that as I lay on the bunk I felt quite dizzy looking up at him.

As he spoke again, I jumped into a sitting position, quite forgetting the low cupboard over my head. The unexpected pain bringing tears to my eyes. Seeing this, Dieter was soon at my side, placing his hand on my head as if to soothe the ache away. However, his action could not remove the hurt that lay in my heart, or the promise I had myself: "From now on he and I are just friends." Remembering this, I flinched, pulling away as if I didn't want him touching me. This had a twofold effect. It strengthened my resolve and as Dieter thought I was repulsed by his touch he too quickly moved back, as far as the small confines of our van would allow.

Now I was standing, it was possible to ensure there was no further body contact. "Hi! Dieter. Nice to see you, how's your family? The boys doing well?"

All this was said in a rush. I knew I was talking too much, but felt powerless to stop, knowing all I really wanted was to be wrapped in his arms, those firm lips passionately against mine. Surrounded by the safe but forbidden world that his love created. This I knew was impossible, especially as I had glimpsed Monique and Birgit standing on the pavement, obviously waiting for us to join them.

Ensuring that the expression on my face was one of cool friendship, I stood, lightly flexing my neck muscles, so as to release some of the stiffness in them due to my cramped sleeping position for the past couple of hours.

"Vicki, it is so good to see you again." He whispered,

Looking up at him my heart ached. Once again I forced myself to remember he was only a friend as was his wife and sons. So long as I never forgot this, we could carry on as I would with any of my family's acquaintances. Never again was I going to let this man know what I really felt for him.

"Come on then friend, let's go and meet your wife." About to take his hand, I thought better of it, dropping my outstretched one before it touched his. I could see a look of hurt puzzlement on his face, but I had no intention of relenting, my resolution had been made --- never to be broken.

I was so intent on getting out of the vehicle as far as possible, I tripped over the little carpet kept near the door, falling out of the van and stepping on Bill's foot as he stood waiting to help me down.

"Watch out clumsy" Don't you ever look where you are going?"

Already hurting, my husband's far from sensitive attitude almost reduced me to the tears that hovered not far from the surface.

Forcing a smile, I walked up to Monique and Birgit giving them both big sisterly hugs who, though they would not have understood what was said, would have known by his tone that I had upset my husband. Not wanting them to think there was any discord between us I laughed, speaking to them in German: "Men, can't handle even a little pain."

Laughing, they both nodded.

Now standing directly before Monique, this time I didn't feel traitorous to her in any way. I had made a decision, I intended sticking to it so she and I could remain friends, simple.

Looking into her sparkling blue eyes, about to say something I was soon interrupted by: "Bloody, hell, you didn't say she was so gorgeous." Charlie voice came over the noise of the children renewing their friendships: The expression of open admiration on his face was nauseating, as Bill repeated the hugs I had given the two women: "Any chance of me getting in a wrestling position with her."

Fighting my annoyance, "Look at her husband, then look at yourself," I replied, in a harsh tone.

"Ouch! Withdraw the claw, I'll always love you best of all sister dear," he replied smiling placing a brotherly arm round my shoulder.

Shrugging it off, I walked away. Pretending to look up the street as if renewing my memories, in reality I was blinking away my tears of pure frustration and agony. Once I felt able to carry on I rejoined the group, who were all studying me intently. The two women smiling, obviously pleased to see me. Bill, looking angry because he knew I was behaving badly, but was unaware of the reason behind it. Charlie, puzzled. And Dieter ---- I had no intention of meeting his gaze at all, terrified what I might see there, or worse still, let him know how I really felt.

During our greetings the children, had been running around. Having been cooped up for long hours in the van, now let loose it was like trying to herd sheep allowed out of a pen. They had no intention of coming when first called. As my voice took on a sharper tone, they came running.

"Mum, it's really nice here. There are farms, football pitches and tennis courts. Lots of things to see and do, Christoph is practising for a football match tomorrow, can we go and watch him." Lottie called as she made her way into the house, with a pleading tone: "Please."

Though I was in a bad mood, I was not about to make the children suffer. So, I nodded my head. And watched them scampering away from the front door, to the nearby sports area.

I then went on to say to Hannah, still standing beside me: "Let her see and do what she wants for now, we won't be here long enough."

"Why not?" I heard Dieter say. Then he turned to the children: "Anything you want to see, come and ask me. I

229

have taken this week as holiday, so we can be together."
looking at me a defiant expression on his face: "Never
mind your mother."

The way in which he said this was meant to get to
me. He did not fail. Tossing my head in his direction I
ran ahead, joining the women who were walking ahead
with Bill and Charlie. In the past I would have smiled at
the picture they made, a great deal of talking in English
and German and hands flying in every direction the
usual way of talking when neither fully understood the
other.

Monique opened the front door, welcoming us in.
She had set up a table in the lounge, a late lunch was to
be served as soon as we were ready.

"Vicki, how is it with you?"

At last a voice I could relate to. Turning I saw Uwe
standing at the entrance to the kitchen, wiping his hand
on a kitchen towel.

"See my sister makes me wash-up for her while she
comes to greet you."

I was so pleased to see him, I launched myself into
his arms, almost knocking him over. He held me close,
for a moment I was in the arms of the brother I so
desperately needed. Prepared to help but asking nothing
in return.

"Hey, what's going on?" Bill asked laughing. "I've
never seen my wife greet anyone like that before.

"When I find out what my brother-in-law has,
perhaps he will share it with me." Dieter mumbled, his
tone bitter as he brushed past us. "It must obviously be
something good."

Uwe, looked up at him then back at me. Evidently
not understanding the situation.

Sitting down to the sumptuous meal Monique and Birgit had prepared for us made things a little easier for me, in that I insisted on sitting near the children.

Conversation flowed easily, with the children chattering away, like runaway trains never stopping. When they did stop for breath Bill or Charlie took up the flow, so it was never noticeable that I wasn't saying or eating much. As Dieter was busy translating, he had no time to watch me either, but I did have a chance to study him.

Whereas the months since I had last seen these two had not in any way appeared to have left any mark on Monique, the passage of time had left an impression on him. Gone was the laughing young man whom I had first met. Instead I saw a person of maturity, someone who had hidden his scars under a false outside skin. Although indiscernible to others, as I was suffering in the same way they were easy for me to see. The telltale lines of restless sleep around his eyes, the tension at his mouth, where lips would often be compressed, so holding back what he truly wanted to say, and his hands on the tabletop clenching and unclenching in an effort to relieve tension., I wanted to walk up to him, lay my head on his shoulder, kiss his cheek and hold him tight in my arms. My heart was breaking and I could see his was too, but we had so many people depending on us, it was impossible for us to take what fate had offered. As I was beginning to feel I could not take any more, Charlie's voice broke in on my thoughts.

"Bill, have you told them about the incident with Vicki and the shower?"

"What did Vicki do in the shower?"

Just hearing Dieter say my name, was like music to me.

I groaned inwardly. Oh! No! Not that please.

With a great deal of laughter and exaggeration, Bill went on to tell the assembled company about my most embarrassing situation when in the camp site at Bern. Not used to showering within an allotted time, I was enjoying the relaxing shower, did not realise that my Swiss Francs had run out, so allowing the next person to come in, when drying myself the door opened and a young Spaniard stood at the door as dumbfounded as I was.

I sat silent, only as the tale ended and Bill, accompanied by Charlie, kept laughing loud and long at what had happened to me, did I hear Dieter mutter, while looking in my direction: "He saw you with no clothes, lucky man. I must find him. He might be able to tell me what I am missing." The bitterness in his voice was obvious, only to me. Then turning his back on me, translated, dissolving his family into laughter.

The meal finished, it was time to clear the table. My offer of help smilingly refused.

"Not today," I was told by Birgit. "But from tomorrow."

"Why tomorrow?" I queried.

"Today you are a guest, tomorrow you become family." Monique said, genuine friendship in her voice, making me feel a heel because I didn't want her friendship, only her man.

My family had left the table and I was about to stand up as Dieter approached where I stood, his hand stretched across in front of me, about to remove an open wine bottle. I could see the whiteness of his knuckles as he bent forward. Knowing for a moment no one was watching us, I gave into temptation and very gently placed my cheek against his side. For a second I was lost in his body smell, thinking he could be unaware of me touching him, so soft was my touch. Only as I heard a gasped: "You do still care," did I realise our contact had been apparent to him. Looking up, his eyes were now smiling, because I had given myself away. Perhaps I had unintentionally wanted my longing for him to be discovered.

I nodded, no further reply necessary.

We were so involved with each other, that I did not at first realise the wine bottle had tipped on its side, spilling white wine over the table cloth.

It was Bill's voice that intruded on our special moment: "Vicki, can't you do anything properly, look!"

Shaking ourselves out of the magic of the moment that had grown once more between us, both Dieter and I looked at the liquid pouring over the table, and laughed, recalling what had caused the accident.

"Bill, it makes no matter," Dieter replied to my husband. "Look, there is no damage. It's only a little wet, see." then dipping the fingers of his left hand in the wetness, I saw him lick his fingers: "Good wine, too. That is the only problem when good wine is lost, it is like love being thrown away, you can never get it back."

I knew there was a hidden meaning in his message. "Come Vicki, taste this." Before I could stop him, the fingers with the spilt liquid, were being put to my lips, ostensibly for me to taste the wine, but as I felt his fingers drawn slowly, gently across my tongue and lips it was not the alcohol that I tasted, but the feel and warmth of an unspoken promise that we would be once more together. Thanking my lucky stars that no one who witnessed our actions was aware of the erotic thoughts running riot in me, now Dieter was aware that my need for him was as desperate as his was for me, he appeared to be much happier.

I was amazed at the ease with which he carried on the conversation.

Turning to Bill, he replied: "Now we have eaten, before we rest I will show where to park your wagon."

As we left the house, I turned to the two women, thanking them for the meal, my voice was more normal than I had expected. I left the house with a much lighter air.

It didn't take long to find the parking space allotted us. We had been allowed to park on the side of the sports field near to the hockey and tennis courts that had so impressed the children earlier, under a great old oak tree, that spread it's bough over us like protective arms. Behind us was a red brick building to which Dieter handed over a great bunch of keys saying: "Bill you will need these for you and your family."

"What are they?" Bill asked.

"You mean without anyone bursting in on us." Charlie laughed, obviously enjoying a joke at my expense.

Dieter, however, turned it to his advantage: "Maybe I will come round, when Vicki is in the shower, then perhaps I will see what the Spanish ma\n saw.

"Yea. Well if you do, let me know. I'm her husband and I don't see it all that much." Bill could not resist adding.

I chose to ignore this.

"Every morning, when you are ready, Monique and I will have breakfast ready for you. You will take all your meals with us, and in the evening we will go out." Dieter informed us, as he turned to walk back to his house, leaving us to follow when ready.

"Hey, hang in there, old son," Charlie called after him. "We are here on holiday, you can't keep us."

"You are on holiday, you are also very good friends. We look after special people, old son." Dieter did a good imitation of Charlie's cockney slang.

For one Bill appeared lost for words, instead he placed a friendly arm round the German's shoulders, an action very unusual for him, giving him little hug: "You're a good friend Dieter."

Turning his face to me, Dieter replied in German: "Not so good, I think."

Only I understood what he said and meant.

Allowing the others to enter the camper before me, I stood and watched the retreating figure of the man whom I was growing to love more each time we met. He never ceased to amaze me, nothing was too much for him to give. I felt sure if there had there been enough room in his house, we would have been living there too, not sleeping in the vehicle.

I returned the little wave he gave, just before he disappeared into the high corn. Dressed in a yellow and black track suit his shape was almost indiscernible with the colour of the vegetation growing around him.

"Hey do you plan on changing, or are you going to Monique's house like that."

Ignoring his sarcastic comments, my mind all the time following each step Dieter took away from me, knowing he was only a few feet away and for now we did not have to dream of each other, we were almost together.

Preparing for the evening was not such chore this time. With the added space of the shower rooms, we did not get under each other's feet, making us all a little better tempered.

Once we were ready, an exodus in the direction of Dieter and Monique's home took place of a much smarter group than had arrive in the village a few hours earlier, now seeming a lifetime away.

Retracing our steps, I was amazed at the difference a few hours could make. When first leaving Dieter's house, the sun had still been high, now it was setting, allowing the moon its freedom. As her golden head rose high over the wheat fields, a sudden deep longing to be held close in Dieter's arms rose up in me. Once again an impossible dream. We had met too late for such dreams. So long as we remembered that being friends was a safer relationship between us, life would be less complicated. A difficult decision, but one that had to be made.

Almost as if my wishes had conjured him up for me, at the sound of a voice I looked up. There in the gathering darkness stood Dieter, smiling: "I thought you would like me to meet you."

"Oh, yes please," I whispered.

"That is good," he replied. The object of my dreams now so close to me, that my softly given reply was just loud enough for him to hear.

"Hey, Dieter what are we doing tonight?" Charlie, called over: "I've heard so much about your local beer, do I get a chance to try a few glasses?"

"Monique thinks as you might be tired this evening we will have a quiet time with some friends and yes beer." Laughing Dieter carried on walking ahead.

"I don't know about the first, but I like the idea of the second." Charlie laughed: "This woman," pointing to me: "Has kept me in a drought, now perhaps I can be off the leash." tapping me on the shoulder showing he was only joking.

In the darkness I could see the whiteness of a smile: "Tell me Charlie, do you always drink as much as the children say?"

"No, only in the act of friendship,"

"Then Uncle Charlie," Hannah shouted back, "you have a lot of friends, because you've always got a drink."

Laughing, we carried on in a little crocodile, heading in the direction of Dieter's home. The children running ahead and meeting up with Christoph and Markus, everything was as normal in this strange place as though we were at home in England.

Charlie and Bill walked behind them, calling them now and then ensuring they did not wander away and get lost.

I walked behind with Dieter. The magnetism between us so strong, it was almost tangible. Each time he moved his right hand, it would brush past my left one, the electricity so strong it caused the hairs on my arms to stand on end. I would see him look at me in the darkness, want to speak, then have to dissolve into silence, because what we wanted to say had to be left unsaid and anything else between us would be unthinkable.

I was so engrossed in my thoughts that as I stepped off the curb my heel caught in the cracks between the stones, pulling me up with a suddenness that Dieter had to put his hand out to stop me falling. So we stood, his hand on my shoulder, unconsciously rubbing the skin where it was exposed. The evening was so warm I had a worn a dress only held up by thin straps. The sound of my family faded into the distance, as we stood face to face in the gloom surrounding us:

"Vicki, I have a need of you," he whispered. I had no answer, seeing all my ready made plans disappearing like the mist in the morning.

"Will you come to me?" He demanded

I had no answer only a silent nod of the head.

"I want to. But when? How?" Now I had found a voice, if only a whisper.

"Soon." He lifted up my hand, raising it to his lips, placing a kiss on the palm. In that moment I felt that he had made me a promise, one that would be kept.

As we hurried to catch up with the others, he insisted we keep a distance between us, making sure no physical contact accidentally took place: "It is too dangerous," he said, at his words a delicious tingle feathered up and down my spine, knowing the power I possessed over this man.

So we continued walking, in silence but in perfect tune. As we approached his house we could see a couple of cars parked in front: "Ah I see that Herbert and Brigitta are now with us. Turning, I asked: "Who are they?"

"Very good friends, of me and my wife."

I still hated the sound of his joining the name of Monique with his own.

As we walked up the path, the moon appeared to be blotted out of a second by the shadow of a man of gigantic proportions.

"Dieter, my friend where have you been, we are three beers ahead of you."

"No problem, Herbert I will soon catch up with you." Dieter laughed, clasping his friend's shoulder in companionship.

"Come I will introduce you to Vicki and her family." He continued leading us into the house.

On entering the small hall I soon realised that the size of this man was no figment of the fading light. He was, in truth, enormous. He was a good-looking man, from the riot of black curls on his head to the hazel eyes that glinted with a hint of the devil in them. His nose was a little wide, but everything about him appeared wide or large, this did not look out of place. His lips seemed to be set in a permanent grin, only just noticeable under the handlebar moustache he wore with pride. His thick neck disappeared into shoulders that would have made a bodybuilder envious. This man gave the impression that life was made for fun and laughter, a sentiment I would once have agreed with. Turning from him to his wife I could not help but be amazed at the difference between the two.

Brigitta, was many inches smaller that her gigantic husband, with thin, mousey-brown hair hanging to her shoulders, over a heart shaped face. Her eyes were a watery blue, appearing to squint every time she concentrated her gaze on anyone. She had none of the robust sun-tan sported by the rest of her compatriots, leaving her looking pale by comparison. A pair of jeans and a large mauve jumper covered her tiny frame. She gave the impression of a person that took life seriously and was perhaps even a bit miserable. I would soon discover that was far from the truth. Once the introductions were over, however, Herbert informing us with pride that he was the baker for the village and that Brigitta made the cakes and worked in the shop. I realised here was a couple, although unsuited in looks but, were certainly the ideal match. Just watching Herbert look at his diminutive wife was enough to make me envious. That was how I wished Dieter and I were free to look at each other - with open adoration.

Having sat down to help ourselves to the buffet and drinks, Dieter began to regale the newcomers with the incident at the campsite in Switzerland. As is the way with all stories, it grew with the telling, now even I was finding it difficult to know the fact from the fiction. So I sat listening, nodding when necessary, all the time wishing the event had never happened.

Once the story was finished and a great many ribald jokes both in English and German being made at my expense, I felt a change in conversation would have been welcome.

"How long have you been married?" I asked Brigitta.

With the self-satisfied expression of a cat who had just finished a bowl of cream, she replied: "We have been married twelve years." then not waiting for me to ask any further questions she volunteered: "We have four children, two boys and two girls."

Thank God, this was a perfect way to change the subject, for all of us were able to join in. the evening progressed in an amiable way with the children watching a famous American soap, dubbed into German, causing the girls to drift into fits of loud giggles, as a star they recognised would appear speaking in a language completely alien to them, with actions and speech out of continuity.

"Your children are enjoying themselves," Dieter said. For the first time since we had entered his house did he look directly at me.

"Like me they always enjoy themselves in your house," I answered. Once again I could see by the gleam in his eyes, Dieter had understood my meaning.

Halfway through the evening, as we sat in the muted light of the table lamps, the children could be seen yawning. Looking at their father Monique suggested the boys go to bed, with a great deal of complaining this action was carried out. Dieter then remembered there were some sleeping bags, so it was decided that the boys use the bags and our girls their bunk beds as once before. This was agreed to with alacrity by all four. So, the children could sleep and not be disturbed when we returned to the camper.

On returning from putting the girls to sleep, I realised that Dieter was missing. Trying to make my voice sound very matter-of-fact, I enquired "Where's Dieter?" Before Bill could answer, Monique replied: "He is in the cellar, we need more wine."

In Dieter's absence the room appeared cold and empty. So when I heard his voice call me from the hallway, it was as if I were being drawn back to a comforting warmth.

"Vicki, come here I have something to show you."

Making a joke of this: "I wonder what he has?" I replied looking at Bill.

"Just go and see," he replied, while at the same time holding an in-depth conversation with Herbert regarding the driving standards on the roads today. It didn't seem to matter that neither man really understood the other, they were enjoying good hospitality, in a relaxed atmosphere.

Making my way into the hall, where Dieter was standing with the cellar door open.

"I thought you would like to choose what wine you want," he said loudly.

"You have such a choice, I replied, trying not to let me voice quiver with the excitement that was building up in me. From the look in his eyes it was obvious we were not going for wine. Dieter was as frustrated as I.

We needed time together, and what better than under the pretence of looking for wine.

I followed him down the stairs. As we reached the bottom Dieter turned, grabbing me by the arms and pulled me into a corner under the stairs. Now his need of me was becoming more evident in the shallowness of his breathing

"Oh!" God, Victoria I need you."

I had heard this before, but now I could feel his desire for me as he pulled me ever closed, till our bodies touched.

Because my dress had only thin straps and I wore no bra it was easy for him to touch me. Undoing his shirt I could see the maze of dark hair that ran up to his neck. I stood for seconds, my face buried in this mat, then slowly I raised my lips to his. It was a long time since we had touched like this that at first I felt a little strange. Then as we renewed our feelings for each other, I felt his hands wandering up my skirt, touching the tender skin on the inside of my thigh. I returned the caress by gently rubbing his manhood feeling the pleasure as it enlarged, knowing I could do this for him.

"Vicki, I know this is dangerous, he whispered hoarsely, as from a distance we heard my husband's voice, "but I cannot help myself."

"Nor me, but oh, Dieter, this is not enough for me!" I replied.

He understood, our need was the satisfaction of complete release of our desires. Tonight it was impossible.

"I will find a way, but for now." They were the last words he spoke for some time, as with my hands clasped round him and him holding me, our lips finally met. His warm, sweet-scented breath mingling with my own as first our lips then our tongues met in total caress. There was no part of our bodies that we had not caressed or held, kissed or licked. The tips of our tongues as busy and warm as the hands that touched each other's bodies.

Finally, as we were reaching the point of no return, Dieter pulled back, panting: "We have to stop here, Schatzie," he whispered. His breathing ragged with is emotions, "or we will have lots of trouble." Once again I understood. Quietly I pulled back, straightening my clothes, thankful I had worn no make-up, so there would be no giveaway.

With shaking hands Dieter tidied his own clothing, then he pulled me to his side, placing a kiss on my cheek. "Tomorrow," he breathed. This I knew was a promise of more pleasure to come.

We left the corner in which we had been hiding, to get the wine we had originally come down for.

There were racks of wines, cases of beer. Turning to Dieter I asked: "Why so much booze?"

"That is for the night before you leave, we will have a party."

At this a shiver of fear ran through me. I did not want to leave him, he was becoming the focus of my life. How could I possibly leave him now. Sensing my sudden unhappiness, he drew me close, kissing my cheek: "It's not a problem now, we will worry about it later," I nodded silently. By now he had chosen some bottles at random.

As we walked away I noticed a small bookshelf on which there was a mixture of family photographs and what appeared to be an old cigar box. Being ever inquisitive, I touched it with the tip of my finger, having the effect of knocking it to the floor. Bending to pick it up I was shocked to see a photo of myself; one that had obviously been taken a few years earlier. Turning to look at Dieter, who had come up quietly behind me, I asked: "where did you get this?"

From Uwe," he replied, a look of embarrassed shame on his face.

"When?" I asked, still stunned with my discovery.

"The first time I came to England. On our return home, when we had the photographs developed, I saw that Uwe had this copy, so I asked him for it. As you can see he gave it to me."

"But I don't understand. He is your brother-in-law, Monique's brother."

Smiling Dieter continued with is explanation: "Uwe and I are the best of friends. He knows I love his sister, but he understands that a pair of deep dark eyes have stolen the grown-up man I am now, from the boy I was. Come we must go."

Pushing me ahead of him up the stairs, we returned to those waiting for us.

"Where the hell have you been?" Bill demanded.

Before I could answer, Dieter had bent his head, planting a kiss on his wife's cheek and apologising to Bill.

"I am sorry, but I have so many bottles your wife did not know what to choose."

Dieter and I rejoined the conversations around us. Wine, beer, Apfelkorn and Cognac flowed freely, as over the air of friendship and camaraderie the music of Strauss flowed. The strains of the Blue Danube Waltz wafting gently around us.

"Dieter, how did you know this is my wife's favourite piece of music?" Bill called over to his friend.

"I do not think there is much about your wife I do not know," he replied laughing. Raising a glass to me: "I think we should drink a toast to Victoria Johnson."

My head shot up as if at the sound of gun-fire. What was he playing at?

"A toast," he continued, "to your wife, Brigitta, Birgit and mine, to all beautiful women of the world."

The glasses were raised as the four men drank to our health. No one could remove the feeling of warmth that ran through me, for though they toasted us all, I was being loved by only one. His green eyes looked long and deep into mine: "Tomorrow is not so far away," they seemed to be saying.

Chapter 15

A sudden movement to my right made me look up to see Bill standing in the doorway that divided the bar from the rooms upstairs. The dogs knowing him made no noise as he came to sit beside me on the settle that I had been curled up on remembering the precious moments of my time with Dieter.

"What are you doing?" Bill whispered even though apart from Dreamie and Vidor there was no one else who could hear us. "Have you any idea what time it is?" Again I just shook my head. Then feeling I had to say something, I muttered: "Just thinking back to the good times we have had here." Bill laughed out loud: "Oh! Yes we have had some fun, great fun." then looking at the cup in my hand: "got any more left." I shook my head going into the kitchen to make a fresh pot.

"I was thinking of the time we hired the camper," I said to Bill, "what fun that trip was and when we arrived here, how Dieter..." here my voice cracked, coming up and taking the cups from my now shaking hands, Bill said: "Look love, don't think the worst, he is an old reprobate he will survive." I looked at the man now sitting beside me, enjoying a cup of coffee, we had now been married over twenty-five years, he was no longer as slim as he once was and his dark hair liberally sprinkled with grey. He was such a dear man, and had deserved so much more than I had given him over the last fourteen years of our marriage but I felt that I had never let him down too much even though my heart had in spirit belonged to another. We, Bill and I were still very much a partnership and parents to our beautiful now quite grown-up daughters.

After he had chatted with me a little. Finishing his coffee giving the dogs a friendly tap on their heads and me a kiss the cheek, went back to bed with the words: "Don't stop up too long." We will be going back to the hospital later on in the day, don't want Dieter to see you looking knackered."

I smiled weakly, gave him a little wave and went back to my memories.

I went to bed that night ecstatic, believing sleep to be impossible.

A bird tapping on the window woke me from the light sleep I had drifted into. No sooner were my eyes open than a smile was once more ready to break over my face. I couldn't help being happy. At this moment it seemed to the most natural state for me to be in.

Strange, there was that tapping sound again. Wondering what bird could be so insistent I pulled aside the curtain. As the children had spent the night with Dieter and Monique, I had slept in their bed.

Blinking at the unaccustomed bright of the dawn sun, I marvelled at how beautiful everywhere looked. I didn't doubt it was the inner excitement in me, bubbling like champagne waiting for the cork to pop.

A sudden movement from behind the large hedge close to the camper made me jump back as a figure moved out. This was so unexpected I almost screamed, until I recognised the man, it was Dieter, gesturing that I should join him. Nodding, I let him know I had seen him and was accepting the invitation offered.

Scrambling out of bed, dressing quietly so as not to disturb the men sleeping, within minutes I had joined him.

"What are you doing here?" I gasped "it's very early."

"Leibchen, I couldn't sleep, don't tell me you could," he said mockingly.

Breathlessly I replied: "No, I couldn't sleep either."

A pleased smile broke over his face. "That is good, we should both suffer together."

We stood for seconds in silence just staring at each other. Green eyes meeting brown, both renewing silent vows to each other.

"I promised we would be together today," he spoke once more, this time taking my hand and leading me. Where we were going I didn't ask, I only cared that for a moment in time I was with him and we were alone.

Quietly I followed him, across the large stone tennis courts, towards the hockey field in the distance. All the time a stillness between us, as if we were afraid that any unexpected sound might spoil the magic of the morning.

I stared at the back of the man whose hand was now tightly clutching mine. His tanned, sinewy arms, tapering down to long lean fingers, excited me as we walked. I remembered them wandering up and down my body, as a maestro fingering the keys of a piano, drawing beautiful music from what was otherwise a lifeless piece of wood. I was the instrument, he, the master.

With great difficulty I kept my rising desire under control. As we walked a gentle zephyr played with my hair, pulling it free from the band holding it in place. I could feel tendrils tickling the nape of my neck. Pulling my hand free to replace these strands, Dieter stopped to watch my actions, all the time smiling:

"Don't mind it," he said, as my annoyance at the trouble my hair was giving became obvious. "It carries out my order."

"Your order?" I replied puzzled.

"Mm. I cannot walk and kiss you, so the breeze places gentle kisses for me on you, till I am able to make you once more mine."

Again desire burnt strong in my breast, my need for him was such that even the mention of us coming together created so heady a feeling that it caused me to trip, stumbling from the path we followed.

We were now in parkland, surrounded by tall trees. Here, the sun had not gained enough strength to filter through, giving the atmosphere a damp, earthy smell.

"We are here," he gasped, out of breath with the efforts of a man who appeared to be in a hurry.

At first I could not make out where we were. All I could see were large bushes and what seemed to be young trees, planted carefully among a variety of roses. Pushing past one of the densest of the bushes, I saw first another garden, it too was filled with young plants, all obviously being nurtured for transplanting once they had reached maturity. Then I noticed a small brown, timbered building. It was to this I was being taken

"I have not been here for many months, hopefully it will be all right." He said pushing open a door that creaked in protest.

I found myself being picked up and carried over some leaves. These I presumed were a kind of threshold. As he placed me on the raffia matting that covered the floor, looking up at the roof, I could see that the shed had obviously been built for the comfort of those who were working on the trees and plants.

"Is this yours?" My voice was so soft, I doubted that he could have heard, as he appeared to be busy searching among the debris for something.

From his kneeling position on the floor, Dieter turned to smile at me: "No, my darling. It belongs to a family friend called Heinrich. He is the gardener of our village, and when I was a small boy in need of money I was allowed to help him with the trees to earn some wages."

My heart swelled with pride, as I imagined the beautiful, proud child he would have been. Too independent to take without giving in return. Like his love making. I nodded in understanding.

"Why are we here?" I asked

"Because this is the only place we can be alone."

Once more that stupid emotion, jealousy, coursed through me: "Oh! Is this where you brought all your girl friends?"

He turned slowly, such a look of pain on his face, I felt as if I had physically hit him.

"Nothing I do for or with you have I done with anyone else." Then, lowering his voice even more: "Not even my wife knows about this place." He turned me till we stood face to face.

"So baby come to me." he whispered.

In silence I walked blindly towards him. We stood for seconds not touching just looking, as if for the moment that was sufficient, until he breathed: "My love, I need you."

"I need you also," I replied.

Without further comment his long, brown fingers were running up and down my bare arms, our breathing coming in short, sharp gasps, as if fighting for air but wanting each other more. Our lips hovered inches from each other, not wanting the culmination of our feelings to come too soon, as the agony was as blissful as would be the ecstasy.

Dieter, began to open my tee shirt. With no bra my breasts were soon exposed. I heard his gasp of pleasure as the round, mounds of flesh were uncovered. Taking each in turn he kissed then placed a nipple in his mouth, suckling them as if seeking sustenance for life. I could feel his hands wander to the belt of my trousers. With shaking hands he undid it, and as my trousers and panties fell to the floor I stood naked before him, not in the least ashamed, knowing what he wanted most I was able to give.

For moments he stood staring at me, his fingers following the outline of my body. Excitedly I began to undress him. By now my desires were racing up and down inside me, causing volcanic explosions all over. At first I found it difficult to undo his shirt buttons and for a second I became embarrassed. However, as he held my fumbling fingers, bending his head to place a kiss on my knuckles he said: "Come baby, don't be shy." His whispered words were all the reassurance I needed.

Having removed his shirt, trousers and briefs soon lay on the floor. So we stood, our bodies naked, staring at each other, yet afraid to dine at the table of love the gods had placed before us.

I placed my hands round his penis that was growing every larger, engorged with the hot blood that flowed through it. Kneeling before him I took the tip of it in my mouth, allowing my tongue to flick around, so exciting him even more. All I could hear were his groans of pleasure, till gently he lay me on my back and joined me on the floor, where we stroked each other. Our hands exploring, finding new zones of joy, bringing cries of ecstasy, building up to the ultimate fulfilment. I could feel Dieter's hands pulling my thighs apart as he mounted me as a stallion would a mare. Slowly our bodies rose and fell together, both covered in the hot, sweet scented sweat that only true sexual desire can bring. For minutes, we continued to work slowly together until the desire we found so hard to satiate began to take over, turning our lust and love for each other into a living, breathing animal, greedy for the satisfaction only the other could give. I could feel his tautness, as he came close to climax: "Baby are you ready?" He breathed, eager that we should reach our peak together.

Once more, lost for words, I nodded. This was answer enough for him. Together we began to climb the peaks that our love has led us to, until, as his body reached its height of desire, I felt him go tense inside me, so urging my body to follow suit, until with a cry of pleasure both of us exploded into each other. Panting we rode the heights of ultimate fulfilment together, until drained and out of breath we were finally still, lying staring at each other.

"Vicki, I love you," he whispered hoarsely.

"Oh! Dieter, why didn't we meet years ago?" I asked, my voice still soft and languorous from our love making.

"Maybe we did, but were not aware of it." then looking at me and smiling he carried on: "No, Leibchen, if I had met you in another life, in any life, I would have known you then as I know you now."

Then pulling me to my feet: "Come we must return, or our families will miss us." As we began to dress, I wanted to cry: "I don't care if the others do miss us. I am always alone, without you."

In silence we left that little hut in which we had experienced such a taste of paradise, feeling sorry for anyone who had not a love like ours. We walked back in the direction from which we had come earlier that morning.

During the time we had spent loving each other, the morning had worn on. Here and there people could be seen wandering around; groundsmen preparing the sports fields and the excited voices of children going out for the day in school groups wafted across the still sunlit air, mingling with the sound of dogs barking and people going about their everyday business, but for us the morning of our new lives had begun in that little hut.

Taking me back to the camper, Dieter looked around to see we had no witnesses, then bending his head placed a kiss in loving farewell on my lips. As I felt him take my lower lip between his teeth the desire that only he could kindle began to rise once more:

"Will you go away," I begged, laughing.

"I will, but only after you tell me what I need to hear."

"Herr Dieter Schmidt, I Victoria Johnson love you more than life itself."

"And I Dieter Schmidt promise to love you for my life and beyond."

Saying this he walked away, in the direction of his home. As I stood watching him I smiled because I was sure at times his feet appeared to be dancing.

Entering the camper, I decided to make enough noise to awaken the men.

"Good God woman, what is the matter with you?" Charlie grumbled.

In a fit of devilment I sprinkled some water over his half-blanket covered head.

"It's time to wake up, the sun is shining beautifully, in fact it's a wonderful day." I enthused.

"Oh No," Bill grumbled, "she's in a good mood, I don't think I can stand it." He joined his brother, both staring at me with looks fit to kill. But today I was impervious to any form of insult.

"What happens at the end of this holiday, when you have to leave him again?" That little voice in my head reminded me of what would soon have to be faced.

"But not today," I answered my conscience.

"What's not today?" Bill asked, struggling into his jeans.

"Oh nothing," I replied, airily walking towards the stove.

"How I hate it when she does this," Bill whined on, complaining to his brother.

"Women!" Charlie huffed in protest.

Laughing I walked away, carrying on with my chores.

It was the sound of tapping on the door that brought Bill to his feet, causing him to knock his knee on the low table top, nearly spilling his coffee.

"Who the hell is that?" He muttered, walking towards the insistent knocking.

"Could be two young ladies, otherwise known as your children, dear." I answered.

"You are so funny, this morning."

No sooner had he opened the door, than two little cyclones stormed into the van ---- followed by Dieter. I could feel him staring at me. For a moment I felt almost shy. This was the first time I had seen him since the

254

incident in the shed and the desire that ran through me was difficult to keep at bay.

"Did you sleep well?" He asked, taking the coffee that Charlie placed in his hand.

"Oh yes," both men chorused together.

"And you Vicki. How did you sleep?" His voice was now just a touch huskier.

"I slept well, thank you,"

"Any dreams?" He was now insistent on getting a more detailed answer from me.

"Yes, if you must know I did have a dream, and it was quite wonderful, but I don't remember what it was about."

"How the hell can you have a dream, know it was great, but not remember?" Charlie mocked.

"Easily, I snapped back.

"Strange," Dieter replied, "but I too had a good dream." The way in which he used the word "good" I felt he meant heavenly.

"Great, maybe you two should get together, and then perhaps you will remember your dreams," Bill butted in sarcastically.

He would never know why at the moment both Dieter and almost choked on our coffee.

Other footsteps could be heard approaching the van, our peace now completely shattered.

"Mum, Dad here comes Monique with Christoph and Markus,"

"My sons are very fond of you," I heard a little whisper behind me, as Dieter walked past to get a coffee for his wife.

Behind Monique stood Uwe and Birgit, accompanied by Maria their daughter. We had seen the couple recently, but their daughter we had not seen since our first visit. Like our own children she too had grown up a great deal. Whereas our girls still contained a lot of the child in them, this young lady was quite the reverse, she appeared to have become a miniature adult.

Maria was dressed in a grey trouser suit, with her long blonde hair permed in the latest style. A light smattering of make-up on her face, highlighting the grey eyes, was complimented with a faint tinge of lipstick on her bow-shaped lips. A pink handbag hung from her shoulder, with matching shoes. I was amazed this was no child, she was the most adult eleven-year-old I had ever met. Compared with this little vision, Hannah and Lottie came over as being a pair of untidy hooligans, but I preferred them that way.

Never stopping for breath, both our children went on to regale us with tales of the night before, when they had slept with Dieter and Monique. How they had helped to do some tidying up, and some of the plans being made for us, all this and more came tripping off their tongues, with a little help from Maria, who had started to learn English and was eager to show what she knew. I was thankful for their eager chattering, as this helped to give me time to collect my scattered thoughts.

A timetable had indeed been drawn up, and for the next few days we would follow it to the letter. Birgit and Monique had even made plans for the days should we have rain. However, luck was on our side, the sun shone brightly day after day.

Dieter and I would probably never have a chance to be together again as we had that morning. But, there were occasions when I would look up and see him staring at me, his eyes burning with the same pent up emotions and frustrated desires that burned in me.

During the day we were shown Germany in the summer, not as we had first seen it, in the dark and cold. No, these days were bright and filled with laughter.

On that first day we were taken swimming, there were snack bars, a restaurant, plus a machine which simulated the waves of the open sea. Periodically these gigantic washes of water would appear, with all the children trying to ride it, like a group of cowboys. This excitement did nothing for Charlie, who sat around complaining until a beer was placed in his hand, improving his attitude markedly.

Another day was spent in visiting Cologne once more, seeing the places we had visited before, together with finding new ones. The moment we entered the Cathedral a little thrill ran up me, as taking my arm, under the pretence of showing me a statue we had not seen before: Dieter whispered "Do you remember the first time we were here?" I nodded, holding up my finger with the ring so that the sun shining in through the stained glass windows picked out the incandescent glow it reflected.

"Good, I am glad to see is still where I placed it," he replied, his look as erotic as any kiss.

When we had finished sightseeing, we would return to the house of either Dieter or Uwe, where we would be introduced to other friends or old acquaintances from the football club, all eager to renew old friendships and enquire about those whom they remembered in Little Barham.

Charlie never complained about these afternoon as they were never spent without a good deal of beer or schnaps in his hand, leading him to a euphoric state of mind.

Each evening we spent at the Hubertus. Drinks would flow like water, but on our second night, frustration set in. I wanted so desperately to be with Dieter, in his arms feeling his kisses, showing him I was his, that I allowed myself to drink too much Appelkorn. Seeing that I was getting tipsy, Dieter placed a hand on my arm, as if to hold me back. But, seeing his disapproval was like a red rag to a bull. Taking three glasses that stood ready for anyone to drink I finished each one in quick gulps, hiding the burning feeling they left in my throat.

"Vicki, you have had enough." Dieter had no intention of hiding his anger. "Behave."

"Oh leave her alone Dieter," Bill answered his friend. "It's easy to see my wife's in a mood, and when she gets like this you might as well forget it."

"Why are you like this?" Dieter demanded.

I couldn't answer him, not in front of so many people. Instead I just stared at him, hoping he would read my mind. Something he did, for with a tremble in his otherwise well-modulated tones he carried on in a whisper: "Baby, it's not good to be like this."

"Like what?" My tones were petulant.

"A child."

The censorious tones in his voice made me even more annoyed. Calling Hildey the barmaid for some more drinks I downed another four glasses - as with the previous ones, all in one gulp.

Glancing at Dieter I could see he had decided to follow my husband's advice and ignore me. This was something I didn't like, especially as it was the one man in the world I wanted to impress who was now turning his back on me. Feeling irritated I looked around me to see if I was still holding anyone's attention, there was

Charlie and Uwe engrossed in a kind of conversation, Bill, Dieter and Birgit had their backs to me talking and Monique was talking to a friend, I was of little to no consequence. About to try something really stupid I felt a hand touch my elbow:

"Don't do it, Liebchen." Dieter whispered.

"Don't do what?" I demanded crossly.

"Make yourself look silly."

"I did that the day I met you."

"Oh baby, when will you understand, it is not for us, we are good. But, look at your husband and my wife."

In my normal state of mind I would have understood, but now I was under the influence of alcohol and self-pity. Shrugging his hand away, I was once more ready to make a fool of myself, until Dieter's next remark: "If we were true married partners in life and spirit then you would have no need to do this thing."

I then spent the next hour apologising. Luckily the liquid I had spilt only covered the table missing the clothes of those present. Turning to look at Dieter I could see by the self-satisfied smile on his face, that once again I had proved he had the ability to shake me to the core.

I promised myself to behave in the future, so as not to spoil the family's holiday or destroy Dieter's love for me.

With great effort I behaved as the perfect wife and guest.

In winter Cologne was beautiful, but in the summer it took on a completely different aspect. The trees in the park lands surrounding the city looking green and lush, beautiful gardens could be found in every village and town we visited. It really was a different city to the one we had seen in December.

"Ah, well it was a good holiday while it lasted, but I won't be sorry to go home," I heard Bill say as we had breakfast on our last full day in Germany.

I was grateful that I was busy tidying up behind our children and my back was to him, otherwise I would have had to explain the sudden tears that rose as an arrow of pain struck at my heart.

"He was glad to be going home."

How I hated the thought of the journey we faced on the following day.

"What are you doing today?" Charlie asked his brother.

"Not too much, I've asked for a quiet day." then turning to me: "I believe Monique and Vicki will be going shopping, then in the afternoon a few old friends are popping round here. The party that Dieter was having tonight has been cancelled instead we are being taken to their new Gold Club.

"That's going to be exciting," I muttered, the sarcastic tone very evident in my voice.

About to give a cutting retort to my remark Bill was stopped before he had begun by a knock on our door. Opening it, standing there were Dieter and Monique accompanied by Uwe and Birgit.

With broad smiles on their faces the women whisked me away. They had decided that I, being a woman, must enjoy shopping trips as they did. Leaving the men to drink and enjoy themselves, with the children playing nearby. I hadn't got the heart to tell these good ladies that shopping bored me to tears. But, I was prepared to spend some time with them knowing in a few hours I would be back in Dieter's company again.

At last my day of torture ended. We had walked into every shop in Cologne, visited more than enough coffee

260

bars, and spoke to a variety of friends that my companions kept bumping into. As I climbed stiffly out of Birgit's car and walked towards our camper I could hear the loud laughter of the men. How I envied them. What a lovely day they must have had.

Looking at the front of the vehicle, I stood with my hands on hips, wondering what had happened to the quiet day, there must have been ten men, my husband and Charlie plus Uwe, Dieter who had been joined by six more, most of whom I knew from the football visits. They in turn were surrounded by beer bottles, barrels and crates. All of them had had more than to drink, something made obvious to me by Bill's remark as he saw me.

Raising his glass in my direction: "Welcome oh wonderful wife," he called in rather slurred tones. Then turning to the others he carried on: "Hey, lads don't you think my wife is beautiful." A rather wasted toast, as apart from Dieter and Charlie no one else understood a word he said, so it was no surprise raising his glass replied: "You are a very lucky man, indeed." About to tell the two men not to be such idiots, the look in Dieter's eyes stopped me.

We were invited to join the men. We sat enjoying the companionship these people offered us, a pleasant breeze reducing the burning heat of the sun. All around us was laughter, from children and adults alike.

I didn't say much, just enjoying the company of my lover. How I wanted to be in his arms, my body yearned for the fulfilment only he could give. I needed to make love to him, the fear that once I left the village the following day I might not see him again was a hard truth to accept. I saw Dieter stand up as if walking towards the wire fence separating us from the mad games the children were enjoying, walking past me I heard him whisper: "I need it also." One more proof that we were in complete tune. Raising my head in surprise I could see he was smiling.

Walking back after some minutes watching the children at play, I saw Dieter bend his head in his wife's direction saying something in a low voice, she obviously agreed to his suggestion, because straightening up, I saw him hold out a hand to me: "Come we need more wine, will you choose."

I agreed, silently following. The earlier desire now threatening to overtake me in a torrent of heated emotions.

"Bill, I am taking your wife to my house. There I will make passionate love to her." Dieter called back as we walked away.

"That's all right, mate, you might be luckier than I've been this holiday," my husband replied laughing.

Dieter and I looked at each other, in our eyes was the message: "We should feel ashamed." But as Dieter squeezed the fingers of my hand in his, we both agreed the emotions that rioted through us was too much for both of us. We could feel nothing but the fever of passion that rose when we were in each other's company.

Entering the house, I was instantly whisked down into the cellar, I heard him lock the door behind us, approaching me as I stood in the middle of the floor, key in hand: "We must not be disturbed, it would be very embarrassing." I tried to laugh, but nothing came out, all I needed was this man.

He stood before me, a tall, dark-haired, green-eyed seducer; one to whom I had given my life and love.

"Well, baby here we are for the last time." Placing his hands on my shoulders, Dieter bent his head to take my willing lips. I could feel the tautness of his body and the rising of the mound between his legs. Standing on tiptoe, my arms found their way round him. Within seconds we were lost to the world, all we needed was each other. We were food, drink and life to each other. I gave and he took, then he would take care of me.

I could feel his hands as they began to undo my trousers. For a moment I stopped him: "Should we do this, maybe Monique." His lips stopped me before I could say anything further, muttering as his mouth closed over mine: "No one will come, I have said we are going to buy the wine, because what my wife wants is not in the house." I laughed a joyous sound, for now I was free once more to love him.

Having undressed each other once more, as we did on a morning so long ago, we stood face to face enjoying the sight of each other's bodies. His tanned, lithe and graceful – every inch of him a man. Allowing my eyes to roam from the top of his head to the long legs, past the muscle that would soon give me an insight to a new life, that of the hidden paradise reserved for those who love in secret.

"Come to me," he whispered, holding out his arms to me.

I needed no second coaxing, I walked where he led. Soon his arms closed round me, holding my warm body to his hot and pulsing one. Our lips and hands fought to gain control of each other. We were vying for superiority, to see who could give the most pleasure. There was no restraint, we both had much to give and much to take. I felt him lie me down, then his body covered mine, as he entered me a cry of pure pleasure left my lips. Only when we were like this did I realise how much I needed and loved this man and what he had to offer. We move in unison, riding the eaves of pleasure together, understanding so perfectly we were each other's alter ego.

"I am ready," whispered Dieter, once again showing how much he thought of me. Never satisfying himself till I too was ready.

My silent nod was all he needed.

Plunging ever deeper into me, he drove like a man possessed and I allowed him. Wanting to give him so much more, but because we were not legally bound unable to do so. Until with joint screams of pain and ecstasy we contented each other. I could feel tears of joy on my face, looking up at Dieter as he stood away from me, I could see he too was feeling the same emotions.

Having dressed, we made our way back to the camper and those waiting for us. I glanced down at Dieter's empty hands.

"Dieter, we didn't get the wine."

Looking down, he raised his hands in the air a look of startled surprise on his face. "Oh Gott! Oh Gott!"

We had to make a mad dash for the local store selling the wine. We could not explain to the good lady behind the counter why it was we laughed all the way in and out of the shop.

"Thank God, they've gone." Bill said as we prepared for the evening's entertainment.

I must agree with you, old son." When these people give you hospitality, they sure go overboard.

"I'm surprised you two know what you're doing, after the booze you must have put away today." I grumbled.

"What about you two. Why did it take so long to get that wine?" Bill queried. I was thankful that I had my

264

back to him, preparing the children for their last night's visit to Andrea and her husband with the boys.

"Well first we had to make passionate love," I tried to laugh.

"Listen to her." Bill's tones were mocking: "She has more headaches than anyone I know. Come on kids if you are ready I'll take you and the boys to Andrea's house."

Watching his retreating back, I should have felt a modicum of guilt, but I didn't. Instead the only emotion I was capable of feeling was great pain that this time tomorrow I would be back in England and away from my love.

We had been informed that the Golf Club, was quite an upmarket club smart informal was the order of the day. The men had dressed in their dark blue suits complementing my strawberry-pink silk trouser suit. My hair was piled up on my head; because I had quite a tan I felt make-up to be unnecessary. My bare feet slipped into sling back sandals.

Once ready we made our way across the village, past Dieter's house, then onto Andrea's where our children called goodnight and went indoors to be spoilt by their new Aunt Andrea.

"Looks more like prison gates," muttered Charlie, as we pressed a bell.

A disembodied voice enquired who we were and whose guests were we. Having given the necessary information a buzzing sound was heard, then, as if opened by an unseen hand, the enormous gates swung open, allowing us to enter.

Walking up a long driveway, it was easy to see the Golf course surrounding us, kept in pristine condition.

"Can't ever cut my grass like that." Bill stated looking at the green surrounding us.

"I'll bet it's expensive to belong to this, Bill said.

"No, my friend, anyone can join, we like to be able to relax and our young people to have something competitive to aim for." Dieter's voice came from behind us.

I had to hold back the cry of pleasure that rose to my lips at the sight of him. He looked wonderful, dressed in a black linen suit, with a green tee shirt that matched the colour of his eyes. I felt that all I wanted to do was stand and stare, he made such a wonderful picture. It was obvious by the glint in his eyes, he quite like the way I too was dressed, trying to ignore the picture his diminutive wife made standing beside him, dressed in blue, that echoed the blue of her eyes, making them appear wide and innocent. How different to me she was.

The three men walked ahead talking quietly, Monique and I following behind. The sun that had been hot all day, was now setting leaving a slight chill in the air. Here and there were little back dots of clouds, hiding the stars that were trying to shine. The gentle breeze that had blown all day was now quite fresh, making us thankful that we had brought jackets with us.

Reaching the end of the driveway, we were faced with a large white building with large plate glass windows, giving the restaurant we were heading for a perfect view over the Green. Climbing the steep steps that took us to the verandah, we were met by a uniformed doorman, who obviously took great pride in his job and surroundings. It was clear that our companions were often guests here, as everywhere we went they were greeted. Momentary pangs of jealousy filled me when realising many of the voices calling out were obviously from young and attractive females.

Looking at Monique I could not help asking: "Don't you feel jealous?"

She smiled: "Many of them are jealous of me, they wanted him and I won." With the self-satisfied look of a Persian cat finishing the best cream she walked ahead of me.

Having left our jackets in the foyer, we walked into the ultra-modern building. The walls had been designed to look like rock covered in stucco paint, a long bar in dark oak ran the length of the far wall. Into the ceiling had been set spotlights of different colours, giving a muted glow to the surrounding area. Tables and chairs in dark oak filled the Indian-carpeted dining room and on each table were set lamps designed to look like old coaching lanterns. The chairs were high backed, with arms in fancy scroll work. It was obvious, though the building was ultra-modern, it had been designed to look like the dining room of an ancient Castle. The décor was effective and most impressive.

Our entry had been noted by our friends who came up to greet us noisily with kisses, hugs and handshakes.

Greetings over, we were led to the table that had been reserved for us. This was the largest one in the room, looking more like a banqueting table, no lanterns here for us, instead we had four sets of lamps designed to look like candelabra. The seats of the chairs were in pink dralon, all adding to the sumptuous setting. Apart from the variety of diners the place was filled with waiters, waitresses who flitted in and out of tables as fleet-footed as any ballet dancer and as quietly.

As Dieter pulled my chair out, he asked: "Do you like it here?" Glancing around, looking out at the expanse of green facing us and the gardens to the side I nodded, adding in a whisper: "I am happy you are here," pleased only I could put that glow in his eyes.

So a very noisy meal got underway, to disapproving looks from diners who had gone out for a quiet night. Looking around us, everywhere were laughing faces, only Dieter, who sat beside me, and I finding it difficult to laugh. Among friends who had come to spend the last evening with us were Walter and Louise from the Hubertus, Herbert and his wife Brigitta. Next to them sat Agatha, a woman of gigantic proportions and heart to match, with her husband Thomas, a small man who would sit and smile while his wife talked incessantly. Then there were the couples who had greeted me on the first night I had come to the village. The cousins Paul and Frank with their wives Helga and Christa. Of course there was also Uwe and Birgit were there too. To the outsider, what a wonderfully happy group we appeared, only two of us would have disagreed --- Dieter and myself.

The food was served swiftly and the drink flowed plentifully. The fact that the group did not understand Charlie and Bill or them the others did not seem to matter, somehow or other they were able to converse. Agatha was telling me that the Club had a sauna, swimming pool and many other facilities free for members to use. I nodded absent-mindedly, my mind taken up by the antics of some field mice that had appeared in front of our window. They ran in and out of the grass not worrying anyone.

As the conversation flowed around us, now and then I would feel the brush of Dieter's leg along mine or the touch of his hand on my thigh. All these little actions filling me with an ache that needed relieving, something from now on would be impossible.

"Vicki, Vicki." I could hear Charlie's voice interrupting my thoughts, annoyed because he had broken into the dreams I was weaving around my lover and myself. I turned, about to give him a rude answer, but the expression on his face stopped me.

"What's wrong?"

"I'm not sure," he whispered, "but I think I've got something under my trousers."

Laughing: "Yes dear, all men have." I answered

"Be serious."

I had never seen such an expression on his face before.

"Call Bill without worrying the others, please hurry."

His order was so unexpected that standing up I walked towards my husband, leaning over and interrupting the earnest conversation he was having with Thomas:

"I think there is something wrong with Charlie, you had better come, quickly."

By now it was obvious my brother-in-law was deeply uncomfortable. His face was purple as he clutched desperately at the top of his left thigh. Having been the expression on his brother's face, Bill needed no second bidding. Walking hurriedly up to Charlie, I saw him bend his head, obviously enquiring what was wrong. Then to our amazement he stood up threw his head back and burst into laughter. By now the two men had the attention of everyone in the room, including the staff.

"You've got a what up your trousers," Bill shouted embarrassing his brother still further.

"A mouse." Charlie called back.

These two words had the most catastrophic effect on all of us. Even the men scattered. There were women on the tables or running for any high ground that was available, including the top of the very expensive bar.

Bill led Charlie outside. His brother now bent almost double as he clutched further up his thigh as the little creature was obviously making its way ever higher up his leg. Standing outside Bill pulled his brother's trousers up, exposing the tail of the rodent. Pulling gently he then held the struggling creature for us all to see. At this the women squirmed. The men, a little shamefaced at their obvious cowardice, clapped Bill for what they considered to have been a very brave act. Placing it in the grass, Bill then brought Charlie back into the restaurant, where he was given a large brandy by the Maître 'D. A drink he swallowed without actually tasting it.

It was quite some time before the conversation returned to normality, as we kept looking in Charlie's direction and giggling: "A bit more entertaining than my shower incident," I felt compelled to remind my brother-in-law. Knowing he would never be rude to me again, as I had more to blackmail him with than he me.

As the customers began leaving I was reminded that the time was rapidly approaching for us all to say goodbye. I was not looking forward to this as our farewell must be made in public, so there would be no tender kisses, or gentle caresses, just the cursory goodbyes' of good friends. Suddenly I felt the sting of tears in my eyes. Bending my head as if minutely studying the table's surface, only the warm hand on my thigh told me that my companion was sensing my heartbreak and feeling the same.

"Meet me outside soon, he whispered under cover of wiping his mouth with a serviette.

I nodded.

Within minutes he had made his excuses.

Having waited for what I thought was long enough, I too made a quick exit, following him. I walked back the way we had come earlier that evening. Reaching the open door I glanced out into the dark, moonless night, hearing my name called in a whisper. There stood waiting for me. I was pulled unceremoniously into outstretched arms. After a hurried kiss on the lips, I was led round the side of the building. Here were no electric lights or windows, making it impossible for us to be seen.

For seconds we stood staring at each other, then Dieter leant against the wall pulling me with some force onto his body. The moment we touched was like an explosion, out lips met in a kiss that we never wanted to end.

"Dieter, you must stop playing games with me," I whispered, pulling back, finding it hard to gain my breathing.

"I don't play games," he answered, obviously bewildered by what I had said.

"Yes, my darling. You do. I have not once heard I love you, only that you want or need me."

I could feel him dragging me back into his arms once more. Trying in vain to fight him off: "There is a difference." I continued.

"Come then, I will show you how I truly feel." with this I was back in his arms, being kissed in a way that drew my very soul from my body. His hands wandered at will all over me, the strength that filled his trousers making it clear that any love I had for him was returned with the same force as my own.

"How can I find a way to show you how much I love you," he spoke: "We are not legally bound. I cannot give you a home. We can have no children together. This is not easy for me, my darling." Pushing me away from him: "Come we must go in now. But please understand I cannot say goodbye to you tomorrow. For me this is not easy." I nodded once more, too full of emotion for any form of speech.

As we had made our exit, so we returned. Separately, so as not to give cause for any suspicion.

As we left the club and said our farewells to our friends, the skies opened and the rain that had been threatening all evening, finally came down, drenching us all with its force, making the seven of us run in an effort to keep dry.

Reaching the house of Uwe and Birgit, our farewells were made hurriedly, in a flurry of raindrops and tears. Then it was the turn of Dieter and Monique to say goodbye. This was going to be a great deal more difficult. Because I was now becoming genuinely fond of the younger girl, and, of course, my feelings for Dieter was going to make it even more impossible.

Uncaring of the rain that fell about us, we stood silently for a few minutes.

"Well, thanks for everything," Bill said to Dieter.

"It makes no matter, you are my friends. I cannot do too much for you," he replied, his voice husky with hidden emotion.

"Thanks, old friend." Now it was Charlie's turn. He was also obviously moved by the moment.

The men then kissed Monique. It was now my turn to say goodbye. I could feel tears burning at the back of my eyes, a lump in my throat making it impossible to speak. Taking Monique in my arms, I kissed her on the cheeks and she returned my salutation; our tears now flowing freely. Then Dieter and I. To my surprise, shock and horror, he did not kiss me. Standing straight, as if an iron rod had been placed through his spine, he held out a hand to me shaking my hand firmly as if we were mere acquaintances. Then ushering his wife up the path to their house, they disappeared from sight, leaving me feeling bereft. I could not believe he had done this to me. What had I done wrong? For moments, as we walked towards the camper I, now thoroughly soaked, I tried desperately to work out what I had done or said. Surely a little kiss, just one brief au wiedersehen, that was all I needed.

As Bill opened the door a breath of wind lifted the hair on the nape of my neck, bringing back a memory of what Dieter had said on that beautiful first morning here: "The wind kisses you, because I cannot." Then a smile broke over my face, as I was sure a voice followed this little caress: "Please my darling, understand."

Falling asleep I smiled a small heartbroken smile replying to the unspoken Prayer: "Yes, my darling I do understand."

Chapter 16

Feeling exhausted with the strength of my memories, giving the two guard dogs a quick pet behind their ears, I decided it was time that I made my way up to bed. Guessing my husband was also awake I took a pot of coffee up with me, walking swiftly and silently past the suite of rooms on the floor below us that belonged to Louise and Walter it wasn't long before I was knocking on our room door.

Opening the door to me, I could see that Bill was also having a bad night and was unable to sleep. This was a time when I knew we should be sharing our times with the Schmidt family together, but my memories of Dieter were so different from Bill's, I knew that in all honesty I could not share all of them with him.

Sitting up in bed coffee cups in hand we started to talk together about events in our lives that had affected us both.

"Bill, do you remember what wonderful times we had together." I had to get the conversation going somehow, making Bill smile and saying: "Do you remember that night when Dieter first stayed with us, and were trying to leave the Club he wouldn't leave." I smiled because I could remember it perfectly. Dieter had pretended he was drunk, and acting silly so Bill had lightly punched him in the stomach, taking Dieter by surprise, he folded over, Bill had thrown him over his shoulder and placed him on the back seat of the car to loud applause.

"Oh yes," Bill said we do have a lot of memories. With a faraway look on his face he too drifted off into realms of long ago. "Yes, the good times we've shared, days and nights I will never forget. Thank God we have photographs. I'll never forget Dieter."

"There won't be anything to forget," I found myself nearly shouting, desperation entering my voice: "he isn't dead, and isn't going to die." My voice now took on a pleading tone: "Please let's not talk about him like that."

Tapping my right arm, Bill smiled: "I'm sorry love, I forgot how fond of him you are. I promise I won't talk about him like that again." So saying he settled down to try and sleep, as he lay there my husband asked me a question I had been asking of myself: "You're a medium, don't you know what will happen?" Bill did not know how often I had asked that question myself and received no answer.

I drifted off into a restless sleep, one in which cars were coming at me from all directions they all appeared intent on my destruction. It was Bill shaking my shoulders that pulled me out of my nightmares, sitting up in bed shaking, Bill looked at me: "Are you O.K.? I have never known you so restless." Shaking my head, as I was still feeling unsettled all I could do was sit quietly in bed with Bill's arms around me while I told him about my night.

"Yes, I feel the same." Giving me a kiss on my lips and walking towards the bathroom, he called back: "Funny, you only think of a car as something warm and comfortable," shaking his head: "You never dream it could be a killer." Having said this, he went into to prepare for the day ahead.

Once we were both downstairs, the smell of fresh percolated coffee and the sight of the normal breakfast laid out for us made me feel sick. For Bill eating his breakfast was not a problem. I couldn't bear the sight of the cheeses, cold meats and yoghurt's, they were too much for me. Declining my husband's offer I drank a couple of cups of coffee and sat filled with envy watching Bill demolishing his food. "You should eat," he said with a mouth of fresh roll: "We have no idea what is going on today." Then looking at his watch: "We should have someone from the family here for us." As there was nothing to say, I sat silent.

Looking out of the dining room that was set aside for hotel guests, I tried not to go back remembering the first time I had sat here and all that had occurred in between. Suddenly, my heart leapt as looking out of the window as I had done on an occasion so many years ago, when waiting for Dieter to come and take us to his house. A tall dark-haired young man was crossing the street, in the direction of the Hubertus, but this time there was no smile on his face, only a look of intense worry. It was Markus, come to take us to his home and then onto the hospital.

On entering the breakfast room, Markus hugged both Bill and myself, telling us that his grandparents were with them at the house today. I knew these were Dieter's parents, in the time that we had known the family we had never met his parents. Something I had long wanted to do but was afraid at the same time. So, it was with some trepidation that we walked alongside this handsome young man to his home and to meet members of his family as yet unknown to us.

Walking up the path the door was opened to us by a man who could have been Dieter thirty years in the future: "If he lives." That little voice came to me again. Shaking my head as if actively pushing it away.

I tried not to stare open mouthed at the gentleman facing me. He stood as tall as his son, with silver-grey hair and hazel eyes. A pleasant mouth trying to smile in welcome. Though not as broad shouldered as Dieter, there was no doubting the relationship between the two. The sorrow on his face and that of the woman who came to stand beside him subsided slightly as she linked her arms in his, while trying to force a smile of greeting to us.

She was a small woman, her grey hair dyed slightly mauve, with light blue eyes, a small nose, and a mouth that quivered in an effort to hold back the tears of worry over her only child. I remembered their names: Heinz Peter and Isolde. About to introduce ourselves I was stopped by Dieter's father, whose smile contained genuine warmth for us.

"You are Vicki and Bill. I know all about you."

In the way he made his statement, I felt he knew more than the rest of the family.

Having greeted the grandparents, I made my way over to Monique greeting her with a kiss on both cheeks and asking if we could go once more to the hospital with her and the family. I hurriedly pointed out that we would wait in line to see him. She smiled weakly at this, stating: "You are family, why would you wait." I smiled and thanked her for the complement. By now more coffee was coming up, the boys now taking great care of their tiny mother and assuming for the moment the role of adult male leaders.

With us all present the small living room appeared to have shrunk even more, all of them smoking and talking in soft tones. Heinz Peter having left his wife taking to Birgit and Monique came over to me. Standing up to speak to him, he took my arm and pulled me away from the others. Feeling he had something to say, and worried as to what it was I was totally unprepared for his next statement: "Vicki, I would like you to know that I know what you meant to my son." And want to thank you for the happiness you have given him." Then placing a fatherly kiss on my forehead, he walked back to his wife and daughter-in-law, leaving me standing dumbfounded. Whatever I had expected it was certainly not this.

I could not explain to Bill why I walked back to him with tears flowing down my cheeks.

Suddenly, I felt myself caught in an embrace that would have made many a wrestler quake. But, this one I didn't mind. It was Frau Hoffmann or Hedwig as we knew her, the manager of the restaurant at the Hubertus. She was a large grey-haired lady, with horn-rimmed glasses and a girth that would make many a man shake with fear, she resembled a school matron more than a lady who was the manager of a very busy restaurant. Like everyone in the room she too had seen all the children grow up, ours included. Had helped us with our variety of hangovers and prevented some friends from being involved in fights during one horrendous carnival night. We were all very fond of this lady. Stretching my arms round her, I felt almost as if the mother touch was there, helping, encouraging and trying to make everything better. We stood and chatted for a bit, then taking my hands in her rather rough ones, smiling she left as the restaurant would now be filling with clients.

Finally, the phone rang. All of us jumping with the shock of the loud trilling of the machine. It was Uwe who answered it. The conversation was soft and curt, a nod of the head and an O.K. Ended the call.

Turning he addressed all of us in the room, "That was the nurse Nicola, she has said some of us can visit Dieter, he has improved a little over the night." This was greeted by loud sighs from every corner. "So we will now go to the hospital."

This began an exodus, those who were friends left to go about their everyday business, and the family went to the waiting cars. As Bill and I weren't too sure where we belonged we waited till Birgit came over to us and invited us to accompany her, Maria and Uwe and travel in their car.

So, it was that a cavalcade of vehicles left the little house to travel to Cologne and see the man who was important to all of us in different ways. From husband, father, brother-in law, friend to lover he was all this and more to us.

As we drove to the hospital, I was remembering an incident when in my pique and jealousy I had almost lost my life.

It was the first weekend that Bill had gone to Germany since I had met Dieter. I was angry and frustrated, complaining to my friends that it was only because we were wives and mothers that we did not go anywhere. My friends were sick and tired of my constant self-pity, so it was decided that we should go to the club that Saturday night. With most of the men not there it was not the most exciting evening, so I decided to drink, not a good idea as this made me throw caution to the winds.

There was a five piece band playing that evening and the guitarist, a good looking young man quite my junior was obviously enamoured with me. So when he asked to dance I didn't refuse. It was obvious he was flirting so I decided to play it his way. Having been a married woman for a long time, I had forgotten just how dangerous this game could become.

Until I went out into the fields around the club house, and he followed. I felt him push me against the outside of the building, his hot nasty breath on my face: "The trouble with you older women, you need a young man." Pushing him away and falling down. Grazing myself, luckily I had trousers on so Angie and Frances, couldn't see the grazes or the blood where I cut myself. I hurried into the club, telling my friends I was feeling unwell and would take a cab home.

As I climbed into the cab, I could hear him calling me very rude names. The driver looked back at me: "Want me to deal with him?" Shaking my head in silence: "Please just take me home."

Putting on my nightclothes, I made coffee, which I took up to bed. It was only as I looked at the familiar things around me the enormity of the situation I had really been in sank in. A shaking took hold of my limbs that I found hard to stop. Turning off the lights, I sat up in bed, bringing my knees up to my chin, hugging them to me. With great difficulty I managed to finish my drink. Then lying down, in the foetal position, I closed my eyes, now with with tears from the trauma I had suffered.

Turning over in bed as if touching someone who wasn't there, I cried out: "Oh God Dieter! I need you." I then fell into a restless sleep.

Chapter 17

Sitting in the back of the people carrier, Bill whispered to me: "I suppose, a bit stupid if we took flowers?" Looking at my husband I tried not to answer him angrily: "No, the man is unconscious, flowers would not be appreciated." Looking at Bill, I felt sorry for him as well. He was now starting to look completely bewildered, feeling as if the situation he had thought he was capable of handling was now slipping out of his grasp.

Slipping my hand into his: "I'm sorry, darling. I guess this is affecting us both." Kissing me on the top of my head, he had to agree.

Making inconsequential talk so as to keep our minds away from the hospital and how he was progressing, we chatted. Talking about our daughters, friends, we even discussed politics. Everything but what was waiting for us in a few minutes time. Until my husband dropped a bombshell on me:

"You do know that Dieter has always fancied you." He said with a little smile.

"Really?" I asked "Why do you say that?" I finally managed to say while trying to appear quite normal.

"Oh, just something he said a few years ago, why?" Then turning to look at me: "Don't tell me it's that important." Shrugging I muttered something like, "It's nice for a girl to feel appreciated."

Laughing I managed to change the subject, giving my fast-beating heart time to slow down.

As we approached the gates that would lead into the hospital grounds, Bill looked at me and anxious expression on his face: "You going to be O.K.?" He asked. Nodding my head, "We did see him the other day, and they have said there's an improvement."

Looking at me Bill said: "A slight improvement." As though he was warning me not to expect too much. He the pessimist and I the optimist.

Travelling up the long curving drive with signs pointing people in a variety of directions and treatment areas, we saw the sign sending us in the direction of the Intensive Care Unit. It was obvious that a great deal of thought had been put into making this a very personal place for families and friends. Surrounding the large glass doors were terracotta pots filled with mini shrubs, flowers and young trees. But no matter how much thought and care was put into the surrounding area. Nothing could remove the pain and fear that the visitors felt. The heaviness that hung between the whole group was proof of that.

Entering through the electronic door, Uwe ushered us along the corridor we had followed on our previous visit the familiar smell of antiseptic everywhere.

It was obvious that the medical team recognised all of us as smiles were cast in our direction, not the smiles you give to a stranger but a friend.

Further along the corridor I could see the tall, thin man we had seen on our first visit. His thick white hair and slightly stooped shoulders, wearing a white coat his stethoscope dangling from his top pocket.

I was frightened when he signalled to Uwe to go and talk to him. Looking at the expression on the families faces I could see that they too were as worried as I was. Eventually, Uwe nodded his head, to our relief he smiled and came back to join us.

Talking to us he went on to tell us that the Herr Doctor Gruber, had informed him though Dieter was in a medically induced coma, he would still be aware of everything that was going on around him. So, we the family should talk to him about everyday affairs. Though we were not allowed to spend too much time with him, each moment was precious to us all.

Monique, went in first, followed closely by both their sons, then his father and mother, Uwe and Birgit, Bill and lastly myself.

Going into the room having seen him the day previous, I was now prepared to see the pale face, the variety of tubes connected to him but it was the one attached to his throat that frightened me the most. Sitting down beside the bed, and taking his listless hand in mine, fighting back the tears that threatened to overtake I started to talk, remembering the smile on Uwe's face when he had said: "You know what to talk about, things that make him happy." Knowing that he had been aware of the situation between Dieter and myself over numerous years, his grin did not worry me in the least.

Pulling up one of the comfortable easy chairs, I sat down, holding his right hand in mine, whispering: "Dieter, Dieter it's me, its Vicki." For a while there was no movement. Then I tried again: "Darling, it's me Vicki. Dieter please let me know you are aware of me." Again I waited for some recognition. Then, after what seemed like hours but can have only been minutes, I was sure that his fingers trembled faintly in mine. This gave me all the encouragement I needed: "He knows I am here," I whispered, giving me the courage to carry on. Once again that was yet another secret between the two of us.

Too soon my time was up and walking out of the room, I turned to have one last look at Dieter, the ventilator breathing for him, because most of his injuries had been on the chest he was not allowed to breath for himself. How I hated that machine but yet how important it was. Walking out of the room and letting the door close quietly behind me, I joined the others.

"What did you talk about?" Bill asked

"Oh, this and that. I mentioned Angie and Frances."

"Typical female talk, well that wouldn't have worn him out." So we joined the others heading back to the vehicles waiting for us.

Entering the lift that Uwe had summoned for us, we made our way down to the ground floor and out of the hospital. Because, we had been allowed to share moments with Dieter, the atmosphere between us all was a little lighter than we had arrived. I was reliably informed that the Herr Doctor Gruber, was the best Consultant that he could have had and with a smile Bill added: Even when he's ill that old bastard has a pretty young nurse to look after him."

Saying this I knew he was talking about Nicola, she was of medium height, with natural blonde hair and blue eyes filled with laughter, but behind the lightness was a deep maturity, showing the care with which this young girl would look after her charges. Her neat slim figure could not be disguised by the blue and white uniform.

Uwe, translated this to Monique, who replied with: "My man is a real man." I kept my eyes on the floor and said nothing.

Sitting in the car going back to the Hubertus, I could not believe that the vibrant man I had known in love and friendship could be lying there, tied to a bed by a variety of cables and wires as if imprisoned by a giant octopus. My pain was so strong I cried silently.

Raising my eyes to Heaven, I asked one question: "Why, dear God, why him?" Of course there was no answer.

Thinking of Dieter lying in the bed, as though asleep, I remembered the only outward sign of his accident, a small scar on his eyebrow. One that would give him a quizzical look something to impress the ladies with when he was better. Yes, my lover would get better I knew it in my heart.

I asked the family if I could return the following day and spend some time with him. As we had been informed by the medical staff talking to him was good, so I was free to visit if only for a short time.

Uwe dropped me off at the hospital the following day, it was raining and seemed to echo my feeling perfectly. Making my way down the corridor I found the room that I knew was Dieter's, opening the door quietly I went in. Never having been in an intensive care ward before I was still amazed at the way this one was laid out, it was not as I had expected to be dull and sombre, filled with an oppressive atmosphere of illness and death. It was quite the reverse, the room was bright, with wide doors that opened out onto a terrace that surrounded these rooms, white lace curtains flapping at the open windows. My eyes wandered round the room, in the direction of the bed and the man lying on it

286

looking asleep. Taking in the heart monitor, a small machine mounted on a plinth half way up the wall, at an easy height for the nursing staff, to view when first entering the room. At the end of this was a plastic clip that was on Dieter's middle finger on his left hand. Then there was the morphine feed into his body keeping the pain at bay. Most important of all was the ventilator. This machine was breathing for him, as his injuries were all to the chest, it would have been impossible for him to breath alone. We had been reliably informed by a member of Professor Gruber's team, once the Herr Professor felt he could manage without it the machine would be removed.

I remembered Bill's reaction yesterday when we had seen Dieter again, never a demonstrative person, the sight of his friend in this position had really quite upset him. So, when we were leaving and I had made my request to come back the following day, Bill had said: "Well darling if I had someone like you talking to me, I'd want to be awake as well." Then in a move completely foreign to him, Bill bent his head kissing me full on the lips: "You really are wonderful, I love you." The fact that this was all done in full view of other people took me totally by surprise.

Pulling up one of the comfortable easy chairs, I sat down, holding his right hand in mine, whispering: "Dieter, Dieter it's me, Vicki." Then I tried once more: "Dieter, yesterday your fingers moved in my hand, could you try it again, please." No movement of the fingers this time but I was sure I saw some movement behind his eye lids, giving me a great deal more encouragement.

About to start talking, I heard the door open. Looking up I could see Nicola, the nurse had entered: "I thought Lieber Frau, you would like some coffee and sandwiches, while you sit with Dieter." Thankfully, I accepted. Placing a little coffee table beside me, she brought in a tray filled with the promised coffee and sandwiches. Still holding his hand, and looking at him I didn't hear her leave, as all my attention was focused on the man lying pale and wan in the bed before me.

I refused to believe that a vegetative state of mind could divide this man and our love from each other. In the fourteen years we had known each other, miles of land and water nor months of separation had never divided us. I was not about to let the unconsciousness he had been placed in come between us. Sitting quietly at first, I could hear the general sounds of the hospital going on around me. From somewhere in the grounds a male voice could be heard shouting instructions to a team of builders. Then the sound of a trolley being pushed over stone tiles. Now and then the swish of tyres on the wet road surface as a car arrived or departed. With all this activity around me, I still had an intense feeling of loneliness, he seemed so still, appearing lost. I needed to know where his mind was, wanted him back with me physically and mentally. Studying his face, I could see the pallor underneath the tan he would have picked up working in his beloved garden and swimming. "I do have something else I like to do," he said nipping the lobe of my left ear: "I like it when we make love." memory of this had me fingering my left ear, smiling. Wishing he knew what I was thinking.

"Dieter, you must remember the good times, we had." I spoke softly, wanting to see his eyes open.

For some moments I sat in silence wondering where to begin, we had shared so many times together, all of them good except for the partings we had to endure. As I sat, my mind running round in circles, his hand held firmly in mine, scenes from the past came back, reminding me of those wonderful occasions, filled with laughter, stimulation and most of all love.

"Do you remember that Chinese dress?" I started speaking, softly, recalling one weekend when I had wandered round the house in a fever of excitement. Wanting to see him yet dreading the eventual parting. Wondering what I would wear, it was Angie who had reminded me of the Chinese dress that hung in my wardrobe. A dress in black silk with hand-embroidered flowers and slits along the side that showed a good deal of thigh.

"If he doesn't like you in that then the man is made of stone." Angie had laughed, when I had nervously suggested "Perhaps he won't like me anymore." this was a statement that often ran through my mind. Each time we met after months of separation, I would have these fears and doubts.

So it was that Friday night, after the men had their usual evening meal without the wives. I had wandered into the club, appearing on the surface, cool, calm and collected, only to turn to jelly the moment Dieter had walked towards me, holding out a hand to take mine, in his usual handshake greeting.

"Hullo, Vicki," he would say, while his eyes said a great deal more.

"Hullo, Dieter." My reply appearing as lame as his greeting had been.

Later than evening, when we had been given the chance to spend some time together, I had asked: "Do you like my dress?"

For seconds that seemed like hours a silence had hung between us. Then, turning to ensure we had no onlookers, from where leaned against the bar, Dieter stood up, running a hand down my side, finding the end of the split and very lightly fingering my thigh.

"I think I like what is in the dress far more," he had whispered. The turmoil of emotion this simple statement created in me made the hand holding my glass visibly tremble.

As the memories came flooding back my voice gaining strength. Reminding him of how he would love to tease me, enjoying the jealous rages I would fly into when any other woman came in too close to him. Looking at me out of the corner of his eye would make a comment, guaranteed to annoy and irritate. Then having gained the results he wanted, walk away laughing, pleased that I had once more risen to his bait.

"Dieter, I will never forget that Sunday morning when all the men were at Frances' house." That was certainly a time that would stay in the furthest recesses of my mind. Only brought to the forefront when I was alone.

This particular weekend the men had paid their biannual visit to England in early October, giving us great anxiety that the weather should prove bad, but as is so often the case we were blessed with an Indian summer. The days turned out to be really warm, the evenings drawing in early, were warm and mellow. This Saturday night Dieter had drunk far too much, making it impossible for Bill to awaken him. Turning to me, my husband had said: "I'll take the kids to Tom's, then onto the club, see what you can do with him," nodding impatiently in the direction of our visitor's room. "After all there won't be any game till he joins us."

It was quite some time after the family had left the house that I decided it was time to try raising our guest from his bed. Walking down the hall, I was about to open the door, when I was forestalled, as the man I had come to awaken was standing before me, naked. No matter how often I saw him like this, I could never get used to the superb specimen of manhood he was.

"I have been waiting, what takes you so long?" He was smiling

"Waiting, what for?" I asked, my voice no more than a thread of sound.

"You," was the only answer.

Nodding, I walked silently past him into the room, still dark as the curtains had not yet been drawn. I stood before him shy, wanting to be in his arms but at the same time unsure of myself.

"Come baby." he held out his arms, then looking down at himself, with a wry smile he carried on: "As you can see, I am very much in need of you." This was quite obvious, as his desire seemed to grow as I looked at it.

Pulling me ever closer to him, he began to undress me, muttering: "You women, why do you wear so much clothes."

"And how many women have you undressed?"

Laughing once more I had risen to his bait: "That's my secret."

I raged at him, wanting to hit him, feeling I should walk away. But, by now, my jeans, shirt and underwear were on the floor at my feet, making escape impossible, had I really wished it.

"You should not make us wait," he whispered, pulling me towards his brown chest.

"Us," I queried.

"Um," he smiled looking down the length of his body. Now I knew what he meant.

The time had come for us to stop talking, as passion and an overriding desire for satisfaction was fast overtaking the two of us. Placing my lips to his, we tumbled onto the bed. Our breathing grew more difficult as each one of us struggled to give the other more pleasure. I allowed my hands to wander at will across his body, fingering parts of him that brought tiny cries of delight. Then he would take over, his lips wandering across my body, taking my nipples between strong white teeth he gently nipped them. Then, following the line of my body, I could feel his lips, tongue and hands all giving me the pleasure that only a mutual understanding of the need and satisfaction could bring.

So we played love games together, until: "Vicki, I must have you, now."

By now I was beyond speech, so once more a silent nod was all he needed.

I could feel his hands parting my thighs as he slipped the length that was him into me. Instantly a torrent of emotion was flooding through me, needing the release that we would eventually give each other.

At first we moved slowly, each enjoying the feel of the other's body. Then, as the demand for satisfaction grew, our rhythm changed growing ever faster. Now not gently asking, but demanding, the other's life. So we shared our sweat as we did our love, until we could take the wait no longer with a sigh that was more a moan of pleasure we gave each other the final sensual contentment.

Saturated, from our sexual sharing of our love, we lay side by side, still breathing hard: "Vicki, why didn't we meet so many years earlier?" He posed the question I had so often asked myself.

"I don't know darling," I had replied. "Perhaps there is a reason; one day we will find out."

As I left him I could hear him singing, happily, bringing a fond smile to my lips. "That man might be able to make love, but he can't sing," I mumbled to myself.

He must have heard me laughing as he left the bathroom, for creeping up behind me he had picked me up and bodily carried me into the bathroom: "So you think Dieter's singing," he said in threatening tones. "I will have to find a way of stopping you." then turning the shower on full, he had soaked us both. Giving a smothered shout, I thrashed round under the water, until, his lips had once more silenced me.

"You can say sorry," he whispered against my lips, demanding retribution.

"How?"

"Like this," he replied, still in a whisper, removing the towel he was wearing.

Pulling my clothes off, tearing at my bra, in his hurry to get to my body, he pushed me against the cold tile of the bathroom wall. Cupping my breasts in his hands, at the same time entering me with a thrust that brought tears of pleasure and pain to my eyes, we made love. Our demands for sexual gratification were so violent, we thrashed about like caged animals, enjoying the pleasure each gave the other, until once more we looked into each other's eyes, knowing that the moment of ultimate joy was at hand. With one final stab he gave me the warm feeling that can come only from true satisfaction.

"You are truly my life, my joy, my wife." he breathed as his face fell onto my neck in complete relaxation.

"Later, he had smiled wryly and said: "How can I play football, you have drained me.""

"Oh, no my lover," I whispered: "I have given you my strength, you could win the World Cup."

This proved to be very true, for after that morning Dieter had played a football game as never before. As Uwe said later, a strange look on his face: "Dieter never played so well, even when he was a professional. I wonder what medicine did he take."

Now I sat silent, staring at the man who wandered in a world I could not share.

"Dieter, you have to come back to me. I will not allow you to leave. Those moments we shared are not lost to us, we can have so many more. Please darling come back to me."

I could feel tears threatening to spill over once more. I realised that our times together had not been a rich tapestry, woven together like other lives. Instead we had more in common with the theatre. Dieter and I shared the faces of laughter and tragedy together.

How I wanted to return to the happier days, feeling I would promise the God who ruled our world anything to let Dieter live. The only thing I could not and would not promise was to give him up. That was as impossible for me as stopping breathing, without him I had no life.

A sudden rustle at the door stopped me from going any further into recollections of the past. Dropping the hand I had held, and picked up the magazine that Nicole the nurse had placed beside me when I had first taken my seat. Looking as if I had done nothing more than sit beside the sick man.

"How is he?" Monique whispered.

Looking at the younger woman, now appearing more her usual self after her the rest prescribed by the doctor with the help of some tranquilliser tablets: "He is still asleep," I replied, standing up and stretching, allowing Monique to sit in the chair I had vacated. Seeing her take his hand in hers, placing it to her lips, I fought the jealousy that filled me.

After all she was his wife, and I merely the visitor from abroad. Giving a little smile I left the room, making my lone way down the corridor out into the fresh air. My pain now too deep for tear.

Chapter 18

Walking along the narrow corridors that had now become familiar to me, I waved cheerfully to a couple of male orderlies pushing an elderly gentleman in a wheelchair. As I passed them I could see Nicole, Dieter's nurse, following behind:

"Hi, how is he?" I greeted her.

Smiling, she replied: "I think perhaps he is better today. He blew me a kiss."

My spirits lifted at this news. If Dieter was appreciating the looks of the young girl, he was definitely on the mend.

My feet quickened in pace. I no longer needed to watch for the signs that pointed me in the direction of the Intensive Care Unit. I had spent so much time there the way had become well known to me.

For a moment I thought back to the first time I had entered this wing. How frightened I had been, not knowing what was wrong with him. The fear that had taken hold of me, as my husband and I had been taken by Uwe to the room in which he was being cared. Terrified he would be paralysed, perhaps some brain damage so many nightmare scenarios, perhaps that he would die. Now, however, all these fears had left me.

With an amazing turn for the better, Dieter had started to improve in leaps and bounds. Each day bringing new and better results. The only thing that worried me was the reservation the Herr Professor had about Dieter's return to a normal ward; something to do with the headaches he still suffered, because of the injury received on impact. But, for now, I could only presume that the learned man's fears were unfounded.

Entering the lift, I tried not to think of the urgency with which Dieter would have first been placed in here, so that he could be transported to the theatre, where his blood-spattered body would have undergone the miracles of modern surgery, then transferred to the room that I had grown used to visiting. Thanking God that all those horrible times were now passed.

As we felt Dieter to be now out of danger, it had been agreed that we would take it in turns to stay with him, today I was happy, it was my turn.

Pushing the glass door open, I stopped, taking in the pleasant scene before me. The windows were open to the warm, summer sunshine and the breeze that gently moved the net curtains. Glancing round the room I could see the ventilator had now been completely removed, as was the machine that had pumped the drugs into him. I could see the heart monitor was still very much in evidence, but this, I had been informed, was only a precaution.

Looking at the bed and its occupant, I was delighted to see he was now sitting up. He must have heard my footsteps, for he was facing the door as I breezed in. Had I ever doubted his feelings for me, the smile that lit his face was answer enough to tell me how mistaken I had been.

As his throat was still very sore from the tubes that had been inserted while he was attached to the lifesaving machine, I didn't expect any actual conversation from him. We had other ways of talking.

"Can I kiss you, or does the Doctor think it's not a good idea." I grinned as he very carefully shook his head, obviously upset at the idea I thought he might be denied a lover's embrace. By the pallor of his face I could see that the head wound still gave him a great deal of pain.

He stretched his hand out for the pad and pen kept by the bed, talking without placing a strain on his throat.

"If you do not kiss me, then perhaps the medical team will have a problem."

His handwriting was proof of the pain and trauma he had experienced. It was not the vibrant, strong, flowing writing of the man before the accident. His writing was almost spidery, in its appearance. With a smile I bent my head, allowing our lips to meet momentarily.

"Not too much, darling not good for you," I laughed lightly, as he strained to prolong our union.

Pulling away from him and bringing the chair up to his bed, I could see he was writing madly again.

"Come join me in bed," I read.

"Now he offers bed. Can't do a thing and wants to make love. Like all men making promises they can't keep." Still smiling I carried on: "Do you want me to take these bits of paper home, to show Monique." At the very idea of this, he made a cutting movement with his hand across his neck. Indicating that he would be a very dead man indeed, if these incriminating pieces of paper were ever discovered. Instead I tore the precious pieces of paper from the pad and placed them carefully in my handbag. Not to be thrown away; instead I would look at them at my leisure, remembering each letter and word lovingly.

"So, what shall we talk about," I asked. "Sorry correction, what shall I talk about and you listen to." this time he did make a soft sound with his mouth, almost as if what he had to say could not be written but had to be voiced.

"I love you," I heard.

With difficulty I managed to play down the effect of these words.

"Don't talk so much, it's bad for you."

However, the smile on my face managed to sweeten the rebuke, making it a gentle caress more than a reprimand.

I turned to look out of the window, afraid to show him how much he touched my heart with his simple soft words, spoken in that harsh, rasping voice instead of the husky tones I had grown used to. Having once more gathered myself together I looked into that dear face, smiling at me from the bed:

"I love you too, very very much."

Then growing afraid that our emotions, if allowed to get out of hand, might have an adverse effect on him, I started to talk, not about anything in particular, just anything that came to mind, until I saw him raise his hand, effectively silencing me.

"Ssh, you make my head ache."

"Oh, darling I am so sorry."

Quickly I was all contrition, kneeling beside the bed.

"I suppose it's the power I've got." I could see a puzzled look on his face. Smiling, I explained further: "I can do all the talking, you can only stop but not interrupt."

Only the jerky movement of his body told me he was laughing, as there was still no real sound coming from him. Grabbing the paper from the bedside cabinet, he quickly scribbled: "My love, you always talked too much, even in bed."

"I should teach you a lesson, and leave this for your wife. How would you explain to her that you know I talk in bed."

For seconds he appeared to contemplate my last remark, then wrote once more: "It is true, I would have a problem. But, my wife thinks I am wonderful, so she would believe what I say. Come leibchen, sit and talk to me of good things. I dreamt last night it was Carnival and we were together.

I accepted the invitation to sit beside him, not on the bed as he had suggested, but on the chair I was fast becoming used to: "I remember that Carnival, when I first arrived and you were so horrible to me." I tried to keep the petulance out of my voice, still remembering the hurt I had felt when he appeared to ignore me for hours after our arrival.

"I was not doing it to hurt you, but protect us. I could feel my love growing stronger, and was not sure what we could do if it grew too big for us," he wrote.

Nodding, I gathered up the stray pieces of paper, placing them in the little secret pocket, of my handbag. with a smile I began to recall that weekend, one that started off so badly, but ended like a dream.

Bill and I had often visited Cologne for the ultimate festival in their calendar, both liturgical and Bacchanalian. We normally went with our four friends, Angie and Tom, Frances and Mark, this time however, we were also accompanied by Connie and David Bright, a middle-aged couple who had their own business. As

Connie had said: "David needs a break, what's better than lot of alcohol and dancing."

That was a weekend I would never forget. Though this event normally lasted for six days, after years of suffering we had decided that Bill and I could only handle the last four days, something our friends had also agreed to.

As usual I had started our journey in complete and secret happiness, because Dieter would be there. The few hours spent in his company were special to me, as I had come to be grateful for any time we spent together.

This time however, things were different. From the moment we met at Cologne station, his coldness towards me was more chilling than the ice and snow holding Germany in its vice like grip.

The unfriendly channel having been safely negotiated, we joined our train at Ostend. Normally this trip was made in our cars, but having been informed to expect heavy snowfalls we had decided this year that we would travel by train. This meant reservations being made on the long trains that wound their way across Europe, filled with all kinds of holidaymakers from skiers to those looking for sunshine further south. Or those just wanting a brief respite from the cold dreary days that followed Christmas.

Arriving at Cologne station was indeed a shock for the uninitiated. As six of us had been before we knew what to expect. But it was obvious from the expressions on the faces of David and Connie, that the scenes greeting them had come as a complete ear-deafening culture shock.

The tunnel that joined the station to the road outside, and the adjoining Cathedral, was filled with revellers dressed in every conceivable costume.

From nuns and monks behaving badly, to known heads of state, including royalty both modern and ancient. Added to all this was a noise unheard of by those of us residing in quiet, almost boring, suburbia. Musical instruments could be heard, being played in far from melodious tones. Trumpets joined in noisy argument with drums; the off key sounds of a piano accordion harmonised with an empty tin bucket that was being struck with a spoon by an equally tuneless youth, seemingly lost in a world of his own.

"If that stupid idiot doesn't stop," muttered Joe, holding tight to a patience that appeared to be disintegrating with each passing moment, "I'll break that bloody spoon over his head, then bury him in the bucket."

Hearing what he said, I smiled vacantly, because for now my attention was focused only on one this, searching for Dieter.

The eight of us stood outside the station in the lee of the Dome Cathedral. The noise around us only slightly muffled by the driving snow. Even the bunting and coloured lights appeared in disarray, swinging in the wind that blew around old and modern buildings. Everywhere was the hustle and bustle of people.

"I suppose Dieter is expecting us," Connie asked, shivering as she huddled deeper into her bright pink ski jacket.

I nodded, for the first time feeling anxious: "He should have been here by now."

So we stood, uncertain what to do, waiting in anticipation of our expected lift.

"If you've given him the wrong day and time......" Here Bill's voice tailed away. I didn't need him to finish the last sentence. We both knew my biggest fault was remembering dates and times.

Being unable to forget the conversation I had last had with Dieter, I smiled: "As if I would."

Then hearing a sound on the ice-laden breeze, I said: "Look there he is now."

"Where?" Bill demanded, peering in the darkness surrounding us.

"Over there by the old bar," I replied insistently.

Once more I heard: "Vicki, Bill, we are here."

"Look, by the taxi rank, Dieter is there," emphasising my point with the use of my finger.

The sudden excitement that had taken hold of me, constricted my breathing, making speech almost impossible.

"I don't know what you are seeing, girl, but I can't see him," my husband replied.

"Shrugging: "I heard his voice, that's all I know."

Then David took up the cry of: "Yes, I see him, standing with two other guys." Then turning to look at me a quizzical look on his face: "How did you hear him, they're standing so far away and there is so much noise." Shaking his head: "I don't understand, you must have the most amazing hearing."

Following the pointing finger of our friend, we could see standing some way away from us three men beside a minibus.

"Bloody hell!" Turning to look first at me then at our friends: "You know it's not really so amazing, I think if that man called her from the grave she'd hear him," shaking his head Bill continued: "If I didn't know better I would have said that my wife and friend were having an affair."

Shrugging, he ducked his head into the glacial wind that blew around us.

I never could explain the shiver that ran up my spine, was it the cold? Or the possibility of my husband's suspicion. I refused to admit it might have been the words "hear his voice from the grave." That caused my momentary discomfort.

Realising they had successfully caught our attention, all three raced, heads bent fighting the driving wind and snow, towards us. The weather being as it was, this was no time or place for introductions, these could wait till later. Instead we were ushered into the warm, waiting vehicle. Once having seen us safely settled in, our driver, a little man whose cross eyes and bandy legs gave him the appearance of a gnome, was introduced to us as Micha, a gentleman who ran his own taxi company.

All the time my husband and friends chatted, I tried to catch Dieter's eye. A contact he appeared to avoid, adroitly. Sensing something was wrong, for the rest of the journey into Kirschweiler, I sat quietly. Staring out of the window, my eyes misted with frustrated tears, not knowing what I had done, but terrified I had in some unknowing way upset my lover. I refused to accept he might no longer care for me: "After all we only spoke to each other a few weeks ago, and he was full of endearments then." I thought quietly.

"Anybody in?" I felt a finger tapping my forehead.

Turning, I could see Bill trying to attract my attention.

"What do you want?" I was annoyed by his patronising tones.

"Gloria's been talking to you for ages, why don't you answer?" He replied.

Turning to my friend: "I'm sorry, I must have been dreaming. What did you want?"

Once again I did not hear what she said, my attention focused on the dark head in the long front seat.

No sooner had we arrived at the Hubertus, the place that was to be home and centre of entertainment for the next few days, than we were being greeted by friends who, unlike Dieter, were happy to see not only our friends but me as well. They too, like those we had seen in the city centre, were dressed in costume. Their dress went from world famous football heroes to clowns wearing ridiculous red wigs and even more incongruous make up.

I was sure, no matter how often I came for Carnival, the sights and sounds that surrounded us would never dull. An air of excitement and expectation seemed to hold everyone in its grip. From the very old to the very young, no one remained untouched.

Stepping from the icy cold into the claustrophobic heat of the bar, still more greetings were thrown in our direction: "It's like coming home," Bill said smiling, obviously pleased to know we had as many friends here as in England.

Taking the beer placed in my hand by Louise, my eyes having now become accustomed to the cigarette haze fogging the air around us. I was able to study the decorations that had been placed on walls and ceilings. Unlike England, any excuse was good enough for decorating and brightening up houses, bars and restaurants. Carnival was just such a reason.

The normally conservative-looking bar had been transformed. The ceiling festooned with balloons and coloured chains, most of them in the red and white of F.C. Cologne. On the walls could be seen cartoons, many quite sexually suggestive. One or two positively obscene. I was not called on to translate the text of these, as the pictures were explicit enough. With all the revellers in costume, it was easy to pick out the foreigners ---- us.

Even though I had been intent on studying my surroundings, it was impossible to ignore the sudden emptiness that filled me. I knew with the same certainty that Dieter had been in Cologne to meet us, that this time he had left us. Without turning my head, I asked of no one in particular: "Where is he?"

"Where's who, dear?" Gloria answered, turning to face me. Her pale blue eyes glinted under the mop of blonde hair that had lost none of its colour with advancing years.

"Dieter," I replied. The noise around us covering the trembling tones of my voice.

"Oh, him" He's gone get get his wife."

One sentence and all hopes of a fond meeting disintegrated around me. I could almost physically feel the blow. He was telling me, in as tactful way as possible, we were about to part as lovers. No words were necessary. His coldness and detachment towards me had already made this intention obvious. Now he had gone to bring his wife, Monique. Tonight would be the first time that I had arrived in this village when he had not found a way of kissing me passionately in greeting, or casting a glance in my direction so filled with love that words were unnecessary.

Due to the lateness of our arrival, we had decided not to change for the evening. This was something I was prepared to accept until… Dieter returned accompanied by his pretty wife. Tonight she looked breathtaking in a black catsuit with tail attached. A tiny cap on her head bore the ears and little whiskers attached to her nose finished off the ensemble. With her blonde hair shining under the cap and white teeth gleaming in a happy smile of welcome, she gave the appearance of a very self-satisfied kitten. Except, in this instance, it was I who had the claws and would have loved to "smack the smug expression off her face."

"Vicki, what is wrong with you?"

Turning I looked blankly at Gloria: "What?" I asked, puzzled.

"Well, all I heard was you wanting to smack somebody." Turning to her husband: "Honestly, I never knew this girl could be so violent." smiling fondly in my direction, she tucked a hand through my arm: "I hope it wasn't me, dear."

Smiling, I kissed her cheek at the same time shaking my head.

"That's a relief." Then, turning once more to her husband: "Look there's Doris and Fredreich." Having drawn David's attention to their personal friends, the couple headed in the direction of the other two now waving frantically in their direction.

With the departure of my friends, I found myself standing alone. My husband and other companions having found others to talk to.

Everywhere I looked were happy, smiling faces, painted and decorated to match their costumes. Why then did I feel so lonely.

"Vicki!"

Hearing my name called, I turned and found myself held in the clutch of a bear-like grip. With some difficulty I extracted myself from Freidrich and his tight hold on me. Standing back in an effort to study him all the better, I was amazed at the costume that he and his tiny wife wore.

Freidrich, a rather short, fat man had decided, mistakenly to dress as a Spanish Don. From white frilled shirt and black bolero to wide-bottomed trousers, all edged with a red braid. A sombrero had been placed on his balding head, throwing the few wisps of hair that he had over his eyes, giving the impression of a rather strange looking Mexican mouse.

"How the hell did he get enough material to put that round his waist." Angie muttered, studying the bright red satin cummerbund.

Laughing I pushed her away, not telling our friend that it was he we laughed at.

"And I thought David was fat."

Gloria was obviously pleased that there were some men larger than her husband.

Her husband having greeted me, now it was Doris' turn. Like Freidrich she too was small and fat and decided to complement her husband and dress as a Spanish Lady. Both costumes were a fashion disaster.

Her frilled dress was in black and red, with the Cuban heeled shoes that were favoured by the ladies of Spain, on her head a black lace Mantilla, fastened with a beautiful diamante comb. The moment they joined our company the conversation became fast and furious as did the drinks, our little clique now being complete.

Leaving the others to talk, I allowed my attention to wander. They had no need of me, any translation that was necessary could be carried out by Dieter and Freidrich who had recently joined us, so I was free to think my own thoughts.

"Now what are you sulking about?" Bill's voice reached me through the mists of gloom surrounding me.

"I'm not sulking." My reply was defensive.

"If you think I'm wasting money on a holiday, and have you behave like this." Bill's tones were threatening.

Knowing he was quite capable of curtailing the holiday, I turned forcing a smile: "Honestly, love," putting an arm round his neck and placing a kiss on his cheek, "I wasn't sulking." Just amazed at the variety of costumes surrounding us. Remember, that fancy dress party we had at the club, only six people turned up and I was one of them.

By the laugh he gave, I knew he had not forgotten that night and the fiasco it turned into. Heaving a sigh, I was thankful that I had successfully taken his mind off my attitude and sent him off onto a different course. Still laughing he turned from me to Mark, drawing his attention to a rather Chaplinesque like character, but one who could so easily have resembled someone else from the late Thirties: "Remind you of anyone?" He asked surreptitiously raising his right arm a fraction in salute.

Though all around me was laughter and music, I felt divorced from the proceedings. The lavish display of colour from clowns to Greek Queens, every facet of costume and fashion seemed to be in this small bar. Yet all I wanted was a pair of strong arms round me, green eyes looking into mine and warm, full lips covering my own. Instead as our eyes did finally meet for a second, mine pleading, his remained cold and distant. Turning his back almost the instant our looks clashed, so that all he presented to me were the mocking designs of the clown printed on the outsize nightshirt he wore.

"So have you a costume for us," Birgit asked, drawing my attention away from her brother-in-law to Uwe and herself.

"No not really."

"Oh, no costume?" she asked, sounding surprised.

"No, actually this time I brought only a mask."

Puzzled: "A mask, is it special?"

"You could say that," I replied, pleased that I had everyone's attention, including Dieter:

"My face."

I could see by the expression on their faces, that my last remark was too deep for all except one of them:

"Why should your face be a mask?" Dieter asked.

"Simple, only I know what goes on behind it."

He had got my message, but had no intention of going any further with the conversation. The rest of the evening passed in an alcohol infused blur for me, I was grateful when all the company admitted to being tired and we went up to bed.

"Why do we always miss ladies night?" I could hear Angie' aggrieved tone as I entered as I entered the Breakfast room next morning.

"Because Vicki hates to see me struggling, fighting against all those beautiful women who want me." Said Bill, laughing.

I nodded smiling relieved to see that he had lost all of the previous night's anger with me.

Looking round at my companions, it was obvious they had enjoyed a good evening. The signs of over-indulgence were there for all to see. The breakfast laid before us was only picked at, while plenty of hot coffee was consumed.

Having caught a glimpse of my reflection in the mirror above the table, I was grateful for their dishevelled states.

Looking out of the window, the fast falling snow had dissuaded us from going for a brisk walk: "In order to blow the cobwebs away." As David had put it: "Blow them away, more likely to freeze them ff." Joe laughed simulating a shiver.

"We must be bloody mad." David grumbled good naturedly: "Coming to a country colder than England, for a few beers and a walk in the snow to see people more stupid than ourselves, all dressed up as idiots,"

"I only hope my feet don't freeze." Connie interrupted her husband's flow.

"Why, got chilblains?" Angie laughed as a crust still on the table aimed in her direction, missed giving Mark a glancing blow across the cheek.

"Hey, hang on a minute, I'm innocent." He protested, rubbing the injured area.

After this, conversation grew desultory as we were all still tired from the previous evening. I was grateful for these silences, as it gave me time to consider the situation I had suddenly found myself in. As I sat, studying snowflakes that landed on the window pane, melting almost immediately on contact with the warm glass. Then racing with all the other droplets coming to rest on the sill in little pools.

I couldn't help thinking how these frozen drops resembled my own life. For so many years I had been a separate entity, then marriage and motherhood made me a part of a family group. My meeting with Dieter, his effect on me consequently dividing me, if only mentally and spiritually from my family. Once more placing me on my own, left with only one thought: "He had now decided to return to his wife, leaving me on the outside. Lying in a pool of self-pity, depression and anger."

"Dieter was a bit silent last night, any idea what was wrong, Vicki?"

Turning to Frances, irritation filling my voice: "How the hell would I know what's wrong? I'm not his bloody wife."

"I'm sorry." She replied, taking a step back and obviously shocked by the venom in my voice. "I just thought, being his friend you would know if anything was worrying him, that's all."

"Why don't you ask Bill, he's more his friend than I am. Added to which had you taken the time to see, you might have noticed we didn't do much talking last night. So, if you are really interested, I suggest ask him personally."

Having had my say, I turned focusing my attention on the pot plants that decorated the window sill.

"Don't mind Vicki, she's always like this when she gets tired." Bill replied defending my ill temper.

This only annoyed me further, as I hated being patronised and that was how I felt Bill was treating me.

"Vicki, now is your chance to see what was wrong with Dieter, I can see him crossing the road."

Slowly, deliberately, I raised my head, following her pointing finger. With great difficulty I kept the expression on my face blank, while my heart did somersaults at the picture he made.

The icy winds seemed to have little effect on him, as his blue ski jacket flapped open. His black hair blowing gently as the wind made little forays into it. Only the slight redness of this cheeks gave any indication of the cold. Under his jacket I could see a thick, cream jumper that fell loosely over the brown corduroy trousers and black boots he wore.

"If ever a man was born to break hearts," I thought, "that one certainly was."

By now he was aware that we had seen him. With a light-hearted wave he indicated we should open the door reserved only for the use of hotel guests.

"So ladies and gentlemen are you ready?" He laughed, shaking the snow from his boots and rubbing bare hands together.

I allowed the others to surge forward, holding back. Afraid to see the coldness I knew would be present in his eyes when looking at me.

"Why? What have I done?" I cried inwardly, as I watched him greet the other three women in the group with fond kisses, and warm handshakes for the men. It seemed his reserve was only for me.

"I'll teach you." I fumed silently, hurting in a way I would not have believed possible: "All those months and years I believed you loved me. God, what a stupid immature fool I was. Well, I'm only made a fool of once. Never again." A promise to myself I had every intention of keeping.

Seeing that our coats and boots were in place, we were ushered out into the bitter cold.

"Where are we going?" David asked.

"I am sorry my friend, I forgot you have not been before. Did Bill not explain?" He asked.

At David and Gloria's silent shake of their heads, his smile grew bigger: "Then you have a nice surprise. You do like beer don't you?" This time they nodded vigorously in agreement. "Then wait and see, you will enjoy it."

Having whetted the appetites of our friends, he walked out of the door without a glance in my direction. His rejection of me now complete and making me feel quite sick. All enjoyment in the forthcoming days, slowly slipping away. Leaving a taste of bitterness both

313

on my tongue and in my heart. But I was not going to show my pain either to him or those around me.

We hadn't walked very far from the Hubertus, before the promise that Dieter had made to David came to fruition. For there, outside a small Italian ice cream parlour, stood a group of people, dressed in a variety of costumes, giving the impression that they might have escaped from the French Revolution.

Even the children were dressed in similar costume, hearing a shout go up I saw Christoph and Markus running in my direction, throwing their arms round me with hugs and kisses they were obviously delighted to see me. The boys were now teenagers and growing tall, I had to stand on tiptoe to kiss Christoph, his brother was still not too tall for a little hug. As I greeted the boys for a second I saw their father look at me, then quickly avert his eyes.

All the children were dressed in the drab colours of late eighteenth century France, from long dresses for the girls to the boys wearing trousers, loose shirts and caps over it all they wore ski jackets.

Monique was of coursed dressed as a lady of high fashion in the early twentieth century. Looking very slim and graceful, in a coat of heavy black velvet, under which could be seen a long hobble skirt in red and green brocade. A jumper of the same colours lying loosely over the waist band. High button boots, her hat in black velvet with a deep crown and wide brim had a feather tucked into a ribbon swathed round the crown, the picture she made, making me feel more like a mule to her graceful racehorse.

"Married to her, honestly how could he love you?" I thought.

"Stop staring," Angie whispered, coming up behind me.

"Who's staring?" I answered.

"You. And the green in your eyes is showing," she continued.

"My eyes are brow..." My sentence was never finished, as realisation dawned. If Angie could see the jealousy I was feeling, then care should be taken that no one else see it.

"Come on girls, let's join them." I forced a laugh, dragging my companions into line so that we might walk along with the others.

"What do we look like," Gloria giggled.

"You can tell we are the English," Frances replied.

Grudgingly I had to admit, compared with the finery of our German companions we eight certainly looked out of place. In our track suits and ski jackets we had not dressed to be seen, only to see. We could not compare with the clowns, Arabian soldiers and Prussian Princes, along with the children and their costumes all designed to complement their parents.

We made a most interesting procession, walking behind Uwe, Theo and Birgit. It was they who had the most important job of the day. The two men pulled a flat wooden trolley on which was placed a large barrel of beer. Birgit's task was to keep all the adults served with beer and schnaps, the children with orange juice and of course the inevitable sausage. This was served with pieces of bread and lashings of mustard.

"I don't believe this. I've travelled three hundred miles just to walk behind a barrel of beer." Gloria muttered, then turning to her husband: "What would you rather have, dear. Me or this Beer."

315

Stopping, he turned staring first at his wife then at the rest of us. Rubbing his balding head, then rubbing his stomach: "Aah, now that's how good marriages end. When the wife wants her man to put her before his beer." Laughing he ducked the hastily assembled snowballs that we threw at him.

The chill wind blowing across farms covered in a blanket of snow did nothing to dampen the spirits of those around me. Conversation was general, as we walked in groups, now and then calling to each other. The children ran ahead, picking up handfuls of snow and rolling in the deep drifts lying at the roadside, unmindful of their carnival finery.

Because of Dieter's attitude towards me, my heart had now turned to ice. So the drop in temperature around me only added to the cold within.

I watched dispassionately as Dieter walked beside Birgit's, dispensing food and drink. Now and then I would hear his laugh, a sound that made me want to walk up, grab him by the arm and beg: "What have I done, please tell me." But it was a question that I would have to remain forever silent.

The raw breeze that had accompanied us on our walk, appeared to pick up speed as we neared the village, that was our destination. It blew across the white fields with a ferocity that could have come from the Arctic. Looking up at the heavy, snow-filled, grey skies I tried desperately to join in with the fun, but found it almost impossible,

Perhaps it was my imagination, but for an instant on that long, cold walk I felt a gentle breeze touch the back of my neck, reminding me of a beautiful, summer morning, when happiness and passion was the only emotion I felt.

A whispered: "When the breeze touches you, here." I could feel Dieter's long fingers playing with the hair that grew at the nape of my neck, "it is a loving kiss from me."

Maybe something of that memory also touched him, for as I turned to look at Dieter out of the corner of my eye I could see an expression, one almost of pain cross his face, but seeing me watching him it was soon veiled, once more leaving me on the outside.

By the lights and noise from the huddle of houses appearing out of the cold, grey, afternoon mists, we were relieved to find the end of our walk in sight. As with Kirschweiler we could see Nachtweiler had also set itself up in festive mood. As the Carnival Procession was to take place in this village, her decorations were far more celebratory. Coloured ribbons, balloons and Chinese lanterns hung from every lamp post, shop-front and door. Music blared from houses where their occupants uncaring of the cold, left their windows open in this way sharing their happiness with all who walked past. Sounds of laughter and chatter could be heard from every corner. Expectancy filling everyone around.

We made our way along streets where the snow had been neatly swept aside, so making it easier to stand in safety and for the floats to progress on their way unhampered, we were led on this walk by Dieter and his friend Micha, looking more like a gnome than ever, dressed in a green, suede coat, with maroon tight trousers accentuating the bow shape of his legs. A spotted kerchief was tied round his scrawny neck. On his ruddy complexioned face I could see that red lipstick had been used to paint designs. These did nothing to enhance his looks, just making his long, thin nose appear more beak like than ever.

"Do you think these two plan on stopping, or are we walking to Berlin?" David came hurrying up to me rubbing his hands in an effort to keep warm.

"We'll stop," I replied smiling, "when we reach the destination where arrangements have been made for us." I looked away, not wanting my friend to see that I was laughing at the expression on his face.

"What arrangements? A deep freeze store?"

"No, David."

My heart raced as Dieter's voice came from behind the two of us: "I think it is cold enough without making you anymore uncomfortable," then laughing he led us to a large, square house, standing in its own grounds. Between the garage and outside wall a large candy-striped awning had been set up, under which was a large oil tin, that had been filled with coals and lit, offering us, the travellers, a very warm welcome warmth.

"Here you will be more comfortable," he said, placing a plastic cup of steaming Gluhwein in David's cold, trembling fingers.

"Dieter, it is good to see you." A man came rushing out of the house, welcoming us. He was dressed as a scarecrow, very much a part of the afternoon's fun. He then explained to us that all the facilities we needed were on the ground floor, and we were free to make use of them as and when we needed or wished.

"Does this mean the loo?" Gloria asked.

At my nod, she took off, followed by Angie and Frances like greyhounds from the stalls.

"So, are you more comfortable?" Dieter greeted my friends as they rejoined me where I stood near a glass front door, with wrought-iron acanthus leaves. Knowing the question was not directed at me, I left the answering of it to my friends. So it was Angie who took up the challenge: "Yes, thank you. Much more comfortable." She laughed, rubbing her cheek where he had bent his head and placed a warm kiss. As he turned away from her, our eyes met once more. I trying to hide the hurt in mine, while his remained impersonal.

Having reached our port of call, we waited in anticipation for the entertainment that was soon to begin. Now and then friends came to greet us. People from the club, that Bill and I had met in the years we had stayed in the Hubertus. Some who no longer lived in the village recognised us and came to talk, discussing the good times we had shared in the past.

"You know as many people in my city as I do." For the first time Dieter had come and spoken to me directly. I was so shocked that I found it difficult to answer. Only as he turned and walked away was I able to speak but by then it was too late, he was already engrossed in conversation with our host.

"Hey, I like Germany," David laughed, beer in hand, his stomach, under his suede coat, appearing to have grown in size since arriving in Kirschweiler.

"You would, drunken bum," Gloria replied fondly to her husband. "I thought you were going to hate standing out in the cold, being forced to drink ice cold beer."

"Well, you know what it's like," he replied, walking up to his wife, placing an arm round her waist and holding her close. "We have to hold out the hand of friendship."

"Yeah," Bill interjected, "and if that hand holds out a beer, then it's a good friendship."

The raucous sound of police sirens, followed by band music heralded the start of the procession we had come to see. Enthusiastically we prepared to watch the spectacle on which many people had worked for months to give us entertainment on this cold afternoon.

I watched with amusement and aching heart as the first floats came into sight. This was a band of housewives, advertising a new brand of cleaner. All dressed as pixies and gnomes, many of them were far from light and fairy-like in shape, making some of the sights that greeted us quite extraordinary.

"Bloody hell, how did that get into tights," Bill muttered as a most enormous pair of thighs marched past.

"We invented stretch material." Theo laughed.

I never ceased to be astonished by the imagination and thought that went into the floats that came past. All sponsored by shops, offices and businesses, they advertised their goods and amused all at the same time. There were farm vehicles decorated with flowers, lorries made to look like Roman chariots and marching groups of people dressed in a variety of costumes denoting their club membership, throwing sweets and little gifts, the crowds rushing to pick up what they could, filling bags they had brought specially for the occasion. Often a friendly tussle would take place on the street, as two or more people went for the same article, giving rise to a rather breathless comment from Mark: "I'm bloody glad the staff in my firm can't see me putting the boot into a nine-year old for some sticky sweets." He laughed brushing the hair from his face.

For the first time that weekend I laughed, at my friend the business man looking so embarrassed.

"That's not so bad, my friend," I heard Dieter's husky tones: "It is good to enjoy and be a child again, if only for a little while."

"Some people never grow up," I replied bitterly: "They take toys, play with them, then walk away leaving them broken."

"Oh!" Now I had his full attention.

"Because like all infants they have no idea what it is they really want." Looking me in the face, a smile spreading round his lips: "There is a difference between children and adults. Children don't know what's bad for them, adults do." With this he turned his back and walked away, leaving me feeling more alone than ever.

As tears filled my eyes, I slowly stepped back allowing others around to enjoy themselves. For me, what little light had shone was now extinguished forever. I stood watching my friends, emptiness the only emotion filling me.

The sudden clattering of horses' hooves indicated the parade was coming to an end. The beauty of these animals held my attention, and brought my mind back from the limbo world of the last few minutes.

There were seven animals in all. The leader a beautiful black stallion, his saddle, bridle and feathered plume bright red, a startling contrast to his dark demonic shade. His rider though dressed in the same colours, a pale shadow of the magnificent animal he rode.

The six horses that accompanied the stallion were beautiful snow white, thoroughbred mares. Their riders were ladies, all sitting saddle, one leg thrown gracefully over the pommel. They too were liveried in red and black, a picture of grace and elegance as the symmetry of horse and rider formed a perfect outline. We stood in open-mouthed and silent admiration as they walked gracefully past. Nothing could spoil the perfection of the impact made on us, until the soldierly gentleman on the lead horse, obviously having imbibed too much of the schnapps from the bottle he held in his right hand, turned in the direction of the crowds to give a wave. In his present condition this proved to be a bad idea, for with a very slow, gentle movement he lost control of his animal. Slipping off the saddle, he moved round the horse's side, rolled under the great animal's stomach, then slipped unconscious onto the road. The horse, as if trained for just such an eventuality, stepped carefully over his master, joined by the ladies and their mounts. The women looked as if they had to fight hard to stop from bursting into laughter, at the picture of the man now lying insensible on the tarmac, surrounded by litter and manure.

"It's all very well looking good," Bill laughed at the spectacle: "But that guy should learn to ride first."

"He can ride." Dieter's indignant tones reached us: "He is the Riding Master and an Olympic Champion."

We turned to stare in open-mouthed astonishment.

"Remind me never to let a German Olympic Champion teach my children to ride." Frances laughed.

Dieter's answering comments were incomprehensible, as he walked away leaving us laughing.

The parade having ended, we made our return in fitful silence. The children tired, clutching onto the bags that had been filled to bursting with sweets, chocolates and the little gifts that had come our way, and the barrel being transported back to Kirschweiler, empty.

Feeling the need to warm myself I stood in the shower allowing the water to course over me. Hoping the heat striking me like hot pokers would bring life back, not only to my cold body but also to my bruised and hurting spirit. For so many years I had lived with the

322

knowledge of our secret love, that now it had been taken away I was finding the realisation of complete loneliness very hard to bear.

"Will you hurry up," Bill's impatient tones echoed round the shower cubicle in our room: "I've arranged to meet the men in the bar," he called insistently.

"As if you haven't drunk enough," I mumbled, towelling myself vigorously, ensuring he did not hear my complaint.

Later that evening, having showered and dressed I joined my companions at the table by the window reserved for us.

"Have you heard David's got a costume?" Frances and Angie were laughing at the whispered information Gloria had passed on.

"No." I joined in with their laughter. Turning to the bar at which our men now stood, looking a great deal smarter than they had earlier. "Is this true David? What are you going to startle us with?" I questioned.

"You may well ask young lady," his reply came back, filled with righteous indignation: "But, I'll surprise you."

With the arrival of the meal, the men joined us at the table. Discussing the afternoon and its events, I listened absent-mindedly to the ebb and flow of discussion around me, having nothing to add, aware of only one thing. Though warmth had been restored to my body, to all other emotions I appeared dead, neither hunger nor thirst did I feel. "If the knife slipped and cut me, I don't think I would feel any pain," I thought as I toyed with the food served before me.

"What's wrong with you now?" Bill demanded.

Gazing blankly in his direction: "Nothing, just thinking."

"Ooh, dangerous," he replied. "A thinking woman, shouldn't be allowed." Then laughed at his own bad joke

About to make a sharp retort at this typical piece of male arrogance, I was forestalled by the sudden rush of cold air as the door opened. Looking up I caught a glimpse of Dieter staring at me, catching me eye his were quickly veiled. Turning he ushered in the little group that had accompanied him.

"If he were mine, I'd make sure he was tied to me on a very short chain." Gloria whispered.

"If who were yours," I asked, feigning ignorance.

"Why Dieter of course. Don't tell me you haven't noticed, he is gorgeous. I wonder what he looks like naked?" She asked, a look of deep contemplation in her eyes.

"Why don't you ask Vicki? She would know," Frances replied.

Keeping my eyes staring at a picture on the wall in front, I tried hard not to show any reaction to my friend's unthinking stupidity.

A whispered: "Is it true then?" Came through to me, cutting across the thick cigarette smoke surrounding us.

"Is what true?" I asked

"The rumours."

"What rumours?" I was now growing ever more irritated.

"Oh, that you and Dieter," here no words were necessary, just two fingers on her right hand crossed one over the other: "You know."

My silence was now beginning to embarrass her.

"You mean have we had an affair?" I was rather pleased with the laugh I gave: "Well to be honest, I think I must have slept with most of the group. So he's nothing new to me. I thought you knew. Everyone else does."

"I knew that bitch Katie was lying." Gloria's relief was evident.

Turning, I looked at my other two friends. In all our eyes the same message written: "Katie would have to pay for this slander."

After this our concentration turned once more to the important things of life, such as drinking and dancing. I was determined that Dieter would never discover how he had hurt me, and ruined my life. I flirted with any man willing to play my game. On the rules I laid down.

As the atmosphere grew heavy with smoke, and because the music was so loud shouting was the only way to talk. My mind and I began to live in the euphoric state induced by alcohol. As morning approached, I took a few minutes' rest from the dancing I had thrown myself into with great gusto. Kicking off my shoes for an instant, giving my feet a rest, I sat watching the others around me.

"Don't you think you are acting a little silly?"

It took a few moments for his voice to cut through the alcoholic haze confusing my brain.

Looking up at Dieter, my eyes found difficulty in focusing "Um, what do you mean?" I giggled uncontrollably.

"The way you are behaving." He appeared to be angry. I couldn't understand why.

"All these men, dancing and holding you close. Even Theo was looking down your front. I don't like it."

"You, don't like it." I squeaked. "Who the hell are you to tell me what you like or don't. I am not yours, you have made that abundantly clear. I will do as I want and when. Leave me alone. I don't need you." With a break in my voice I ran towards the ladies' room, locking myself in a cubicle. For the first time that weekend I

325

allowed the tears to run free. When I had calmed down, I made up my face to present the usual laughing countenance to those around me.

On my return I was glad to see no sign of Dieter, the others appeared not to have noticed the little scene that had taken place minutes ago.

As I made my weary way to bed in the early hours of the morning, my mind was in a turmoil. I wondered what my husband and friends would say if they knew that all I really wanted was to go home. I needed the solace of my own four walls and the protection of my children. But it would be impossible for me to request we cut short our holiday by two days. Too many questions would be asked. Instead I fell into be an exhausted mess of emotions.

"Rosen Montag or Rose Monday," as the penultimate day of Carnival is known dawned bright and cold. Though the skies were clear, the chill wind continued to blow, ensuring we wrapped up warmer than ever, as we had learnt from the experiences of previous years. Whereas the smaller processions lasted a couple of hours, the great even of Cologne went for much longer. As with Carnival in Venice, Rio and Mardi Gras, Carnival in Cologne attracted people from everywhere, making it one of the most populated places on the continent of Europe for a few hours.

Making our way to the station the next morning, heads bent against the buffeting wind, we were joined by a number of people all heading into the city for the same reasons - that of taking part in the greatest event of the year.

In common with those we had met in the past few days, even the spectators had dressed to complement the pageant we were going to view. From families dressed and made up as clowns in tatty costume, to Pierots and Pierrets. A group of teenagers dressed as hippies, walked nosily past pushing a pram. This held not a squalling baby but, a beer barrel. Everywhere was noise and confusion.

I smiled as we neared the station, a single storied brown, brick building. Looking more like a Hollywood set for a war film than a modern suburban commuter centre. Today no need for tickets as all travel was free.

Walking along the tunnel that linked the platforms, we answered greetings thrown in our direction. Coming out from the dingy darkness of the subway, we made our way towards the place where we were to meet Dieter and Uwe.

Looking ahead in expectation of seeing Dieter's dark hair, I was disappointed to see only Paul and Frank. The ladies I knew would not be joining us, in the past this had not been a problem, because normally this was one day that Dieter and I had eventually to ourselves. While the Carnival was in full force and all the company busy drinking and enjoying themselves, Dieter and I would slip away and find an empty place, where we would make passionate love. We would return later to our companions satisfied and happy.

Today this was obviously not going to happen, for he was nowhere in sight. Pretending a nonchalance I was far from feeling: "Where's Dieter?" I asked.

"He isn't coming with us today, but we have been told where to stand." Paul replied

"Great! Thoughtful of him isn't it," I replied, anger and frustration in every word.

The sound of the siren signalled the arrival of the train. At this a great cheer went up. No sooner had it come to a stop then there was a mad scramble for any seats that might still be vacant. As Cologne was the last stop on the line, this was almost impossible.

Fighting my way past a man in a bear suit carrying a beer barrel, I finally found myself on the train. Standing in cramped conditions no London Commuter would accept, there was only laughter and fun. From somewhere at the back of the train a young male voice started to sing a Carnival song, that everyone joined in. As each carriage interconnected with the one in front or back the message of Carnival was carried all the way through.

As the train pulled into the station, we found ourselves being picked up and carried by the motley crowd that flooded out of its vast doors. Everywhere I looked people moved like wave on a restless ocean.

Following Frank and Paul, we made our way out of the station, past its shops, now doing a roaring trade, into the precinct that lead that led to the vast square. From shopping centre the cathedral and along the side roads the pavements were thronged with people.

"I don't believe this?" Connie breathed the excitement taking hold of her.

"Yes, it is rather magnificent," I replied, taking pride in this city as if it were my own. For a moment I looked at the great church beside which I now stood, looking down at the ring I refused to remove. I couldn't help wondering did Dieter ever think of that Saturday afternoon when he had given it to me; had he really meant the words he had used, or were they like feather in the wind, easily blown away.

"Come, or we will lose the place reserved for us." Paul pulled me along, making sure our party did not break up.

Having seen the small villages and towns decorated, Cologne in all her beauty outdid them. Flags, bunting and confetti. Excited faces could be seen hanging from every window overlooking the streets we now walked along. The flags that held the heraldic motto of Cologne hung from every lamp post and doorway. Tiny pieces of confetti feathered down on our heads and shoulders, thrown by revellers from above. A group of policemen walked past laughing and joking with the people, today was a day of fun but they were always vigilant should trouble arise. They walked along with roses tucked in jacket pockets or in their hats. A sergeant not complaining when one of juniors was grabbed and kissed by a woman in the crowd.

Making our way past stalls selling a variety of edible foods and drink from gluhwein to apple fritters or hot dogs. Today no one cared how much they spent. It was Rose Monday, today the people were to have fun, leave the cares of everyday behind and just enjoy life. As Dieter once said "Today we enjoy, tomorrow we worry."

"We are here." Paul led his cousin and the rest of us to the doors of a multistorey car park. On this occasion there was no use for its usual purpose, no vehicles allowed in the city apart from the floats and the backup transport. Instead it was to be used as a viewing point for the parade.

Making our way to the third floor, this had been set aside only for the friends of the car park owner. Here we were serenaded by a lone guitarist and enjoyed food from the sausage and soup bar that had been placed in the corner. To the delight of the men they discovered that beer was also close by.

Having seen us settled, Bill and Frank went for the important stuff, beer. As we stood together once more my husband raised his glass: "To Dieter, thanks mate." This was chorused by all present.

As with the previous day, our first indication that the parade was about to begin came with the howl of police sirens. Then the excited crowds began to cheer, turning the already intoxicated atmosphere electric. I stood for a second or two looking around me, as with the passengers on the train not a miserable face was present, even I was beginning to smile.

"This is fantastic." Angie called over to me, as the horses leading the procession came into view.

"No matter how often I come, I will never grow tired of this spectacle," Bill joined in.

During all this I suddenly found myself being grabbed by a youth, who had decided to make a procession of his own. All standing in that area of the car park had soon joined us and we were doing a German version of the Conga.

"I've never danced round a multistorey car park before." Frances called breathlessly, as we laughingly rejoined our husbands.

By now the outrider had passed by, making way for the more impressive floats. Accompanied by dance bands, girls in costumes, majorettes wielding batons all seemingly oblivious to the cold. They were joined by Roman Soldiers and other characters linked with the history of Cologne. The floats that followed were built on gigantic vehicles. Covered in flowers, all the characters made out of papier mache and pointing derogatory fun at their political leaders. This was the big procession, all the sweets, cakes and presents thrown were larger than in the smaller one of the day previous. From bottles of perfume to boxes of chocolates each time a well-aimed parcel arrived on our floor, there was yell and a rush to see who could get to it before anybody else, everything was done in fun and good humour. Finally at the end of the parade came the Princes and Prince in floats of their own, magnificent and regal with not usually the most beautiful or handsome person sitting on high, it was the person with the most money and very influential in business.

As the afternoon wore on I threw myself wholeheartedly into the proceedings, fighting the void that filled me, determined that nothing would spoil this day, I could cry later when alone.

So the time passed in a haze of fun and laughter, with the collection of quite a few bruises. Gloria the smallest in height was the biggest sufferer.

"Hey, girl," David cuddled his little wife: "Next time I'll bring a chair for you to stand on." Laughing out loud as a box of milk chocolates glanced off her shoulders once more. "See what I mean."

Returning to the station, we were amazed to find that the streets, which only minutes earlier had been littered with everything from beer bottles and horse manure to pieces of paper were now being cleaned up, leaving it clean and smart for the following day.

We walked along the platforms looking for our train, laughing at those who had drunk a great deal more than us. On one side were some frustrated railway workers trying to get a young man off the tracks before a train came in. Another group of revellers had decided to share the gifts they had collected, these were being showered over anyone unlucky enough to be standing near.

"This lot are mad." Frances called over to Paul.

"No, my dear," he smiled: "Not mad, we work very hard, so when we can enjoy ourselves we do."

"That's a good bit of logic." Mark nodded: "I approve."

The return journey was quieter, as many people would have stayed in the city. The rest of us were too tired to jump and shout. So we sat talking quietly with Frances fast asleep.

"What are we going to do tonight?" Gloria asked.

Quietly from the depths of the brown coat that encompassed Paul came a reply that shook me to the core: "That's why Dieter did not come with us today, he and Monique are having a party in their cellar."

"Can I wear my costume?" David asked.

"Yes, they would like that." Frank replied for his cousin.

A party, Dieter was having a party in his house. How could I bear to be in such close proximity to him and be unable to touch him.

Our arrival back at the Hubertus was filled with the turmoil that accompanies preparations for an enjoyable night out. After primping and preparing we were all ready. In honour of the Carnival theme Bill, Mark and Tom dressed in Bermuda shorts of horrendous colours, clashing madly with the lime green and orange cotton shirts they also wore.

We women had dressed more conservatively, Frances in a red blouse and long, black skirt. Angie wore a high waisted dress in bright orange, a colour that suited her perfectly, Gloria had dressed in a plain, black, straight dress with a gold belt. I had worn a pair of very tight Lycra trousers in blue and white, over which was a white lace blouse. We stood on the landing waiting for David to join us. When he did there was no disappointment; his costume was unique and dumbfounding.

David had dressed as an Arab. His costume was a white cotton kaftan, over which he had placed a brown and cream shapeless robe. On his head was a hood worn by the nomadic people of the desert, held in place by a series of coloured ropes. His bearded face sported a pair of dark glasses and on his feet a pair of open sandals finished off the costume. Our amazement was such that for seconds we stood in silence. Then a clamour of hands congratulated him on his originality.

"Well done, old son." Bill clapped him on the back, as we made our way out of the warmth of the hotel and out into the bitter cold.

"I congratulate you." Angie kissed his cheek. "What made you think of it?"

Pleased with the effect he on us, David went on to explain the idea had come to him after watching a play on television.

We walked heads bent against the wind that had grown colder with the setting of the sun.

"I presume that is their home." David laughed.

Following his pointing finger we all joined in with his laughter.

"Yes," Bill replied: "I think that possibly that is the home of the Schmidt family."

In the dark no one could see the silent shake of my head. Ever the exhibitionist, Dieter had placed a number of coloured lights all over the house. They covered walls, windows like a multitude of stars, glistening and shimmering, lighting up the dull evening.

As we made our way up the path, past the little bush in the tiny front garden, I smiled. On this he had hung balloons, now swaying agitatedly in the night breeze.

Raising my eyes to the black and silent heavens I wished that I could be free, free from the torment that comes from loving a man whose very name had become life to me. But I was no longer an essential part of him. He had turned his back on me and the memories we had made together.

Sighing, I waited beside the man who was my husband, placing an arm on his we stood together waiting for our host to let us in. I was leaving my broken dreams on the outside, entering the house of my husband's friend a different woman.

As Dieter ushered us in, greeting my friends with kisses, warm smiles and handshakes, it seemed it was only for me that the distant smile of one stranger acknowledging another had been reserved.

I was learning to accept this until: "What is the matter, have you and Dieter had a row?" Angie whispered as we removed our coats, prior to joining the rest of the group in the cellar.

"If I knew what the problem was, I would be able to tell you." I returned, furious that my friend had unknowingly opened up the wound that I thought closed.

Walking quickly, I followed the sounds of voices drifting up from the beer cellar. Listening to the sounds of admiration ad congratulations that David's costume was receiving. All the time trying not to think of that week with the camper when he and I had made such beautiful and passionate love in this very same place. Looking at him smiling and playing the perfect host, I wanted to shout out: "How could you?"

As from a distance I heard Gloria: "Thank goodness everyone likes his outfit."

I was so engrossed in conversation with my three friends, that I was not concentrating on where I was walking, until, with a sense of shock I came in contact with the hard, muscular frame of a man heading up the stairs. As my arms in an involuntary movement closed round his waist, I knew it was Dieter whom I held. Unconsciously, my head went on his shoulder, in a familiar and loving gesture. We stood arms round each other, until I felt him push me roughly and rudely away.

"Vicki, what are you doing?" though his voice was whispered, I heard the anger in it.

"I am sorry Dieter. You really must widen this stairway. Allowing two to pass comfortably." then turning to look at the faces watching us: "Hi gang, gosh I'm hungry. Moniqe can we eat now? Do you know how cold it is outside?" Before I could carry on any further, I felt Angie's hand on my arm: "If you don't shut up, I personally guarantee to push you down the stairs. Do you have any idea what a fool you sound?"

In an instant sanity returned. I could not believe that one touch from Dieter, and all my self-imposed and rigid rules regarding his effect on me turned instantly into bubbles, blowing easily away and bursting.

"That was quite an entry." Paul smiled. "You and Dieter look good together."

"I am the sort of woman who looks good with any man, even you. Please, can I have a drink," I whispered, my voice hoarse from tears that were choking my throat.

In an effort to regain self-control, I wandered round the area reserved for the party. Not too many people had been invited, making it possible to dance on the concrete floor, while allowing others to move around comfortably.

Most of the guests were in costume. There was Paul and his wife Helga, dressed as sixteenth century peasants, they had chosen the colours of green and orange. A Doctor friend of Dieter's came as a bird, with all the plumage of an Ostrich. There was an elderly gentleman whose name I never knew, came as Einstein

335

and of course David who had been taken to the hearts of our friends, His gentle humour, loud laugh and larger-than-life personality endeared him to all. Connie happily basked in his reflected glory.

Tonight, there was no waiting for the party to liven up, all were eager to enjoy what was left of Carnival. No sooner had the music started then so did the dancing. Even I threw myself into the atmosphere surrounding me.

Dancing having taken its toll of me, I decided to take a few moments respite. Looking at the long table, on which the food prepared by Monique, Helga, Christa and Birgit had been laid, I could see Dieter standing with his arm round his wife

"What a perfect pair they make." A little voice tormented me.

I had to acknowledge tonight they looked just right together. Him so tall and dark, dressed as a Roman soldier, and Monique, small, feminine, dressed as a lady of high birth from ancient Rome. She had chosen turquoise, a colour that contrasted perfectly with her hair, making her skin appear like alabaster, and leaving me with the feeling that compared with her I was no more than a pea-hen. A feeling that did nothing to enhance my own self-esteem.

After this, I decided that the best course of action for me was one of total and complete enjoyment. No time for thought, just vigorous movement.

There were times during my pursuit of happiness when Dieter's laugh would impinge on my subconscious, bringing me once more to the brink of the disaster that can come from too much soul-searching.

"I like this. Are you coming again next year?" Gloria asked. "If so, then David and I will certainly join you."

I stood silently, watching Dieter as he danced with Helga, laughing fondly down at her. A feeling of jealousy raced through my blood stream. "No Connie, I think this is going to be my last year for Carnival. In fact I don't think I'll be coming back to this village again." It was obvious from the look on my friend's face that the venom in my voice had taken her by surprise.

"Did you hear that Bill, Dieter," I heard Mark call laughingly to my husband and friend: "Vicki says she isn't coming back to Germany ever again." This message was called across the bunting-decorated room at the same time that a lull appeared in the music and conversation. Every head seemed turned in my direction, a look of consternation on all their faces, except that of Dieter. His expression was different, a look almost of fear and pain was there for a brief few seconds.

"Thanks, Mark. When will you learn to keep that shut." I said pointing to his mouth.

Realising he had said something wrong, Mark walked hurriedly away from me.

"I wasn't aware that we weren't coming to Germany anymore," Bill said annoyed by what appeared to be my high-handed attitude in telling him what to do.

Walking up to my husband, pulling him unwillingly onto the little dance floor, I explained that Mark had been joking.

"Not funny." Bill was not ready to easily accept any explanation I might give. After much cajoling, I could see he was giving in, the smile I was searching for appearing on his face. "I know what you mean." He muttered, holding me close in his arms: "Mark does have a sick sense of humour, but you should be careful what you say in front of him."

Relieved he had accepted what I said, I quickly turned the conversation to other things, including the people around us.

As the night progressed, the emptiness that I tried to fill became hollower. Everyone around was laughing happily. Looking at Dieter I could see that he was not missing our closeness at all. He moved freely around his guests, uncaring of my own feelings. I had seen him dancing with my friends, but never approaching me. It was only as I saw him dancing once more with his wife, that the pain I tried to contain burst out. The pair were close together, his dark hair resting on the lightness of hers. Then I saw her stretch up, arms round his neck and place her lips against his, a kiss that was returned passionately and promptly by Dieter.

"Hey you two, behave yourselves. You are not supposed to behave like that, please remember you are married." Mark laughed.

The sight of their happiness was too much for me. With an excuse I could not afterwards remember, I made my escape up the stairs and out of the front door, into the safe anonymity and protection of darkness.

I stood gasping for air, my hasty retreat having me quite breathless. For minutes I stood alone. After the almost stifling heat of the house, the biting cold was a relief. I stood staring at the skies, as if searching for an answer. The stars had now come out in full, now and then a moving light giving the impression that one of the heavenly lights had taken flight. Only the gentle drone of an aeroplane's engines giving the truth to this flight of fancy.

"Why will you not come back to Germany, again?" I had been so engrossed with my own thoughts, I had not heard Dieter's approach across the frost-covered grass.

"Do you really care what I do?" I turned, my hurt emotions turning to anger: "After the way you have treated me? No Dieter I think it would be a relief for you that I don't come any more." Turning my back, I hoped he would leave, but the hand on my arm made a shiver run up my spine: "You are cold," he whispered.

"No," before he could continue further: "And don't flatter yourself, you make no impression on me any more either."

"Then why are you moving away from me?" In the light reflected from the street lamp, I could see the smile on his face.

"I'm sorry I wasn't aware that I was. Look I am now standing still, satisfied."

"You have not had a good Carnival?"

"Ha, funny you should say that. No, I have not had a good time. Turning to stare at him in the face: "Do you know how I feel? Do you even care? No. Well I am going to tell you." Now I was holding his shoulders, making sure he heard every word I had to say. "Some weeks ago, you might remember, we talked on the phone. You ended the conversation by saying how much you loved me. I carried the memory of that with me, waiting till we could be together again. I arrive and you are colder than an iceberg. Explain!" Now I was shaking with frustration.

"Oh baby if only I could make you understand," he whispered.

"Please, show me how to understand. I need to know."

There was no answer. We stood in silence: "Tell me you never loved me, that all you wanted was an affair. All those wonderful things you said, and this." Lifting up my right hand so that the ring glistened in the winter

339

moon-light: "Was all this just an expensive excuse to get me into bed?" I waited for his answer, dreading the truth, yet needing his reply so that I could be set free and allowed to live again.

"It is not an answer I can give, easily." He turned his back on me.

With the removal of his hands from my shoulders, the cold that had been kept at bay by anger, hurt and frustration, began creeping into me. Setting up a shivering I found it impossible to stop.

"I'm cold, do you mind if we go in?" Again there was silence from my companion: "Did you hear me, I am cold."

"I wish that you were, leibchen." For the first time in days, I heard him use the endearment he had always reserved for me. This stopped me from taking flight.

"What did you call me?"

"I said, I wished you were cold." Turning to look at me: "Oh baby, it is not good for us to be together. But I do need you." Stretching his empty arms out to me.

I stood hesitant – for a while, was this yet another game of his? Would I be walking into a new and even crueller trap he had invented, could I not see that he was the cat and I the mouse? Not till I looked into his eyes, watching the tears that formed there, falling onto his cheeks glistening in the dark like tiny diamonds, was the truth confirmed. He did love me, with a soft cry I flew towards him, filling his embrace with my body.

"Oh God Dieter, I thought you didn't care about me anymore," I whispered as we covered each other's faces with little kisses. Why did you make me suffer so?" I demanded.

"Don't you realise we have no future together. I have a life and family here, yours is on the other side of the channel." He was touching my body, investigating it. "We should stay only as friends."

"Friends! Is that what you really want?" My voice a whisper my eyes searching every inch of his face.

"No."

"If that is really what you believe, then why have you made me suffer so?" My arms held him, as a drowning man a raft.

"If you have suffered, I have too," he whispered, his lips now busy decorating my face with kisses.

"Then stop wasting time," I demanded. "Kiss me." An invitation he carried out with vigour and vitality.

I stood, held in his embrace, feeling the strong beat of his heart, its tattoo like mine growing ever faster as our kisses grew more desperate. For days and months I had dreamt of this, and now at last we were in each other's arms. Once more my dreams coming true. He drained my life, I was aware of nothing only the touch of his lips and hands as they made little rivers of fire. Everywhere they touched molten pools appeared. I was standing at the base of my own personal volcano, I had helped cause an explosion now it was up to me to help assuage it.

"Dieter." My voice not its normal tones but a soft breath of air sounding his name, "I need you."

"I need you too, but for me this is not enough," his lips now exploring the valley between my breasts. "Oh, Vicki! The smell that is you, is always with me." Further words were unnecessary.

The fast growing hardness between his Roman costume was proof of his growing desire: "We both have a great need of you," he smiled slightly, looking down at himself: "It is good, beneath he will not be seen so easily."

Pulling slightly away, I looked down at the masculinity growing there, wanting to take it in my hands and caress it, giving it the freedom we both needed.

"We would have a problem, if your wife and my husband could see that."

Laughing together, we embraced once more.

"So, how will we get the chance to make love," I asked. "It must be tonight, or I will not sleep."

"Ssh, baby we will." Tapping his nose: "I am clever, we will do it but now we must return."

We entered the house once more, a far happier couple than when we had walked out earlier that evening.

"Where the hell have you been?" Angie grabbed my arm as I reached the bottom steps making our return to the cellar extremely public.

I pulled myself free of her restraining arm: "Why do you want to know?"

"Oh, no not me dear, but your husband. You do remember him."

"No need for sarcasm." I was now feeling annoyed.

"Well he has been looking for you. What was I to say, you were having a bunk-up with his best mate."

At any other time I would have laughed at my friend's crudity, but tonight I couldn't. Perhaps because it was almost true.

I could understand my friend's anger, but was not going to let her denigrate our love by turning it into a sublimation of the basic human instinct, sex.

"We love each other, Angie. There is nothing either he or I can do about it. Not everything is basic, I wish you could experience a little of the feelings we do." With a little side-smile, I tapped her on the shoulder.

"Well, I must admit, I wouldn't mind trying him. In that costume, with those legs, he does look worth a try."

Now I knew my friend was teasing me: "Go get your own. He's mine."

"From the way he's looking at you, my dear, that's bloody obvious."

A tingle of anticipation ran down my spine, as our eyes met. His making promises of things to come, that we would once again walk through the gates of heaven together.

"I have been telling my wife we were looking at the place where she wants her rock-garden put," Dieter called across the room.

"You have?" Realising that I was being given a way out of explaining why we had been so long: "You have Oh! Oh yes, that's right." Monique I like the ideas you have for improving the garden, I think those bushes will look very nice." About to say more the look on Angie's face stopped me.

"I'd quit while you're ahead. She believes you. Now shut up before you hang yourself." Angie tugged my arm leading me towards the bar and food.

"You have got to be the biggest liar," Frances laughed.

Smiling, I replied: "Love my dear, can turn the nicest of us into the biggest liars."

"And you, my dear, were never the nicest," I heard Angie call, as I allowed myself to be whirled onto the dance floor by Uwe.

The rest of the evening passed with me in a daze of happiness. Dieter and I never spoke to each other again. But, when we thought ourselves to be unobserved, our eyes would meet, many secret promises being made.

As the hour grew later and guests were leaving, I began to grow worried as to how Dieter and I could get time to be together. Once Bill decided to leave I would have to go with him and our friends.

"Vicki, can you do me a favour?"

Suddenly the centre of my thoughts was there before me. Looking down on the tiled floor, appearing to study the wine stain that had appeared recently very intently, afraid he might read my mind.

"We are going back now, but Dieter and Monique asked if you wouldn't mind helping them tidy up."

My head shot up, as if my hair had been violently pulled. Looking across the room, I could see Dieter's slight nod of his head.

"Yes, yes, I don't mind. Are you staying too?" He didn't hear the tone of my voice. Hoping he would reject my offer.

"No, I'm going back to the Hubertus now. Dieter will walk you back." Tapping my face, he placed a little kiss on my cheeks.

"I knew you'd help. You really are a good girl."

He walked away pleased with his wife and her selfless attitude.

I on the other hand should have felt guilty at the lies, I was helping my lover to concoct. But I felt no shame at my duplicity, I wanted and needed Dieter. That was the only thought that filled my mind.

Eventually five of us were left in the Cellar, the boys already in bed. Dieter, Monique, Uwe, Birgit and myself, all the other guests having left. Quickly we worked together, returning the little room to its normal tidy state. All the time we worked, my heart beat a tattoo of fear and trepidation, while my mind ran round in circles. "How could we make love? His wife was here and very much awake." What did Dieter have in mind. I didn't have long to wait.

The clearing having been finished, Uwe and Birgit said their good byes, with Dieter taking them to the front door, he then joined us sitting on the sofa to relax. Monique was by now yawning hugely, Dieter straightening himself up from the sofa, said "Would you like a coffee, or shall I take you back to the hotel now." The way in which the offer of coffee was made, it was obvious he wanted me to refuse.

"No thanks Dieter. I think I should go back to Bill now, you don't mind Monique?" I said, turning to look at the younger woman.

Smiling sweetly, she agreed that I must be as tired as she was. "Dieter you will make sure that Vicki is in before you come back."

"Yes, my sweet, I will make sure she is in," he laughed

Only I knew the double meaning behind his seemingly innocent remark.

We walked through the frozen, quiet, night streets. With only the street lamps to light our way, we walked in silence, a shiver of anticipation coursing through me.

"You are cold?" Dieter had seen the shiver.

"No, just puzzled."

Turning to look at me in the glow thrown from one of the lights: "You are worried. Why? We have done this before," a smile lighting up his face.

"No," I replied insistently: "Not worried, just wondering where we are going."

"Wait, you will soon see." Now he was whistling, tunelessly but happily.

Our walk continued in silence, till reaching the neighbourhood of the Hubertus. Here, there was no peace. For though it was the early hours of the morning, revellers were still out enjoying themselves. As we neared what was my destination, much to my surprise I realised that he was not leading me to the large front door, instead I was being walked round the side. The entrance reserved only for guests of the hotel. With a sinking heart I began to realise that Dieter had changed his mind. We would not be making passionate love, instead I was being returned to my rightful place, in bed, beside my husband.

About to take out the key that I had in my handbag, I noticed that Dieter had walked ahead, and the door normally securely locked was now standing open, with a very happy looking Dieter grinning at me: "Will you hurry, I do not have all night," he whispered, kissing my cheek.

"How did you get this open?"

He gave no reply, just held up a bunch of keys that he had taken from his pocket: "I have a room here."

"You reserved a room. What about Walter and Louise do they know about us?" I whispered, as he ushered me in through the door, shutting it with a click behind us. Quietly we made our way up the stairs to the first landing. Here he opened a door leading to a room I had never seen before. Unlike the other rooms, this was decorated in a less utilitarian manner. The walls were a simple mint-green, bedspread in pale grey and the carpet blending with the walls. It was completely en suite. However, it was not the colouring of the room that held my attention, but the ice bucket holding the bottle of champagne that stood on the bedside cabinet.

"Did you arrange this?" I was dumbfounded.

Looking as if he had just become Chancellor of Germany, Dieter nodded: "You like it."

"Well, yes. But."

"No buts. Yes Walter knows about this, but not his wife. And we have no need to worry about him, he thinks I am very lucky now come to me."

Walking slowly towards him, we stood facing each other, wanting to take him in my arms, but afraid, holding back until: "Leibchen, be happy, we are together now." He whispered, moving towards me.

With a soft cry I found myself in his arms, our lips taking and holding possession of each other. Hastily, we ripped each other's clothes off. Once naked we allowed our hands and lips the pleasure of investigating each and every part of our bodies.

The desire coursing through my body, set me on fire, giving unspoken permission to his enquiring lips, hands and tongue to make their discoveries of my body bringing from me only sounds of pleasure as we learnt new ways of inviting and giving satisfaction, until we could hold back the ultimate demand no longer. As I lay on the bed, taking his now fully extended, vibrating, manhood in my hands, caressing it: "Are you ready?" I whispered, finding it difficult to talk, my lips sore from the rough way his teeth had bitten them. He nodded, his green eyes aglow with a light I found difficult gauge. Slowly parting my legs, I waited for him to possess me. Fingering the wet, pulsing opening, with a sigh he slipped tenderly in, a cry of contentment coming from us both. We needed each other, and now at last we were in the place reserved for us, as one.

At first our movements were slow, luxuriating in the feel of our bodies rubbing against each other. My nipples rubbing against the hair-roughened surface of his cheek. Allowing my hands to wander over his back, I could feel the shiver of desire running through him as I found and

347

toyed with his erogenous zones. Returning the enjoyment, his lips and hands wandering over my body. Pulling up on his elbows, looking down at my breasts, which were now full, waiting for the rapture that was soon to come: "Oh baby you are beautiful," he breathed. Those were the last words either of us spoke as our rhythm grew faster, sweat pouring from us as the demand for pleasure and satisfaction grew with his driving into me.

As I felt I could no longer hold back my own climactic sexual urge, I felt his body begin to tauten. The moment we both desired was near. His legs straightened. I could see his face, eyes closed. Dieter was with me in another world, that very special place, reserved only for those truly in love; those who know and understand each other. With a cry, deep-throated but soft we gave to each other the elixir of life, the juices that are an intimate part of the human body.

Moments later, having regained our breath, Dieter opened the bottle that stood beside us and in a silent toast we raised our glasses to each other. Tears of happiness in our eyes. One thing I was beginning to know about the man I loved: He was not afraid to show his emotions. Whether happy or sad, Dieter shared everything with me, as I with him.

Hours later, it was time to part. Me to go upstairs; Dieter returning to Monique.

After much tossing and turning beside Bill, I dozed off into a fitful sleep. One in which I returned once more to the arms of my lover. Tonight we had climbed the pinnacle of love, with a beauty that transcended everyday life. I had memories that would last my whole earthly life and into eternity.

I spend the rest of the next day in a dream, with pleasurable memories of the previous night and silent dread that this was my last day in the village. Today when we said goodnight, it was also goodbye.

As we prepared for our impending departure, shopping and packing, I was forgiven my taciturn and silent manner because, as Bill reminded all our friends: "She did stay behind to help clear up, while we were in bed." I should have felt some modicum of guilt, but as that night had felt so right it was impossible.

As this was the last night of Carnival, no one dressed up. For the first time in days I was seeing people I knew coming into the Hubertus dressed normally. Though the party theme still existed, it was more subdued, as were Dieter and I.

We sat at our usual table, Dieter ensuring we sat next to each other. Under cover of the table our hands met, eyes searching and finding answers we needed.

"Did you sleep well?" He asked, the light of laughter in his eyes.

"Um. It was difficult. I had such a boring evening, I really wasn't very tired."

For this bit of teasing, I felt a gentle pinch on the back of my left hand.

I drifted through the night on a cloud of happiness, with now and then the little voice of sanity saying: "Tomorrow night, you'll be back in Little Barham." At this a shiver of fear would make its way up my spine. I didn't want to leave him. It was obvious from the look on his face that he too had read my thoughts: "Come Vicki, let us have one last dance together," he said pulling me up and leading me to the far end of the bar, the only place open for dancing on the last night.

I felt his arms close round me, my head coming to rest naturally on his shoulder.

"You smell nice," he whispered.

There was no need for any reply.

In silence we danced. Happy because we were together, sad because we both knew this time tomorrow water and miles would be separating us.

As the song that finishes Carnival played round us "Am Asche Mittwoche ist Alles Vorbei" translated On Ash Wednesday everything is ended.

"Oh Dieter, I wish we had met years ago."

"So do I," he replied to my heartfelt wish. "But perhaps God has a reason for us to be like this. Perhaps in another life we can be together."

I didn't want another life, I wanted only the now. Our loving should not be curtailed. Ever since I had known this man our lives had consisted of partings.

Eventually, the time came for us to say our farewells. We had to leave early the next day.

With fast-beating heart and a lump in my throat that made breathing difficult, I stood quietly behind our group, watching the exchange of handshakes and kisses.

"Are you all right?" Angie whispered, as she and Frances came to stand beside me. They understood the predicament I was now in, with my husband and his wife looking on. Our farewell kiss could be only the superficial one of friends, last night had been our greeting and farewell in one.

"So, Vicki, we will see you again soon, perhaps," he whispered. I had said my goodbyes to everyone else, we now had only each other. On legs grown suddenly wooden, I walked towards him my arms outstretched, a farewell smile on my face. I felt his arms close round me, a slight dampness on his cheeks s they were held against mine, proving this parting was as difficult for him as it was for me. The kiss he planted in my lips was one of gentle movement, telling me silently: "I will always love you."

So the group that comprised our German friends walked out into the cold night air. I could hear their voices, drifting back to me on the still, night air. There was only one I did not hear, perhaps he was having as much trouble with speech as I.

Making our way for the last time to our rooms, I was reminded of something I had seen scrawled on a girl's jacket in Cologne on Rose Monday:

Love is difficult to find
Wonderful to have
Easy to lose
Hard to forget.

How true it was, Dieter had become my love; the centre of my existence. That night I cried myself silently and heartbreakingly to sleep. I did not think any pain could be as bad as the one I now suffered. I should not have tempted fate.

With the ending of my recollections, I looked at the man now lying on the hospital bed. A smile and colour I had previously not seen on his face was now present. Obviously this had been as good a memory for him as me.

"There will be more Carnivals for us, baby." He spoke softly, his throat still sore.

I nodded: "I'm going now." Standing up, I bent down to plant a kiss on his lips. The sound of the nursing trolley told me I was now going to be ejected from my place by his bed, leaving him to the medical team. There were times when love had to give way to reality.

Chapter 19

It was now three days since Dieter had been taken off the ventilator. Six days since the accident that had rocked all our lives, creating as much turmoil in this little village as an earthquake.

From today, however, the fear that had held us in its grip had begun to relax a little. The interminable hours of tension and worry, as we watched by the silent bedside, talking in soft tones as instructed by the Professor all seemed to have been successful. As I entered Dieter's room, I could see that colour was slowly returning to his pale cheeks. Those beautiful green eyes that had seemed closed to me forever were now open and sparkling. With all the artificial aids, that had helped him to stay alive. Removed, my lover appeared to be returning to his normal self. Even having begun to eat a little.

As the trauma of his illness began to fade, Monique felt she was able to return slowly to normality. Spending slightly longer hours with her sons and less time with Dieter. These times were handed over to me with the gentle remark:

"Vicki, you go and stay with my husband, I know you can make him smile."

As I was about to leave her house in one of the taxis I had come to know well, she called back: "But, remember he has been very ill, do not take advantage of him."

I smiled and waved in return; "What advantage could I take," I muttered, as I settled back into the soft leather of the car's interior, "that I haven't already taken."

Now that I knew Dieter was well on the road to recovery, I felt able to resurrect all the thoughts and dreams I had held at bay over the past few days.

Though everything seemed to be returning to normal, one little thought niggled at the back of my mind.

"If he is getting on so well, why has the Herr Professor not transferred him out of the Intensive Care unit." My face screwed up as I tried desperately to some up with an answer. However, the only one that seemed to keep coming to the forefront of my mind was one that I did not want to accept: "Perhaps, Dieter is not yet completely out of the woods," I thought as I got out of the yellow Mercedes that had driven me swiftly and silently to the long, low, white building standing in its own parkland.

Shaking this thought away as swiftly as it had entered my mind, I entered the hospital.

As both Bill and I had been seen so often in the company of Dieter's family, my entrance into the hospital went unchallenged by security and nursing staff alike.

In my eagerness to reach the room in which Dieter lay, I was unaware that I hurried, almost racing, along corridors unlike any I had seen in an English hospital. Here were no trolleys or beds left cluttering the progress of patients and visitors alike. Nurses and doctors appeared relaxed and happy, unlike their English counterparts, who, because of overwork and lack of support, appeared to look as tired and unhappy as their patients.

"Slow down, Vicki," I stopped to catch my breath: "Otherwise Dieter is going to think you've been worrying about him, and won't his already outsize ego just love that." I stood for a few seconds allowing my heart to steady its frantic beating, and my throat that had gone suddenly dry began to return to normal.

About to open the door, I felt a pressure on my fingers:

"Wait one moment, Lieber Frau," the gentle tones of the Professor in charge of Dieter's case addressed me.

Turning, I stared at the tall, thin man, my heart once again starting to race: Was I about to be told something awful?

"What's wrong, is Dieter…?"

Before I could finish the man who was now leading me away from the door stopped and bending from his great height, a smile spreading across his thin face said:

"You can set your mind at rest, my dear Vicki."

Leading me farther up the corridor and away from Dieter's room: "There are no further complications."

Was there just a slight hesitation in his voice, or was it my imagination. Deciding that I was really letting the situation get the better of me, I forced myself to pay attention to what the learned man had to say, and why I was being led away to what was obviously his private sanctum.

"There's something that's puzzled me," I asked, as we walked, his arm linked in mine. "We've never spoken before, yet you seem to know me, how?"

354

He stopped, bending, to stare at me for a second, his eyes never wavering from mine. Then, once more with my question unanswered, he walked on.

I was not about to be led from the path I had chosen: "You knew my name was Vicki, even my surname, yet at no time were we ever introduced to each other."

By now he was a few steps ahead of me, frustration taking the upper hand, like a child I stamped my foot: "Will you please answer me," I almost shouted.

"I know a great deal about you," he replied. "After all a lovely young lady such as yourself must have many admirers, I must be one of a long line." This was said with a huge grin accompanied by a flirtatious wink.

"You Germans are full of charm, but it doesn't work on this lady." My voice was now stronger, as it was obvious the good doctor was teasing me, feeling that nothing could be seriously wrong with Dieter, if the consultant was prepared to play little word-games with me.

"No," he had now stopped outside a smooth, walnut panelled door bearing his name and status in the Hierarchy of the hospital, "but I think perhaps the charm of one of my countrymen did reach your cold, English heart."

I was now completely mystified, what was the man talking about. Baffled I turned, about to ask him for further information, only to see that he had opened the door, leading me into his office. Ignoring any questions I had been about to ask, he continued talking as I was led ceremoniously to a leather armchair and seated with great panache.

"Victoria my dear, you are right, I knew you before we met."

Walking behind his large oaken desk, he took a key out of his pocket. As he bent to open the centre drawer, I mumbled: "I'm sorry Professor what did you say?"

Having taken a small envelops out of the open drawer he was now free to give me his complete attention. He stood, staring at me: "I said I knew you before we met." The tone of his voice was as one talking to a slightly backward child.

"How?"

"I'd like to say it's a secret but I know Dieter would have no objection."

Seeing my confusion, he silently handed the small, white envelope over to me. With shaking hands I tore it open, gasping as its contents were revealed to me. I found myself staring at a photograph I could never forget. It was me; taken by Dieter when he and I had shared some precious days together.

"Where did you get them?" My voice was a whisper. The woman who stood on the Austrian mountain, laughing so obviously happy and in love with the photographer, now seemed a million miles from the woman who held the picture between nerveless fingers.

As I stared at my image, I could hear the doctor explaining: "When Dieter was brought in, the nurses were puzzled as to what it was he kept mumbling. When conscious he spoke in German, but on lapsing into moments of unconsciousness he would speak in English. In an effort to ease his agitation I was called, and before he was placed under the anaesthetic, I understood that in his breast pocket he carried something that was very important. Only when the photograph was placed between his restless fingers, and he kissed the face there, did I see it was not his wife, but someone else. Turning to look out of the window, his voice growing softer he continued: "I did not realise that I was looking at a man who had found what we all dream about, but seldom find, true love. You are both indeed very lucky.

The silence in the room seemed to stretch from seconds into hours. I was dumbfounded, never at any time had Dieter ever hinted that he carried a picture of me. A little smile flickered across my face, it was the only secret we had from each other. Dieter did not know I also carried a picture of him, in the secret pocket of my hand bag.

"You don't condemn us?" I whispered.

"No, my dear," the doctor replied, his voice still soft: "It is not for me to condemn or apportion blame, that is for your conscience." A smile that revealed nothing was cast in my direction.

"Now, I think there was something you wanted to ask." He said his voice regaining its gentle tones.

Once again, the man's intuition took me by surprise.

"How did you know I would like to talk to you?" I asked, quickly.

"Perhaps it is the way in which you watch everything I say to Frau Schmidt or her brother, almost as if you don't believe." He stared at me, his pale eyes never wavering from mine. Each of us studying the other.

"Are you speaking the truth when talking to the family, or is there something you are keeping from them." I demanded. His knowledge of my relationship with Dieter giving me the courage to demand answers, I could not normally have felt to be my right.

"Why do you think I lie?"

"If you are not lying, then why is he still in the Intensive Care Unit; especially if he is doing as well as you say?"

Walking back to take my arm: "When a man has suffered the injuries of our friend over there," he nodded indicating the room across the hallway, "it is natural that a very close eye is kept on him. If he remains stable for the next twenty-four hours, then I will ensure he is placed in another room, with less attention." Giving a sly wink, and an even wider smile: "Now come, we must go. I have work to do and you have a young man who has need of you."

Our conversation ended, we left the room with its desk covered in papers and walls lined with expensive, accomplished medical books. My heart should have been happier, footsteps lighter, yet it was the words "twenty-four hours" that hammered incessantly in my head, sounding like a vast bell, tolling a danger as yet unknown.

Entering the room, I stood leaning against the door frame, one hand clinging to the handle as though it were a safety-line to sanity, blinking my eyes rapidly, in an effort to clear the tears that had inexplicably risen misting my sight.

From outside, the sounds of summer rain could be heard, along with the bird-song that accompanied these sudden showers breaking up long, hot, dry days.

The railings that had for some days been erected round Dieter had now been taken down, leaving only the heart monitor still attached to his chest.

Silently, I approached the sleeping man, thanking God that the ventilator was now no longer necessary.

"You are not always so quiet when coming to my bed," his voice came in a hoarse whisper.

Had someone once told me that the sound of a man talking to me would create such ecstasy in me, I would have laughed at them. This, however, was the case.

Hearing him, awakened within me a gentle reminder of out euphoric moments together, this time the tears that filled my eyes were ones of happiness, making speech impossible.

At last, I was able to talk to him. Not only was he conscious but we were alone.

Swallowing the lump in my throat, "Hi, how do you feel?" I whispered back.

"O.K. You don't have a sore throat, so there is no need to speak so soft." In the faint light filtering in through the drawn curtains his smile was just visible. My face relaxed into an equally happy expression, approaching his bed, with hands outstretched, ready to take that beloved face and cover it with kisses. He delayed this moment, however, by asking:

"Leiberlein, the curtains, I need to see you."

The endearment "little love" whispered in a voice still husky after hours spent in unconsciousness, had my heart missing a beat.

Having drawn the curtains, I stood, staring out of the large plate glass windows, across the balcony that surrounded all the rooms on the second floor.

"Please make the window open."

I resisted the temptation to smile at his very bad grammar.

Having pulled the windows, the room was soon invaded with the scents that filled the afternoon air. Watching the rain making large puddles in the almost empty parking area, the scent of damp earth assailed my nostrils, once again reminding me how sweet life could be. I had come so close to losing the most important thing in it, Dieter. Was I now to be given a second chance?

Stepping out onto the balcony, mindless of the rain now soaking into my shoulders, I raised my eyes heavenward, making a promise I would keep forever, if my Prayer to the Deity, who ruled our lives and fates were answered.

"Please let him live and I in return would give up his love, return him to his wife and never see him again. It would be enough to know he lived."

So rash are the debts we offer to pay when those who truly love are in danger.

"What are your thoughts, my love?"

Dieter's voice, still sounding gruff and a little hollow, queried.

"Um, just remembering the first time we met," I replied turning with a smile.

"Oh no Leibchen, I prefer to remember the last time we were together."

The tone of his voice deepened at the last three words.

Walking back to join him, leaving behind the sounds and smells of life, now overpowered by the disinfectant odours pervading every corner of this room.

Pointing to a chair that stood not far from where he lay, Dieter suggested I sit close to the bed. Hands clasping each other's, trying desperately to be close, feeling the weakness of his hand in mine, hurt. It upset me to realise how weak his injuries and loss of blood had made him. Yet those green eyes still had the ability to make my blood race, sending shivers of yearning and desire up my spine.

"Remember Salzburg and the Feldenburg," he whispered, lifting my hand shakily to his lips.

How could I forget "The mountain fields," as the mountain we had shared was called.

I nodded my head in silence, he carried on, "what were you doing when I telephoned you that morning?"

It was not difficult to cast my mind back to that dull June morning. I could remember to the last second what I had been doing when he had called me at home.

As a medium, my work was to help and try to counsel people with the help of Spirit, though on this particular morning I was finding it very difficult to do my work honestly as my thoughts were constantly full of Dieter and what he might be doing at that particular time. It had been many months since we had last seen each other, and my life felt empty without him. Our daughters like his sons were now young people, my husband had his work, true I had mine but Dieter had for many years been so much a part of mine that any time without him was empty.

Waiting for my next client to arrive, I was thinking how my life had changed over a period of fourteen years. In the past when giving a reading to my sitters and there had been the problem of one or another partner falling in or out of love, to me that had always been just a reading with Spirit giving me the answers. Now, it was different, I truly loved one man and that man was not my husband. Occasionally, when talking to a client and giving them the advice passed onto them through me, I would feel a hypocrite. Dieter and I knew that our relationship was wrong and yes we had tried to end it but with no luck, we were as important to each other as breathing. So, it was before I did any work I would always ask Spirit to help me, guide me so that my work could be done with integrity and honesty and I could leave my other self outside the room.

It was the strident ringing of the telephone that brought me out of my unhappy moment, one of self-pity not a state a medium should be in as we do know better.

Thinking the person on the other end was a prospective client, I answered the phone in my usual professional manner: "Hullo, Victoria Johnson speaking, may I help you."

The laugh in the voice that answered was so clear he could have been in the room with me.

"You are the psychic, who do you say it is? Um, and can you tell me my fortune?"

"I don't know," I replied laughing: "I need to ask Spirit for guidance to help you."

"Do you have many men ring you for appointments?" He asked. "Not sure I like to think of you sitting in one room with other men." He continued.

"Of course they also need the help that I can give and believe me they see me as nothing more than a helper of Spirit."

After a moment's silence he continued: "What are you and Bill doing for a holiday this year?"

"I'm afraid that we are travelling with our friends to the Greek Islands, I do not want to go." I could hear his disappointment when he answered: "So, you will not be coming to Germany at all this summer."

Keeping the sob out of my voice, I nodded my head as though he could see.

"This I do not like," he replied, in a voice that echoed my own feelings. "I have to see you Leiberlein. It is not possible for me to go till next year without sharing some time with you."

My heart raced as I knew what he meant. The thought of his nearness, the feel of his body in my arms and the touch of his lips on mine were so tantalising I was unable to stop the shaking that took complete hold of my body, causing me to knock a book off my table.

Into the silence that once again hung between us, he asked: "Can you go away for a few days on your own."

I had been asked to work in Berlin for a time and as yet had made no decision: "Well, yes," I then went on to explain about working in Germany. Before I could finish he interrupted:

"Tell Bill you are working in Germany and meet me in Salzburg." I sat down on the chair, my heart racing, could I really be so naughty. Steal not just moments but days, I knew that my husband would not want to accompany me on a trip abroad if I was working, having done so once and been bored he now left me to travel and work on my own.

"We can be Herr and Frau Dettweiler, on holiday."

Hearing my nervous giggles did nothing to lighten the mood he appeared to be in: "Why do you laugh? You do not want to stay with me?"

"No, no." Afraid he might think I was not interested, I quickly interrupted. "No, it's just in England, when people go away, they are called Mr and Mrs Smith, but as that is already your name…"

"Yes, so."

By now my voice had faded away, realising he did not understand what I was saying.

"Well," he was now showing definite signs of impatience, "I wait for your reply, will you come, please?"

"Where will we go?" My voice had gained no strength, as the excitement rising like a flood tide was robbing all my powers of speech.

"We will go to Austria."

"But, Dieter."

Before I could begin another argument he continued.

"Have no worry," his English was now showing signs of deterioration, "we do not go where our families visit, I know a mountain called The Feldenburg, it is there we will stay.

No sooner had he mentioned the mountain's name, I was ready to go. Over the years that my family, sometimes accompanied by Dieter and Uwe with their families had visited the picturesque country of Austria, we had got used to villages being at the base of mountain ranges with the most beautiful names, and this one certainly sounded perfect for us.

"I will tell Bill and the girls that I am working in Berlin.

This idea was readily accepted by the man whose impatience for my reply was beginning to show.

"Ich Leibe disch," he quickly whispered, before ringing off, leaving me holding a silent telephone while trying to still a heart filled with turmoil.

I had lied to Bill before but never to this extent. For the rest of the day my moods swung like a pendulum. From the dizzy heights of happiness to the deepest, darkest depression.

First I told myself I could not accept the invitation. Then I would return the argument by asking my conscience why I was unable to go. All these and many more thoughts raced round in circles, filling my brain with more feathers than could be found in a pigeon loft. Having made the decision to go, I was so excited and feeling guilty that I took the unprecedented step of cancelling my appointments for the rest of the day, knowing my mind would be incapable of helping me to work well.

So, I sat in my living room guilt, happiness, fear of discovery and many other emotions running through me for the rest of the day. Deciding it was time to prepare the evening meal for Hannah, Lottie and Bill, I waited for the inevitable ring on the front door letting me know my daughters had come home from work.

Lottie was the first to fly in, hugs and sticky kisses for me in between her chewing on a large lump of chocolate. I smiled how grown up my daughters looked now, both having been through university. Lottie tall and slim was now working in a marketing team in the City of London, her long brown hair tied in a knot on the top of her head.

Hannah, equally as tall as her younger sister but not so fond of sweets, was putting her handbag in her room, before asking: "What we got to eat?"

I answered her question with a smile, "Chicken"

"Oh, goody," she replied: "the food at school today was diabolical," she replied.

Hannah, had always been good with children, so it was no surprise that my eldest should decide to teach, the real surprise was that it was history and geography because when at school she had not excelled in these subjects at all. Her hair was not as long as her sister's, cropped so it was convenient for the young people around her. As she was teaching twelve to thirteen year old children, she felt her hair kept like this was most convenient.

As I laid the table and the girls helped, I said: "Got some news for you," two heads came up at the same time: "What?" a joint chorus: "You know I have been invited to work in Berlin for the past few years," both girls nodded: "Well a gentleman phoned from there this morning and asked if I could go over in June." I tried to justify this by the "a gentleman" and June this year was also not strictly speaking a lie. I waited to hear what my daughter's replies would be. The replies I received I was not sure if I felt disappointed or relieved.

From Lottie, "Oh! Goody can you buy me perfume at the airport."

"No," I mumbled" as Dieter and I had agreed to meet at Salzburg Station.

"You go Mum," from Hannah, "we can look after Dad, how long for?"

I mumbled, "Two weeks, might be longer." My tongue falling over itself at the lies and afraid of discovery.

"That's fine," Hannah continued, "you stock up the freezer and we will do the rest."

Heaving a sigh of relief, one hurdle over. I still had to face my husband. I did smile a little, so much for worrying they might miss me.

Having slipped into my house clothes of tracksuit and bare feet, I pottered round the kitchen. Hearing the girls sharing their plans for the evening. Tensely, I waited, listening for the first sound of Bill's car in the driveway, I didn't have long to wait.

"Hullo love, coffee on?" I heard his customary greeting at the same time as I felt the peck on my cheek as he breezed into the lounge, then up the stairs to the bedroom.

There was no need for me to answer his question, in the years we had been married he had never changed his greeting, nor had he ever waited for a reply. Shrugging I carried on with my own tasks, of setting the table and calling the girls down.

My mind was so busy with thoughts of Dieter and our forthcoming holiday, I settled all the family at the table without thought for anything. Until, I heard the three of them laughing: "Where are you brains my dear?" From Bill.

I looked at him and the laughing girls blankly: "What? What's wrong?"

All three looked down at the food, serving utensils knives and forks, finger pointing to where plates should have been. Looking a little shamefaced I walked back into the kitchen.

"Is this because of your forthcoming trip?" Bill asked

"What trip?" I called back guilt coming to the forefront of my mind. "Oh, yes you mean my trip to Berlin." He nodded, "The girls told me." Then coming over to help with the plates and serve dinner he carried on with: "Good for you, time you got your name out abroad." That was the end of any discussion about my trip.

My guilt was still there, because over the years I had lied to my family so much, I had now become quite good at doing it, I did not like it but neither could I stand the thought of my family looking at me with hate in their eyes if they really knew the truth. As Mum I was expected to set the rules and the standard in the family, yet here I was breaking every sacred oath I had ever made and completely unable to stop it.

Only once did I ask myself one question: "How will I pay for it?"

Finally the day we had set to meet had arrived. The journey from Little Barham to Salzburg would take over twelve hours, so I had decided to travel overnight. Leaving home in plenty of time to get the boat to Ostend then in a reserved carriage that would go all the way into Salzburg Station in the early hours of the morning.

On arrival at Ostend, I made my way to the station to catch my train, I knew where the train would be for Cologne having done this before for Carnival but I needed one that would go further so I made my way up and down the carriages till I found one going to Splitz, that I knew would be mine. I then had to find my reserved carriage, with the help of one of the Stewards on the train, I was soon settled comfortably with coffee and sandwiches being provided. I had chosen first class, knowing I would be on my own and well cared for. This time the expense was immaterial.

It wasn't long before the train pulled out, settling back in my seat, I opened the suitcase. Now, I could readjust what I had packed. At present the top layer consisted of clothes I believed I would wear if giving big meetings or Private Readings. The lower layer were the clothes I knew would be worn in Feldenburg. Having been to Austria on numerous occasions this was something I knew by experience. My only problem had been did I take a nightdress or not? So, I settled for just one.

Settling down with the coffee the steward had provided and sandwiches, for the first time I actually felt hungry. Feeling the sudden jolt as the train was pulling out of the station. Quickly the train picked up speed leaving the lights behind, heading into the darkness that was gathering. As we raced through towns, villages and across farms, I gazed out of the window. Tonight there was no scenery to be admired, only my own reflection gazing back at me.

The face I saw was not the young woman Dieter had met, but a woman of more mature years. "One old enough to know better." Once more my conscience whispered back. A little smile quivered round the lips I saw reflected in the slightly misty glass. Allowing my hands to run through the short hairstyle I now wore. I wondered how much change there had been in Dieter since I had seen him the previous year. Was he much different? I doubted it. I could still hear the tone in his voice when he had phoned me once more, when I was between appointments. "I cannot stay long, darling. I love you and cannot wait for our days together." He had then hung up leaving me no time to reply. Again, I smiled. He had sounded so happy, why then was I filled with so many reservations. It was with relief that I heard my door open and saw Leon the steward enter with my supper tray. I suddenly did not want to be alone.

"Leon," I called to him, as he was preparing to take his leave: "Please wait," then apologetically "I'm sorry you must be busy." I looked at the little man who wearing his black suit, white shirt and bow tie with his mousey hair bore a strong resemblance to a Penguin.

"No little lady, for you I have all the time you need." His tone was neither patronising nor ingratiating. In the instant I knew he would be a true friend.

"Your English is very good," I couldn't help remarking as I ate the food he had brought. I was sure it was very delectable but tonight I had no appetite at all.

"In my young days I was a stage dresser and worked often in the London, so I learnt a great many things," he said with a sly smile. As though he too had secrets to hide: "One of them was the understanding of human nature."

So we sat for what seemed like hours talking, discussing a variety of subjects but never the one closest to my heart, until with a screech of brakes the train began to slow down, making her first stop of the long journey: "I must leave you now, we are at the German border of Aachen, here I must greet the customs officers and let them see all the passports as well as greet my new passengers. "We can talk later if you want." This was added because he had seen my hastily stifled yawn.

About to close the door behind him, Leon turned, walking back he lifted my left hand in his, gently touching my wedding and engagement rings he said: "I think perhaps these should come off, but leave the beautiful one on your other hand it suits the occasion."

"I don't understand," I whispered.

"The man you go to meet, I do not think he is English. Neither is he your true husband."

Silently I shook my head.

"No, I thought not, but in spirit you are truly man and mate."

This time I nodded.

Blowing me a kiss he left the compartment, leaving me more scared than I had ever been before. Were my feelings for Dieter really so obvious or was it just that the little Belgian penguin really was a witch in disguise.

I slept fitfully that night, aware of every jerk and stop the train made, guilt coming to the forefront when the train made a lengthy stop at one station. Looking out of the window I realised it was Cologne. "Just think as you travel to meet Dieter, his wife and sons sleep not far from here, completely innocent of his duplicity," a voice taunted me.

"Yes, but she has so much more of him than I have."

Not till the words echoed round the empty carriage did I realise that I had spoken aloud, in my own defence.

As the light from the large station filtered through the curtain I had not closed properly, it picked out the gold of the ring Bill had placed on my finger so many years ago. Silently and deftly I removed the outward sign of more than twenty-five years of marriage, wrapping them in a tissue then placing the rings carefully in my handbag. At first it felt strange but somehow the weight of the ring on my on my finger of my right hand felt so right."

"Come little one, it is time to wake up. Today you live for a short time a new life and that makes the sunshine brighter than ever." I could hear Leon speak in gentle tones as he shook me out of the sleep I had finally fallen into.

As my eyes became accustomed to the daylight, I could see that Leon was not wrong, the day did indeed promise to be beautiful. Dressing hurriedly in the mint-green tracksuit I had decided to wear, it wasn't long before I heard the tinkle of cutlery and the wheels of the breakfast trolley heading in my direction.

"Ah good you are awake and dressed," Leon greeted me, this time his tones more normal. "Unlike those bloody Australians down the corridor." The way he used the epithet made me mile. "Why, what's wrong with them?" I asked, trying not to laugh in case I should hurt his feelings.

"Because they have purchased a ticket they think I have also been purchased. I am neither their servant nor their slave." Saying this he left the meal behind and stomped off, obviously to carry out some bidding of the much maligned antipodeans.

With a final check I made sure all my personal items were once more safely tucked inside my suitcase. A loud click and I was ready for the next part of my journey. Feeling too keyed up to sit down any longer, I stood looking out of the window. Now there was no more darkness to shroud the countryside, instead I was able to see the Austrian mountains covered in the familiar blue haze of early morning. The sun slowly spreading her golden fingers across each peak appeared to bring them to miraculous life. Here and there, where snow lingered or glaciers were visible, the sun cut orange paths across the pristine white of snow and ice, as though advising the climbers who would be walking that day, the safe route to take.

With a sigh I turned from my vantage point. Case in hand I headed towards the door only to have Leon take the cumbersome weight from me. "Let me help you, Madame." He smiled, "You look nervous, why?" I could only shake my head in silence, there was, after all, no answer.

With a final long screech of brakes the train came to a juddering halt. Opening the door that led onto the platform, not only allowed in the early morning chill but the noise of porters running up and down offering assistance. Little flower stalls were also plying their trade. New passengers were doing what I had done the night previous, checking train numbers and their reservations. This reminded me that though I had reached my destination, Salzburg was in fact the jumping off point for so many other countries. Cities where dreams were made, places about which songs and played had been written: Venice, Budapest and Istanbul to name but a few...

"So Madame, we part," Leon's high pitched voice cut in once more on my thoughts. "It is a pity we part so soon, but who knows..." With an almost Gallic gesture he shrugged, placed my case on the hard platform surface, put his cap on his head and saluted. This action touched me to such an extent that for a moment tears welled up choking me, as I fought vainly to stop them bursting forth.

This little Penguin like creature had proved to be a good and understanding friend. Would we ever meet again, I wondered. Then, as the train began once more to move, he leapt onto the step calling out: "I say farewell to a lady, may you know only true happiness." At this, that shiver of foreboding I had come to expect ran up my spine once more. Were we asking too much? Were we really so wrong to steal just a few short hours of life together? I didn't know. I was short of answers.

With the train's departure the station had once again fallen silent. Looking up and down the platform, no sign of Dieter anywhere. Having said goodbye to the steward I was now completely alone, I felt bereft. What was I doing here, had Dieter been playing a sick trick on me. Checking frantically in my bag I looked over my ticket, yes it was an open one so I could make my return the same day if my lover were not with me in the next few minutes. I almost felt relieved, having decided to return home on the next train.

Walking disconsolately up and down, I watched as the few people still left were finally greeted by those who had come for them. From an elderly couple, obviously meeting children, to sisters and brothers holding each other in family embraces. It was the passionate union between a young couple that finally brought my complete aloneness home to me. I had followed a dream but it was not to be.

Turning unhappily, and following the arrow that pointed in the direction of the opposite platform and customs post, I walked with slow dragging footsteps, my suitcase packed some twenty-four hours earlier with such excitement now feeling heavier than ever.

"I see a damsel in distress, perhaps I can help?"

Turning, a sharp retort ready on my lips for any railway Romeo who might be approaching me, I was struck dumb. For here was no greasy, Lothario, no unwholesome stranger, it was the man I had travelled hundreds of miles to meet. We stood face to face, no film-like acknowledgement. To anyone watching, we might have appeared more like protagonists in a fight than story-book lovers.

The tension holding him like a fine-honed knife transmitted itself to me. Nervously, almost like a bride on her wedding day, I allowed my footsteps to lead towards him. Silently, I walked with measured tread, not understanding what it was that held him in so tight a grip that he stood unsmiling and rigid.

Standing in the early morning sunlight I could see little specks of white now nestling in the midnight blackness of his hair. Around emerald green eyes there were little lines of worry, making me want gently to soothe them away. I looked at the full, sensual mouth. Today it appeared to be pursed in pain. I was more used to see it smiling or feeling it placing hot passionate kisses on my own lips or gently touching and teasing more vulnerable parts of my body. The desire I always felt when this man was around, once more began to well up in me. I needed his arms round me, wanted to hear him say how much he loved me, yet it was the expression on his face that held me at arm's length. Instead of flying into his waiting arms I heard myself say: "Hi, I thought you weren't coming."

How banal was my greeting. I hadn't said anything I wanted just, "Hi." What had happened to the romantic meeting I had envisaged? It had disappeared like the train. Dieter's eyes were lacklustre, no arms stretched

374

out in my direction, instead he stood as if divorced from me and our surroundings.

Quietly I was led out into the nearby car park, where I was ushered into a red Mercedes. "This isn't yours," I mumbled fiddling with the seat belt.

"No," he replied while checking over his shoulder that it was safe to pull out, "I thought it was best to hire a car."

I nodded. No need for words. In this one sentence I had been informed that he wanted nothing left behind that might later incriminate him with his wife.

We drove from the station in a heavy silence that seemed to last for hours. The car with its powerful engine appeared to swallow the miles easily. Seated beside the man who now appeared to be more stranger than lover, I examined the old-fashioned houses built during a more graceful era, when the music of Strauss was popular and horse carriages were the fashionable way of travelling. It wasn't long before we had left the crowded roads behind and were driving past the airport, finally finding ourselves on a wide road bounded by mountains through whose valleys we journeyed. Cutting across meadows we followed the route of the River Saalach around whose banks the city of Salzburg and its accompanying suburbs had grown.

My frustration at his attitude toward me was the only thing spoiling the beauty of the day. Giving him a sideways glance, I could see his profile. His jaw set in uncompromising lines, cheek bones so rigid they looked as if carved from granite.

"Why?" I kept asking myself. "I didn't want to come, this was his idea. He could have called it off anytime he liked." Terrified I might burst out in temper, or worse still break down in tears, I allowed my common sense to lead me away from danger and into enjoying the beauties nature had provided.

The mountains surrounding us stood strong and silent, like sentinels guarding a million secrets, man should never discover. They stood, these prehistoric monoliths of granite, a memento of millennia past. I felt, as I watched the blue haze still lingering at their base, that if my eyes closed for a second these stone edifices would disappear taking us with them into a timeless world of dreams.

My fanciful thoughts continued to take wing, joining the birds that flew all around us. Accompanying them on their mysterious flights were bees and insects who, like their larger counterparts, seemed intent on carrying out the tasks nature had designed for them, that of keeping this part of the world a haven of beauty and peace.

So lost was I in the harmony surrounding us--- the meadows ablaze with colours from the blue of the cornflowers and the pale cream of the edelweiss to the reds of the poppies. Everything was in perfect synergy. Except, that is, for the tension that held me tightly. Suddenly, I was blind to the green of the long grass and the gold of the wheat.

"Looking down at my hands, clenched tightly in my lap, it was obvious the warm mountain air now blowing through the open car window nothing to ease the discontent running through me. This was only one solution. Taking a deep breath, holding it for a second, I let it out in a rush: "I'm hungry, can we eat?" I was furious with myself, what had I said? Why? For what seemed like weeks I had been imagining our first magical hours together. Now we had met Dieter's reaction to me had not been as in my fantasies. So, when I should be questioning him on it, why had I instead requested food. It was the last thing I wanted. I needed Dieter, nothing more and nothing less.

"You are hungry?" His voice came to me soft on the balmy air filling the car.

I could only nod.

Minutes later we pulled into the car park in front of a small timbered building surrounded by tables and chairs. The smell of fish being grilled filled the air, making my stomach rebel quite violently at the aroma. Steckerl fish, was a meal I normally enjoyed, but today the thought of eating barbecued fish, brown bread and sauerkraut on paper plates in the open was more like a nightmare.

Having been served, we carried our paper plates with bottles of ice cold beer, to an empty table. As it was still quite early in the day there were many to choose from.

"Do you like this food?" Dieter asked, his mouth full of home-made brown bread.

"God, he doesn't even know what I like to eat." His last remark had once more reminded me how little we knew of each other.

Trying not to stare at my companion, afraid he might see the pain I felt sure was mirrored in my eyes, I stared up at the tree under whose branches we were sharing our first meal together. Alone.

Having felt I had studied the tree to its minutest detail, I looked once more at my plate. The fish normally so tasty, had no more flavour today than a plate of ashes. Looking at Dieter out of the corner of my eye, I was furious to see that the atmosphere between us had in no way affected his appetite, he seemed to be enjoying each mouthful with gusto. I watched enviously as he systematically devoured everything on his plate.

"I suppose you'll even manage to chew the bones." I muttered.

"No," he smiled "they will stick in my throat."

"Yes, then perhaps you might choke," I replied waspishly.

"Sorry," he looked up quickly, "what did you say?"

"Nothing," I said, glancing down at my plate, still almost full. "Would you like to eat mine as well?"

Pushing his plate away, wiping his fingers, he smiled: "No thank you, I think I have had enough."

The temptation to hit him over the head with my plate, was very strong. The picture of him wearing my lunch over his dark head was so ludicrous, that I started to giggle. A sound that took the man sitting beside me by surprise.

"Why?" What do you laugh for?" He asked.

"Because I'm an impressionable fool." I stuttered, my laughter now showing signs of hysteria.

With a muttered expletive in German, Dieter dragged me from my chair. With a barely concealed anger he took our plates to the large metal bins provided, then with a force I had not been expecting he pulled me across the grass to the waiting car. It was obvious that the astonishment now filling me was shared by our other dinner companions, who were staring at his actions with as much surprise as I felt. Once we had settled in the car, the only sound to be heard was the screech of tyres on the gravel as Dieter pulled away, anger in every move he made.

The laughter had faded, filling the car once more with an uneasy silence. Suddenly, a memory came back to me, one that stemmed from hearing him order our food. "Why did you say, "my wife" when ordering our meals." I asked quietly.

"That is how I see you." His voice was as quiet as mine.

I had wanted to reply: "Like hell." instead I said: "Then why this performance?"

From his look it was obvious that at first my question had not been understood. Only as comprehension dawned did his expression lighten, and the speed of the car slow from suicidal to just fast.

"Oh, Schatzie, you do not understand." Placing a hand on my knee he glanced momentarily at me: "I had hoped you would, that perhaps you too would feel the same as me."

Then turning to stare at the road flashing past us, he carried on in a tone that was quiet and filled with pain. "For me you will always be my wife, my woman, the soulmate all men desire but never find." A quick glance in my direction accompanied by a smile that made an already bright day sunnier. "Did I not give you my ring? Don't you know I love you now and will forever." There was no mistaking the meaning and emotion in his voice, making me feel quite selfish. I had been so wrapped up in my own little world of self-pity. There had been no thought of what pain my lover might be suffering.

"Then why have you been so quiet?" I asked once more, still needing an answer.

"Oh baby don't you see? I have wanted this for so long. Needed you alone with me so much that now I am frightened."

"What are you scared of?"

"Us."

At this one word I turned my head, puzzled. "Please explain."

"Moment," he replied. As he manoeuvred the car off the main road, seeking one of the minor, tree lined roads that fed from mountain tracks and farms onto the main thoroughfare.

Finally we came to rest on a quiet road in the middle of a field. Here we sat for some seconds, looking at each other. This time none of our feelings were hidden. We had no need for words, passion and need for each other was easy to read in each other's eyes.

Taking my right hand he placed his lips to the ring put there so long ago by him. As if by this act he renewed the vows made in the cathedral that winter's afternoon. This simple act of love and devotion brought such a surge of feeling that my breath caught in my throat.

"It is because I know you are the right one for me, that I have great fear, my darling." he hesitated slightly before carrying on: "What frightens me is that when our days together are over, I will not want us to part."

This was a sentiment I too could agree with, for in this stark sentence he had echoed my feelings. If our partings had been painful after so many years of grabbed moments, secret looks and guarded words, how much more agonising would our farewell be after days, hours and nights in each other's company. Learning every intimate detail, finally knowing each other as we longed to, how then could we say goodbye?

I could feel the heat coming from his arm, as it lay along the back of my seat. In silence I turned to him, feeling the familiar tingle of anticipation running up my spine. Hearing the gasp that escaped his open lips, as he saw the promise of what I had to offer mirrored in my eyes. My soul was bared to this man, my love my life.

"Lieber Gott," he whispered as our lips finally met in the kiss I had craved for so long. It was a kiss that seemed to have no ending. All our frustrations and desires slowly being released until, finally, kisses were not enough. It was not just the taste of each other's lips that was needed, but the closeness that could come from the joining of our bodies. I needed the feel of him, the scent of his hot body close to mine. Allowing my hands the freedom they desired I could feel Dieter moving restlessly beside me.

Knowing only I could give him the release he needed. I slowly and deliberately began to undo his zip so giving his penis the freedom it so obviously required.

"No, baby," he whispered, gently stopping my groping fingers. "Not in the car, we are close to the house where we stay," here he stopped. No further need for words, his eyes finished the sentence. They promised joys and pleasures that could not be spoken about but shared only between true lovers.

Having tidied ourselves the last leg of our journey was restarted, this time the air between us heavy not with tension but longing.

Sooner than expected I saw a small, wooden, hand-painted sign, appearing to point up at the sky, stating we were two kilometres away from "Die Feldenburg." It was only as we turned up what appeared to be no more than a track cut by tractors, that I realised the distance given us had not meant the length of road, before reaching our destination, but, in fact, the height.

With skill Dieter manoeuvred the large car round hair-pin bends, seeming to cling to the side of the mountain like a limpet. Pine trees that had appeared small and insignificant from the main road were soon taking on a new aspect. They were growing in stature and density. Looking over the side, I would hold my breath to stop giving an involuntary scream. Looking out of the car it appeared as if there were no more roads for us to travel on. But gradually my fears gave way to my admiration of the scenery unfolding about us.

Finally we came to rest on a tiny plateau, where a small farm wagon filled with hay stood beside a car that must have first seen life during the latter days of the war.

Opening the car door Dieter, invited me to alight; then to my amazement he walked over to the old barn near where we had parked, here he appeared to be searching for something. I stared puzzled at this rather erratic behaviour, until with a grunt of satisfaction he appeared before me carrying two large rocks: "Just why have we got those?" I asked, unable to contemplate the answer.

"Extra brakes," he muttered. Walking to the back of the car the giant stones were placed under each wheel. Rubbing his hands together the look on his face made me smile. He was so happy with his inventiveness he looked for a moment like a school boy.

"Come we must meet our host and hostess, but first…" I wondered what was to come next.

"You must walk slowly, here we are very high so breathing is very difficult when you are not used to it."

I was tempted to state that his warning had come a little late. Walking away from the car, carrying a couple of small bags, I had attempted to stride in my normal fashion, only to be brought up short as my breath seemed to disappear leaving me gasping like a fish out of water.

As we walked from the car to the little chalet in the distance, Dieter explained we were now in the "Pinzgauer Valley." this mountain, like all those surrounding us, had its own name Feldenburg or translated "Mountain Fields." A name I felt suited it perfectly.

Standing still for a few seconds, dieter took one of my hands in his. Raising it to his lips he whispered: "You like."

I nodded silently, overawed by the magnificence surrounding us. We had left the pine trees behind us and now stood in a meadow filled with long, waving grass, Edelweiss were everywhere, the little cream flowers truly looking like snowflakes amid the lush green. These blooms were accompanied by the blues and yellows of other wild flowers. I marvelled how each blade of grass and flower appeared to cling tenaciously to the side of the mountain. The air around us was filled not with the sounds of motor engines, only the lowing of cattle, accompanied by the tinkle of their bells.

"How beautiful it all is," I whispered, too frightened to raise my voice to its normal pitch.

"Here you can forget everyone, but me."

He replied, his voice as soft as mine.

This simple sentence reminded me more starkly than anything else he could have said, that we had no right to be here. We were stealing a moment out of time, turning, without permission dreams into reality and all thieves get punished in the end.

We walked in silence across the meadow, following a path that had been made by the constant use of heavy booted feet. Under the azure-blue skies, past a mountain stream that emptied itself into a clear lake that reflected the sky above in its shimmering waters. Here and there birds flitted silent as ghosts as though they too feared disturbing the peace surrounding us.

Perhaps it was my unaccustomed silence that drew a question from Dieter: "Liebchen, what is wrong?" You are not happy?"

Only as he turned to stare at me did he see the tears I had been trying to hide.

"There is something wrong." He demanded an answer.

"No," I replied, shaking my head, leaning against him for a second: "there is nothing wrong, it is just I am so happy that I am frightened."

Placing a little kiss on my lips, he smiled: "Women, I will never understand them!" then picking up our cases he began walking towards the house that had now come into view.

How could I explain my fears? They were so intangible to him but real to me. I was sure somewhere close at hand could be heard the mocking voice of fate, advising me to take what I had now and enjoy it because the future was unpredictable and not always pleasant.

"So what do you think of our home for the next few days?" Dieter asked, turning to smile at me, obviously pleased by the expression on my face.

"It's more beautiful than I could have imagined," I replied.

The chalet nestled in a fold of the mountains, bounded by trees and wild flowers. It looked like something out of a story book. From the slanted roof made of hand-carved wooden tiles, to the porch surrounding it, the little house was unbelievable. I could see that logs had been cut into uniform length and stacked neatly along three sides of the little wooden house. Looking up I could see smoke rising from a chimney that was the only thing visible not carved out of a tree.

This was no normal guest house, but a working farm house for dairy cattle. Chickens and ducks meandered around the footpath, not in the least nervous of strangers.

"See up there." I followed Dieter's pointing finger to a balcony that appeared to be covered in pink geraniums, adding a splash of colour to the drabness of the weathered wood.

"That is where we will sleep." Something in the tone of his voice told me that the last word was the one thing we might not be doing too much of.

A slight movement on the porch brought my thoughts and eyes back to the front once more. Here I saw a lady of uncertain years, her skin tanned by the extremes of climate creating an almost leathery effect. Smiling at us she showed the magnificent sum of two teeth, clamped tightly round a long, wooden pipe, black from age and constant use. As she puffed, surrounding herself in a noxious smelling cloud of smoke, she wheezed: "So, your wife has now arrived." Then turning she spoke to me, her dialect strong and difficult to follow. It was Dieter who translated, while trying not to laugh.

"She said," he began, "she is glad you are here, for last night when I was alone it was clear that I was finding sleep difficult." then bending he whispered in my ear: "Tonight it will be impossible."

I nodded silently, feeling any answer to be unnecessary while finding it difficult to climb the two steps that took us to the verandah, as my knees had been turned to jelly by the expression in Dieter's eyes.

Entering through the solid wooden door, I was amazed at how spacious and tidy the inside was. Everywhere was pine, scrubbed clean till every surface shone. A large, black, iron range took up one wall in the kitchen that also doubled as dining and sitting room for warmth, economy and companionship. Nearby stood a large dining table surrounded by hand-made, high-backed chairs with beautifully embroidered cushions in a rich deep red on the seats. Along all the walls could be seen shelves holding iron pots and bric-a-brac all original in design and make.

On a wall by the door was a photograph of the farm. This, like the lady we had already seen, had been affected by the passage of time, as it was now a sepia colour. In it stood a young man dressed in the style of the early twentieth century, with Tyrolean hat and beard resembling one the Kaiser might have sported himself, between his lips was a pipe. The same one I felt sure, that the old lady now clung to so lovingly.

My hostess was bending before the cooker, wearing a green and white check Dirndl, her blonde hair done up in a chignon on the nape of her neck. As she turned to face us, a welcoming smile breaking across her face, I could see that as yet the harsh weather of the mountains had not touched her, for her gleaming skin and fresh faced complexion were as perfect as any child's. Bertha, as I discovered her name to be, was the epitome of the country woman. She had no need of high heels and glamorous make-up. Instead she wore her rotund figure, ankle socks, and flat shoes with pride. Her handshake was firm. Only in her clear, blue eyes did I detect a slight shadow.

"Ah, guten abend." A voice filled the room with the sound of a bass-drum booming. Turning more in shock than in surprise, I was faced with a man who looked as if he had been carved from the granite of his beloved mountains.

Willi, was a giant of a man. Taking his hat in one hand, he held the other out to me in greeting. I had to stand on tip-toe to try to face him, finding even this difficult. I felt for a moment as David must have felt when looking at Goliath, except this man did neither threaten nor terrify. Instead, from the top of gleaming black hair to the fresh ruddy complexion of his face, his grey eyes looked out on the world with the knowledge of centuries of education about nature, that comes to all those who live in amicable friendship with the earth, neither giving nor taking, only borrowing. He was indeed a gentle giant. Taking my hand in a grip that would have crushed rock he welcomed me into his life.

I watched as he greeted first Dieter then his wife, dressed in the leder hosen that was natural for all native Austrians. His, "Welcome to the Feldenburg, I am sure that you will have a good holiday," was thrown over his shoulder as he disappeared out of the room, obviously to prepare for the evening meal that was being cooked, delicious smells reminding me that I had not eaten since much earlier that day and most of that had been thrown away.

As Dieter sat at the table, a cigarette between his ling fingers, I stood hesitantly, wanting to be alone with him yet unsure. As if reading my thoughts Bertha suddenly stood up, her face redder than usual from the heat of the stove: "Come, I will show you to your room." then as Dieter made a move to follow us: "No, you stay here and talk to Willi. Coffee is ready and the food will not be long."

I followed her out of the room, up a short flight of steps, which like everything else in the house was made from well-scrubbed pine. After leading me along a dark, narrow hallway she opened a door into a room that was bright, sparkling and perfect in every detail.

No wallpaper to be found her, only timbered walls on three sides, the fourth did not exist as this was the window I had seen earlier that looked out onto the verandah on which the flower-boxes stood in all their glory. From here I could see we had a perfect view of the mountain ranges surrounding us.

Once left alone, I did a little exploring. Apart from the French windows, I had noticed a couple of other doors. Opening one I found it lead into an en suite shower-room and toilet. This was done in a delicate shade of lilac as with everything else in the house it was surprisingly modern and not at all as I had expected.

Wandering from the bathroom, I opened the other door only to find myself faced not with a room, but a walk in cupboard. Feeling the brush of a jacket on my face and a familiar smell assail my nostrils, it was with a start that I realised Dieter's clothing and mine would for a few days hang together. Entering the bedroom once more I could not believe what an erotic sensation the thought of our clothes hanging together gave me. With shaking legs I walked once more round the room not just regaining my composure, but still admiring the room in which I stood.

Like the bathroom and kitchen it was bright and airy. As with everything else I had seen in the house it was filled out in polished wood, from the fitted bed and dressing table to the little bedside units on which rested two lamps their bulbs shaded in pink cotton. Looking down I could see that even here the floorboards had been polished with just a few rugs in pink and grey scattered around the room to give it a slightly warmer appearance.

A sudden feeling of excitement filled me. Turning round and round like a child on its birthday, my bare-feet making no sound on the floor, I raised my arms above my head and sighed: "Our room." With a final look at the bed and its pink and grey duvet, I made my way down the stairs to the family waiting below.

During the meal I tried not to let Dieter's glance meet mine, for fear that I might give myself away. All the time wondering what these good, honest folk would think were they to discover we were married ---- but not that is to each other.

Having finished our meal, a delicious one of the native part of the country, we were led out onto the porch. Here, under a moon gaining in strength with the disappearance of day and the onset of night, we sat talking. The men drinking beer, while Bertha, her mother-in-law and I shared a large earthenware pot of buttermilk.

"How long have you two been married?" Bertha's voice came out of the dark.

"Fifteen years," from Dieter

"Ten years," from me.

Thankful for the darkness that covered our blushes, at this mistake, Dieter and I laughed, hoping they would not question us further.

We were both wrong, for the interrogation period had only just started.

"So, we know you are both married, though you are not sure for how long."

"That's not a problem." Willi laughed, settling back in his chair: "But do you know how many children you have?" This question was directed at me.

It was Dieter who answered, however: "Yes, we have four children."

At this I gave quite a start. Turning to look at him, I heard him explain further: "We have two boys and two girls."

Silently I nodded. He had placed both our children under one protective paternal wing, his own.

It was Bertha who heard the sound of my hastily smothered yawn. Standing up she took the mug from my hand placing it on the cane table that stood before us: "Come, Dieter, can't you see your wife is tired, she has come a long way today." Then, placing my hand in his, she carried on: "Take her to bed." An invitation she had no need to repeat.

Jumping up with an alacrity that I thought seemed overzealous for a married man of many years, he waved a bright goodnight to our companions saying, as we walked once more into the brightly lit kitchen: "My wife is not very good at staying awake once the sun has gone down. My good lady is no longer as young as she once was."

Our host and hostess were not aware that it was my well-aimed foot, coming in contact with Dieter's ankle, that made him try to smother a loud groan of pain.

Once more entering our room, this time by the side of my lover, I stood for the second time that day nervous and hesitant.

"Would you like a shower?" I mumbled as Dieter began to turn the duvet down.

"You go first," he replied.

In my eagerness to escape, I stumbled catching my foot on the corner of one of the mats. As Dieter held a hand out to catch me, he realised I was trembling.

"Why Vicki, you are nervous."

I nodded into his shoulder, no need for words.

"But darling we have been together often, why are you so frightened."

Looking up into his passionate green eyes, how could I explain that though we had made love together often, in the past. It had not been on so complete a basis as this. Our moments together had been short and stolen, but tonight was almost like a honeymoon. There would be no one to disturb us. We had hours, days together. I was so frightened that I might in some way disappoint him. Maybe I would not come up to his expectations. All these fears were soon put to flight as I felt his warm lips seeking mine. Once finding and taking possession of my mouth it was not long before our embrace became one of desire needing satisfaction. Suddenly he pulled away, his breathing heavy: "Come little one, shower, then we can go to bed."

Having dressed myself in the nightshirt I had brought with me, I once more entered our room, only to find it empty. I stood silently wondering where my lover was, the only sound filling the room coming from the fields surrounding us, that of crickets and cow bells. So lost was I in thought that when hearing Dieter's voice I was startled.

Searching the dark for him, it was long seconds before my eyes picked him out of the gloom heading towards me from the balcony. The moon made a silver path across the wooden floor, lighting his sway. The only scent accompanying him being that of jasmine and hibiscus coming in through the open doors. He stood before me completely naked, his masculine beauty filling me with awe and desire.

"Why are you wearing this?" He asked, lifting my arms over my head as he slipped my nightshirt from me. Then, as it drifted silently to the floor his fingers began an exploration of my body. My need for this man was so strong that my body began to shake from the warmth of his lips as they explored my body. Making their way down me, leaving little rivulets of fire where they touched, I was unable to stem the trembling that gripped me.

His long brown fingers caressed me gently, then, taking my hands in his, I was shown how to pleasure him. We stood for what seemed an eternity reacquainting ourselves with each other's bodies. Learning and teaching, sharing and giving. There was no need for words now, we knew instinctively what each other needed and wanted.

"Sweetheart, you are so beautiful," Dieter mumbled as he lay me down, not on the bed but the floor. Our desire having reached fever pitch we had no wish to move from where we now were, knowing only that we had to take possession of each other. As we lay together his hands and mine exploring, touching, I felt his lips finally close over mine, with a groan I opened my mouth allowing his tongue to take full possession of me.

So we stayed, each one taking pleasure in the other. Hearts and minds in unison, until the waiting became a kind of delicious agony. Then I felt his hands pushing aside my warm thighs, feeling his body covering mine. The sudden thrust of his penis as it penetrated me came with a shock. One that took my already overheated brain into another world. One where there were no sounds other than the groans of ecstasy coming from us as we writhed in passion on the floor. For us the present was all that was important.

At the moment of his hotly uttered: "Ich lieber disch," I knew his ownership of me to be complete. In that instant I had become his wife and lover. Never again could there be a dividing line between us, spiritually and physically we were now one.

As we lay side by side on the bed, exhausted by our earlier demands of each other, I was grateful that the moon in her wisdom and silence would hold forever the secrets of lovers everywhere for eternity. In the light coming from her golden glow, that lit up our haven of pleasure, I could see the happy and rested smile that crossed Dieter's face. The tension that had held us both in its grip during the day finally melted away under the heat of the assuagement of our passions and desires.

"So, you are now happy." this was more a demand than a question.

"I am always happy to be with you," I whispered in return.

He nodded, obviously pleased with my answer.

I could feel his head go once more to my breasts, kissing each one in turn, then taking and sucking each nipple. I could feel the desire I had thought spent in our earlier love-making start to rise once more, like a river reaching its barrier at flood-tide.

"Stop, don't do that," I muttered, placing my hand over his lips.

"What is wrong, you don't like this" He queried.

"I love it, but you will only start me wanting you once more," I replied, hesitantly.

"So, we have all night, darling. This is for us."

These were the last words spoken for some time, as the horse that was passion rose on his hind legs, needing to be ridden once more.

Finally, all passion and energy spent, we lay in each other's arms. A whispered, "Thank you," from me brought a puzzled, "For what?" from Dieter.

"For loving me."

Chuckling, he replied, in tones still husky from the heat of our love making. "Go to sleep liebchen. For now our dreams have become reality. There is nothing we have to lose."

Lying quietly on the bed I could hear the dawn chorus starting. My body was filled with a delicious lethargy, limbs hurting after the heated ecstatic movements of the night before. Turning my head to gaze at the man still lying asleep beside me, the need to touch him filled me with a yearning so deep it bordered on desperation, but I was reluctant to disturb him as he looked for the first time completely relaxed. While he lay like this I felt him to be only mine. In this quiet period I was free to study him for as long as I liked, without his being aware of my gaze.

Giving a sigh I cuddled closed, feeling the warmth of his body burn into mine. Feeling his arms brush against my breasts, once again the rising tide of passion coursed through me. In an effort to keep my feelings in check I pulled hurriedly away, surprised when a voice said: "You don't like the feel of me?"

With a quick move Dieter was on his back, pulling me down on top of him, his lips covering mine. It wasn't long before the actions of the night before were re-enacted. This time it was better, we had by now learnt how to pleasure each other. Earlier we had been students in the art of love, now we had become proficient, masters in the age-old practise of love.

The sun rising over the Grossglockener and her sister mountains was the only witness to the promises we made to each other. Finally, our desires once more satisfied, I rose from the bed, walking slowly to the open French-windows. From here I could see the panorama spread before me. In the distance were the range of mountains that divided Austria from Italy. These stately ladies of stone, with their snowy tops, appeared so wise, for a moment I wished we could learn some wisdom from these granite antiquities. I was still fearful that the happiness now filling me would be snatched away, never to be returned. Looking away from the mountains I could see the cattle being led out pasture by Willi. His mother wandering in a field close to the house, appeared to be picking up stones and odd piece of wood. So lost was I in studying my surroundings that Dieter had to repeat himself twice before I heard what he said:

"Why are you so far away from me?" He mumbled.

"No darling, not far, just afraid."

"Of what?"

"Losing our happiness, you and I both know this is wrong. We shouldn't be here, we have responsibilities, families." Turning from the window to look at the man now sitting up in bed, on his face the same expression as mine --- that of guilt.

"I know what you say is true," he replied, his voice wavering slightly, "but I cannot say we avoid our duties. No darling, we steal from each other, our families lose nothing."

I knew this to be true. For though pain, need and frustration had long been companions of ours, we had never put our families at risk. Dieter and I had carried on our chosen tasks caring for those in our care diligently. Choosing to suffer the pain ourselves, rather than pass it on to those innocents around us.

I climbed back on to the bed, holding the man who had given me so much pleasure tightly in my arms. This time it was not with passion, just the simple way of showing him I was aware of his feelings, both the agony and the ecstasy. So we sat, silently, content to know each other was close. Into this peaceful moment Willi's voice could be heard summoning us to breakfast. Glancing at each other we knew that one precious moment had been broken, never to return.

Entering the kitchen we joined our host and hostess at the tables, both looking bright and fresh from their labours of the morning and the cool, crisp mountain air.

Bertha enquired as she poured my coffee: "You slept well?"

I could never explain to how so innocent a question could bring gales of laughter from her guests as Dieter and I glanced at each other, finding the passion of the night before and the following morning something impossible to forget.

Our laughter having subsided: "What will you do today?" Willi enquired, placing a large chunk of bread and cheese into his mouth.

"I shall show my wife Salzburg," Dieter replied, staring at me. The pride with which he used the words "my wife," brought a momentary ache to my heart.

"Oh, how I wish it were true," I could not resist thinking.

Breakfast finished: "Now we have work to do. You and your man must go and have a good day." Bertha ushered us out of the room, before I could offer my services as washer-up.

Again I felt an immeasurable amount of pleasure at the simple words used by my hostess. Glancing up at Dieter, I could see the tide of passion rising once more in his eyes, as if the words had evoked memories of the times we had spent together. His hands gently lifted my right hand, pressing his lips softly and with all the love he could show against the ring he had placed on my finger so long ago. We stood for a moment in time, living statues locked in a time warp where dreams and reality had become indefinable.

"It is good to see two people still so much in love, after many years of marriage."

It was Bertha's sigh and her words that brought us back to the present with a shock. We had been so lost in our world of love, that we had forgotten we were not alone in the kitchen.

Driving down the mountain, the fresh winds blowing through my hair, though I had travelled to Salzburg many times before with my family, this time I made the journey not as a wife or a mother but as a lover. So the scenes that opened up before me, though familiar were strangely new and different, like myself they too had become reborn. The golf course nestling in the valley, riding school nearby, the meadows and pastures all had taken on a new glow. Today was definitely the first day of my life. I felt nothing could go wrong. Looking at Dieter, as he smiled and hummed tunelessly but happily, I defied the gods to take away what I now had. Oh! What a mistake to make.

My eyes closed as I tried to make my mind photograph every scene. A memory to be filed away, kept for the times when I would once more be alone. Suddenly intruding into my happy thoughts came a voice I had not heard for many years: "When the Purple Michaelmas Daisy blooms your life will change." Jim's words echoed once more.

I wanted to shout for joy, thinking: "Jim if only you were here, I would hug you. I am so happy."

Only as I thought of the last word did Josie's words also come to me, like a dark cloak being placed over the bright sun: "Vicki, my dear, don't be too greedy, please be careful what you take and from whom."

"What could I lose that was so important to me?" I had replied flippantly. In my naivety, convinced that my life would forever run on lines that appeared to be chosen for me. Not for a second thinking that even the best run tracks could suffer derailment.

"What is wrong, baby?" Dieter asked, as a shudder ran through me.

"Nothing. I think the wind was a bit cold then."

For a second he looked puzzled, as it was obvious that the nearer we got to the valley the air grew warmer, the early wind losing its bite as the sun gained in strength.

In an effort to lighten the atmosphere he soon had me laughing at silly things he said, our hands often reaching out for each other. Glances, finding and holding secrets only for two.

"Think. What is the thing you would most hate to lose?" Once more Josie's voice teased me. I shook my head, as if to remove the cobwebs of fear that hung around me, filling my soul with an anxiety that made me want to cry.

"No, dear God, you cannot, must not take Dieter from me." Turning to look at him so full of life, love and fun, I realised my fears were ridiculous. "It's a guilty conscience, my dear, that's all." I admonished myself. Then, placing a kiss on the side of Dieter's mouth, I gave myself over to the joys he had in store for me.

Our first stop that morning was at the water games of Hellbrunn, a palace built by a capricious archbishop with a sense of the ridiculous.

Having enjoyed our visit to the Baroque Palace and beautiful park we headed into the city, both looking decidedly dishevelled from the hidden sprays of water we had endured during our adventures in the water gardens of Hellbrunn.

"Where would you like to go first?" Dieter asked, as we blinked trying to accustom our eyes once more to the bright sunlight, after the darkness of the underground car-park.

"The cathedral." His smile was all the answer I needed. In our hearts we knew there were those who would condemn us. Say we were irresponsible, uncaring and adulterous. Only Dieter and I knew we were lovers in the true sense. Husband and wife, man and mate since time immemorial. Neither distance in life nor the final separation of death could divide us. So sure was I of our feelings for each other. Yet I did not want ever to face my final thought. Life without Dieter would be no life at all.

After our visit to the beautiful Gothic church, our day was spent in a haze of tourism. We walked and ran, laughing and giggling. At times behaving like the teenagers we saw everywhere in the city's many squares. All the sights we witnessed were for us the first time, no action repeated, no word duplicated. For us life had begun today, how I wished it could never end.

"Hungry?" He asked, looking down at me.

I nodded.

Taking my hand in his, I was led into a part of the old city I had never seen before. I was amazed at how he could find his way around the dark alleyways that infested this medieval memorial to the salt miners of years ago. As we walked he promised me a meal such as I had never tasted before. After much turning and twisting we were eventually faced with a large wrought-iron gate.

Here I hesitated.

For a moment I had forgotten how sensitive he was to my every thought and action. Sensing my hesitation Dieter looked down at me: "What is wrong, liebchen?"

"Have you ever been here with your wife?" I blurted out.

"No, schatz. Neither Monique nor my sons have ever been here." Taking the hand I had slipped out of his: "Come, I am very hungry and there is someone special who wants to meet you."

I felt so elated, knowing I was being taken somewhere his wife had not been, but no amount of self-satisfaction could stop me curiosity, who was this mysterious person that wanted to meet me.

We gained entry into the courtyard beyond by Dieter pressing a button on the lion's head carved in iron and answering the disembodied voice that enquired who we were.

I was led, dumbfounded, across the square, unprepared for the beauty of the garden in which we found ourselves. The complete garden had been designed around a large pond, filled with a variety of fish in every size and colour. From its centre rose a fountain in the likeness of Aphrodite holding a water jug. It was from this the water spilled. Looking away from the fish and water lilies that floated gracefully before us, my gaze was caught by the riot of colour coming from flowers and trees. Adding lustre to an already beautiful scene. Everywhere I looked were rhododendrons, roses, geraniums protected from the heat by the tall, graceful linden trees.

"I think perhaps you like my garden." A soft husky voice spoke, his English perfect.

Thinking I could not be surprised any further, I was once more proved wrong. For the man standing before me could have been Dieter's double, a much larger and older version. But, everything about him was Dieter.

Turning to look from one pair of laughing green eyes into another I thought: "I know he is not his father."

In the next instant I found myself in an all-enveloping embrace, "So, you are the lady who has given my favourite nephew so much happiness." My puzzlement had been answered.

Finally, extricating myself from the powerful arms that had held me for some suffocating seconds, I heard Dieter's laughing reply: "Uncle, I am your only nephew."

"Makes no difference, you are still my favourite."

This logic took some understanding. Having failed to do so Dieter and I looked at each other, smiled and followed our host into the cool interior of his restaurant.

We were led away from the garden, along a narrow cobbled pathway and through a high, arched gateway, almost Moorish in style. From here we were led into an entrance hall of marble, where two flights of steep stairs led into the dining room. Reaching the bottom of the stair I realised this was no small salon but a refectory, with long, wooden tables and heavy benches made from dark oak taking the place of chairs. A solid iron candelabra stood as a centrepiece on each table.

While Dieter and his uncle discussed the menu, I allowed my gaze to wander round the room, admiring the ornately worked iron grilles on the stained glass windows, each one depicting a scene from the Bible. The walls were painted in pale cream. No carpets graced the floor, just cold marble, which after today's heat was cool and welcoming.

"What are you looking at?" Dieter asked, his attention attracted by my silence.

"Trying to read this." I pointed to what looked like a memorial stone in the centre of the floor, inscribed in Gothic German.

"I cannot read this."

Before I could ask him anything further he added: "My uncle cannot, either."

"What is this place?" I asked, puzzled.

"It was an old cloister. Then when the monks left, it became a school, now it belongs to my uncle."

"Your uncle knows about me?"

"Of course, it's how it should be. He is also my godfather."

I could not reconcile myself to this. Surely his uncle must feel loyalty must be given to Monique, Dieter's wife. If that was the case, how then could he accept me so readily. Before I could ask any more questions the meal was served. It was brought to the table in small, sizzling iron skillets. A feast of noodles, cheese and bacon. We drank no wine, only a beer made by our enterprising host. We dined in silence, only the occasional touch of hands meeting, of eyes uniting us in mind, body and spirit.

About to make our farewells, Alois placed a small package into my hands: "A small present for a lady who is delightful, and is making my nephew very, very happy."

Standing beside the pond, the sound of bird song filling the warm, gardenia-scented garden, fingering the prettily packed box I decided to open it before we left the restaurant. Opening the box I was amazed at its contents. Lying in a bed of rose pink tissues was a small basket woven in porcelain, nestling in its pristine base five tiny silver fishes accompanied by two loaves of bread, all made in warm glazed ceramics.

"Why?" Was all I could think of asking.

"To make sure you do not forget me, also it confirms that you will always have what your heart desires, most."

I smiled up at him in thanks, this benediction from his uncle was amazing but in my heart I somehow felt that somewhere the fates were laughing at me. Placing a gentle cheek on Dieter's cheek I felt a tear escape from the corner of my eye. Why? I did not know. Perhaps it was the emotion of the moment or was I being prepared for things to come. I did not know, nor did I want to find out.

Placing the present carefully in my bag, along with Dieter I waved a final goodbye to Alois, who stood at the entrance to his kingdom. I was never sure whether if it was tears in my eyes that misted the older man's eyes, or did he like me feel the emotion of the moment and so shed a few of his own.

"How long has your uncle known about us?" I asked as Dieter and I headed once more for our mountain retreat.

"From the first time we met," he replied matter of factly, keeping his attention on the treacherous road.

"But, that was years go."

"Um, I know it. You see he is not only my uncle but also my best friend. When as a little boy I was in trouble with my parents, or I needed someone to talk to, Alois was always there. A good friend and confidant, he is for both of us.

This last statement filled me with a warm glow, for with these words he had placed us both into a special and secret compartment, where nothing and no one could intrude.

The sun was setting behind the mountain ranges as we showered, preparing ourselves for the evening meal. Our bed still untidy and tousled from the passionate interlude we had shared on our return from the city.

Walking down we met the old lady, who smiled at us, showing the two teeth she still possessed. "She must have kept those for her pipe," Dieter remarked, taking my hand and leading me, giggling in to join the others.

The meal was superb, almost as good as the one we had eaten earlier. However, Dieter caused me great embarrassment with a mocking comment when we were served with the dessert. It was vanilla ice cream, topped with raspberries marinated in a hot rum sauce, called "Heisse Liebe" or "Hot Love." Innocently remarking that I quite liked the ice cream served in this way, Dieter replied, while filling his mouth with a spoonful of the tasty sweet, and all the time staring into my eyes: "I think it is you who makes the love hot." In an effort to hide my embarrassment I picked up the serviette and spilled dessert over the table. "Ah, I was right," Dieter's mocking cry echoed round the room, "I think this time the love was too hot." He ducked, laughing, as a well-aimed roll hit his forehead.

The meal over we accompanied Bertha and the coffee pot out onto the verandah, here we sat in a companionable silence, broken only by the stentorian tones of the old woman's snores. Relaxing into the cane chair, I closed my eyes enjoying the pleasant and relaxed atmosphere around us.

"Do you think my home is beautiful?" Bertha whispered into the darkness creeping around us.

Silently, I nodded.

Opening my eyes, I allowed myself to look around, with the setting sun the lapis sky, was now a deep indigo from which the silver of stars and moon created a new universe. So clear was the smiling face of the queen of the night, I felt sure she was indeed the goddess around whom so many myths and legends had been written.

Now and then a shooting star would flash overhead, a burst of flame then darkness. Sudden death. A shiver coursed down my spine as if I had once more been given a warning, but of what I did not know. The muted sounds of restless cattle was joined by the rustle in the undergrowth of night creatures waking up.

Looking across to the neighbouring mountains, little lights could be seen twinkling, as if the earth was trying to outdo the night sky with her own elegant symmetry.

"Who gave you the duvet that covers our bed?" My voice broke the silence.

"It was made by Willi's mother," Bertha answered.

With a start I sat up, studying the hands of the woman opposite me.

"It is hard to believe that she was once beautiful. Tall and slim, with hands that could create such wonderful embroidery." Bertha went on, voicing my own thoughts.

Silently I shook my head, finding words difficult.

"We cannot always stay young, old age and death come to us all. Some lose their lives when young and others are lucky to be given a long stay on this earth of ours," Willi continued, with a philosophy I wanted to dispute but could not as in my own work there were many who came for a reading having a young child, brother or sister in the Spirit World, I knew and for a brief few minutes I am allowed to enter and share their pain at the passing and in the joy of knowing they still are around.

"Age, I can understand," I answered. "But I refuse to accept why it is that God takes our little ones from us, or a person who is so greatly loved and can achieve so much while on the earth and then their lives are cut short." Holding onto Dieter's hand as though trying desperately to keep him by my side, I finished with: "I refuse to accept God is right in this."

"You are so young, my friend." Bertha answered.

In some way I did not feel she was referring to my actual age, more that where life was concerned.

I had remained untouched by pain, sorrow and sadness. How wrong she was?

"Before you go back, Vicki, we will show you a little of our real life." This cryptic remark puzzled me as I felt sure, with the things Dieter and I had been told in the past few hours, that we knew our host and hostess well. Shrugging I sat back in my chair, waiting quietly till Dieter called me.

"Come liebchen, I am sure you are tired. We will go to bed."

Standing up, I took his hand knowing by the way he held mine that sleep was the last thing on his mind. With my body filling with desire for this man at my side it was difficult to say goodnight while keeping the quiver out of my voice.

"Vicki, what would you do if I was to die before you?" Dieter's voice came to me from the darkness of the balcony surrounding our room.

The feeling of shock and horror that filled me was so great, that I found myself sitting on the bed, my legs having lost all control and strength.

"Don't even think it," I whispered: "You are my thoughts, my words, breath and life. I cannot live without you." Tears were now filling my voice and eyes.

"But, you believe in life after death don't you?" He continued joining me in the bed, our naked bodies wrapped around each other.

"Yes, I do and always have," I then went on to explain the strange things that had happened in my life as a child and young adult until I joined a Development Circle: "So, it goes to say if I am dead before you we will still meet." He continued, his hands beginning to reacquaint themselves about my body.

"Yes, my darling we will meet but it is very different," I knew what he was talking about, as it was my work to give proof of life every day, bringing happiness to people who had loved ones in the Spirit World, but though I had my mother in Spirit she had been elderly and my father too. Looking for his lips in the dark, I could not believe that what we had physically would or could end. My readings had always been a little detached from me. I knew about Spirit, I worked for them but yet was afraid of a loss that would touch me and hurt beyond belief.

As if he had to keep a distance from me, he stood up from the bed and was walking back onto the balcony, a god of a man. Tall, slim and naked. As there were no neighbours there was no one to hide from.

"It is something we must face. I live so far from you, how would you even know what had happened."

Standing up I hurried across to him, placing my own nakedness in his arms: "Do you honestly think I would not know something had happened to you." pulling away slightly, so that I could look up into his green eyes: "You and I are one, our hearts beat together." I placed my hand against his chest, feeling the very heart of him, that with my nearness had lost its natural tempo and was now beating hard and fast. "How then could I not know what events befall you." Taking his hand I led him towards our bed: "Come make love to me, for now we are alive and together."

Only once during the night did I awaken, a shiver running up me as if a cold hand had been laid on my shoulder. Turning, I studied the man sleeping beside me. Watching his strong chest rising and falling in the regular rhythm of those in a relaxed and peaceful sleep. Relief filled me. It was only a nightmare that had disturbed me, no portent of horrors to come. No, warning of pain beyond belief to fill my life. Holding him in my arms: "Our lives will never change, we will always find a way of being together," I thought, as I lay down, sleep once more overcoming me.

"Remember, Vicki," Jim's ghostly voice seemed to fill the room: "All pleasures must be paid for by pain."

Shaking this off as a ridiculous thought, I relaxed into sleep.

The next few days were filled with laughter, the sharing of each other's innermost thoughts and dreams. Our love bloomed into the perfect partnership of man and mate. It was the night, however, that finally was ours. In these golden hours of darkness we shared not just words, but actions. Giving to each other in a way that we would have found impossible with anyone else. Each one of us knew the other's secret desires and needs. With the joining of our lips, hands and bodies two worlds united, leaving us satisfied, happy and tired.

I sat at breakfast pensive and thoughtful, this was our last full day together. Glancing at the cuckoo clock that hung on the kitchen wall: "This time tomorrow you will be leaving Salzburg," my thoughts reminded me.

"Are you O.K.?" Bertha's concerned voice came to me. I nodded "Yes, I'm fine." I spoke softly.

"Baby, what is wrong?" Dieter whispered taking my hand and holding it tightly in his own.

Fighting back the tears that filled me: "I just remembered where I will be tomorrow."

"That is right," Bertha answered, not knowing the truth so misunderstanding me: "You will both be away from here and on your way back to see your children. Then my friend you should be happy. Perhaps you will bring them here one day to see us." I nodded, unable to give her a truthful answer, all the time knowing that our parting would be final.

"We still have today," Dieter said: "and today I will take you somewhere special."

Now we had the interest of Willi and Bertha.

"Oh, and where is that?" Willi replied, his cup of coffee held suspended between table and mouth.

"Die Maria Kirchental."

At this the older couple nodded, smiles breaking over their faces.

"I approve, that is the best way to end a visit to the Pinzgauer Valley," Bertha replied, her approval made evident by the smile crossing her face.

Mystified, I took my place in the car.

"Where are we going?" I asked, as we made our way down the road that had become so familiar to me.

Turning, a broad smile crossing his face: "Wait and see," Dieter replied, tapping me slightly on my nose and laughing happily.

I was now growing very irritated but felt if I were to show it Dieter would only tease me further. So, sitting back in the car, I allowed myself to be driven from a place that I knew and recognised to a village completely new to me. This was more of a small town than a village, the kind that tourists enjoyed, with its many little inns, large shopping area and high-spired church, in the usual Baroque design. I was annoyed to think this was where he had brought me, knowing I wanted to spend our last few hours together.

"No, schatzie we do not stop here." Once more, here was proof that we were both aware of each other's thoughts.

Leaving the town behind, we followed the road until we turned off into the car park of an old Inn that stood all alone, nestling in the lee of the mountain range unknown to me.

"Put these on," Dieter had taken our mountain shoes from the boot of the car.

Once ready for a long walk, I stood up, looking around, my puzzlement growing with each moment he kept me in ignorance. "O.K. Lover boy, what now?" I asked, staring up at the mountains facing us.

"See that path." he pointed to a rough road that led from the car park and seemed to disappear into the pine forest that covered the mountains.

I nodded.

"It is there that we go. Now, come we are wasting time." So saying, he took my hands and led me to the grey stone footpath that cut its way like a pale ribbon into the mountain.

We climbed slowly and steadily up the steep path. This was no ready-made tarmac route, but one that had been trodden in by generations of walkers. Why? Was still a mystery, something Dieter was at pains not to reveal. For everytime I asked the question: "What is so important up in the mountains, why are we going there?" He would turn to smile at me, touching the tip of his nose, then taking me by the hand would carry on walking, never answering my questions.

I was amazed at the untouched beauty that surrounded us.

Everywhere I looked were bushes and trees, their translucent greens giving the wild flowers in bloom a vividness of colour that I found breathtaking. Birds and butterflies seeming to be the only other users of this path. Once a butterfly landed on Dieter's head, seeming to lose itself in the night darkness of this hair.

"See, now I am as pretty as you are," he laughed.

Leaving the creature with its gossamer wings of blue where it rested, we carried on walking.

Feeling that nothing on this walk could surprise me anymore, I was soon to be proved wrong. Before I could ask Dieter how much longer we were to climb, as I was now feeling quiet and breathless and tired, I realised that we had come to the end of the unmade road and that a more modern surface faced us.

"We could have driven here," my tones were accusatory.

"Yes, my darling but would it have been so beautiful."

The quizzical tone of his voice brought a shamed smile to me face: "You are right, nothing could have been better than our walk," I replied.

"Shush, my love. The best is yet to come." He spoke in lowered tones, while placing his forefinger to my lips.

The road surface here, though better, was much steeper, taking every ounce of strength from me. Now and then we would have to step aside as cars drove past us either heading up the mountain or making its way down. Having walked past some pillars on which I could see hand-painted scenes from the death of Christ, I began to feel that perhaps this was some kind of Pilgrimage route

Rounding the bend where the road was steepest, I was relieved to hear the sounds of voices telling me the end of our gruelling, though satisfying, journey was at an end. For the next few minutes I was to be faced with one surprise after another, each one more beautiful than the one before.

My first one came with the gigantic crucifix that was set into the granite of the mountain. This massive wooden masterpiece had been placed at the top of the road, as if guiding penitents to it, while at the same time protecting those who left its mountain. From the large eye, painted into the blue canopy over the cross signifying the all seeing eye, to the life size statue nailed on the wooden structure, I was soon aware that was indeed a special place.

Making our way past the cross I could see buildings on either side of the path. Here was a Gasthaus, with people sitting on the terrace, enjoying the sun while eating their midday meal. The shake of Dieter's head, as I went to join the other diners, told me that the end of my walk was not yet at hand. Though it was now feeling more like an ordeal, the heat from the sun having completely enervated me, breathless and hot I stopped for a second outside a souvenir shop to wipe the sweat from my forehead:

"What more?" I asked, trying not to sound childish and bad tempered.

Stopping for a second he gently placed his hands over my eyes, closing the lids. Then, softly leading me by the hand we walked a few paces: "So, my darling welcome to the true heart of Austria, come open your eyes."

At these words I did as I had been commanded. Once my eyes were once more used to the bright sunlight surrounding us, at first all I could see was a rickety wooden gate that led into a meadowland where the flowers and blossoms that we had seen on our walk up appeared to be duplicated. Birds of startlingly bright colours swooped around us as if dancing to their own waltzes between trees and bushes. Butterflies and bees skipped from one brightly coloured flower to another, this was indeed a scene tranquil beauty. The sound of voices having been left behind, the only noises to break the unearthly silence around us were the grasshoppers in the bushes and the ringing of church bells.

Dieter pushed open the gate, standing aside so that I could enter before him. "Now we come to the real end of our journey. Look."

Following his pointing finger I stood in complete wonderment at the sight before us. There, in a valley on the top of a range of mountains, was the most perfect little cathedral, having been designed from plans made by an architect of the most prominent buildings in Vienna and Salzburg. Fishcer von Erlach had given to the people of the Pinzgauer around the fifteenth century a jewel that could never be bettered nor copied.

"Maria Kirchental," was the name given to this place, Dieter informed me, going on to say: "It is a long time since I was here last, but its beauty is always a surprise and never the same."

Silently, I nodded. Looking at the mountains surrounding the cream painted Baroque building, with its narrow, high windows and massive wooden doors, I could imagine how it would look as the seasons around it changed. From the heat of the summer to the snows of winter, yes, this truly was a place of ever changing beauty, never boring but always magnificent.

Making my entrance I was amazed how small it was. This was no museum-piece but a place for the truly reverent. We walked in silent wonderment, studying the icons on the walls. Here and there were votive offerings, little paintings done by the simple valley folk thanking God for some prayer answered or miracle granted. From the roughly made drawings of a rescue at sea to the health of a child being restored, I felt that the Maria Kirchental was indeed a place of all kinds of emotion from heartbreak to happiness, all were brought to the lady whose statue stood next to the high altar.

Taking my hand in his, Dieter once more walked me down the aisle as he had done so many years ago in Cologne, kneeling before the main altar we once more pledged our lives to each other. Kissing me gently on the lips, then my ring, he once more made a Benediction to our love.

About to take our leave, a soft sound arrested our attention. Turning, I was amazed by the sight that greeted our eyes. We had thought ourselves to be alone in the church. Now we discovered we were wrong, for sitting in the corner by the oaken doors was a little old lady dressed in black from head to foot. She shuffled in our direction waving a claw-like finger in Dieter's direction: "Please can you do something for me?" she asked this in a rough voice, her dialect proclaiming she was truly a child of the Pinzgauer.

"If I can I will," Dieter replied.

"Gut," was all the answer she gave, as she took Dieter's hand in her rough calloused one.

She led us slowly to the last pew in the Church. Nearby was a little table on which rested a large visitor's book. Taking the pen that lay in it, she placed this in an ungainly fashion into Dieter's hand.

"Come please put my name in here," her voice quivered whether it was old age or emotion, I was never sure.

"Why is it so important that your name is in the book?" I asked, bending so she could hear me more clearly.

"So that God may know I was really here. I know this is a book where people make requests for health and help." Shrugging she stood up to her full height, her

414

fading blue eyes staring into mine: "I have only one request, not the curing of my old age, I know that is impossible, but I should like to be with my loved ones who have already gone ahead." A smile crossed the old, gnarled features, making them appear almost beautiful: "Wouldn't it be wonderful to spend eternity with those you love most."

Through the tears that clouded my vision at this woman's simple, uncomplicated faith, I watched Dieter's hand shake as he signed the name she gave. We had both been moved by this simple philosophy.

The two of us walked out once more into the sunshine, leaving the old lady to say her prayer of thanks.

"It would indeed be wonderful to spend eternity with the one I truly love," Dieter whispered, looking down at me.

I smiled back, silence reigning between us, both of us full of the moment.

"I have something to buy for Bertha," Dieter muttered, disappearing in the direction of the souvenir shop, returning moments later with a paper bag.

That evening our meal was a quiet one, Dieter and I filled with the parting that was imminent. Glancing at our hosts it was obvious that they too had some deep thoughts filling their minds.

"Come we will have one more coffee together on the verandah, then we have something to show you." Bertha said, carrying the tray and its contents outside.

We followed in silence, each one of us taking up the positions that had become ours over the past few days.

Dieter sat on the large high-backed wooden chair that I had thought appeared uncomfortable, till I had sampled the relief it had to offer. I sat on the stone floor at his feet my head on his lap. Watching the look of pleasant relaxation coming over his features, I looked up at the sky, secretly hoping that God the one the old lady and I believed in so much was looking down on us and would, in his mercy, grant me the opportunity of spending eternity with this man.

"So, we must go now, before it gets too dark."

Willi stood up from his position by his wife on the large swing lounger. Going into the house he soon reappeared with the paper bag that Dieter had brought with him from the church that morning.

Puzzled as to where we were going I accompanied the other three. We walked out of the brightly lit house into the gathering darkness of the mountain. We followed a path I had never seen before. Past a large lake, glistening like ebony in the dark. Perhaps it was the lateness of the evening that subdued our voices, or was it something else? I didn't have long to wait. Once we had gone past the lake, we followed the pine-scented forest route, quietly walking round a sleeping herd of cattle, across a field that climbed the mountain, till out of the darkness I saw before us a small area surrounded by a low fence. Opening the gate that led into this area I saw Willi take two candles from the bag he carried. I recognised these as being those that people bought and placed by grave sides. Little night lights placed in red, plastic coverings with a cross cut into the sides.

"Where are we?" I whispered to Dieter.

"These are the graves of our father and our son." Willi's voice was deep with emotion.

The shock I received at these words was more violent than if I had fallen into the cold mountain lake.

"Your son!" I exclaimed.

I was not surprised at finding the grave of the old woman's husband, but the thought of a young man lying up here on the lonely mountainside was more difficult to accept, once more bringing home to me how important a job it was that I did.

"Yes, his name is Josef." Bertha spoke. Her voice completely lacking in emotion as she spoke, the empty darkness filling with the ghosts of the past. Suddenly I was becoming aware of a young man I had never met, yet one I wanted to cry for.

"He was thirty years old, and working on the land with a small tractor, it overturned and killed him." Her voice was soft and lost as she carried on with: "Willi was with him and tried to help, we had the doctor and the helicopter to take him to hospital but after two days he left us." Turning to place her hand on her husband she carried on with: "We know how he loved the farm and his grandfather so we kept them both together," turning with a smile she continued: "We will all come here together one day."

In the dim light coming from the stars I could see her hand pointing in the direction of the grave.

"Perhaps the Good God has a special task for our son, that is why he took him." So saying, she turned, placing the now lit candles at the foot of each grave. Then she and Willi knelt to pray, at this point Dieter and I left our host and hostess alone, their grief was not to be shared.

The next morning dawned bright and beautiful, as had been all the days since our arrival. Making our farewells to Bertha, Willi and the old lady brought tears of regret to all our eyes. In the few days we had shared in this mountain retreat, a good friendship had been struck, one that I would have liked to keep, but knew it was impossible.

"It is because we have become such good friends that I took you to meet Josef last night." Bertha whispered, speaking as if her son still lived. My belief in the spirit world accepted this, but I could see from the way Dieter shook his head and smiled he found this a little hard to believe.

Our journey to Salzburg and the station was made in silence, unlike the one that had filled the car on our journey out. That had been filled with misunderstandings and fear, this time it was the sadness of partings to come that kept out thoughts busy.

"Don't you believe in life after death?" I blurted out.

"I don't know darling, I have never been dead, so how should I know," Dieter replied smiling at me: "Why do you ask."

"I do, and I believe Bertha's son is as much in the house as he ever was," I replied.

"You are so innocent my love, you believe everything you are told. Of course he is alive for his parents, they loved him so he lives in their hearts and minds, not reality."

I was not going into my work and the proof that I had given to so many people, this was neither the time nor the place.

"I Dieter Schmidt, do promise when I die to come back and visit you, my love. That is a promise I make and will keep."

Dieter's voice came to me as if through a tunnel. Turning to look at him for a moment, his face was covered in a glow as the sun poured in through the windscreen, filling the car with heat. Yet I found myself shivering with a cold I could not explain.

My train journey back was made in total silence, no friendly steward to help through my pain. Only memories filling every mile that carried me away from Austria and my love.

I thought once more of our last night together, how our lovemaking had been filled with desperation and tears, happiness and sadness. We wanted to give so much yet were unable to do so, then I remembered how we had clung to each other as we said goodbye at Salzburg Station having to leave each other yet fearful to do so. As the train gathered speed my last sight of Dieter had been as he wiped the tears from his eyes, I wanted to leap from the train and rejoin him, but that was impossible. Taking my seat in in the compartment reserved for me as we headed into the right sunlight, I heard his voice: "I, Dieter Schmidt, do promise when I die to come back and visit you my love." Shivering I pulled the blanked on my bunk round me, once again feeling cold, yet the barometer over my head showed that the heat was really quite intense.

As my eyes closed, allowing me to drop off into an uneasy sleep I heard: "Remember I love you," Dieter's whispered words as we said farewell. "Nothing will ever part us, I believe it, you must too."

Reaching the end of this reminiscence I realised that for the last few minutes he had been very quiet. No sly comments, nothing added to our joint memories. Studying him more closely, I realised that his eyes were closed, his breathing weak and his face very pale. The smile now completely gone from him. Hearing a sound behind me I realised that the family had come, turning to look at Uwe with a helpless look on my face and hands outstretched, he and Bill soon too charge of the situation.

Running out of the room both men called for Nicola the Nurse and she in turn rang an alarm that alerted the medical team. As Dieter's breathing became more laboured all those involved in his health had gathered.

Quietly and firmly we were removed from the ward, as Surgeon and Nurses accompanied a mysteriously covered trolley into the room.

"Come my friends, you must leave now. It appears that Dieter is a little uncomfortable we must help him." Only as the Herr Professor placed an arm round my shoulders did I hear him whisper: "Pray for your love."

We stood, Dieter's wife and sons, his brother-in-law and Birgit, Bill and myself in total silence just staring at either the floor or each other. We were completely mystified by the sudden turn of events.

"Was he all right when you were with him earlier?" Bill asked.

I nodded: "There was a time when he did say he had a slight headache, but would not let me call the nurse."

Birgit and Uwe stood a little way from us, talking, as we did, in undertones. Suddenly into the silence a loud alarm sounded sending shivers of anxiety down my spine. From another door, four nurses appeared, pushing yet another trolley, which I knew carried the resuscitation unit kept for those who had gone into heart failure.

"Dear God, don't let him die," I cried. My prayer for help of necessity being silent. So we stood for what seemed like hours. Each one of us lost in our own thoughts and prayers for the man lying behind the heavy doors.

Then, when we felt the suspense becoming unbearable, we saw the door to Dieter's room open. First, one trolley was taken away, then the other. Next the Professor came towards us. Placing an arm round Monique, he explained: "Dieter has a small pressure on his brain, we must take him into surgery and relieve this."

Quietly, we stood, like soldiers, as Dieter was wheeled from sight. For a second a faint smile lit up his sleepy eyes as he saw me before he was once more swallowed up by the thick plastic, doors that led into the mysterious world of the surgeon and his knife.

A further period of waiting ensued. One in which we drank numerous cups of coffee, all the time finding speech impossible, as each of us was afraid we might echo the other's thoughts. Walking up and down the corridor we would smile wanly as we passed each other. On a number of occasions Uwe tried to light cigarettes, but these attempts were unsuccessful, as each time he had one held between shaking fingers a passing nurse would take it, extinguish it and then admonish him.

At last we heard movements from behind the swing doors. As one person we turned to see the Professor come through, his face pale and lined, his shoulders stooping more than normal, eyes appearing sunken and tired.

Sighing, he held out his arms to Monique, then as she silently went into them: "I am so sorry, my friends but Dieter has just died."

Such simple words, but Oh God the terror they strike in the hearts of those who love and are left behind.

From their expressions it was obvious Uwe and Bill were dumbfounded. With a little moan Monique slipped out of the Professor's arms and fell to the floor in a faint. Markus and Christoph stood with tears in their eyes their world completely shattered.

I was numb. This was my end as well as his. All I wanted at that moment was to join him, wherever he was.

Last Chapter

I watched as the tall, thin man walked towards us. His footsteps once quick and decisive, now slow, dragging and very tired. He and his staff had fought valiantly and long to save Dieter's life. A courageous attempt that had failed.

As he approached us, I had the feeling that if I were able to run away the news he had would not exist, it would all be a nightmare.

"If I am not here, then nothing can have happened."

My mind began to run in circles, the only part of me capable of movement, the rest was numb. Every ounce of blood having drained away.

"I am so sorry, Monique," I heard the Professor's voice, soft, gentle and consoling. Only my subconscious realising that he had called Dieter's wife by her first name, instead of the more formal Frau Schmidt.

"We did all that was possible, but he had a Cerebral Oedema." The Surgeon then went on to explain what the problem was and how it occurred. I found it very difficult to follow what he said, so I allowed my mind to wander.

As if my body and mind were divorced from each other, I could see Bill standing still, staring at a blank wall, now and then rubbing his eyes surreptitiously. Perhaps he was afraid his masculinity would be called into question if he was to be seen crying for a friend.

Turning, I looked around, trying to take in my surroundings. As if in some way the mere act of concentration would help to steady my shaking, shivering body. I could see Uwe deep in conversation with the Surgeon, their voices soft as if they tried not to disturb anyone.

I heard Nicola ask Uwe: "A Priest?" He nodded.

"We have one at the hospital I will call him, now." Nicola hurried off to carry out her promise.

Still the whispering went on, I wanted to shout: "Don't whisper, you can't disturb Dieter now, he is dead," but the words wouldn't come. My throat was dry, tongue swollen to twice its size. Looking along the corridor I could see that the two nurses who had come to Monique's aid were sitting beside her and taking care of her. Dieter's two sons just stood holding each other's hands, like the rest of us finding it incomprehensible their beloved Pappa, that bundle of energy, a man with so much life could have it all extinguished in a manner of moments.

Instead I turned my thoughts to wondering what had happened to all those who had taken part in the attempt to revive Dieter, but they, like my dreams of happiness, had disappeared into the background of the hospital, like wraiths in the evening mists.

It wasn't until I heard a little whimper, going over to where she was seated between the two nurses, they moved aside to allow Birgit and myself to sit and try to help her. Always a slight, small girl, she now appeared to have shrunk even more. Sitting on the hard, leather bench she tore a paper tissue to shreds, letting the pieces

424

drop from lifeless fingers, covering the grey, tiled floor with an untidy carpet of hand-made confetti.

Placing my arms round Monique, I allowed her head to drop on my shoulder. For once we shared the same emotion, that of the loss of the man we loved.

"Vicki, remember The Feldenburg, our mountain." His voice seemed to echo along the now empty corridor. For a moment my eyes scoured the area, as if hoping the news we had just received was all part of a very sick joke. Perhaps, nearby, one of the male nurses was standing beside Dieter, both laughing and enjoying the situation.

"No," my mind insisted, as my eyes ensured that only the seven of us now inhabited the corridor. All the action of moments ago had now abated, leaving only the stillness that follows all catastrophes.

About to leave the hospital, Nicola suddenly joined us talking to Uwe who then spoke to the family and last of all us. "Would you like to say goodbye." This was an invitation that was accepted by us all.

First Monique and the boys were taken through the plastic doors that Dieter and the team had disappeared behind what seemed hours ago. I wasn't sure how long they stayed but all three came out crying and helped by the same two nurses who had been with us earlier. Then it was the turn of Uwe and Birgit, who also came out in tears lastly Bill and I were invited to go in and make our farewells.

The room was a stark white, with a variety of surgical instruments on trolleys, and heavy white lights over the trolley on which Dieter lay, a white sheet covered him up to his neck. As I approached I heard Bill say: "Good to have known you mate, perhaps we will meet again." touching Dieter's face, he left unable to say much more.

Finally it was my turn, approaching the trolley I could see the dark hair with streaks of silver, uncovered by the white sheet. His green eyes now closed in the sleep that lasts forever, the pallidness of his face could be seen through the normal summer suntan he had, I found it impossible to accept that the life, spirit of the man I knew and loved had all gone. Bending down I placed a kiss on his cold, lifeless lips. Then turning to look above me, for the first time I spoke out aloud.

"Dear God, I have for many years spoken to people about you and your generosity to us on the earth. That there is a life that continues when the one we know is gone. Please help me now to understand what has happened and why?" Turning to look at my lover, desperately needing him to move but knowing this would never happen again. I turned and walked away, leaving him alone in that stark, white, surgical room.

Slowly we walked the many passageways, now slowly coming back to life. I walked behind Uwe and Birgit as they supported Monique out of the hospital. Bill and I walked with the two boys now allowing their tears to flow with the realisation that all their plans for looking after their father when he came out of hospital would come to nothing.

There was one thing I had to do and do it now, a barrier had to go up round my emotions. I was not able at any time in public to let anyone know how I truly felt.

I could feel Bill glancing at me: "How are you?" I shrugged, no answer to give.

"Yes, I know what you mean." He said as we once more and for the last time came out of the main doors of the hospital.

Approaching the parking area, I could see that the rain which had been falling during the early part of the day, had now stopped, allowing a watery sun to shine through. Standing in the open air, away from the antiseptic smells invading every passageway in the building behind me, I breathed in deeply, filling my lungs with fresh air hoping in this way I would wipe out of my life the events that had just taken place. I remembered I had not even said good bye to the Herr Professor.

About to join the others in the car, I stood once more gazing back at the place where dreams unfolded constantly. A building where miracles could be achieved, but failures were difficult, almost impossible, to accept.

About to shut the car door, we heard: "Is there anything I can do?" Turning, we saw Nicola, the young nurse who had been so good at looking after Dieter. By the tears in her eyes, and the pale parchment appearance of her face, it was obvious that her patient's death had had a deeply moving effect on her too. Monique and Uwe shook their heads, holding out their hands in an effort to show their gratitude, at the same time refusing her kind offer.

As we pulled away from where the young girl stood, tears streaming down her face. I wanted to stop the car, run back, grab her by the arm and shout: "Yes, there is something you can do. Go tell the two bastards who caused the death of this wonderful man what they have done. Let them know, through their uncaring attitude, I have lost the one man who meant my life to me." But I couldn't say anything. Just stare unseeingly out of the window, aware of only one thing --- my life had ended that day. I was also seriously thinking of never working as Medium ever again. I felt that the Spirit World had let me down. In my selfishness thinking not of Monique and her sons, or the other members of the family just myself.

I could hear Uwe, Bill and the boys now suddenly grown up and facing responsibilities. Each man finding it difficult to understand the other, but somehow with the help of the boys who had learnt English getting some form of comprehension. Decisions had to be taken, about funeral arrangements, and the passing on of information to all those involved in the club both English and German.

Having reached the conclusions the two older men drifted once more into silence. The younger men now consoling a heavily sobbing mother. As we travelled back to Kirshcweiler, I would glance often in Monique's direction. Listening to her heartbreaking sobs, see her sons now men, no longer boys, holding her, while she twisted and turned her wedding ring, almost as if by doing this some magic genie would appear and restore life to her husband my lover. For years she had been known by the title Frau Schmidt, the wife of Dieter. Now she had to get used to the new one that all women feared, the label: "Widow."

Once again I thought of the farewells that were made between us and the surgeon. I knew he had kissed Monique on the cheek and seen him shaking hands with the rest of the family. However, watching him walking in my direction, had brought a new fear. Knowing he was aware of the secret between Dieter and myself, afraid any sympathy he offered might dissolve my resolution. That of standing firm and hard. I would lean on no one, but there was a little weakness in my self-control, neither I nor the wall newly built round my heart was yet strong enough to handle the kind of assault his kind, well-meant pity would have. Perhaps, if the barriers were to collapse, I would give away the truth between Dieter and myself, so destroying not only my own marriage but the memories of Monique and those two special young men sitting beside her.

As the man came closer, I found myself physically backing away as if silently begging him to keep his distance. Correctly interpreting my move, I saw him falter, then stop in mid-stride. With a slight nod of his head I was informed he had understood my situation, so it was only with the briefest of handshakes did the learned man pass his condolences on to me.

I had decided the best way of handling the next few days was to keep busy. As I was not a member of the family, there would be no need of us to be involved in making any preparations. Bill had already spoken to David Bright, who once getting over his shock would contact club members and arrange for flowers to be delivered.

While arrangements were being made Bill and I would help as and when necessary, talking to the boys, helping their cousin Maria. Bill and I would often take long walks in the forests that surrounded the village, talking quietly among ourselves about life and death and the suddenness in which it all occurred.

"You are the expert on death," Bill said to me once.

"Me! I'm no expert I only know what I have learnt over the years and had Spirit teach me," I replied. "Yes, I know there is a different world, I know it exists but apart from the passing of my mother and father I had never been associated with anyone so young." I didn't add, "and someone I loved so much." So I carried on with: "At this moment in time I am as lost as you."

Though I went through the motions, talking and eating, being supportive to everyone who needed it, I desperately wanted to come back home. Be with our daughters and find a bolt hole in which I could hide, lick my wounds and yell and scream at God and the Spirit World and think seriously of not working for them ever again.

I knew Bill wanted to share memories but I could not add too much, because all the thoughts in my mind were of two people, myself and Dieter.

There was one evening when all my new found strength was tested.

"Vicki," Emile, a friend of many years, called out to me. He was a charming much married man, not very tall but quite wide. His hair was silver-grey and grew long almost to his shoulders. With laughing, blue eyes, and aquiline nose, a mouth as perfect in shape as his musician's fingers, this pianist had been a great confidant of Dieter's and one with whom he would often play mischievous tricks on the others of the club.

Today, he had not much more than a glimmer of the old twinkle in his eyes.

"I have something for you."

As he said this I felt a piece of paper pressed into the palm of my hand: "Uwe asked me to give it to you. It is a memory."

Glancing down at the piece of card, I felt a choking gasp begin to escape me. Breathing, deeply, gaining as much oxygen as possible, I studied the little memorial card before me. I found myself looking at a mountain scene, with a lone cross on the pinnacle. For a second I was transported back to the Feldenburg where I had seen two crosses. And, that night, how passionate had been our lovemaking. Perhaps in the deepest recesses of our minds, we knew this would be our last time together.

Opening, up the card, I had yet another shock coming to me. Inside was a picture of Dieter. The cry of pain that rose to my lips was held back with great difficulty. I remembered the night this photograph had been taken. It was during a summer visit to Kirschweiler with our girls. I remembered the night the photo had been taken, Bill had made a joke that had caused Dieter to collapse with laughter. It was then that Uwe the photographer had snapped his brother-in-law. Now this picture was part of his memorial. Gone was the bright face, sparkling green eyes so full of life, and the voice that grew husky with emotion. Beneath the photograph was a little prayer, and on the opposite side details of his family, plus the time and date of his funeral. I stood for seconds staring at the card before me, finding it hard to believe that in one moment a spark as bright as my lover's had been extinguished.

The night before the Funeral a cortège brought his body down to the church in the village, everyone was there from the Burgermeister to friends of his family. With silent ceremony his coffin was carried in and placed on the stands at the Altar. The Priest started to say Mass and hymns were sung, we were then invited at the end to stay for a while in quiet prayer and contemplation. This we did until as the evening grew dark we left and made our ways to different destinations. Home, Bars, and Bill and myself quietly to our hotel room needing to be alone.

The morning of the funeral dawned dark and dismal. There were little drops of rain beginning to fall as we left the Hubertus in the company of Walter and Louise. For once neither of us had anything to say. We walked in sombre silence towards the church, filled to capacity. Having been at the service the night before I knew the

Coffin was in the centre of the Altar but it still came as a shock showing the finality of life.

We walked up the aisle, now and then a faint smile breaking across one of the mourner's faces, as a friend or acquaintance was recognised. Bill was deep in thought as he preceded me towards the front of the Church, so it was he never heard the soft "Gruss Gott," that made me falter in my progress behind him. Turning, I saw Dieter's Uncle Alois. For long seconds we stood staring at each other, once again united in secret memories of those beautiful days in Austria. Realising Bill had stopped to see where I was, I hurried along, after Alois and I had exchanged surreptitious nods of acknowledgement.

"Who was that?" Bill questioned

"Dieter's Uncle."

"How did you know him, I don't remember meeting him." Bill continued.

I was in no mood to carry on this question and answer conversation, and somehow changed the conversation so he forgot to pursue the matter.

Now the priest and the servers had come on to the altar and the Requiem Mass was about to start.

Before his body had been brought into the church the night previous, Dieter's body had lain in the little chapel in the cemetery for two days, in this way allowing friends and family to make their farewells. Bill had been but I had refused Monique's invitation as I needed to remember him vibrant with life, not lying still, silent and cold. With Dieter's last breath every magic moment we had shared in the last thirteen years was taken from me. Our lives ruled not by a fairy godmother but the cruel Fates.

Not only had Dieter been my friend and lover, he had also been every dream and fantasy come true. Now all gone. As if preparing for battle, I squared my shoulders and stood straight, awaiting the moment when I would follow the mourners out of the church, into the grounds and so make a final: "Auf Wiedersehen."

I followed the service, going through the motions as though living a nightmare. Seeing the number of people filling the church, it was obvious he had been a very popular and likeable personality. As though from far away I could hear the priest giving a little homily on the young man Dieter Schmidt. The boy he had baptised and taken him through his first Communion and Confirmation and then his marriage and fatherhood. Then his father spoke with a break in his voice, followed by Christoph, telling us what we knew that Dieter had been as a father – perfect. Now and then a little memory brought out would make us smile as knowing the man we knew and understood the words.

For me, though, there were other thoughts running round in my mind. The realisation that there would no longer be any need for me to visit Kirschweiler. No doubt Bill would come with the men, but for me it was over. No more Carnival, or long weekends here. Perhaps on returning home I would ring Monique once or twice a month, to ensure she was coping. Even this would eventually stop, so that both of us could go on with living, though for me life would now be an empty shell. Having been so cruelly robbed of my one and only true love.

A little involuntary smile did reach my lips when I heard the priest, talk about Dieter's marriage to Monique and what happiness he had found with her. In my heart there were the secrets that only we two shared, no one would or could talk about it as it belonged to only two people – us. And, knowing this brought a little touch of warmth for the first time in days to my cold, dead heart.

In a strange way I envied Monique. Although she was his widow, once this young woman had been "his wife." Now because of the carelessness of two men, Monique was now alone, so entitled to all our love and care. But, what about me? I too was eligible to what was left, for to the outside world and my own family we were friends, nothing more. I also thanked God we had been nothing less.

It was the shuffling of feet informing me that the service was ended, I now had to prepare myself for the hardest part since saying goodbye to him in that white surgical room. We now had to make our way across the village to the cemetery.

As Bill helped me from my kneeling position, preparing to leaving the church, I grabbed his arm, once again trying to delay the inevitable. I saw Markus and Christoph, joined by their Grandfather, Alois, Uwe, Frank and Paul walk to the Altar here they very carefully shouldered the coffin and started the slow walk to the door of the church, held open by the ushers allowing a draft of cold, wet air into the church. As we all stood in silent prayer and tribute to the man who was now being carried by those closest to him, I wanted to break into tears, scream and shout, I had never known pain like this. I was being torn apart inside, everything I had ever learned as a child, my own development as a Medium, all the readings I had done giving people proof of life I suddenly began to feel was a lie. Had I been subconsciously fooling myself and other people? Were the so called scientists right, there is no Spirit World? So many questions and no answers. As the coffin came past me in my heart I asked: "Dieter, you promised to come to me, will you?"

The men carefully placed the coffin in the car, then following Monique and the family we walked through the village to the cemetery, a silent crowd of people, with many standing on the side of the road, heads bowed unmindful of the now pouring rain, like our tears there appeared to be no stopping. By the time we reached the graveyard, Dieter's coffin had been placed in the little chapel where it had stood for two days, here the priest said some more prayers and then he was carried to the burial site. This time he was carried not by the family but those whose job it was to place him gently in the space provided.

The priest gave the final blessing at the same time that a sound I wish never to hear again. It was the tolling of the chapel bells, this was a true test of my stamina. With head held high, eyes dry and throat aching from the self-control placed on myself, I followed Bill and the family to the graveside, as the coffin was gently lowered into the earth, Monique, who had suffered so much strain over the past few days, finally gave in and with a silent murmur she fainted at the feet of her father-in-law. Before anyone could come to her aid, a man was seen striding out of the crowd surrounding us. He was as tall as Dieter, with blond curly hair that clung wetly to his forehead. Eyes framed by thick horn-rimmed glasses, he had blunt features, totally opposite in appearance to Dieter.

"Who is that?" Bill enquired of Herbert.

"That is Peter, he was engaged to Monique before Dieter came back from the army."

After this there was no need for further questions, it was obvious that the arrival of Dieter had broken up any romance that had existed between Peter and Monique. Something I could fully understand.

Once the young widow had been revived, the service was able to continue. All the mourners were invited to take a flower from the table near the graveside. These would then be thrown in a final farewell gesture onto the coffin. There was an assortment of blooms from carnations to roses.

Blindly stretching my hand, I picked up the first blossom that came to hand. Only as I was about to throw the bloom, did I realise I had picked up the most perfect flower there. It was a red rose, still in bud. With its petals closed as if waiting for something special to open it. The tiny green leaves surrounding it, appeared to be protecting it from the unknown.

As I picked up the rose, with a little wince of pain, I realised that the flower held fast between my thumb and forefinger had pierced my skin. This perfect blossom was now stained with another colour, this time the scarlet that was my blood. Feeling this was a symbol, kissing it gently I threw it to rest with the others on the coffin. I had made my final farewell, but somehow I felt the flower that I had thrown was indeed special, for I had placed my own blood on this bloom for Dieter and our love.

The service now finally over, we made our way back to the house. Here food had been laid on for the benefits of those of us who had been invited back. We were joined by some of Dieter's friends from the bank. All coming up to speak to Bill and myself, their English almost impeccable. Talking of the times Dieter had told them of our exploits either at Carnival or on days that we had spent together. I enjoyed listening to this, because it made me feel more a part of his life than ever.

Alfredo, one of the football group, and Friedrich seemed to have taken it on themselves to look after Bill and myself. Wherever we went, or whatever we needed, these two men were there to obtain and provide it.

Sometime after we had entered the house, I felt that my self-restraint was slipping. Feeling it would be better if I slipped off somewhere on my own, I went and sat on the bottom stair.

Following the line of the stairs I knew these led to the room that had been Dieter's and Monique's. In the other direction was the beer cellar. Here I had my own memories of the man. Fun and laughter shared by many here today, and the times when we had been alone in our lovemaking, those were the special moments that neither the passing of time nor the physical absence of Dieter could erase.

Sighing, I looked up to be confronted by a photograph that had been taken during the time that Dieter had played professional football. How proud he looked, holding the medal and cup that had obviously just been presented to him. I knew he wanted one of his sons to follow in his footsteps, playing for the team that had so often supplied an international goalkeeper.

With no one to witness what I did, I approached the picture: "It's not fair, you entered my life like a tornado. Now you have left me bereft and alone, what am I to do?"

Where I had seen only bright sunshine in my life, now all appeared to be darkness and shadow. As I carried on talking to a lifeless photograph: "Your wife has the children and her knowledge of the past you two shared. All I've got are a few snatched hours," This was nearly the end of my very well-kept self-control, I could feel myself coming to the end of my tether and in danger of total collapse. Deciding to rejoin the others, this way I could hold on to my sanity.

The dull day had given way to an even more miserable evening. Summer today seemed to have disappeared. With the appearance of a moonless evening, those of us still left in the house took our leave of the family, leaving them to mourn in private.

As I shook hands with Alois his softly whispered: "Remember, only the good times," left me silent as Bill and I walked back to the Hubertus with Walter, Friedrich and Louise.

Hearing the sound of running feet, we stopped in our tracks to see Uwe slightly out of breath coming up behind us. "I have here some money, from Dieter's father. He would all his friends to drink his son's health tonight."

"That is not necessary." Walter pushed away the hand holding out the notes. "Tonight, we give a party for our friend." Yet another piece of proof of the esteem that Dieter had been held in, for Walter a true businessman had never been known to give anything before.

As we neared the Hubertus, I suddenly realised my sorrow was turning to anger. "Why the hell had we met, if we were to suffer in this way?" I asked an unrelenting blackness, a night without moon and stars.

Entering the brightness of the Hubertus, leaving the darkness to itself, I stopped, allowing the men and Louise to enter before me. Looking back along the now quiet village street, I vowed then never again to visit this place. When I left the following day, Germany would never see me again.

Standing in the bar, I stared around me. Finding it hard to believe how, in the space of a few years, all our lives had been interwoven together, like a giant tapestry.

Once having been knitted and joined, the fates had stepped in and torn asunder the material, so making us once again separate entities.

"I'm going to bed," I whispered to Bill, feeling unable to take anymore.

"Why so dramatic," he replied. "We haven't finished drinking to his health." I could tell by Bill's slurred speech the drink he had been given at Monique's home was doing more talking than he was.

"I'm tired. I have been through a great deal," I answered determined not to lose my temper.

"Listen to you, anyone would think you were his wife, not just a friend."

As he spoke, I felt the ring on my right hand tighten, as if I was being reminded more of the promise that was made so many years ago. To love truly and sincerely even beyond death.

I wondered what he would have said had I continued with: "Well actually Bill, Dieter and I were husband and wife – spiritually." Instead I just smiled and said, "Goodnight to all present, with a final wave of the hand I closed the door to the bar behind me and made my way up the stairs.

Throwing myself fully clothed on the bed, I lay with empty eyes staring at the ceiling, until thankful oblivion took over, allowing me to sink into the unconscious state of exhausted sleep.

I was never sure what awakened me the next morning. Perhaps it was because I had fallen asleep so early, or maybe the morning bird song, informing all who would listen that the previous day's rain had disappeared and there was the promise of a good day ahead.

Feeling in need of some fresh air, I glanced at the sleeping figure of my husband. Thankful to hear the even tenor of his deep breathing, showing he was in a restful sleep. With the long day's journey home ahead of us, a good rest in advance would be helpful.

Realising I was still dressed, it was not difficult to slip on my trainers, creep down the stairs past the doors of a sleeping Walter and Louise. I paused momentarily outside the door where Dieter and I had shared those magical moments that Carnival, the one that had started off so badly and ended up ecstatically. Tiptoeing past the sleeping forms of Vidor and Dreamie, I made my way out of the hotel.

I began to walk slowly along the main street. Everywhere I looked were reminiscences of the past. The supermarket where I had gone shopping with Monique and Birgit, while the men had enjoyed drinks in the Hubertus.

Further along, just past the traffic lights, was the men's boutique that Dieter, ever vain, liked to frequent. I stood for some time outside the ice cream parlour, remembering the afternoon when we had sat and shared friendly conversation, along with outsize ice creams. It was here the Dieter had given me more proof of his feelings for me. As we had been surrounded by friends and family during one of our visits, there had been no chance for us to be alone together. Instead, as we had sat in the rays of a bright summer afternoon sun, he had picked up the coffee cup I had just placed on the wrought-iron table top, turning the cup so that his lips were placed exactly where mine had recently rested, and raised it to his own lips. With eyes full of meaning we had stared at each other. Mouths silent, no need for speech, our hearts did all the talking that was necessary

I thought back to the previous day, when the fat, jovial, little Italian who owned this parlour, had looked at Bill and myself. This time no laughter creasing his already lined face only tears streaming down chubby cheeks, and misting up his thick glasses.

Sitting down at an empty table outside the ice cream parlour, so many memories came flooding back, from events at Carnival to family visits.

I remembered the first the first time I had entered the church in which we had the day previous said goodbye to Dieter. The little priest who yesterday very solemnly and sadly celebrated the funeral service. It was our first Carnival visit and as Dieter's sons were involved with the local school they were among the children who along with teachers and nuns and older children had acted in little playlets written by them all dressed in costume and full of fun and laughter.

The other event was one of embarrassment for me, it had been a hot afternoon, with the children insisting on an ice cream before they left the village the following day. This we had done. After we had been seated for some minutes, Monique reached into her handbag. With a smile she produced a package from it. Puzzled I took what was held out to me:

"What's this?" I asked.

"Just a little something I thought you might like," she replied her smile growing ever wider.

Opening the package, I was touched to see it was a book of German Fairy Stories, from different regions of this vast country. I was so touched by this thoughtful little gift, that in my rush to say thank you I had used the wrong word for present.

Puzzled, and not a little annoyed at the laughter that had greeted my words of thanks, it was quite a few

441

minutes before Bill and I could gain any form of sense out of our friends. When asked for an explanation of the laughter: Between bouts of hysterical laughter Monique had replied: "You have just said, thank you, I like sex on the table," That made my face flame. Trying to make matters better I hurriedly replied: "I meant to say I like the present on the table."

"Yes, my darling." Dieter had replied still giggling helplessly, but you used the wrong word." Then looking around to see if we were unobserved: "You see for my wife it was the wrong word, for me it is the best." He had then given me a look that had melted every bone in my body.

With all these memories and so many others flooding in, I stumbled to my feet and began running. Now no longer in the public eye, I was able to finally let my tears break through the self-imposed barriers. With my face soaked by the tears that had been held back for so long, and finding it difficult to see, I finally had to give up running and slow down to a walk. Gasping for breath, I stopped looking around me, trying to gain my bearings.

My desolation was now complete. I was alone not only in the village but in my world. Taking stock of my surroundings, with a surprise I realised that in my headlong flight from sorrow, I had run to the source of it. I now stood outside the cemetery gates. An involuntary shiver ran up my spine, as I recalled the events of the previous day.

With my sense of loss growing ever deeper, I felt an urgent need to enter this quiet place. But, how to was the problem. The gates now securely locked were too high for me to climb. So I began to walk round the walls, hoping I might see a way in. It wasn't long before I saw my opportunity, and seized it. Though the complete area was surrounded by a high wall, I found a corner where bricks and mortar had been replaced by a rather thin bush. Forcing myself through the leaves and twigs, uncaring of the scratches I received, only knowing I had to spend some more time alone with Dieter, I was thankful when I eventually made a breakthrough.

Once inside I had no idea which direction to take. My feet seemed to have a mind of their own. Though I set off in the direction that I thought would take me to the chapel and from there I felt sure I would be able to find the newly dug grave, it wasn't long before I realised I was walking round in circles. After many abortive attempts, I would end up either in an enclosed area, or a dump for dead flowers. It was only as I came close to giving up, what I thought was fruitless task that I suddenly recognised the cement path we had walked along the previous day. With shaking feet, heart racing, and breath coming in short, deep heavy gasps, I stood before the earth mound now covering the body of my beloved.

Never sure how long I stood there, with the sun growing ever warmer, now and then a powder puff of cloud would glide across its face, as if a veil had been drawn across. Everywhere I looked was peace and serenity. Marble remembrances to lost loved one, all with a different memorial, many with photographs enamelled into the marble. Branches of trees waved slowly in the gentle breeze now blowing through them.

For moments I stared at the newly moved earth, remembering the man who lay beneath it. In the seconds that followed, I thought once more of the people I had in Spirit. Dear, wonderful friends, three had themselves been visitors to this little village. Then there had been the death of my own darling mother, but somehow the pain of their loss could not compare with the searing agony now filling me at the emptiness left by the abrupt curtailment of Dieter's life, and the gap left in mine.

Within minutes the pain that had been creeping up, needed full and final release. This could come in only one way. Uncaring of any early passer-by who might me, I raised clenched fists to the sky, with eyes blinded by tears I screamed one word: "Why?"

Over the centuries this question had been posed numerous times, and always hollowly it echoed back question for question, no answer ever being received.

"I have worked for you in Spirit all my life, this is the way you repay me!"

In my heart I knew that from this day I would not longer work as a Medium, as all my faith had been destroyed.

Uncaring how I would explain the mud covering my clothes, I threw myself in the attitude of the abandoned across the grave. My misery now reaching its zenith, with the tears of pain, sorrow and anger falling in earnest, I was unconscious to the world and all others around me.

I wasn't sure how long my tears lasted, only that as they subsided my eyes and throat were sore, while my head was dizzy from the depth of my emotion. Sitting up, then pulling away from the position that had been mine for the last few minutes, I tried to look at my life dispassionately. For so long Dieter had been my every thought, whether waking or sleeping. Now that had all come to an end, what was I to do?

So deep in thought was I that it was quite a few minutes before I realised that I may not be quite as alone as I had at first imagined. With the return of sanity, I began to feel embarrassed should the caretaker, or whoever it was now keeping me company in this garden of peace, have witnessed my earlier performance. Worse still, it might have been a mutual friend or member of the family. About the turn round I heard: "Vicki, Victoria Anne, I am here to keep my promise. Please look at me."

"Oh, God! Now I have flipped."

I prayed, quickly crossed myself. For the voice I heard was that of Dieter. This was no imaginary voice, as in the hospital. I could almost smell his after shave, a very distinctive perfume and one I had never known anyone else to use.

A feeling of unease was creeping into me. Here I was all alone. No one knew I was here. What if someone here was a good mimic having witnessed my grief of earlier that morning anything could happen and no one would know till too late.

Once again I heard the whisper: "Vicki, Schatzie. Please look at me. I have a need of you." Then silence for a second: "I cannot stay long."

It was at this last that had me whirling from the graveside, fury written in every tone of my voice: "I don't know who the hell you are, but if you don't bugger off I shall personally call the police." Just to make sure I made the announcement in both English and German: "No one fools with me," I muttered.

For some time after I had called out to the invisible person, there was silence. Leaving me in peace to go back to saying my silent prayers by the graveside. My passions had been spent, now there was no more anger, only a terrible sense of loss. One I had to grow used to.

"Vicki, I remember The Feldenburg."

Once again I heard his voice. This time I knew there could no cheap imitation, for only two people in this village knew about the mountain. I was one of them, the other..... I looked once more at the grave, what I expected to see I wasn't sure but it was obvious no tampering had taken place. Everything was as it had been the moment the grave diggers had left the scene.

Feeling a gentle breeze lift eh hair on the nape of my neck, I gently touched the spot where the zephyr had rested. Only to run cold all over as a voice came back to me borne on the wind: "When you feel that, it is I who kiss you."

My belief in the world of Christian Spiritualism was indeed a strong one, had been tested to breaking point. However, everything I had learnt in Circle and at the Church Meetings, had not prepared me for anything like the materialisation that I suspected was about to take place.

Very slowly, almost as if I had been filmed in slow motion, I turned, afraid what I would find. Yet even more scared was I to be disappointed. Once more the voice, as in a whisper "Vicki, I will always love you. Nothing will ever part us."

After this I could wait no longer, I swung round as fast as I could. My eyes had long been accustomed to the early morning light, so I was a little disappointed on checking my bearings to see that I was still alone.

"Vicki, look here, near the trees."

This time I searched, God how I searched, trying to see but finding nothing... A movement between two willow trees caught my eye.

What I saw, was so breathtaking, I heard my own breath coming in harsh gasps: "Dieter is that you?" I asked prepared to laugh it off quickly if I discovered it to be some sick prankster.

"At last Leibchen, you know me." this time his voice was stronger, as was the figure coming towards me. With each passing moment his shape grew more definitive, till he appeared almost solid.

The shock of his appearance was so great, for seconds I clung to the large, wooden cross that had been placed at the head of his grave, with a number and his name written on it. This would stay there until a marble surrounded and headstone could be put in place.

As I watched him come closer into view, I felt all my disbelief in Spirit and God begin to dissolve. Everything I had been taught, all the messages I had given to people over the years were true there really is a Spirit World and I was being given the perfect proof by my lover.

With hungry eyes, I studied the man now standing smiling before me. He was dressed as I best remembered him, on that first morning in the mountain hut, after having spent the night in passionate lovemaking. Dieter, had looked relaxed, not pale and lifeless as I had last seen him in hospital. With a light, blue open-necked tee shirt, tucked into tight fitting dark blue jeans, and sandals covering his bare feet. A look of immense satisfaction in his green eyes.

"What is wrong Schatzie?" Came his voice, as clear as a mountain stream. "Do you not want to see me?"

I nodded, too stunned for words.

"Then…" He carried on: "Talk with me please."

Again I shook my head: "No you are not here, I am dreaming."

Shaking his head, he denied my earlier statement: "Nein, Leibchen I am here. Feel." With this he moved closer to me. I saw and heard him, yet as he moved through the grass, not a blade moved or leaf was crushed. It was as if he were not there.

Seeing my hesitation, he smiled once again: "Don't be frightened."

"How can you be here?" I begged once more.

"Because, we love each other, that keeps us always together."

To this sentiment I could only agree, if silently.

"But, how do I see you so clearly? And feel your touch." Once again I received his heart-warming smile.

"The power of thought and the World that I am now in, my darling, for that is what I am to you now. The feelings that we had, our minds are one now. Though I no longer live in the body I once had, it does not mean I have ceased to exist. My world is different but I will be forever alive, in your memories, photographs and conversations. From the Spirit World true love like ours cannot die. The life, the energy, the Spirit that was me, it goes on like the wind, the rain and the sun... forever.

Then I heard called above the trees: "Remember, du bist mein ganzes herz." As he used this endearment to me, one I recalled him using to me, one I recalled him using to me after we had first made love: "You are my very heart." Something akin to a kiss touched me gently on the lips. Then I was alone, no puff of smoke. No magic noises. Only a gentle sighing to tell me he had taken his leave of me.

I was sure for minutes after he had left, his husky gentle voice could be heard in loving laughter, pleased that he had made contact with me.

Completely stunned by the events that had taken place, I stumbled to me feet, subconsciously brushing away the dried twigs and damp earth. Then I walked back down the path I had followed I had followed what now appeared to have been centuries ago. Leaving the graveyard in the same way I had made my entrance, I began to walk back to the Hubertus, my mind distracted and still finding it difficult to accept the vision that I had been witness to. My thoughts in complete turmoil, I argued with myself that it was all imagination. Dieter had not been there. What I had seen was only wishful thinking and the need to know that my beliefs in the Spirit World were real.

As I neared the traffic lights that would lead me to the hotel and my husband, I felt once more a breeze on the back of my neck. Raising my hand in a gesture I had carried out so often before, as if an unconscious with to keep hold of the ephemeral touch, a smile crossed my face... at last I understood, completely.

Dieter had come back to tell me that death was no divider of true love, be it parent, lover, sibling or friend. Only a change in dimensions separated us from the loved ones who we thought had left us.

I found myself running back to where my husband lay still asleep. The sun was now completely free of the chains placed on it by night. Somewhere very close a bird sang a song of joy, to welcome the new day.

With a heart much lighter now, and a smile on my lips, for the first time in days, I asked forgiveness of God for ever doubting Him, and thanking him for the Gift granted to me this day, and for the rest of my life.

The simple realisation Dieter was not lost to me at all, as I was not parted from him. Though we could no longer be together in the physical sense, I would still hear his husky laughter in the wind, see the beloved shape of his face in the clouds that floated by, hear his voice in the everyday sounds surrounding me and feel the passion of his kisses in the warm summer rain that would touch my face and lips.

My lover had come back to me, not to say farewell. Instead, he had returned to make his continuance known. After what I had witnessed, how could I doubt it. Dieter lived as I did and one day, when my time was ended, I too would join him, as he waited for me at the end of the tunnel that divides life from death.

The song of songs, which is Solomon's
O that you would kiss me with the
kisses of your mouth
For your love is better than wine.

The End